DEAD
ALREADY

MIKE KRENTZ

Relax. Read. Repeat.

DEAD ALREADY
By Mike Krentz
Published by TouchPoint Press
Brookland, AR 72417
www.touchpointpress.com

ISBN-13: 978-1-952816-18-5

Editor: Jenn Haskin
Cover Design: Colbie Myles

First Edition

Printed in the United States of America.

To Kathryn. Best friend, critic, soulmate.

CHAPTER ONE

In the year his heart stopped, Dr. Zack Winston checked his watch as he headed to the ER suture room for his next patient. Four p.m. *Two hours left.*

Strident blare from the EMS radio stopped him in mid-stride. His experienced ear caught the gist of the paramedics' report.

"Three minutes out . . . Full code . . . Fifty-two-year-old male . . . Seen in your ER yesterday."

Zack's heart plunged. *Who?* He turned from the suture area and hustled to the resuscitation room.

Paramedics burst through the doors, wheeling their patient on a narrow gurney. Zack recognized Carl Barnett, even with a plastic LMA tube protruding from his mouth. A medic squeezed air into the tube from a green football-shaped neoprene bag. Another medic straddled the gurney, performing vigorous chest compressions. Another held an IV bag aloft, its tubing plugged into a catheter in the patient's arm.

Carl's skin looked waxy, pale gray-blue, and mottled. He'd had a healthy pink complexion when Zack saw him in the ER the previous day.

A medic spoke into Zack's ear. "Wife found him in full arrest on the floor in their home. She's a nurse, doing good CPR when we arrived. No pulse or rhythm on scene or during transport. Down time at least twenty minutes. Unknown how long he went without CPR."

1

A strong grip on Zack's arm swung him into the florid face of Janice Barnett, Carl's wife, ICU head nurse.

"Do not lose him." Stern. A swallow. Softer voice. "Please."

"We'll, uh, do our best, Jan."

Zack followed the paramedics into the resuscitation room. The cardiac monitor showed a wavy horizontal line with an occasional bump that resembled an inverted U. Agonal rhythm. Dying heart.

Odds of save, zero to zilch.

Zack recalled a favorite saying: A thin line separates cardiopulmonary resuscitation from assault on the already dead. His gaze swept from the monitor to the patient. Carl Barnett, already dead.

From behind, Janice bumped into Zack, scowled, and moved to pass. He blocked her path. "You shouldn't be in here."

She flipped a frizz of frosted platinum hair off a sweat-dotted forehead. Hazel eyes pierced him. Her tone pleaded. "I must be with Carl."

Zack nodded to Monica Harris, ER head nurse. She steered Janice to a corner from where she could watch without interfering. Zack turned to his patient, his back to the man's wife.

Carl's skin color had not improved from arrival. The monitor displayed the same wide bumps, at a more ominous rate of thirty. Zack had never seen anyone recover from prolonged agonal rhythm—not to useful life. He started the protocol for managing pulseless electrical activity. *The algorithm for the already dead.* Protocol. Routine. They needed an outlier, something to reverse the man's status from already dead to almost died. *When you hear hoofbeats, think horses not zebras.* Zack needed a zebra. "Continue CPR," he said. "Get the ultrasound machine."

Zack performed a quick cardiac ultrasound, looking for heart-wall motion, contractions—maybe a dilated right ventricle to suggest massive pulmonary embolism. Maybe cardiac tamponade. Zebra hunting. The test showed ineffective heart contractions, nothing more.

He recalled his interactions with the Barnetts the previous day. Fit and healthy, with no cardiac risk factors, Carl had come in with chest pain that began at rest. The pain had resolved in the ER without treatment. Zack had run a gamut of standard tests and calculated a low probability for acute heart disease. He had explained everything to Janice, whose subtle mistrust had never waned, even when she agreed to take her husband home. What happened in the interim?

Zack could not accept defeat. He went off protocol and tried other medications. Atropine. High dose epinephrine. The entire arsenal.

"Asystole," a nurse said. An undulating line snaked across the EKG screen. No bumps.

"Respirations?" The tech paused the ventilator. A minute passed. No breaths. Zack felt over the carotid arteries in the neck. No pulse. He listened over the chest. No heartbeat.

He turned to look at Janice Barnett weeping in the corner. "I'm sorry," he said.

Tears ran down her face. "I know."

He looked at the clock. "Time of death, 1536." *Already dead, around 1425.*

Monica Harris seized Janice's arm and led her toward the door. "Let's go to the quiet room while the staff cleans up, then you can come back and say good-bye." Her grip tightened until Janice winced.

As the two women left the resus room, Zack froze. His feet refused to move. His mind lurched far away from the familiar milieu of Bethesda Metro Hospital ER. A young woman's body lay lifeless on an operating table in front of him. Blood ran down the sterile sheet and dripped onto his shoes.

He took a few seconds to return to the present, then headed to the suture room.

A twenty-something disheveled man with a scruffy beard-shadow, unraveled brown ponytail, and hostile features sat on the edge of the gurney. He held his arms tripod-like beside him, hands pressing on the thin mattress, body leaning forward—a gorilla poised to lunge. As Zack moved closer, the distinct odor of recycled booze assaulted his nostrils. The man sported a purple-and-maroon swollen and busted lip. The dirty, yellow-encrusted edges of the laceration suggested it was a day old, if not more. Dark blue and light purple bruises around the man's face and upper torso completed the picture.

The patient told Zack that he had started drinking the previous night, got into a fight that he somewhat remembered, continued drinking, passed out, slept most of the day, and awakened an hour before coming to the ER.

"I need this fixed good, Doc. Got a job interview tomorrow."

In a calm voice, Zack explained that if the man had sought treatment soon after the injury happened, they could have cleaned and repaired the laceration with good results. "Too late for that," he said. "One-hundred-percent probability it's infected. If I suture it now, germs will get trapped inside and create an abscess that will get ugly. Best we can do is clean it up, put a dressing on it, and let it heal on its own. It's going to leave a scar. If that's a problem for you after it heals, you can get a plastic surgeon to fix it." *At a hefty price.*

Irate, the young man leaped off the gurney, pushed Zack aside, and stormed out of the suture area. "Just another fucking ER doc. I'll go where I can get some real help."

Straight to the nearest bar, Zack thought. *Too bad about that job interview.* He shrugged. Not the first time he'd been called a "JAFERD." Many emergency physicians had withstood similar, or worse, cheap shots. On a popular ER docs' social media site, a colleague had devised a counter-acronym: BAFERD ("Bad Ass Fucking ER Doc"), a badge-of-honor adopted by emergency physicians with multiple years on the front lines taking on the worst life-and-death battles, the most serious and unusual illnesses and injuries, suffered by a diverse cast of humanity; yet handling it all with aplomb and unimaginable self-esteem.

Back in the day, Zack Winston had considered himself a total BAFERD. *Now . . .?*

CHAPTER TWO

Heading to the main treatment area, Zack passed the resuscitation room. Janice Barnett stood by her husband's body; Monica's arm draped around her shoulder. The women didn't notice Zack in the doorway. The staff had cleared out the post-resuscitation debris and had extinguished the bright lights. In natural lighting, covered to the neck by a clean sheet, with the ventilator tubing, monitor wires, and IV bags removed, the dead man appeared to sleep. Janice caressed his forehead and sobbed.

The scene caused Zack to back away as a surge of emotions threatened to suffocate him. Hyperventilating, heart galloping, skin clammy, he bolted from the department to the nearest men's room, hit the first stall, and bowed to the commode. Dry heaves. Gasping, he knelt on the cool tile, collecting himself, easing his breaths, willing his rapid pulse to slow. Not his first visceral reaction to a failed resuscitation. He doubted that other emergency physicians suffered such symptoms. They hadn't been to hell; not Zack Winston's hell.

He forced himself to stand. Living patients awaited his care. Whatever he felt now, however related to past terror, must wait until he could be alone—for the sake of his patients and the ER staff.

At the sink, he saw Walter Knowles, unit secretary and perennial seer of the ER; a bearded, taciturn, enigma who seemed to know everyone's thoughts. He anticipated most requests before they were spoken. None of the current staff knew for sure when Walter had started working in the ER, or how old he might be. Steely eyes beneath bushy eyebrows scrutinized Zack. "You okay, Doc?"

Zack put on his game face. "I'm fine, Walt. Rough resuscitation."

A conspiratorial half-smile. "Because of who it was?"

Zack shrugged.

"Good luck with that."

Zack furrowed his brow. "Walt, can you please make a printout of Mr. Barnett's ER record from yesterday? And today's code record?"

"In your cubby by end of shift."

Zack took deep breaths and headed back to the ER; once again the confident emergency physician, braced for the next patient, the next challenge, the next opportunity to touch another's life, ideally for better, not worse.

"God save us from emergency physicians!" The epithet greeted Zack when he returned to the main treatment area. He recognized the bombastic voice of Dr. Jeremiah Hartman, medical director of the ICU and chief of the medical staff. Hirsute, stout, and loud, he could verbally eviscerate the most confident of colleagues; and he didn't care about witnesses. Oblivious to the patients in the curtained cubicles lining his path, Hartman bore down on Zack like an eagle on a wounded gerbil.

"Did you not realize Carl Barnett was my patient?"

Concerned about confidentiality and his pending humiliation in earshot of patients and staff, Zack gestured toward the ER lounge. "Let's talk in private." He led his accuser into the room, shut the door, and turned to face him. "I did treat Carl. I noted you are his physician."

"Why the hell didn't you call me?" He barked as if Zack had stolen a favorite bone. No doubt his baritone voice projected to the treatment area.

Zack retreated a step. "No time. He was full code."

Hartman sneered. "You should have had someone contact me. I was in the ICU. Jan just called to tell me her husband is dead, and she doesn't understand why."

"He arrived in non-survivable cardiac arrest."

"You should have summoned me."

Jerry and Janice were tight professional colleagues based on their complementary ICU roles. The hospital grapevine sometimes buzzed about a secret personal relationship. Zack didn't care. *Until now.*

"He was dead when he hit the door. No one could have saved him." Zack moved to leave the lounge. Patients needed him, and he had another hour to go before he could retreat to solitude and a bottle of Tuscan red at home.

The hound blocked his path. "We're not done."

Zack stopped. "What?"

"You saw Carl yesterday. Sent him out with acute coronary syndrome."

Zack folded his arms, squared his stance. "Not true. I did evaluate him yesterday. He came in with atypical chest pain and I ruled out cardiac etiology. HEART score was zero, including two negative troponins four hours apart. He was pain-free when I discharged him."

Hartman's voice dripped with contempt. "You had him in the ER four hours and didn't think to inform me?" The man could blow like an IED if not contained. Jerry Hartman had the political clout and authority to hurt Zack Winston.

Zack struggled to maintain a reasonable tone. "We don't contact the private physician in all cases. We exercise clinical judgment. Most attendings appreciate not getting called every time one of their patients comes to the ER. I repeat, he was pain-free, without treatment, at discharge. I referred him to you for follow-up."

Jerry moved closer, snorted into Zack's face. "Yet he suffers a fatal cardiac arrest the next day? You missed something, *Doctor.*"

"No. I did not." Zack reached for the doorknob.

Jerry stopped him. "This death was preventable. I will review the record. If I find a single discrepancy, you will answer for it."

Zack scoffed. "Do what you wish. Now get out of my face." He pushed past Jerry and returned to the main treatment area, ignoring the curious eyes looking for a cloud of smoke billowing from his rear. He bowed his head, picked up a chart, and scurried into the first cubicle. A distraught young woman, her face a paled question mark, held a crying infant in her arms. As the full brunt of Jerry Hartman's assault unsettled his soul, Zack ignored his pounding heart, took a deep breath, smiled at the mother, and spoke in a reassuring voice. "I'm Dr. Winston. How can I help you?"

CHAPTER THREE

B ridget Larsen fought a too-familiar battle in District of Columbia
Superior Court. The judge, a tired-looking man in his early sixties,
massaged his temples and spoke in a detached tone. "Ms. Larsen."

"Thank you, Your Honor." Bridget pushed back from the defense
table, stood, buttoned her navy-blue suit jacket, and flipped her wavy
blond hair over her shoulders. Seated next to her, Dr. Julie Dawson, a
thirty-two-year-old emergency physician from George Washington
University Hospital, gazed at her with anxious eyes.

In a stately walk toward the witness stand, Bridget smiled at Roger
Meadows retaking the seat next to his client at the plaintiff's table. "Just a
few questions for the good doctor there," she said as she made deliberate
eye contact with as many jurors as possible. She paused in front of the jury
box and faced the plaintiff's expert-physician witness waiting to parry her
cross-examination. Her eyes scanned his well-groomed appearance: salt-
and-pepper hair with no errant strands, manicured fingernails, custom-fit
charcoal suit with red silk tie, monogrammed shirt-cuff kissing a gold
Rolex on his left wrist. She had observed his rich Italian footwear when
he took the stand earlier. *Quintessential peacock doc.*

Confident of everyone's attention, she addressed the witness. "Dr.
Sanders, I'm Bridget Larsen, and I represent the defendant." She gestured
toward Dr. Dawson, pleased by the young physician's demure pose in an off-

the-rack half-size-large dark-gray suit, pale blue cotton blouse, absence of make-up, and dishwater brown hair drawn into a modest chignon—just as Bridget had coached her. *Unpretentious as a sparrow.*

"To summarize, in your opinion Dr. Dawson here missed classic EKG signs of ST elevation myocardial infarction, or 'STEMI' as it is called. Is that right?"

"As I stated to Mr. Meadows a few minutes ago."

Bridget glanced at the jury. "In layman's terms, you believe she missed a heart attack, right?"

The physician sneered. "She missed a heart attack."

Bridget tugged on an ear lobe and turned toward the jury. "You further opined that George Watkins, the late husband of Mr. Meadows' client, suffered wrongful death as the result of Dr. Dawson's alleged misdiagnosis, right?"

The doctor scoffed. "As the result of her negligence, yes. She sent him home to die."

Bridget wheeled toward the judge. "Move to strike that as speculative and prejudicial."

"Sustained. The jury will disregard the witness' response. Just answer the questions, Doctor."

The physician turned to the judge. "Sorry, your honor. May I hear the question again?"

The court reporter repeated Bridget's question.

The doctor harrumphed. "Yes."

Bridget smirked. "Thank you for finally answering a question without your personal embellishment."

Behind her, Roger Meadows, all sixty-four doughy inches of him, bounced to his feet. "Object!"

Bridget waved him off. "I'll withdraw that." She moved closer to the witness. "To be explicit, Doctor, you've rendered an opinion about the cause of Mr. Watkins' death. You did not state an absolute fact, correct?"

The doctor folded his arms. "I have given my expert opinion based on training and years of experience, yes."

"Could another emergency physician with similar training and experience have a different opinion?"

Meadows objected. "Calls for speculation." He shot Bridget a sinister look.

"Sustained."

Bridget shrugged. "Okay, then. Let's review the relevant EKG together, to be sure I have it right." She stepped to a large video monitor next to the witness stand, on the screen a magnified computerized EKG tracing. "Earlier, under questioning from Mr. Meadows, you pointed out details in this EKG that, in your opinion, confirm the diagnosis of STEMI." She used a laser pointer to identify a segment of the tracing. "These elevated lines between the S and T waves, right?" She pointed to areas on the EKG representing single heartbeats.

"Yes."

"In a normal EKG, you would expect those lines to stay even with the baseline, am I right?"

"Yes."

She pointed to verbiage printed near the top of the EKG. "What's this, Doctor?"

His voice spat impatience. "That's the computer's interpretation of the tracing."

"Not an official reading by a trained cardiologist, right?"

"Correct. It's an AI thing. They can be pretty accurate."

Bridget furrowed her eyebrows. "AI thing? I don't understand."

The doctor huffed. "Artificial intelligence. The computer analyzes the tracing against programmed algorithms and comes up with a preliminary interpretation."

"Got it. Thanks." She looked at the jury. "Can you read that interpretation from your seat?"

"Sure. 'Abnormal EKG. Unconfirmed. Cannot rule out anterior infarct.'"

Bridget nodded. "So, this artificial intelligence thing could not validate a STEMI, or heart attack, on this EKG?"

He waved a dismissive hand. "It's a machine. EKG interpretation is an art. There are nuances, often esoteric and not relevant to this case."

Bridget smiled toward the jury. "Too esoteric for us lawyers and laymen, eh?"

Roger Meadows jumped up. "Object. Badgering."

"Sustained."

Bridget cast a skeptical eye at the judge. She looked back at the jury. "I'll restate it. To generalize for our slower minds, Dr. Sanders, sometimes a 'normal' EKG can have an elevated ST segment for reasons other than a heart attack, correct?"

The doctor crossed his arms. "Can have subtle nuances, yes."

"Might other physicians reach different conclusions based on those subtle nuances, regardless of the computer's analysis?"

The doctor stared at her. "Again, not applicable to this case, which is a straightforward misinterpretation of a pathological EKG."

Bridget cocked her head. "No doubt about your interpretation?"

"None whatsoever."

She turned back to the EKG. "Okay. I'd like to ask you about some other features on this tracing." She led the doctor through several technical aspects of the EKG tracing, then pointed to a small wave on the EKG. "This little bump at the beginning of the elevated ST segment, what's that called?"

The physician stared at her for a few seconds before answering. "J wave."

"What other condition, besides STEMI, might demonstrate a J wave like this one?"

The man flushed. "Early repolarization, but this patient had STEMI."

Bridget smiled, patronizing. "Early repol, as you ER docs call it, is a benign condition that can mimic STEMI, right?"

"Yes, but—"

"It's not the same as a heart attack, right? No one dies from early repol, do they?"

"No."

She paused for a few seconds, walked back toward the witness. "Dr. Sanders, do you know an academic emergency physician, Dr. Evan Reed?"

"I've heard of him."

"He's famous in your specialty, is he not?"

"He has a solid reputation."

"Are you familiar with Dr. Reed's study, published in the ANNALS OF EMERGENCY MEDICINE in 2013, wherein he describes a formula for differentiating early repolarization from STEMI?"

"No."

Bridget squinted at him. "You do read medical journals, don't you, Doctor?"

The man scowled. "Of course."

Bridget smiled. "What if I tell you that the formula Dr. Reed derived in that study establishes, as independent predictor of early repol over STEMI, the same findings we just reviewed on this EKG; that a competent emergency physician, such as Dr. Dawson here, might correctly interpret that EKG as benign, non-life-threatening early repolarization, not STEMI. Not a heart attack?"

Meadows roared. "Objection. She's testifying, and badgering."

"Sustained. That's enough, Ms. Larsen."

Bridget raised her hands. "Sorry. Let's move on." She walked toward the jury. "Dr. Sanders, when did you last treat a patient in an ER?"

The man bristled. "I don't work ER shifts anymore. I'm a consultant."

Bridget lifted her eyebrows. "You don't see patients? Since when?" Roger Meadows fidgeted behind her, but no objection came.

"Roughly five years."

"Wow. How do you stay current in your profession? A lot could change in that time, right?"

"I read—" He stopped, catching himself.

"Medical journals?"

Shoulders slumped. "Yes."

"Just not the ANNALS OF EMERGENCY MEDICINE."

Roger Meadows yelled from his seat. "Objection."

"Sustained." The judge scowled at Bridget. "Wrap this up, Ms. Larsen."

"Yes, your honor." She stepped away from the doctor, turned to the jury. "What consulting do you do, Dr. Sanders?"

"Various projects, on request."

"Expert legal testimony?"

"I am in demand for that."

Bridget spun away from the jury and faced the witness. "Isn't that the only 'consulting' you do?"

The man looked away. "I support both plaintiff and defense attorneys."

"No other consulting beyond expert testimony?"

"No. I mean, yes, that's all I do."

She moved within two feet of him. "You get paid for your testimony, Doctor?"

"I receive remuneration for my time."

Bridget inched closer. "How expensive is your time, Doctor?"

"I devote many hours to researching the cases and preparing my testimony."

"But not—" She made a pretense of catching herself in mid-sentence. "Whoops. Almost mentioned ANNALS again."

She felt the judge's glare and turned to him.

"Thank you for your patience, Your Honor." She swung back to the jury. "And for yours, ladies and gentlemen. One final question for the 'expert' here."

She inspected him from head to toe. When she spoke, her voice rose in a steady crescendo. "That's an Armani suit, right? Custom-tailored shirt? Rolex watch? Gucci shoes? All paid for by remuneration for your precious time, Doctor?"

Meadows nearly toppled the table in front of him. "Objection!"

"Withdrawn." As she strode past the jury, Bridget caught a few smiles. She stood next to her shy client. "No further questions."

CHAPTER FOUR

A fter calming the baby and reassuring the young mother, Zack hustled through the remainder of his shift to clear out the workload before his relief arrived. ER docs' unwritten code: Never leave unfinished work for the next physician. The policy fostered not only collegial respect, but also patient safety and liability avoidance. Medical errors tended to happen at turnover.

Three patients remained in progress when Dr. Paula Cho arrived at seven p.m. She put a hand on Zack's shoulder. "Go home. You look exhausted."

He shook his head, loath to burden a favorite colleague.

"I have it, Zack. Get out of here."

Of course she had it. Paula Cho was one of the most skilled and efficient doctors he'd ever met. After a quick report on the remaining patients, he thanked her and headed to the ER physicians' combined office/lounge/locker/sleep room behind the main treatment area. Sometime in the past, a harried emergency physician had sought refuge in that space from a belligerent, threatening patient. "I'm diving into the bunker," he had said. The name stuck, and now the entire staff referred to the room as "The Bunker."

Walter the Inscrutable had left copies of Carl Barnett's records as promised. Zack sat on the edge of the thin single bed and tried to study them, but the print turned into a blur that his spent brain could not process. He set the pages aside and buried his head in his hands. Random images crossed his mind, reflections of the failed resuscitation, of a healthy Carl Barnett the previous day; and a fleeting shadow of another already dead patient, the young woman, at a different time, in a place far away, at the alcove to hell.

Zack picked up the papers and placed them, along with a plastic bottle containing the dregs of his homemade energy drink, into the small backpack he carried to and from work. After changing into street clothes, he intended to go home, pour a glass of wine, eat, and dig into those documents to figure out why Carl Barnett died.

B y the time Zack reached his silver Lexus in the physicians' sweltering parking lot, a solitary evening of chart review and soul-searching had lost appeal. Ange would be home. Still early for a Friday night.

He backed the car out, departed the lot, turned toward the District of Columbia—opposite direction from his Bethesda apartment—and commanded the hands-free phone function to dial her.

She answered on the second ring. "Yes?"

"Want to get together? I'm in my car headed your way. Could meet you for dinner somewhere in Southeast."

Audible gulp. "Still at the office, working a brief on a tight deadline. Ate a salad earlier."

Zack scowled. "Tomorrow? I'd like to talk to you."

"Are you okay? You sound upset."

"Hard day; rough case near the end. Husband of one of our nurses died."

"Sounds awful."

"I treated him yesterday. Checked out fine."

"Not your fault he died, right?"

"Not that I know." Clacking from a computer keyboard in the background. Zack let up on the accelerator.

"Sorry I can't talk. I need to work on this brief. Dinner next weekend?"

Not long ago, they couldn't stand two days apart. "I work nights then."

"I'm sorry. I have to present this brief in court Monday. I'll be working it up to the last minute."

Zack sighed. "Okay. Maybe I can switch shifts for Friday night." He let the car slow down to the speed limit. "Call me tomorrow?"

"Can't promise."

He brushed off a wave of disappointment. "No problem either way. Good luck on that brief."

"Later gator." She clicked off.

Zack made a U-turn and accelerated back toward Bethesda.

A fter a short detour for Greek takeout, Zack parked the Lexus in its assigned space beneath the five-story luxury apartment building and rode the elevator to the top floor. When he crossed the threshold of his two-bedroom electronically enhanced man-cave, he felt not peace but utter exhaustion.

He dumped the backpack in the spare room/study, returned to the living room, flipped on the 65-inch UHD TV, and tuned to the Washington Nationals game from New York. In the second inning, the Nats trailed the Mets by three runs; not auspicious for deterring a fall from first place in the National League East. Like many capital-area faithful, Zack hoped to see the revitalized home team in the post-season. He wanted to treat Ange to her first in-person World Series.

From his well-stocked wine bar, he opened a bottle of Sangiovese and poured a full glass. He set the glass and bottle next to the Styrofoam food container on the coffee table and plopped onto the mahogany leather couch to eat, drink, and watch the game. The routine made a welcome contrast to the distressing events near the end of his ER shift. Although he'd bounced back from traumatic cases before, no recent event had distressed him like this one, on both an emotional and professional level. A specter of Janice Barnett's tear-strewn face popped into his mind. Behind her, Jerry Hartman shook a threatening fist. Behind him, the phantom of past clinical disgrace that nearly destroyed his professional life.

A game-tying home run by Juan Soto chased away the visions.

The wine soothed Zack's brain while the dolmades and spanakopita satisfied his gut. The copies of medical records from today's disaster languished in the next room as he savored baklava and quaffed a second glass of wine. With the weekend off, he could postpone the clinical review for a rested mind. Nothing new would happen tonight. He disposed of the food remains, poured another full glass, and settled into the couch. Sixth inning in New York, and the Mets regained the lead.

Damn!

The Nats tied the score in the top of the ninth and shut down the Mets in the bottom frame. The contest went into extra innings. Zack fell asleep in the middle of the tenth.

CHAPTER FIVE

Janice Barnett turned her metallic deep-blue Mercedes 450 SEL off Democracy Boulevard into the circular drive of the three-acre Barnett estate in Potomac, Maryland. She suffered a violent migraine headache. Instead of driving around to the three-car garage on the side of the house, she turned into the front portico, parked, and entered through the massive oak door. When she glanced left into the ornate parlor, she frowned at the displaced rococo furniture, splotches of dried vomit and blood on the ivory-white carpet, and leftover debris from the paramedics' vigorous efforts to resuscitate Carl. The housekeepers could clean up the mess tomorrow. Even if they obliterated the stains, she planned to replace that carpet with something more vibrant, less pretentious, a whimsical display of her rejuvenated existence. One of many changes to come, including a dog—a Labradoodle. Maybe two.

She swung right, stepped past the grand piano and French provincial chairs in the sitting room, and crossed to the credenza under the vaulted window. From several framed photographs, she picked up the fading glossy black-and-white of two young US Army officers pressed together at a lookout along the South Korean demilitarized zone. Oblivious to the jumbo-sized North Korea flag fluttering from a high tower a mile behind them, Captain Carl Barnett and Second Lieutenant Janice Klinefeld gazed with passion into each other's eyes—her left hand posed to highlight a sparkling engagement ring, her body rotated away from the camera to obscure the bump in her belly.

Janice clutched the frame and moved through the formal dining area into the kitchen. She flipped on the wall switch, then swatted it off when the brilliant fluorescent beam aggravated the pain pounding the right side of her head. In the fading ambient light from the window, she opened a drawer and rooted around until she found a meat mallet. She propped the bronze-framed photo in the sink, raised the mallet, and smashed the picture with full force. The glass shattered, spicules flying in every direction. She swung the weapon again. And again. And again. The hammering stopped only when she'd pounded the glass to splinters and hacked the photograph into fragments. Not caring that shards pierced her fingers, Janice ripped the picture scraps into tinier pieces. Mixed tears of rage and remorse flooded her cheeks. She rinsed the blood off her hands, wiped them on her blouse, dried her eyes, and turned to the refrigerator.

The adrenalin surge had somewhat soothed the headache. Exhausted and starving, she should eat something—despite the migraine-induced nausea. A few mouthfuls of yogurt did somersaults in her gut and she scrambled back to the sink to vomit. She used the sprayer nozzle to blend the puke with the glass dust, photo remnants, and blood; then splashed water from the faucet onto her face. That helped her retain a few sips taken straight from the spigot. *Leave the mess for the housekeepers.*

The migraine returned with unrestrained fury. Dizzy, Janice stumbled back through the foyer and clung to the banister to climb the stairs to the second floor where she braced herself with a hand against the wall to traverse the long hallway to her bedroom. The effort worsened the pounding inside her head. She avoided looking into Carl's bedroom when she passed it. In her bathroom, the empty medication bottle on the counter mocked her suffering. *Call for a refill in the morning.*

In her bedroom, she opened the bedside-stand drawer. From beneath a pile of old magazines, she extracted the framed grainy photograph of Chantal at age thirteen. With gentle strokes, she caressed her daughter's dark-skinned image, kissed it softly, then set the photo atop the bedside stand. Tomorrow, she would put it on the shelf downstairs from where she'd removed the old photo of Carl and her in Korea.

Closing the drawer, Jan looked at the packet of white powder peeking out from beneath the magazines. A drug rush might alleviate the headache, but she didn't want to use it now. *Don't know when I can get more. Save it for a happier occasion.*

Back in the bathroom, she extracted a container of Percocet, her final resort for intractable migraine, from its hiding spot behind the nifedipine and extra-large bottles of Motrin in the medicine cabinet. She swallowed three of the yellow tablets without water. Janice knew the risks of opioids, but so what? *Won't get addicted in one night. Or any time. Never lose control.*

The narcotic soothed her head as she dropped her clothes to the floor and fell naked into bed. She burrowed under the covers and slithered toward the middle, grateful for the solitude, craving sleep. She needed to awaken pain-free and rested the next day. *So much to do.*

She had just dozed off when her phone buzzed. Groggy, she answered it.

"What are you doing?"

"Sleeping. Migraine." She yawned on purpose.

"Sorry."

"I'll make the calls tomorrow."

"Right."

"I gotta mourn for a while."

"I know."

"Then I'll be around."

"Uh-huh."

"Okay. Later."

"Sure."

The phone clicked off. In less than a minute, Janice Barnett fell into a deep, pain-free slumber.

CHAPTER SIX

Saturday morning, Zack awoke on the couch with a massive headache and sore neck. He looked at his watch. Eight-thirty. *Hungover? I had, what? Two glasses of wine?* Last he remembered, the Mets were threatening with two on and one out in the bottom of the tenth. He turned to the TV, where a static *MLB.com* logo mocked him. On the coffee table, a wine glass with a half-inch of Sangiovese red sat next to an empty bottle. *So, more than two . . .*

He fumbled to find the TV remote on the floor and checked the scores from last night. Mets beat the Nats in twelve innings. *Damn!*

When he tried to stand, the room lurched into a violent spin that forced him back onto the couch. He would have remained there, except his taut bladder felt larger than his head. After arising in slow increments, he staggered to the bathroom and stared into the mirror to stop the room from rocking so he could pee. Once relieved, he doused his face with cold water and changed into running attire. Zack's sure cure for a hangover: a long, sweaty run.

Outside his apartment building, muggy morning air covered the city like a heavy tarpaulin trapping dense pollutants beneath it. The mid-

July heat wave showed no signs of relenting. With the weekend off, he could stay in his air-conditioned digs and let the tourists and adventurous locals deal with the heat. After this morning's therapeutic run, he would work out the rest of the weekend in the apartment building's well-equipped gym.

By the time he completed a brisk four-block walk to the Capital Crescent Trail, Zack's head had cleared enough so he could break into a steady run. He found Noelle waiting at the usual spot around a tight curve. She ran alongside him. Her spectral stride matched his as if floating on air; almond-brown skin glistened without sweat; brunette hair billowed in the still air. In silence, they headed south, dodging other runners, a few cyclists, and a couple of elderly meandering pedestrians. Zack's head deflated to normal size.

Hanging on the edge of hypoxia, he rehashed the events of the previous day. "What the hell happened with Carl Barnett?"

On an objective scientific basis, Carl's demise—even if coronary artery disease were the culprit—was unpredictable, unpreventable, and untreatable. No physician, however skilled, could have saved him.

Noelle interrupted. "Not so fast. Did you not sense something odd about this case from the beginning? Why go to extremes trying to save him if he was already dead? Why go off book with heroic efforts using atropine and high dose epi? Why not quit once you reached the end of the protocol? No one would fault that decision."

Zack scoffed. "Because Janice Barnett. She doesn't trust emergency physicians. I knew Carl Barnett was DOA. I followed my gut and took heroic measures for Jan's sake—and for mine. I didn't want to be responsible for her loss." Zack quickened his pace. Noelle kept pace without effort. "I had to convince myself that Carl was really dead."

Noelle needled him. "How much proof did you need? Dead is dead, as you well know."

Zack's breathing became labored. He slowed to a moderate jog. He cast a pained glance at Noelle, whose pace mirrored his. "Don't. Please, don't."

"Quit clouding your brain with bad memories, Zack. Think through it. What about the day before his death? Atypical chest pain, minimal risk factors, no concrete evidence for coronary artery disease. Then he crumps the next day? How convenient."

Disheartened, Zack made a 180-degree turn back toward his apartment. Noelle did not follow. Throughout his emergency medicine career, he had learned to trust his clinical instincts, a practice that seldom betrayed him. He had followed those instincts both times he saw Carl Barnett. Naval aviator Noelle relied on hard data. Zack would have no peace until he produced it.

B ack at his apartment, Zack finished dressing, cleared the wine bottle and glass from the coffee table, then made his standard post-run kale/fruit/whey/yogurt/almond milk drink and a mug of Starbuck's Komodo Dragon dark roast. Thus fortified, he sat at his desk and opened the copies of the ER records, starting with Carl Barnett's first visit the day before his death.

Two hours later, Zack threw down the files in frustration. He'd detected no missed clues during Carl's original visit. The man had presented with abrupt onset of pain across his entire chest, not localized to the precordial area over his heart, not radiating to his left arm, and not producing nausea. Resolved without treatment. Nothing in the assessment, including Zack's calculation of the standard HEART risk score, suggested cardiac origin. No warning of potential demise the next day.

Carl had pleaded to escape the ER. "Release me before I get sick, Doc." Janice had asked if he should undergo stress testing or angiography.

Zack had countered. "Uncharacteristic chest pain in a healthy, fit, fifty-two-year-old man with no risk factors or previous history, a negative workup, zero HEART score, symptoms relieved spontaneously; the evidence-based literature suggests no useful value in further evaluation."

Janice had stood her ground. "What about CPU?" Like many ERs, Bethesda Metro featured a dedicated chest pain unit, or CPU, for twenty-four-hour observation of patients with symptoms ambiguous for acute coronary syndrome—a less costly option than admission to the hospital.

Carl had bristled at his wife's suggestion. "I want out of here."

Zack had pressed to reassure her. "He's too low-risk to justify CPU. I feel safe sending him home; especially with you, a competent ICU nurse."

In hindsight, Janice's frown at his attempted reassurance should have prompted Zack to admit her husband. Did he spurn her request to exert his authority? Noelle would say he did. Now Janice suffered the consequence.

Bottom line, Carl Barnett died, and Zack Winston didn't understand why. He stared into the middle distance, eyes unfocused, mind spinning. Nothing more to accomplish that day. Further analysis of the clinical data would be futile, frustrating, and self-defeating.

Zack had put off calling Dr. Dennis King, the director of the emergency physician group, known as Emergency Health Associates, or EHA, until he'd scrutinized the records hoping for an easy explanation of Barnett's death. Now he had to notify his boss of a "situation," as Dennis liked to call it, that might cause legal problems. Reluctant, he stared at the phone. *Like telling dad I wrecked his car. Just do it.*

Dennis was pulling a rare (for him) Saturday duty shift, so Zack dialed the ER and caught his mentor and friend between patients.

"What's up, Zack?" Dennis had a curt, business-like demeanor that belied an underlying loyalty to his colleagues. He might be abrupt, but he cared. A good guy to have on your side. If he believed in you.

"Janice Barnett's husband came in yesterday as a full code, non-resuscitatable, despite extraordinary measures."

"I heard."

"I saw him the day before with atypical chest discomfort that resolved in the ER. We found nothing on workup and discharged him pain-free."

Dennis sighed. Over the phone it blew like a gust of wind. "Did you consider CPU?"

Zack's stomach did a flip. "Janice asked, but his risk assessment was zero. I couldn't justify holding him."

"Then he goes home and dies."

Ouch.

Another gush of wind. "You know Janice won't let it go."

"Why I'm calling you now."

A brief silence, during which Zack pictured Dennis frowning and rubbing his forehead. "Okay. I'll review the case then inform our insurance carrier. Expect a call within a week or two."

Zack squirmed. "Okay."

"We need to sequester the records for the lawyers, just in case. I'll take care of that." A pause. "You make any copies?"

"Yeah."

Dennis' voice turned stern. "Get rid of them. You should know better."

"Okay."

"Now."

"Will do." *The hell I will.*

Dennis seemed distracted. "Gotta go. I have patients. Don't discuss this with anyone. Not even your girlfriend. For the record, you called to tell me about a case, nothing more."

"Got it." Zack planned to discuss it with Ange.

"We discussed no copies of records you didn't make and don't have, right?"

That seemed excessive. "Right."

Softer voice. "Another thing. Don't obsess on this, okay? Sounds like proper care on your part."

Zack smiled. "Thanks. That means a lot."

"Enjoy your weekend. Get laid if you can." Dennis hung up before Zack could react.

He recalled how Dennis had taken a chance hiring him after his navy tour in Japan; when he returned to the US broken and pessimistic, skeptical whether to stay in the profession. Zack owed Dennis King his career, indeed his life. This exchange with his mentor reminded him that Dennis also had a steely side.

An oft-told ER anecdote described how Dennis had once faced down an aggressive gang member twice his size. The man had come in with a deep but not serious gash on his right forearm. As the story went, he reacted to the painful injection of local anesthetic by taking a swing at Dennis with his other arm, coming within a half-inch of damaging his face. Dennis pushed him away, grabbed a scalpel from the suture tray, and held it up for his assailant to see. "I make my living cutting people," he had said. "I know just where to cut you. Be still if you don't want to feel this blade where you least expect it." The man settled down, after which—according to the legend—Dennis proceeded to repair his laceration, without anesthetic.

Zack would comply with Dennis' instructions. He fought off a heaviness in his chest and hardening in his stomach.

Please, not again.

CHAPTER SEVEN

J anice Barnett awoke with an aching low back, but no headache; despite the brilliant light streaming through the sheer curtains on the bedroom window. She blinked her eyes open and checked her watch. *Slept nine hours*. In a precise sequence of postures to protect her spine, she rolled out of bed, stood, and bent backward until she felt a crack. *Maybe lose weight now*. The soreness abated, and she stepped in moderate discomfort to the bathroom. The empty pill bottle mocked her again. She swept it up and tossed it in the trash.

Downstairs at the kitchen table, she sipped coffee, munched dry toast, and started her phone calls. First was to her local pharmacy for a medication refill. "I know it's early, but I've had a tough month, more migraines than usual. Plus, I dropped pills down the sink—because of the pain."

The pharmacist cleared his throat. "I'm sorry. We can't refill it without an order."

Janice thumped the *End* button on the phone, then jabbed a speed-dial. "Yes?"

"Need a new prescription. Pharmacy won't refill the other one."

"I'll handle it." The line went dead.

She poured another cup of coffee, then called the housekeeping agency for clean-up of the debris from yesterday.

Next, Janice used the speed dial on Carl's phone to call the private number of Cedric Alworth, the Barnett's accountant she had never met.

"Good morning, sir." Cedric's supercilious tone thinking she was Carl annoyed her.

"It's Mrs. Barnett. Carl died yesterday. Heart attack. Sudden."

The man gasped. His voice quivered, fumbling for words. "Oh God. So, uh, sorry for your loss, Mrs. Barnett. He was a . . . fine man."

She swallowed the bile that rose into her throat. "I appreciate that sentiment, Cedric." She paused a few seconds for transition. "I need to access our accounts to pay expenses."

A long pause. "You can use your personal account, ma'am. As for the others, I thought you knew that Mr. Barnett put everything into a private trust account that only he could access."

"His death doesn't change that? I'm his sole heir."

"Perhaps in time it will change, after probate. For the interim, you can subsist on your personal account. Surely that will be sufficient."

Janice Barnett knew that it wouldn't be, not for her to continue as she was before Carl found out about Chantal.

"I can write checks on our joint account, right?"

Another long pause. "Mr. Barnett opened a new account and closed the joint account. You're not a co-owner or signatory on that new account, ma'am. So, uh, no. You cannot write checks on it."

That bastard! She blew into the phone. "Very well. My lawyer will be in touch." She ended the call before the flustered man could respond.

J anice poured another cup of coffee and paced the kitchen before deciding to make the next call. As she dialed, she stared at the photo she'd retrieved from her bedside drawer the previous night. "Yolonda, it's Jan."

Detached voice. "I know."

Janice paced the floor. "How is she?"

"She okay. Got a bit of a cold. No big."

"Does she need a doctor?"

"Nah. Just a cold."

Janice's voice quivered. "I could send—"

"She doesn't need a doctor. Just needs rest. I got this."

Janice swallowed hard. "Of course, you do. Can't help but worry, you know."

"Yeah."

Janice cleared her throat. "So, uh, bit of bad news."

Silence.

"The cashier's check won't be as much this time. When my husband found out, he put his money where I can't get it."

A short pause. "If you say so."

"I have some of my own. I'll send what I can."

Rush of air through the phone. "We got along okay before you. Can do it again."

Janice's head began to ache. She rubbed her eyes. "I'm sorry. It will turn out okay."

"Uh-huh."

"I've got money coming. A lot of it. Chantal and you will never want for anything."

"Uh-huh."

"It will take time."

"Whatever."

"Can you hang in there awhile? Give me a chance?"

Yolonda sighed. "Sure. Why not?"

"Thanks." Janice took a deep breath. "I wonder if— if there's any way I could see her sometime."

Long pause. "You think that's safe?"

"It is now. Carl's dead."

Another pause. "I'm sorry for your loss."

"Don't be. Maybe now I can spend time with Chantal."

Longer pause. "You're not her mother now."

A numbing dread fell over Janice. "I know, but I want to be in her life—somehow."

"I don't know, Mrs. B. I have to think about that."

"After what I've done for her—" Janice stopped herself, took a breath, forced herself to calm. "I understand, Yolonda. Take all the time you need. Trust that I would never insert myself between you and her."

"I said I would think about it."

"Thanks. Meanwhile, I'll send what I can; and trust me, I'll have more money soon."

No response.

"Give her a kiss for me, okay?"

"Sure."

That didn't sound sincere. "I hope she gets over the cold soon."

A sigh. "Always does."

"Let me know if she needs to see a doctor. I can help with that."

"Yeah."

"You take care, Yolonda."

"Sure."

The line went dead. Janice ran her finger over the photo she'd taken from a distance when she'd finally found Chantal at the Kennedy Krieger Center in Baltimore, playing with a half-dozen other girls. She raised the image to her lips and kissed it, ignoring the frozen face and distant stare that made the girl look more like the other children than her own mother.

No need to hide this now. She walked to the sitting room and placed the photo in its new prominence on the credenza.

Janice returned to the kitchen, quaffed the rest of her coffee, took a sharp breath, retrieved a piece of paper from her purse, and dialed the new number.

"Roger Meadows."

"Good morning, Mr. Meadows. Sorry to disturb you on a Saturday. My name is Janice Barnett."

"I've been expecting your call."

CHAPTER EIGHT

Sunday morning, Zack awakened to air-conditioned chill blowing over his naked body atop damp, tangled sheets. He groped across the bed. No one there. *Good.* His blurred eyes adjusted to the familiar trappings of his own bedroom. *Home. Alone. Good.*

A dull cranial throb reminded him of last night's sortie to follow Dennis' advice to get laid. He had ventured into the unfamiliar Saturday night singles crowd in Bethesda, where he had met up with José Cuervo— a sadistic influence. Shots too numerous to count had turned him into "That Guy" and rendered him unfit to execute his mission. Defeated, he had made it back to his apartment, somehow.

The bedside clock announced 5:00 a.m. in annoying red LED. Zack's body felt like it had gone too many rounds with Hulk Hogan, not José. Without turning on the light, he wobbled to the bathroom. A satisfying pee and bracing splashes of cool water to his face lifted the fog. Returning, he flipped on the bedroom light. The chaotic bedding bespoke tossing and little slumber. Perhaps a bad dream about . . . what? The stench of sour sweat suggested something nasty. Details scurried into subconscious lairs like cockroaches.

Amber pre-morning light seeped through the curtains. Resolved to escape reminders of nocturnal terrors, Zack straightened the sheets and flung the bedspread over the top to hide the evidence. The apartment gym would not work for him this morning. Spurning his exhausted body's protest, he donned fresh running shorts and singlet, tucked into his Nikes, and pushed through the door and down the elevator.

The heat wave had vacated the region. Zack relished the cooler air as he took to the trail in emerging light, choosing the opposite direction from yesterday. He didn't need Noelle's jibes, friendly or otherwise, about last night's escapades.

Serene, his path seldom crossed by another runner or cyclist, Zack's brain drifted into an endorphin-enhanced trance, fueled by mental and physical fatigue. Remnants of tormenting dreams yielded to the here-and-now of running; more salubrious than drugs, or alcohol, or sex. In the zone, he maintained a mindless, steady pace—until memories of Carl Barnett crashed through the tranquility.

He pulled up, took a hearty swig from his water bottle, and reversed course.

Back in his apartment, Zack pulled off the sweat-soaked singlet and shorts, cooled down under the A/C vent, then showered. Dressed in shorts and tee shirt, he fixed a late breakfast of boiled eggs, sliced tomatoes, and feta cheese, then sat at his desk to re-read the clinical records from Carl Barnett's ER visits. He searched medical websites and downloaded articles from peer-reviewed journals. After hours of study, he had discovered nothing new; yet he could not quell the nagging sense of something missing.

He needed the autopsy results. Barnett's out-of-hospital cardiac arrest and subsequent death would have been a coroner's case. The pathologist would have studied the coronary arteries visually and under a microscope. Signs of coronary artery disease would suggest that Barnett's chest pain *was* cardiac in etiology, and that an exercise stress test might have led to the diagnosis by stimulating recurrence of his symptoms. An EST was not justified by the standard protocol, but a professional witness, such as Jerry Hartman, might claim poor clinical judgment by the attending ER physician. *Bullshit, but a jury might buy it.*

The postmortem had occurred on Friday, but Zack could not access the official report until Monday. Unwilling to endure a day's wait, he called Eric Wolfe, the chief pathologist at Metro Hospital and frequent running buddy. Zack had treated his daughter's asthma several times in the ER. More pertinent to the moment, Eric served as a deputy coroner for the Montgomery County Medical Examiner—a common arrangement in busy metropolitan areas that would otherwise overwhelm the understaffed tax-funded government office.

His friend answered on the second ring. "Hey, Zack. I was thinking of calling you. Dodgers are in town this week. Thought we might catch a game."

"I've got shifts tomorrow and Tuesday. Wednesday night?"

"Sounds good. I'll get tickets." A pause. "You called me. What's up?"

Zack cleared his throat. "Hoping you did a coroner's case Friday on an ER patient named Carl Barnett."

Eric waited a beat before responding. "You're the third person to ask. Jerry Hartman and Dennis King both called about it yesterday. Barnett's wife works at the hospital, right?"

Zack's heart reeled. "Head nurse in the ICU. Jerry was the man's attending physician. I treated Barnett in the ER, which would explain Dennis' interest."

"Okay. Negative autopsy except for minor cardiac findings. Other than bruising on the anterior myocardium, which I attribute to aggressive CPR, I found nothing. Coronaries were clean."

Zack's eyebrows furrowed. "No plaque? Don't most men in middle age have some degree of atherosclerosis?"

"We do, but not this guy. His coronaries were smooth as new PVC pipes."

"No cardiac pathology other than the bruising?"

"That's right."

Zack rubbed his forehead. "Cause of death?"

"With negative postmortem results, including no evidence of stroke, brain hemorrhage, or other causes of sudden death, we go by exclusion. I listed 'cardiac arrhythmia' as the presumptive cause. It's not a pathologic diagnosis, as you know, since arrhythmias don't result in anatomic changes. Without a cardiac monitor on him you wouldn't see it when it happened."

"He was in full cardiac arrest when he arrived."

"In that case, all we know for sure is his heart lost its natural rhythm sometime before that."

Zack remained perplexed. "Any thoughts on what caused the arrhythmia?"

"None for sure. Coronary artery spasm comes to mind, albeit rare. Not a pathology diagnosis. You might have reproduced it with EST, but that would have been a crap shoot."

Zack's cheeks burned as his voice went flat. "Thanks, Eric. I should let you get back to your Sunday."

"Sorry I couldn't shed more light."

Another thought struck Zack. "What did Jerry say when you told him your findings?"

"He didn't. Thanked me and hung up. Odd duck."

Odd, and threatening. "Thanks again, Eric."

"I'll get back to you about the baseball tickets."

After the call, Zack paced the floor. *How did Carl Barnett die?*

CHAPTER NINE

Monday back in the ER, Zack was slammed with patients. In addition to the expected tide of individuals who put off ailments and injuries over the weekend to hoard precious leisure time, a morning-rush-hour multi-vehicle fender-bender on the nearby Capital Beltway added to the workload. A flock of would-be victims walked in to "get checked," many with visions of insurance settlements dancing in their heads. He spent the morning "meeting and streeting," triaging and treating a mix of sick, injured, and worried-well. The latter tended to be the most demanding.

The pace slowed around three o'clock. He used the hiatus to guzzle his homemade health drink (like his post-run concoction but with more protein). He was still hungry. *Screw it.* He hustled to the hospital food court, bought a half-pizza, and hurried back to the ER lounge to eat while he had the chance.

Dennis King entered as Zack shoved a second wedge of pepperoni and cheese into his mouth. Dennis carried a manila folder in his right hand. He was on "admin time," a day of desk-riding and computer-clacking, not a revenue-generating clinical shift.

Still chewing, Zack greeted him with a head nod.

Dennis saw him glance at the folder. "Autopsy report."

Zack wondered if Dennis knew he had spoken with Eric Wolfe. He swallowed the food. "And?"

"Clean coronaries. Cause of death signed out as arrhythmia."

"Good news, right? Not for Carl Barnett, but for us. He didn't have pre-existing coronary disease, so how could we anticipate his cardiac arrest?"

Dennis scowled. "We can't discuss that case. I have a document in my hand. I never mentioned a patient's name."

Monica Harris appeared in the doorway. "Doctor Winston, chest pain in One."

Zack tossed the pizza crust into the box, took a quick swig of his drink, and followed Monica to the treatment area.

They reserved Bed One, closest to the resuscitation room, for evaluation of patients with acute chest pain. Carl Barnett had occupied that space three days ago. Today's tenant was a sixty-two-year-old pudgy fellow in obvious distress. Monica spoke into Zack's ear. "Abrupt onset of crushing pain in his mid-chest while mowing the lawn. Wife drove him here."

Pellets of sweat dotted the man's forehead. Wide, frightened eyes surveyed the surroundings while nurses and techs started an IV, positioned a green-plastic nasal cannula to deliver oxygen through his nostrils, and pasted EKG leads to his chest and extremities. Zack shook his hand. Calloused yellow-stained fingers, sallow skin reeking of stale tobacco. "How long since the pain started?"

"Maybe an hour."

"Ever had it before?"

"Not like this." Breaths came in shallow, rapid puffs.

A tech handed Zack the completed EKG. What he'd expected. "ST elevation in the precordial leads. Call a STEMI. Start the protocol."

The unequivocal EKG, along with the acute symptoms, age, obesity, and smoker status, confirmed ST-segment elevation myocardial infarction, or STEMI; an evolving heart attack. Sudden blockage in a coronary artery had interrupted blood flow to a region of the heart. The muscle—myocardium—was dying but not yet dead. Zack recalled the axiom: *Time is muscle. Muscle is life.*

At Bethesda Metro Hospital, "Time is muscle" meant urgent heart catheterization to open the occluded artery with a tiny balloon threaded to the heart via catheter from the femoral artery in the groin. They had a narrow time-window in which to restore circulation to the compromised heart muscle before it became a hunk of inert tissue; or worse, the damage spread and killed their patient. Their goal: "door to balloon" in less than thirty minutes.

"Code STEMI, ER. Code STEMI, ER." That announcement over the PA system summoned a specialized team to the patient. Meanwhile, the ER staff administered chewable aspirin (as a blood thinner), morphine by IV (to relieve pain and anxiety and reduce stress on the heart), and IV heparin (another blood thinner for the catheterization).

Zack stepped aside for the clamorous arrival of the STEMI team, led by Dr. Sevati Prakash, head of cardiology.

He passed her the EKG. "Textbook."

Sevati skimmed the tracing, nodded, and approached the patient. "Sir, I'm Dr. Prakash, a cardiologist. You are having a heart attack, but we will do all we can to reverse it. I am taking you upstairs for heart catheterization. We expect to remove a clot in one of your coronary arteries, then we will place a stent to keep the artery open. Understand?"

The man nodded, a mask of terror frozen on his face.

Sevati gestured to the team. "Go."

In an instant, a gaggle of six attendants wheeled the bed with the patient, attached IVs, oxygen tank, and heart monitor out of the room.

Zack stood alone in the abandoned space and looked at the timer on the wall. Twenty-two minutes from the patient's arrival.

Time is life.

CHAPTER TEN

The ER intercom interrupted his self-adulation. "Doctor Winston, Resus STAT." Zack turned and hustled to the resuscitation room.

A thirty-something woman wearing chartreuse, pink, and gray running attire with matching Nike shoes sat up on the gurney, wheezing and gasping for air; her skin red and swollen, a telltale three-inch red welt on the left side of her neck. Nurses bustled around her, placing an oxygen cannula in her nose, hooking up a monitor, and starting an IV.

"Name is Melody Snyder. Bee sting while running," one nurse said. "History of allergy to same. No results from two EpiPen injections at home. Husband drove her in."

"How long ago?"

"They estimate fifteen minutes."

The woman became more agitated and breathless, started to panic. Zack's quick assessment confirmed the diagnosis of impending anaphylactic shock.

"BP 60 over 40," a nurse reported. "Sinus tach at 140."

Scratch impending. She's in shock.

"As soon as you get an IV, push point five milligrams of epi." If two intramuscular injections of epinephrine from the EpiPen hadn't worked, likely due to her low blood pressure, they needed the intravenous route.

The woman thrashed, gasping for air.

"Start albuterol by nebulizer," Zack said. A respiratory therapist began the treatment, but the patient became more anxious, fought the treatment, tried to pull the nebulizer out of her mouth. Then she slumped back, semi-conscious. Her breathing turned rapid and shallow.

A young nurse, whom Zack didn't recognize, had trouble starting the IV. He started to take over the procedure when a senior nurse grabbed the patient's other arm. "I have this," she told the junior nurse. "You get the epi." The veteran nurse succeeded on the second stick. IV access at last.

Zack raised his voice. "Push that epi now."

The next few seconds seemed to pass in slow motion. The veteran nurse plugged the IV tubing into the cannula she had just inserted into the patient's vein. While she bent to tape it down, the junior nurse reached over her with a one-milliliter syringe, thrust the 23-gauge needle into a port on the IV tubing, and pushed the plunger to inject the full contents into the patient's bloodstream. It took two seconds for the mistake to travel from Zack's eyes to register in his brain—about the same time it took for the concentrated dose of epinephrine to flow from the woman's arm to her heart. Zack yelled, "Stop!"

Too late. The young nurse wheeled around, puzzled, while the senior nurse looked up and her face paled. She and Zack stared at the syringe in the junior nurse's hand: a one-milliliter syringe designed for subcutaneous injections. For IV injections, the epinephrine should have been diluted in ten milliliters of saline. The young nurse had just pushed the full-strength drug, a powerful cardiac stimulant, into rapid transit to Melody Snyder's coronary arteries.

As if on cue, the woman lurched forward, clutched between her breasts, and cried out. "My chest!" The monitor showed intermittent abnormal spikes of premature ventricular contractions. Those soon combined into a row resembling shark teeth. The patient's hand slumped off her chest. Her head fell back. Unconscious.

"V-tach." As if anyone in the room needed Zack to articulate the life-threatening arrhythmia. "Lower the head, bag her, get ready to intubate." As the head of the gurney rolled back to a flat position, Zack pounded his fist on the woman's chest. Nothing. He pounded again on her sternum. No change. Her skin turned pale blue.

Beads of sweat broke out on Zack's brow. He sucked in a gulp of air and held it in his lungs. *I will not lose this woman.* He pounded a third time, so hard that he thought he might break her breastbone. On the monitor, the shark's teeth stopped and for seconds that passed like minutes the tracing went flat. Then a beep as a normal EKG complex popped up on the screen. Then another. Beep. Beep. Beep.

Zack let himself breathe. "Back in sinus." With his fingers on the patient's neck, he felt a weak, thready pulse. Through his stethoscope on her chest he heard a heartbeat and shallow breath sounds. "She's breathing. Assist with the ambu, please. BP?"

"Seventy over forty, rising. Now eighty over fifty." On the monitor, sinus rhythm with occasional abnormal beats.

"Keep her fully oxygenated." The patient began to move. Zack spoke into her ear. "How are you doing?"

To his relief, she opened her eyes. "What . . . happened? My chest exploded then everything went black."

Zack gripped her hand. "Quite a scare, for all of us, but it's over. You'll be fine." He stood by her side and watched as her condition improved over the next five minutes. With enough epinephrine on board to kill a bear, her anaphylaxis was well under control. Without knowing it, she had dodged the bullet of adrenalin-induced near-fatal cardiac arrhythmia—caused by medical error, not pathology.

Once satisfied she was stable, Zack left her with the nurses and went to find the patient's husband. A niggling voice in the back of his head wondered why the woman's EpiPens had failed to work.

Zack found Douglas Snyder, Melody's husband, filling out forms at the ER registration desk. A mask of terror crossed the young man's face when Zack approached him.

"You wife will be fine," Zack said as he touched Snyder's shoulder. He summarized what had happened in the resus room but did not mention the near-fatal medical error.

"Thank God," Snyder said. "I was about to leave for work when she came in from her run." He wore a rumpled but expensive business suit. "She was already wheezing. I ran and grabbed the EpiPens, but . . ."

"Do you have those EpiPens?" Zack asked.

Snyder shook his head. "They would be in the trash at home."

"Any idea how old they are?"

Snyder's rubbed his chin, shook his head. "She hasn't had an episode for almost three years, so . . ."

"Please do me a favor," Zack said. "Retrieve them when you get home, then call the ER with the expiration dates. Better yet, if you could bring them in so we can examine them. I'm wondering why they didn't work."

"I'll try. Can it wait till I get home from work? I'm already way late for some important meetings."

Zack stared at him for a few seconds. "Sure. Now that she's out of the woods, it can wait."

Doug Snyder shook Zack's hand. "Thanks so much, Doc. You saved her life."

"Why we're here." Zack turned and left the room. *Why do I feel like I just shook hands with a used car salesman?*

Paula Cho arrived to relieve Zack at seven p.m. She gestured toward the resus room, where Melody Snyder continued to improve. "What's in resus?"

"We tried to kill a woman. Fortunately for her, we failed." Zack described what had happened.

"Nice save," Paula said.

Turnover complete, Zack hustled to the bunker to change from scrubs to street clothes. He'd spent enough time in Metro Hospital for one day.

On his way out, he spotted ER secretary Walter Knowles in the lobby, speaking on his mobile phone. *Does he ever go home?* When he noticed Zack, Walter clicked off, stuffed the phone in his back pocket, and regarded him with penetrating, prescient eyes.

"Hope your evening goes better than your day, Doc."

Zack nodded and walked past him. *Creepy guy.*

After wrapping up that last case, debriefing with the staff, and comforting the young nurse ("We've all made mistakes, and will again."), Zack drove home—two hours after his shift officially ended. As he turned onto Old Georgetown Road, unfamiliar elation buoyed his short journey. He should inform Dennis King about this new "situation," but it could wait until later in the morning. The case should not generate any legal problems because of the positive outcome and the rapport Zack had established with the patient and her husband. Not like the Barnetts.

The hospital hierarchy, however, would demand accountability. Therapeutic misadventures always incurred intense scrutiny, given that medical errors remained among the leading preventable causes of death in US health care. Zack anticipated another volatile encounter with Dr. Jerry Hartman, who would no doubt demand that he appear in front of the medical staff executive committee to talk about this case, and Carl Barnett. So be it. For now, he welcomed the elation.

He parked in the underground garage, shut off the car engine, and reflected. Thanks to Zack Winston, Melody Snyder would go home with her husband, to whatever life they had before she almost died. He imagined them through future decades; raising a family, guiding their children into adulthood; growing old together. He had resuscitated that future life through sheer determination. No one, not even Jerry Hartman, could take that satisfaction away from him. In fact, Jerry could take his bullying arrogance and shove it up his crack. Zack Winston would take no more of it.

CHAPTER ELEVEN

The next day during a lull in the ER, Zack consulted Dr. Sevati Prakash in her office. He handed her the copies of the serial EKGs from Carl Barnett's first visit, with the name, social security number, and other identifying information blacked out to avoid breach of patient privacy—and his own possible embarrassment. "I interpreted these as non-diagnostic for coronary artery disease. What do you think?"

Sevati was one of the most respected physicians on the staff, not only for her rich knowledge of cardiology but also for her collegial personality. Zack would trust her with his life. She arranged the papers on the desk in front of her and regarded him with gracious eyes. "Before we get into that, I will give you a report on the STEMI case from yesterday. He had near-total occlusion of his left anterior descending coronary artery. Angioplasty went well, and we achieved complete reperfusion of his myocardium. He is now pain-free, and his EKG has returned to baseline. I plan to send him home tomorrow. A clean save, Zack."

He flushed. "Thanks. I needed that."

Sevati smiled, took a caliper from her desk, and measured several segments of Barnett's initial EKG tracings. Zack scrutinized her face for clues to her thinking, craned his neck to see which elements commanded her interest. After a minute, she put down the caliper and regarded him with kind eyes.

"I concur with your interpretation. Non-diagnostic for acute coronary syndrome." Something in her tone worried him. His throat tightened. She cleared her throat. "How did the patient present?"

"Moderate distress at first, but the pain resolved without treatment. He demanded to leave."

"A positive sign." Her forced smile did not convince.

"Be straight with me, Sevati. Did I miss something?"

She tilted her head. "I would need more information."

How much to disclose? What the hell, he needed her expertise. Without identifying Carl Barnett by name, he summarized the two-day case history and handed her the EKGs from the attempted resuscitation on the second day.

She skimmed those, tossed them aside. "These show a dying heart, or one already dead. Nothing to do to at that point. Did you get a post?"

"Coronaries were clean; no pathological evidence of infarction. Cause of death probable fatal arrhythmia, perhaps from coronary artery spasm."

"Coronary spasm in a fifty-two-year-old?" Sevati stroked her chin. "Question would be what caused it. Medication history?"

"None other than occasional ibuprofen."

She pursed her lips in thought. "Toxicology screen?"

"Didn't order one."

Sevati frowned. "So, you do not know what caused his chest pain."

Zack shrugged. "That happens." Something gnawed at his gut. "Do you consider my care negligent?"

The corners of her mouth tilted up into a half-smile. "No. At worst, less than ideal clinical judgment."

He flushed as if he'd been slapped. "Would you admit a patient like this to the hospital?"

Sevati did not hesitate. "Yes, but I am an interventional cardiologist. I would bring him in for provocative angiography, which sometimes demonstrates coronary artery spasm."

Zack's mood darkened as he stared past her. "Could that have prevented a later episode of spasm that produced a fatal arrhythmia?"

She shrugged.

"Was his death preventable?"

Sevati leaned back, sucked air through her teeth. "In retrospect, it is possible."

Zack had to get out of there. He stood. "Thank you, Sevati."

He bolted out the door. Fighting a wave of nausea rolling up from his gut, he rushed to the nearest men's room and heaved into the toilet. His stomach empty, he leaned back on bent legs and wiped his lips. He stumbled to the sink, rinsed his mouth, and stared at his reflection in the mirror. He looked like he felt, morose and unglued. Negligent or not, he had fumbled the chance to prevent Carl Barnett's death and Janice's loss.

Zack Winston knew the grief of losing a spouse. He would not wish that suffering on Janice or anyone. Alone in the stuffy bathroom with his thoughts and memories, he buried his head in his hands. *Whatever made me think I should be a doctor?*

He took several minutes to compose himself. Nothing more to do. Zack had climbed too far from the abyss to slide back now. *Man up and carry on, sailor.*

Leaving the hospital, Zack gulped the fresh air as if it were 100% oxygen. He thought about the previous day, the STEMI, and the rescue of Melody Snyder. His spirits lifted. Zack Winston was a BAFERD. No plaintiff's attorney or emergency physician "expert" could match him head-to-head on the Barnett case. He gave proper care. He did not cause Barnett's death. Whatever threats might materialize, Zack intended to win.

CHAPTER TWELVE

Friday evening at six p.m., halfway from DC to Alexandria to pick up her fourteen-year-old son from baseball practice, Bridget got summoned back to court. The jury had reached a verdict on the Dawson case, just two hours after her closing argument. She had expected them to adjourn for the weekend and deliberate the following Monday.

Damn. She maneuvered her Range Rover back toward George Washington Memorial Parkway as she issued a voice command to her phone. "Call Marshall."

Her husband's edgy baritone Southern drawl filled the car's interior and drowned out the traffic noise. "Let me guess. You're running late."

"Right. Heading back to court. Jury's returning already. Not good." She made the turn onto the Memorial Bridge. "I'm sorry, Marsh. Can you pick up Justin and drop him at home on your way to the fundraiser? He can order a pizza on my credit card. That should hold him till I get there."

She heard only his amplified breathing for several seconds.

"I'll try to meet you at the fundraiser," she hoped her tone didn't sound as disingenuous as she felt.

Marshall spoke in a calm voice. "You won't be in the mood to party if your verdict goes south. I'll tell them you got held up in court. Folks will understand. We'll have plenty of other opportunities to show you off."

Bridget scrunched her forehead. "Thanks. I owe you one."

"I'll add it to the list." The smile in his voice attenuated some of the sting in his words.

After ending the call, Bridget reckoned that the honorable Marshall Hilliard, United States Attorney for the Eastern District of Virginia, would be happy to call in his wife's IOUs once he started his formal campaign for attorney general. Who ever said that a dual-professional marriage raising an active teenager would be easy?

D r. Julie Dawson was pacing the hallway outside the courtroom when Bridget arrived. The young physician's eyes bristled with tears when she saw her advocate approach. "That monster Meadows sneered at me." She gestured toward the court room. "They're all in there."

"Let's see what we got," Bridget said. "This may not be good. No matter what happens in there, it's not the end of your life."

Julie's jaw dropped. "You mean—?"

"Juries are unpredictable. Whatever this one does, we must stand tall." Bridget put an arm around the young physician's shoulder and steered her into the court room. She had been in the same situation too many times. Cynicism had become habitual, for valid reasons.

T he jury foreman bellowed the verdict in a strident pharisaic voice. "We find in favor of the plaintiff, to whom we award two-million dollars in compensatory damages. We further adjudge the defendant's care as gross negligence and award the plaintiff an additional two-million dollars in punitive damages."

Julie Dawson shrieked. "No!" She wheeled on Bridget. "I didn't do anything wrong. Tell them again. Please. I did nothing wrong."

The judge pounded his gavel. Bridget hugged Julie, pulling her in close to avoid another outburst. "Shhh. Be quiet or the judge will hit you for contempt. Hold tight until these people get out of here. This is not the end."

Behind her, the judge ended the proceeding. People filed out. Over Julie's shoulder, Bridget saw Roger Meadows approach with lips curled, eyes icy daggers. She cast him a withering stare, a warning not to come closer. He ran his tongue along his upper lip and followed his client out of the room.

Alone with her client, Bridget let go of the devastated Dr. Dawson, sat her down, and took her hands. "I'm sorry, Julie. I thought we had a solid case and discredited their expert. We'll look for a reason to appeal."

Julie's lips quivered, "Gross negligence? Punitive damages? I never—"

Bridget put a finger to the young woman's lips. "That is nonsense. The jury made an emotional decision based on the dramatic display of grief that Roger coaxed out of the widow. They chose to give her all they could and stick your insurance company with the bill. We'll try to get that reversed."

She felt a presence behind her, turned to see three people on the periphery. Julie's parents and fiancé. She nodded to them, and they stepped forward to hug Julie. When they were done, Bridget faced her client and put reassuring hands on her shoulders. "Your world is not dead, Doctor Dawson. Your life and career will move forward." She gestured around the court room. "This . . . is not the real world. You are a great physician. Believe in yourself. You can treat me or my family anytime."

Julie hugged her. "Thanks, Bridget."

"We're not done fighting."

As she walked out of the courthouse ten minutes later, Bridget shook her head. *No more ER docs. Their odds are too damned low.*

CHAPTER THIRTEEN

Across a narrow table, Zack compared Angela Moretti's honey-almond complexion and shoulder-length chestnut-brown hair to Noelle's somewhat darker complexion and jet-black hair. Similar yet different. For their dinner date, he had chosen RASA on 1st Street in southeast DC for its fast and casual service of exquisite Indian cuisine—and for its walking proximity to Ange's apartment building. He had commuted by Metro from Bethesda, to avoid any risk of driving home under the influence should their night together end sooner than he desired.

Ange pushed away her half-finished plate of tikka masala and fiddled with her napkin.

As the server cleared away the entrée dishes, Zack realized he'd monopolized the conversation since the first bites of garlic naan. She'd taken only a few sips of house white wine, while he had almost finished his second Bengali IPA. He cleared his throat. "That's everything you'd want to know about the latest ER misadventure and threat to my career."

Ange stared into the distance for a few seconds, then focused on him. Her deep-brown eyes reminded him of Noelle's. No coincidence. "You've never been sued?"

He looked away. "Not sued, censured. The navy thing I mentioned."

"You didn't tell me much about that. It seemed too painful for you."

He re-engaged eye contact, saw sympathy in hers—or pity. His nervous gaze darted around the crowded restaurant. "Can't talk about that here. Maybe later when we're alone."

She did not respond. They sat in silence, sipping strong coffee. Her expression turned thoughtful, her tone gentle. "Your case doesn't meet three of the four pillars for malpractice."

"Pillars?"

"Duty, negligence, harm, causation. You had a duty to treat, but that's the only fit. If you did not deviate from the standard of care, it's not negligence. No negligence, no harm, no causation. Ergo, no malpractice."

Zack's mouth curled into a slow smile. "So, no worry."

Ange frowned, reached out to touch his hand. "Here's the real deal, Zack. Whether a physician committed actual malpractice seldom matters. The plaintiff's attorney aims to motivate the defendant's insurance carrier to settle before trial. They bet that the threat of losing a case in court, with the resulting disgrace and baggage, will force the doctor to cave. Let the insurance company pay off the plaintiff. Put an end to it with no money out of pocket." She withdrew her hand.

Zack reeled. "I should admit guilt? I'm innocent."

She gave him a clenched half-smile. "It's not like a murder trial. 'Guilt' is not a factor. No matter how 'innocent,' you can't trust a jury. They might feel sorry for the 'victim,' want to compensate her for loss of her husband, his companionship, his earning power. Insurance companies expect that, and they know up front how much they can spend. The plaintiff's attorney gets a sizable percentage of the settlement, reduces overhead by not going to trial, and avoids any chance of a verdict for the defense." She shrugged. "That's the malpractice game, Zack. The plaintiff and the doctor are bit players. You have little influence on the outcome. Being right doesn't count."

He slumped. "Thanks for the uplifting summary, counselor. Should I shoot myself now or later?"

Ange waved him off. "Don't be dramatic."

Zack retorted. "The 'game' you describe involves human suffering, on both sides. I may have professional angst, but Janice Barnett lost her husband. How can you lawyers be so cold?"

Ange's eyes flared. "Not so. The law touches humanity, all facets, including suffering. You know my empathy. That's why I practice here and not with a bloated firm in northwest DC."

Zack admired her commitment to those who could not afford expensive legal support. "One of your many endearing qualities."

Ange looked away. Silence descended. Both pretended to sip from empty coffee cups.

After a minute, she spoke, voice flat. "In regard to big law firms, I have news."

"You're joining the dark side?"

"Not me, Keisha."

"Keisha? You two are partners."

"We share office expenses and a conviction that the practice of law is about helping people, not getting rich." She sighed. "She accepted a lucrative offer as associate to Roger Meadows, arguably the most successful personal injury attorney in the area. She starts in two weeks."

"Wow. What are you going to do?"

She spread her hands. "Try to get more cases, cut expenses. See if I can survive solo."

"If not?"

Her eyes dimmed. "I have options. I'll figure it out."

The server filled their coffee cups. They sipped. Ange put down her cup. "How are your kids, Zack?"

He fumbled for words. "Fine."

"Talk to them much?"

"It's, uh, complicated. Time difference with California and all."

"When was the last time you spoke to them?"

He turned in his chair, blinked. "I tried to call Annie on her sixteenth birthday, Christmas Eve."

Ange's eyebrows raised. "That was the last time?"

"I've left Facebook messages."

She scoffed. "Facebook. How nice." A pause. "Do you ever talk to their mother? You never said much about your divorce."

Zack took a few seconds to calibrate. "Not since the girls got older. It happened long ago. Natalie left me for another guy. Said I was too bottled up for true intimacy."

Ange smirked. "Imagine that."

"Psychobabble. She's a shrink. A psychiatrist."

"You never mentioned that."

"Like I said, ancient history."

She smiled. "I appreciate the honesty, Zack. Sorry if I opened an old wound."

He understood honesty, vulnerability, pain; how death could rip out your heart. He couldn't find the words to tell her, so he responded with a stupid shrug. She touched his hand.

The restaurant had reached peak time. Patrons waiting for seats glared at them. He nodded toward the exit. "We've overstayed our welcome. Walk you home?"

She pursed her lips. "Sure."

The walk to her apartment took ten silent minutes, tension building with each step. They held hands, but hers stayed limp. Like a confused adolescent, he released his grip. She did not reattach. At the entrance to her building, she stopped and faced him, forcing a foot and a half of space between them. The amber gleam of streetlight accentuated her Mediterranean beauty. "Thanks for dinner. I hope your legal situation turns out okay. Best case, it goes away."

Zack moved closer, muscles tense. They stood in place, neither one moving. He tried to break through the wall by gesturing with his head toward the front door.

"I can't sleep with you."

His heart plunged. "Tonight, or ever?"

"For certain not tonight. Don't know about ever."

Zack's gut twisted. "What's going on?"

Her eyes softened and her skin flushed. She lifted her head, holding her gaze on his. "I care for you, Zack. We've had a great fling. We both knew it wouldn't last." Her tongue wet her upper lip, her breathing quickened. Then she looked away.

Zack felt a tightness across his shoulders. "The age thing."

She nodded.

"That's why you brought up my kids and first wife."

Ange took a breath. "Sometimes I fantasize that we met in another time and place. We didn't. Can't change that."

Zack blinked his eyes to reconcile conflicting emotions. "I get it." A deep breath. "You deserve a chance with someone else, not a once-divorced, once-widowed older guy. I can't deny you that."

She shrugged. A tear wet the corner of one eye. "Yeah."

Zack rubbed the back of his neck. "We can stay friends."

Ange smiled. "Always." She moved closer and kissed him on the lips, soft with a tinge of passion.

He pulled her close. She pushed away, then reattached. Their breathing deepened in synchrony as they kissed.

Zack broke the embrace. "I don't suppose we could . . ."

Her face broke into a full smile. "One last time?" She grasped his hand and led him into her apartment building.

When Zack left Ange's apartment early the next morning, he felt buoyant. He appreciated that Ange had taken the initiative to do what they both needed, to end their affair before it became a ridiculous obsession. After a night of unburdened passion, they had parted on a different level of intimacy. Friends. Zack could not remember having a female friend that didn't involve sex. He relished the possibility.

Riding the Metro toward Bethesda, he thought about his past post-divorce recovery as a US Navy flight surgeon in Japan. Enjoying off-ship liberty in Hong Kong during a *USS Kitty Hawk* port visit, he had joined the fun at an aviator party-suite at the Harbor Grand Hotel. He noticed her at once: Lieutenant Noelle Robinson; Junoesque, flowing brunet mane, sensuous as hell in that white gauze pantsuit, gold chain with naval aviator wings adorning a silken swarthy neckline. The most beautiful woman he'd ever seen. When they talked, their minds melded in a way he had never experienced with any other woman. He came on to her with a clumsy line about being a flight doc required to assess her physical readiness to fly jets. She rewarded him with a conspiratorial wink and smile. They soon discovered a shared affection for single malt scotch, and for more sensuous pleasures.

As the Metro train rolled north, Zack drifted into half-sleep—content in the memory of when he first bonded with Noelle, ten years ago.

CHAPTER FOURTEEN

Saturday night, Bridget treated Marshall to her specialty, pasta Bolognese accompanied by a properly aged bottle of Antinori Tignanello. Now that their son was engaged in teenager pursuits like this night's movie outing, they found themselves with more time together. Certain past topics remained off-limits by mutual agreement.

Halfway through the meal, Marshall poured each a second glass of the Super Tuscan. "What are we celebrating?"

"Not celebrating, commiserating over losing the Dawson case."

"Damn. Sorry, Bridge. I know how you hate to lose, especially to that ass-wipe Meadows."

Bridget shrugged. "For me it's a number in the loss column. Julie Dawson's life, in spite of my efforts to reassure her, is forever changed. She talked about getting out of the profession. I tried to convince her that losing the case is not a judgment on her ability. She didn't cause that patient's death."

Marshall looked at her with a strained smile. "You are one of the few lawyers I know who takes the term 'counselor' to the full extent of its several definitions."

Bridget felt her neck redden. After an uncomfortable silence, Marshall put down his glass and leaned toward her. "I meant that as a compliment, Bridge. Sorry if it gouged an old wound."

She tried to lighten her voice. "It's okay. Anyway, it's done. I hope the good Dr. Dawson comes to her senses and gets back in the saddle. We need doctors like her." Bridget shuffled in her chair. Their interactions had been strained since his return from a case in Norfolk a week ago. "How are things on the prosecution side?"

Welcoming the shift in focus, Marshall leaned back, took another sip of wine. "We've opened a new investigation that I can't talk about."

Bridget gave him a flirtatious smile. "Since when do we not have husband-wife privilege in our personal communications?"

He smiled back and shrugged. "It has to do with docs and drugs."

She stroked her chin. "Do tell."

He chuckled and shook his head. "Further affiant sayeth not."

She laughed; relieved to have steered the conversation away from her penchant for over-engagement with her clients. Eventually she would have retaliated by challenging him about his affections for female subordinates. Both subjects better left off the table. "Are you up for dessert? I picked up some cannoli at the Italian grocery store."

"Deal, counselor. But only if you let me brew a suitable espresso."

Bridget smiled, genuine. "As you wish, Mr. US Attorney."

CHAPTER FIFTEEN

When Zack got home at 6:45 a.m., he remembered he'd promised to meet Eric Wolfe for a run at 7. He threw on running clothes and shoes, swallowed microwave-reheated coffee in three gulps, grabbed a water bottle, and charged out the door at a half-sprint to the trail. When he arrived, Eric was pacing the ground at their usual spot. Zack was five minutes late, but Eric was punctual to a fault. Without ado, they started down the trail.

"You look like re-heated shit," Eric said, slowing his pace to match Zack's slower-than-usual strides.

"Rough week. Getting too old for shift work." He thought of telling Eric about his encounters with Janice Barnett and Jerry Hartman, or his last night with Ange, but he didn't. They were running buddies, not soul mates. Passing his special bend in the trail, Zack looked for Noelle. Of course not there. She never showed when he ran with someone else.

The two men completed the ten-mile run in near silence, each lost in his own thoughts. At the end, Zack bid Eric adieu with a half-hearted agreement to run together the next weekend. By the time he jogged home, a shroud of fatigue and ennui enveloped him. Skipping the post-run smoothie, he threw off the damp running clothes, fell into bed, and slept until four p.m.

At six p.m., Zack strode through the ER door, rested, showered, nourished, and confident. With effort, he'd left the Barnetts, Ange, and even Noelle, back in his apartment. The patients he would see in the next twelve hours deserved an unencumbered mind.

Typical for an ER Saturday night, a constant stream of humanity flowed through the ER, keeping Zack busy throughout his shift. On most nights, he could get a few hours of sleep around two a.m. Not this night. In addition to the usual complaints of stomach aches, headaches, respiratory infections, fevers, sprained ankles, broken wrists, cuts and scrapes, and babies who would not quit crying, he treated victims from two serious automobile crashes, a young woman who overdosed on opiates, a drug-dealer who got himself shot ("Two dudes just jumped me, man."), a septuagenarian male with unmistakable acute coronary syndrome, and a sexagenarian female smoker who suffered a major stroke.

At five a.m., while he finished charting on the stroke victim before sending her to the ICU, EMS called in with a full code. "Fifty-five-year-old male, witnessed arrest, immediate CPR on scene, V-Fib on AED, shocked twice, converted to sinus brady at forty BPM, weak pulse. Request atropine."

"Atropine approved," Zack said.

Two minutes later, the paramedics rolled through the door with an obese male whose color appeared somewhere between pink and light blue. "We got a pulse," the first medic said. In short order, the ER team got the patient under control. His heart rate, in normal sinus rhythm, came up to seventy. His blood pressure returned. He woke up, stable. "Welcome back from the already dead," Zack said. A flash of memory hit him. "Carl Barnett should have been so lucky." The man stared at him, befuddled.

In the workstation Zack shook the paramedics' hands. "Nice save." He meant it. Their quick actions had snatched the man from the jaws of death.

After his shift, Zack visited the hospital cafeteria for a quick breakfast of eggs, bacon, toast, hash browns, grits, and orange juice. (Sundays were his designated "don't need to eat healthy" days). He headed home with a full belly, took a long shower to wash off whatever detritus he had picked up in the ER, turned off his phone, and crashed into bed. He slept through the day until his alarm awakened him at five p.m. to prepare for another night shift.

All this and a paycheck too.

Unlike Saturday nights, where the action began late and lasted long, Sunday night shifts tended to be busy early before tapering off after midnight. Aside from an occasional adrenalin-charging true emergency, Sunday evening's clientele featured people looking for a quick tune-up from ignored injury or illness because they could not take the time to visit the ER or their own physician's office on Monday.

By one a.m. the ER was empty of patients. While nurses and techs restocked the treatment spaces and resuscitation room, Zack wandered out to the triage area to check status. The two receptionists busied themselves breaking down and filing the records from the previous patients, while the triage nurse took a coffee break—no doubt his first of the night. Zack noted the empty chairs in the waiting area, then walked outside to recon the parking lot; vacant save for vehicles belonging to the staff. Most folks in the region were now in bed, prepping for Monday; one more weekend in their lives gone forever. Zack stood outside for a few minutes to savor the tranquility of deep night.

How time flies when you're having no fun at all.

Satisfied that no immediate tragedy, pending illness, or anxious parents loomed over the horizon, Zack went back inside, nodded to the nurses, and headed for the bunker. With luck, he would get a few hours of uninterrupted sleep. From well-honed practice, despite several cups of coffee throughout the shift, he nodded off within seconds after his head hit the pillow. He never had problems sleeping during a night shift, and could wake up, alert and coherent, immediately upon notification that he was needed up front.

A tap on the bunker door awakened him. Zack looked at his watch. Just past seven a.m. He'd slept for six uninterrupted hours. His weekend of night shifts had ended. Jesse Berg, his relief, entered the bunker to change into scrubs.

"What a charmed life you lead," Jesse said.

"If you only knew," Zack said.

Unexpectedly rested, Zack went to the cafeteria for breakfast. He'd just started to eat when Monica Harris rushed in. "They need someone in ICU, STAT. Dr. Berg is tied up with a full code in the ER."

In rare instances, when the ICU was short an intensivist and the patient's attending doctor was unavailable, the emergency physician on duty got the call to intervene in a life-threatening event. Zack put down his fork, dashed out of the cafeteria, and rode the elevator to the second floor.

When he barged into the ICU, Janice Barnett met him. Stone-faced, she directed him to a cubicle where a muscular young male lay unconscious, purple-cyanotic from upper chest to scalp, neck veins standing out like Tiparillo cigars. Zack recognized him as one of the trauma victims he'd admitted for observation Saturday night.

The monitor showed a rapid pulse at 130 and a dangerously low systolic blood pressure at eighty. At the head of the bed, a nurse assisted the patient's respirations with a bag-valve-mask apparatus. A technician was running a twelve-lead EKG.

"Let me see that EKG." The tech handed him the tracing. ST elevation in all leads. He showed it to Jan. She glanced at it but said nothing. He put a stethoscope to the young man's chest and heard the expected muffled heart sounds. "Pericardial tamponade." Blood had collected in the sac covering the heart. The accumulation prevented the vital organ from normal filling.

Zack pulled on a pair of sterile gloves. "Needle, please. You know the procedure."

A nurse handed him a 20-cc syringe with a five-inch long 18-gauge spinal needle attached. Another nurse cleansed the skin below the man's breastbone with an antiseptic solution. *As effective as spitting on it.* Zack nudged her hand away. Holding the needle at a 45-degree angle to the patient's chest, he inserted the point just below where the lower rib cage joined the sternum on the left side. With steady pressure, he pushed the needle toward the patient's left shoulder while maintaining slight back pressure on the syringe's plunger. He wished for an ultrasound machine to visualize the needle's path toward the heart, but he could not afford to wait. Before ultrasound became the standard, Zack had learned to rely on wits and feel performing this lifesaving procedure.

Within seconds, he felt a distinct "pop" as the needle penetrated the taut pericardial sac. Dark red blood flowed into the syringe. Zack pulled back the plunger and withdrew 10 cc. The patient's blood pressure rose, and his pulse slowed. Skin color changed to mottled pink and he began to writhe.

"Be still, sir." Zack spoke in a commanding voice as two nurses restrained the patient. "I have a needle next to your heart, and I'd hate to puncture it."

The man went rigid.

Zack addressed the nurse at the head. "Make sure he's awake." She flipped open the man's eyelids and nodded in the affirmative. Another nurse reported vital signs normal.

A rough grunt from behind diverted Zack's attention. He glanced back to see Jerry Hartman, scowling.

"Pericardial tamponade," Zack said. "He was crashing. I did a pericardiocentesis."

Jerry's eyebrows arched. "Without ultrasound?"

"No time to get a machine."

Jerry tilted his head toward the corner of the room. Zack had not noticed the portable ultrasound unit when he'd rushed into the unfamiliar environ of the ICU.

Hartman sneered. "Nurses know how to use it."

Nice of them to tell me. Zack checked that the man's vitals remained normal, then pulled out the needle and handed the syringe to Jerry. "My shift ended a half-hour ago."

Hartman did not reply. He dropped the syringe onto the instrument tray and turned toward the patient, his back to Zack.

At the ICU door, Janice Barnett blocked Zack's path. "Document the record before you leave, doctor."

"Of course."

She walked away without a word.

Zack drove home on a high note. His weekend of successful night shifts had restored his confidence. By the time he ascended in the elevator to his apartment, his mood tempered. He paused at his door, key in hand, recalling his doubt after he'd reviewed Barnett's EKGs with Sevati. He had questioned his life-choice to become a doctor.

Might as well not live. No one ever held a gun to my head and forced me to be an emergency physician. I chose it, for both the highs and the lows. ER doc is who I am.

He sighed, unlocked the door, and stepped inside his apartment. Noelle reclined on the couch, hands clasped behind her head, radiant in that white gauze pantsuit, the naval aviator wings-of-gold pendant sparkling on her umber chest, her smile alive with affection. "Welcome back, BAFERD."

CHAPTER SIXTEEN

As usual, Noelle didn't remain after Zack got home. His spirits rode the wave of her "BAFERD" praise well into the next month, when his days seemed to normalize after the turbulence of Carl Barnett's death and aftermath, Zack's mutual split with Ange, and his pivotal save of Melody Snyder. He had not heard from Janice Barnett or any lawyers. No signs of Noelle.

Then a summons arrived from Jerry Hartman for Zack to appear before the medical staff executive committee.

A week later, Zack sat alone on one side of a long, polished cherry table in the hospital board room. His inquisitors on the opposite side were the eight heads of hospital departments. Across from Zack in the confrontation seat, Jerry Hartman stared with cold eyes while his alter-ego, obstetrician Sebastian Barth, railed about the incompetence of emergency physicians in general and Zack Winston in particular. When Barth finally shut up, Hartman summarized the case of Melody Snyder, "who almost died of an egregious nursing error. Dr. Winston should have stopped that nurse from giving the wrong dose of epinephrine."

In counterpoint, Dennis King stated that Zack could not have predicted the nursing error before he saw it happen; too late to intervene. He reminded the committee that Zack had saved the woman's life through quick thinking and bold action.

Hartman shifted focus to the death of Carl Barnett. "The man needed CPU admission and provocative angiography. Instead, Dr. Winston sent him home to die."

Sevati Prakash defended Zack. "Easy to opine as much in retrospect, knowing what happened, but we must not second-guess Dr. Winston's clinical judgment made with the data he had at the time." She glanced sideways at Zack when she said, "I might have made a different decision, but I don't know. I was not there, and I am not an emergency physician. I do know, without reservation, that I would trust Dr. Winston with my life. Anytime."

Zack had to look down and stare at the table to cover his stunned emotions.

In the end, the committee threw Jerry Hartman a bone while sparing Zack from significant consequences. They issued a non-punitive letter of caution, a harmless document that would not be included in his credentials file.

As Zack left the meeting room, Jerry Hartman met him at the door. "This isn't over. Screw up again and you are meat a starving dog won't touch."

As summer gave reluctant way to autumn, Zack's life entered a new normal. He put on the persona of a middle-aged male not on the prowl; a dedicated emergency physician, head down, focused on his job, avoiding controversy or unwanted attention—in and out of the ER. Not the adrenalin-driven live-on-the-edge élan he had relished in his young BAFERD days, but a mindset less risky and more consistent with his present age and station. Renewed clinical confidence motivated an improved lifestyle. He all but quit drinking, stopped disrupting his healthy diet with junk food, and stepped up his running routine.

By the time Halloween decorations appeared on store shelves, Zack began to doubt he would need legal advice. Maybe Janice got through the stages of grief and accepted reality. Maybe she'd seen a lawyer or reviewed the records with a medical expert. An ethical physician or objective plaintiff's attorney would tell her she had no case. An experienced ICU nurse should intuit as much. Competent advice might have convinced her.

The Washington Nationals fell out of the post-season picture, and with them Zack's hopes of treating Ange to her first World Series. They were still friends, after all, albeit without much contact.

One chilly morning in late autumn, Noelle surprised Zack at their usual spot on the Capital Crescent Trail. They ran in silence for a few miles before she stopped and turned on him. "Why did Carl Barnett die?"

Frustrated, Zack stopped and put his hands on his hips. "From fatal cardiac arrhythmia, probably due to coronary artery spasm."

Noelle cast him a frozen smile. "Not how did he die. *Why* did he die? Don't say it was God's will or 'just his time,' or some other crap. What happened to him, and why—or who?"

Sometimes Noelle could be a pain. Zack rubbed his forehead. He could not ignore the lingering doubt. "I need to figure that out."

CHAPTER SEVENTEEN

The following morning, Zack arrived in the ER rested and in high spirits for his day shift. His mind had already buried Noelle's provocative questions. After the run, he had pulled out his copy of Carl Barnett's records from beneath deferred personal financial folders. Perused for the first time in over two months, the ER records seemed stale and boring. He thought about using his remote access to the hospital's electronic medical records to search for other clues in Barnett's history file but thought it would be a privacy violation. Not worth the risk. *Sorry, Noelle.* The Barnett case had faded into the past. *Let it desiccate there.*

The ER tempo remained slow throughout the day, typical for mid-week in autumn when summertime activities had faded into memories, children languished in school with faint anticipation of winter holidays, and lives mimicked the drifting tempo of falling leaves. Near the end of the shift, Zack discharged a young man with a two-day-old sprained ankle. No other patients remained. He resisted the temptation to run to the food court for pizza and settled into the lounge to finish off the five-ingredient turmeric smoothie that he had sipped throughout the shift.

Dennis King entered the room, holding two white envelopes in his hand. He gestured for Zack to follow him. Expressionless, he led Zack to the bunker, closed the door, and handed him one of the envelopes. Zack's pulse quickened as he noted an embossed formal font with his name as the addressee. His eyes scanned the return address:

Cooper, Meadows, and Clark, LTD
Attorneys at Law

Dennis held up the other envelope, addressed to Emergency Health Associates. "Hospital got the third one."

Heart pounding, Zack opened his envelope with trembling hands and extracted two sheets of expensive stationery. He squinted at the raised letterhead. *Roger Meadows.* Where had he heard that name?

The text, in pedantic legalese, notified Zack of Janice Barnett's intent to file suit for the wrongful death of Carl Barnett due to Zack's negligence. The lawyer offered a meeting to discuss settlement without going to trial. Zack read the letter three times, then threw it at Dennis. "This is bullshit. Doesn't come close to the truth. 'Acute coronary syndrome?' No way in hell he had that."

"I agree. Now we have to prove it."

Zack paced the floor, fists clenched. "Five-million dollars? Screw that bitch."

Dennis spoke in a calm voice. "Get your anger out now, Zack. You can't afford it as this moves forward. Like it or not, bullshit or not, this will move forward."

Zack met Dennis' eyes, not a foot from his face. "I'll pull it together. That woman will not ruin me."

Dennis nodded. "I don't need to tell you not to contact that attorney, right?"

Zack snorted. "Duh."

"Tomorrow I'll get up with our insurance carrier. I'll let you know what happens next."

"Thanks." Rage boiled inside Zack.

Dennis put both hands on Zack's shoulders, like an older brother soothing a pubescent sibling. "We'll beat this. Nothing more we can do today. Finish your shift, go home, have some stiff drinks. Get laid if you can."

Zack groaned to himself. *He needs to drop that stupid line.*

A fter Dennis left, Zack stayed in the bunker to compose himself, to overcome the urge to race up to the ICU and throttle Janice Barnett. He remembered Noelle's challenge from the previous day. A familiar gloom descended over him. The life that he had rebuilt over the last nine years had just plunged like a wounded jet into the sea.

CHAPTER EIGHTEEN

An urgent knock interrupted Zack's emotional storm. Without waiting for a response, head nurse Monica Harris leaned into the room. She did a fleeting double-take at his pained facial expression. "EMS on the line. Full code."

Why summon him in person? Why didn't she get the information from the medics and pass it to him?

Monica read his thoughts. "They want the doctor on duty."

Zack hurried to the EMS radio in the workstation. "Dr. Winston."

The medic's voice sounded shrill, his words racing over each other. "En route your facility five minutes out sixty-two-year-old male unwitnessed cardiac arrest. Partner found him unconscious and started CPR. On our arrival patient in V-fib. Defibrillation achieved return of spontaneous circulation with regular rhythm and ST-segment elevation on twelve-lead EKG. Patient remains unconscious with weak pulse at sixty, intubated and ventilating with ambu bag."

The report seemed routine. *Why so anxious?* "Proceed."

After a beat, the medic's voice came back, higher pitched. "Patient works at Metro Hospital as ER secretary."

Walter Knowles? The medic could not say the patient's name over a public EMS channel, but Zack got the message. Collective gasps around him indicated that Monica and other staff within earshot got it too.

"Copy all," Zack said. "Expect Code STEMI on arrival." He didn't wait for their response, turned to Monica. "Call the STEMI code. Now."

F our minutes later, the medics and the STEMI team all converged on the resus room. Everyone recognized Walter Knowles, the enigmatic augur who for years had been a constant presence in the ever-shifting milieu of the Metro ER. As the team transferred him from the ambulance stretcher to the ER gurney, Zack blinked as he recalled his cryptic encounters with Walt after Carl Barnett's death.

The tech handed him an EKG, which he shared with Sevati Prakash standing next to him. They spoke in unison. "Infero-lateral STEMI."

"Get him to the cath lab," Sevati said.

The ER staff had barely enough time to finish drawing blood for protocol lab tests before the STEMI team rushed their patient out of the room toward the dedicated elevator to the second-floor where the cath lab and intensive care units were located. Once they departed, Zack looked at the clock. Door to cath, eight minutes flat.

Time is life.

C atching his breath, Zack leaned against the ambulance gurney that had carried Walter Knowles into the ER. Moisture seeped into the back of his scrubs. He turned and found the sheet soaked. Had the medics spilled something on it? Saline from the IV tubing? Too much for an IV spill. He sniffed the sheet. Urine, and sweat. *What the . . .?* People who collapsed often lost bladder control. But sweat? Why sweat on a temperate autumn day?

He questioned the medics and confirmed that Walter was sweating when they arrived on scene. "The carpet was damp with it; the room seemed warm. Like he'd amped up the heat. Strange odor in the place too. Like someone cooking with garlic."

Zack scratched his head. *Typical inscrutable Walter Knowles.*

B ack in the main treatment area, seven new patients waited to be seen. All had arrived during his meeting with Dennis and the triage of Walter Knowles. None appeared in imminent danger, so Zack began seeing them in order of arrival. He was examining the third patient, a woman with a two-week history of vague abdominal pain, when Monica Harris drew back the curtain. "Dr. Prakash on the phone, needs you STAT."

What the . . .? Zack excused himself, hurried to the phone in the physicians' work area.

"It is not a STEMI." Sevati's muffled voice indicated she was talking through a surgical mask, still in the cath room. "No coronary stenosis. No clots. He is crashing. BP bottomed out."

"On my way," Zack said. "Run fluids wide bore if you're not already doing that." He hung up the phone and rushed to the elevator. "Where are those labs on Knowles?" A nurse thrust a printout into his hand just as the elevator door closed. On quick scan, the results did not make sense.

At the cath lab door, he donned a surgical mask and charged into the room. Walter Knowles' sallow skin glistened with sweat. Beside him, in surgical gown, gloves, and mask, Sevati looked at Zack with wide eyes. A nurse struggled to start a second IV, while another pushed a pliable plastic nasogastric tube into a nostril, aiming for Walt's esophagus and stomach. Streaks of recent clear brown vomit pooled around the endotracheal tube, ran down his chin, and puddled on the sheet beneath his head. Zack detected a slight odor of rancid garlic.

Sevati spoke in a trembling voice. "We cannot get his blood pressure above sixty, and he remains hypoxic. Pulse ox is eighty on one-hundred percent O2." As competent as she was, Sevati had entered a chaotic, unfamiliar world—a patient trying to die from undetermined pathology. This was a BAFERD's domain; Zack Winston's domain.

He took command. Sevati let out a sigh of relief and stepped back. "How can I help?"

Zack showed her the lab results. "Cardiac enzymes are negative. No surprise based on your cath findings. Blood gases show severe metabolic and respiratory acidosis."

"Very severe. Metabolic, not cardiac," she said.

"Agreed."

The nurse had succeeded in establishing a second IV. "Run both IVs wide open with normal saline," Zack said. "Squeeze the bags if you have to." He looked at Sevati. "Can you get a line into his femoral vein?"

"Of course." She withdrew the angiography catheter from Walt's femoral artery, then inserted a large bore intravenous catheter into the femoral vein that ran next to the artery. A nurse connected a bag of normal saline to that catheter. They now had three IVs going wide open, but Walt's blood pressure did not improve.

"Start a dopamine drip," Zack said. "Alert ICU we have a critical patient." The other nurse had finished inserting the nasogastric tube and used a large syringe to withdraw fluid that looked like filthy dishwater from Walt's stomach. Sudden acrid stench exploded through the room as Walter's bowels evacuated a gush of watery diarrhea. Stifling a gag, Zack looked him over again. His skin still glistened with sweat. Tears ran down his face. Saliva drooled from his mouth. Clear snot flowed from his nose. "How are his pupils?"

A nurse lifted Walt's eyelids. "Constricted. Not quite pinpoint."

Zack looked at Sevati and saw in her eyes the same terror that surged through him. "We're going to need a boatload of atropine," he said. "And we need to lock down the hospital. Now."

CHAPTER NINETEEN

Z ack's gaze swept the cath room. Three women and two men stared at him, astonished by his last statement.

"No one leaves the room," he said in a commanding voice. "We need to decontaminate him before moving him. Wash him down with soap and water. Quickly. Bag all his clothing." Two nurses started to do as he had ordered. He glanced at Sevati then back to the group. "We have to decontaminate ourselves too. Everyone here must discard and bag all their clothing and don fresh scrubs from the shelf there." Hostile eyes glared at him. "All clothing. Underwear too. Sorry, not the time for modesty. Keep on your surgical masks."

No one moved. Zack whipped off his scrub top, stepped out of his Crocs, and loosened his pants. "Do as I say. It could mean your life." After a few seconds, everyone complied, doing their best to turn their backs on each other as they disrobed. Once he finished changing, he spoke to Sevati without looking at her. "Can you contact ICU from where you are?"

Her strained voice through the surgical mask sounded far away. "Yes."

"Tell them to clear a path to their isolation room, and for everyone there to don personal protective gear—including neoprene gloves and aprons. Charcoal cartridge masks, if they have them. We'll need atropine, a lot of it. Ask if they have 2-PAM. If not, they need to get it ASAP." He grimaced. "And I need to speak to Dr. Hartman." He turned back to check Walter's status. No change.

Sevati hurried to finish dressing, then lifted the wall-mounted intercom and relayed Zack's message. After a pause, she beckoned him. "Dr. Hartman."

Zack leaned over Walter to take the receiver from her hand. He didn't wait for Hartman to speak. "Organophosphate poisoning in cholinergic crisis. Unknown source or route of contamination. We have to assume it's weaponized." A quick glance around the room satisfied him that all had complied with his instructions. "Heading your way now." He paused. "It's Walter Knowles from the ER."

He was about to hang up when Hartman replied. "I hope you're wrong, Zack."

"I wish. If it's on his skin, he contaminated the ER, and from there the whole hospital. We need to decon the ER and lock down the hospital."

Hartman's voice turned gruff. "We'll discuss that."

"No time for discussion. At your door in ten seconds." He dropped the receiver and gestured to the team. "Go."

Jerry Hartman and Janice Barnett met them at the door of the ICU, both wearing full protective gear but each recognizable by their defiant eyes. As the cath-lab team carted their patient to the isolation room and transferred care to the ICU staff, Zack gave Jerry a quick summary of Walter's history. Janice hovered a few feet away, hanging on every word.

Hartman shook his head. "I doubt it's organophosphate toxicity. You may not know that he's immunocompromised. HIV."

"I didn't know that."

"He's my patient. We've kept it out of his record. This could be many things besides organophosphate poisoning. Severe viral gastroenteritis with dehydration seems more likely."

Zack's neck and shoulders tightened. "Even if so, we're already treating it with massive fluids. Without response." He knotted a fist, spoke in a sharp tone. "It's not gastroenteritis. Do you know the DUMBELS mnemonic for organophosphate poisoning? Defecation/diaphoresis, urination, miosis, bronchorrhea, emesis, lacrimation, salivation?" Hartman stared back in silence. Zack squared his stance. "It's organophosphate toxicity. The garlic odor suggests parathion. We need to lock down the hospital. Now. People may have been exposed in the ER and spread it elsewhere."

Hartman stood erect, feet apart, arms locked over his chest. "Lockdown will not happen."

Zack's nostrils flared. "If he got it through his skin—"

"Where was he?"

"At home."

Hartman scoffed. "When was the last time you heard of someone exposed to parathion in an urban environment? You think he picked it up at Home Depot, sprayed spiders with it, and got enough on his skin to cause cholinergic crisis? What have you been smoking?"

Zack moved forward; fists clenched. "We don't have time for ego games, Jerry. This man is dying. He needs atropine and 2-PAM. Now." He huffed. "We must lock down the hospital." Eyes flaring, he poked a finger into Hartman's chest. "If you refuse and people die, it's on you, not me."

Hartman pondered for a few seconds, then his body relaxed. He stepped back. "Okay. You take care of Knowles. I'll talk to administration." He turned and left the ICU, doffing his protective gear as he went.

Zack looked at Janice Barnett, unclear which of them seemed more surprised at Hartman's abrupt attitude change. "Start with one milligram of atropine IV push, then double the dose every five minutes until we see a response." He remembered the previous medical error when the young nurse misconstrued his order for epinephrine on Melody Snyder. "To be specific," he said, "start with one milligram, then two milligrams five minutes later, four milligrams five minutes after that, then eight milligrams five minutes later, then sixteen milligrams after another five minutes, and so forth until we get a response. No way to tell how high we'll need to go." He looked her in the eye. "Clear?"

Janice stared back with blank eyes. "Understood, Doctor." She moved away and approached the patient, as if walking through Jell-O.

What's with her? Zack felt like he'd stumbled into The Twilight Zone.

CHAPTER TWENTY

$\mathbf{A}$s if through dense fog, Janice approached the nurse responsible for Walter Knowles and repeated Zack Winston's atropine order. She needed to get away, at least briefly, but she sensed Winston's close presence. He had followed her into the isolation room. "Did you get the 2-PAM?"

Janice looked at the nurse, who nodded.

"Start with a low dose. One gram IV," Winston said. He paused, seemed to reconsider. "To be clear, I want one gram of 2-PAM, that is pralidoxime, by slow IV push. Give it over five minutes." Jan was about to relay the order when Winston interrupted. "Repeat that to be sure we both have the same understanding."

Puzzled, Janice squinted at him, repeated the order. He nodded and turned toward the patient. She looked at Walter Knowles for the first time since his arrival. A sense of doom overwhelmed her. He looked already dead.

Overhead, the hospital PA system blared. "Code Orange, Code Orange. All personnel remain in current location. Hospital is on lockdown. ER is on divert and closed to all personnel." The announcement was repeated three times. Jerry Hartman had convinced the administration to follow Zack Winston's instructions.

Janice saw him cock his head, no doubt smiling under his mask. She sensed he would protest if she left the isolation room to the other nurses, so she stood next to him for thirty-five minutes, watching and hoping for some positive sign from Walter. After the sixty-four-milligram dose of atropine, she noted a subtle change. Walter's pulse rate had come down a bit and his blood pressure had risen slightly. She glanced at Zack Winston. He had seen it too.

"Check pupils," Winston said. "Take another twelve-lead EKG and repeat the blood gases."

"Pupils are three millimeters, slight reaction to light," a nurse said. Winston exhaled with relief. So did Janice.

A few minutes later, he looked at the new EKG, then handed it to her without speaking. "Sinus tach," she said, "rate's decreasing. No ST elevation."

"Agreed. We may be coming out of the woods. No doubt it's organophosphate toxicity."

Janice shrugged. "Cholinesterase level?"

"I ordered one," Winston said. "We won't get results for several days. It should confirm the diagnosis, but not in time to help us." A nurse handed him the blood gas results. He looked at them, then handed the paper to her. "Looking better. Still acidotic but improved. Let's repeat these labs every half-hour."

Janice seized the opportunity. "I'll call the lab. Anything else you want to order?"

"Yes, repeat the full metabolic panel and CBC."

"Will do." Leaving Winston at the bedside, she doffed her protective gear in the isolation room changing area, then phoned in the lab order from the main desk. After that, she stepped into the women's bathroom, checked stalls to be sure she was alone, pulled out her phone, and dialed a number that picked up at once.

Her words hissed through clenched teeth. "What the hell did you do?"

CHAPTER TWENTY-ONE

An hour passed, and Zack had not moved from Walter's side. With the ER locked down and no reports of critical patients, he would not be required there. Zack needed to stay with Walt until he was for sure out of the woods. For reasons he could not fathom, he felt some affinity to this man, a subliminal connection to his current condition.

Walter continued to show slight but steady improvement. He remained in deep coma, not moving, not breathing on his own; but his blood pressure had risen to eighty and pulse had come down to one hundred. His pupils showed slight reaction to light. *Still in shock but holding his own.* Survivable if they could keep his brain perfused. In addition to massive IV fluid infusions and 100% oxygen by ventilator, Zack sought to boost Walt's heart muscle with cardiac stimulants. "Hang a dobutamine drip in addition to the dopamine."

A PA announcement seized everyone's attention. "Cancel Code Orange. Cancel Code Orange. Resume normal hospital operations. Repeat, cancel Code Orange and resume normal hospital operations. ER is open, no longer on divert." Zack stared at the PA speaker as if it were an impostor. *What the heck?*

Jerry Hartman burst into the isolation room, not wearing protective gear. "All clear, Zack. You can relax the isolation. It *was* parathion, but he didn't inhale it or absorb it through his skin. He swallowed it."

Zack scowled. "What?"

Jerry puffed out his chest, spoke with an authoritarian tone. "When you lock down a hospital in the National Capitol Region for chemical exposure, you get a lot of attention. While you were isolated here trying to save his life, we got swarmed with law enforcement and Homeland Security agents. The cops found an empty container with Chinese characters on it in Knowles' kitchen. Took a while to identify it as China-manufactured parathion, which anyone can purchase over the Internet. The medics didn't find it because Knowles collapsed in the living room. Everyone assumed it was cardiac arrest."

"I don't get it," Zack said. He had not removed his protective gear, although the others in the room had.

Jerry cocked his head. "He left a note in the bedroom. Cops are calling it a straightforward suicide attempt. Homeland Security packed up and left."

Something bothered Zack about that story. "What did the note say?"

"Don't know for sure. Apology of some sort."

"To his partner?"

"Who else? Don't know all the details. Contact the police if you have questions. For now, we'll get the hospital back to normal while you work to save his life." He started to leave, turned back at the door. "Strong work, Zack. Overdid the lockdown and isolation, but good job on the diagnosis and treatment."

Damned with faint praise? Did Zack perceive a subtle threat in that "overdid" statement? He scrutinized Jerry for a second. The man seemed sincere. "Thanks," Zack said. "Now if we can keep him alive."

"Stick with it. I'll take care of the rest, including telling the boyfriend that his guy may survive the suicide attempt."

As soon as Jerry left the room, a shrill alarm from Walter Knowles' ventilator captured Zack's attention. Walt bucked like a rodeo bronc, fighting the ventilator. Zack moved closer. Walter looked alert, stared at Zack with terrified eyes. Zack pushed him back with a hand to his shoulder. "Whoa, take it easy, Walt. You need that tube. Let the vent do its job." He spoke to the nurse. "Ativan." Walt's head and upper torso rose off the bed toward Zack, his eyes so wide that white encircled each iris. Legs thrashed as arms strained against the restraints intended to keep his IVs in place. Zack feared he would dislodge the endotracheal tube or occlude the IV, either of which would be disastrous. "Push that Ativan. Two milligrams." Walt's panic increased. His eyes pleaded with Zack. The nurse injected Ativan into the IV. In seconds, Walter fell back onto the bed. A minute later, he lay still under full sedation, no longer fighting the ventilator, blood pressure and pulse stable.

Zack's own pulse raced. *What the hell was that? No way he's stable enough to extubate. He could crash again.*

He addressed the nurse. "We need to keep him down so we can control his breathing and vitals. Propofol and fentanyl." The nurse started to the door. "And get Dr. Hartman," Zack said.

When Jerry Hartman returned, Zack summarized what had happened with Walt. "Right choice to put him down," Jerry said.

Zack ignored the compliment. "We need to make a decision. As you know, an ER doc can't admit a patient. This has been one very long resuscitation since Sevati called me three hours ago, but I can't continue to manage him." *As much as I want to.*

"You've done above and beyond already," Jerry said. "I'm his attending physician and an intensivist. I'll take over."

Zack blinked. *Why is he being so agreeable?* "Thanks. Please keep me informed. He's a mainstay in the ER. I feel responsible."

"Sure." Jerry turned away, spoke to the nurse. "Start the fentanyl and Propofol."

Thus dismissed, Zack removed his protective gear and left the isolation room to return to the ER. At the ICU workstation, Janice Barnett sat with head down, typing on a computer keyboard. She'd been in the ICU all day. Would have had no contact with Walter Knowles before he arrived.

Noelle's voice whispered in his ear. "Why that thought, Zack?"

CHAPTER TWENTY-TWO

Zack stumbled off the apartment building elevator at 10 p.m., four hours after the scheduled end of his ER shift. From the ICU he'd returned to the ER, where staff hustled to reclaim the department from the lockdown, decontamination, and onslaught of law enforcement and Homeland Security agents. He stayed to help Paula Cho meet and street a horde of curious people who had made up reasons to come to the ER after seeing the news on TV. He took extra care not to miss anyone with a real illness. When the surge died down, he commiserated with staff members upset over Walter's status, then absconded to the bunker to change into civilian clothes and retrieve his belongings. Defying his profound emotional and physical fatigue, he returned to the ICU to check on Walter before heading home. Jerry Hartman and Janice Barnett had left for the night. Walter remained stable, albeit in deep sedative-induced coma. Zack had conferred with the night intensivist, left his phone number for contact if any change, taken one last look at Walt, and departed the hospital.

At his apartment door, Zack hyperventilated until he became lightheaded and air hungry. Calming himself, he unlocked the door, stepped inside, flipped on the light, and looked for Noelle. No joy. His home seemed foreign, cold, sterile. Slamming the door behind him, he flipped off the light, tossed his backpack aside, and bolted to the bedroom. Leaving his clothes in a heap on the floor, he dove into the bed, buried his head in the pillow, and willed his pulse to slow down. The room felt afire, like a crucible charring his flesh, stopping his heart, consuming his soul. He rolled onto his back, stared at the ceiling, concentrated on deep, steady breaths. He crossed his hands over his chest. Like a man already dead, a corpse.

His phone vibrated and lit up, a familiar icon on the screen. *Ange?* He took the call. Ange's comforting voice filled his ear. "Zack, I saw the news about your hospital. I worried that you were involved."

Emotions he could not decipher engorged him. "I was in the middle of it."

"What happened?"

He told her about Walter's near-death, his decision to lock down the hospital, and the aftermath. He waited a beat, but she did not speak. "On top of all that," he said. "I'm being sued over that cardiac case from last summer."

After an interminable pause, she spoke in a voice laced with empathy. "I am so sorry to hear that. Truly. You don't deserve it. I wish I could help."

Zack sat up in the bed. "Talk to me. I need to talk."

"Sure."

He talked and she listened. He started out angry yet firm, but that thin veneer of courage broke open like an egg shell, and he confessed his chronic self-doubt, the frequent need to throw up after bad clinical outcomes shook his confidence; about how he had questioned his decision to become a physician.

"Surely you're not the only ER doctor to feel overcome by the tragedies you see. It doesn't mean you're a bad physician, or that you shouldn't do emergency medicine."

He scoffed. "Easy to say, Ange."

She paused before continuing. "I don't know much about medicine, but I know people, and I know you. You're a good person. You care. You always try your best. Those are the qualities I look for in a physician."

Zack swallowed a sob. "Thank you."

"Always."

His heart soared at the word. He yearned to see her right away, but he didn't have the strength to leave his bed. After a long silence, his breathing normalized, and—for the first time since he opened that letter—he did believe in himself. He had saved Walter Knowles. He could save himself. "Thanks for listening, Ange, and for being a good friend."

"I'm here if you need me." Zack knew that the "here" had limits. He blew her a silent kiss. They ended the call with no follow-up plan. Zack went to the bathroom, washed his face, returned to bed, and burrowed into the covers.

Janice Barnett can burn in hell.

In the darkest of nights, Zack Winston slept—until at two a.m. his phone again vibrated and lit up. *Noelle? Ange?*

He rolled over and stared at the caller ID: Jerry Hartman.

CHAPTER TWENTY-THREE

When she closed the garage door and entered her manse at 8 p.m., Janice Barnett still seethed about the response to her earlier phone call from the ICU ladies' room. *No big deal?* On the day he got notice of her lawsuit, Winston ended up a fucking hero. How would that affect her case? She let out a deep breath and headed straight for the kitchen. Walter Knowles had remained stable, so she could finally leave the ICU after fourteen hours on duty. *No thanks to Zack Winston.*

Now that the lawsuit had launched, she had expected to feel elated, relishing the end in sight. She had planned to call Yolonda, to tell her that more money would soon be on the way; maybe convince her to relent and let Janice spend time with Chantal. Then Winston blew into the ICU with Walter Knowles. *What the hell?*

Janice uncorked a bottle of vintage Chardonnay, grabbed a long-stemmed glass, and headed straight for the marble bathtub in the master suite. There she soaked for forty-five minutes, long enough to finish the bottle, smoke fine dope, and let her brain turn to mush. Tomorrow she would feel more like engaging with Yolonda, a task that had become more vexing with each successive interaction. Did Yolonda intend to make a clean break? Not likely, given her financial reliance on Janice; even with the reduced stipend over the last months. Still, Janice needed to keep her close.

She got out of the bath, dried off, and put on silk pajamas. From the medicine cabinet she retrieved the bottle of Percocet, no longer hidden behind the Motrin. She popped two yellow pills into her mouth and headed for bed. Sweet oblivion soon followed.

Oblivion succumbed to terror as the too-familiar nightmare broke in full fury through her alcohol-, pot-, and narcotic-weakened inner walls.

Camp Casey, a stone's throw from the Korean DMZ. Her last night on temporary duty. Three fierce US soldiers, armed and dangerous, taking turns on her. The bayonet at her throat when they finished. "Tell anyone and you die." Her tears making small rivers in her face caked with mud. The searing pain as she stumbled back to her barracks room and buried herself beneath the covers on her rack. Wanting to die. Her decision never to tell anyone, least of all Carl.

A dog barked outside the barracks. She tried to ignore it, but it persisted. She woke up, realized it was her own phone that she'd set to bark instead of ring when he called. She tried to shut it out of her mind. Failed. Picked it up. Clicked to answer.

"Knowles is dead," he said.

CHAPTER TWENTY-FOUR

The next morning, while Marshall lingered in the shower and Bridget finished dressing, she turned on the TV to watch the news before heading to work. A "Breaking News" banner caught her eye. "Bethesda Metro Hospital Locked Down in Fear of Terrorist Attack."

The video showed an aerial view of the hospital, engulfed by flashing-light emergency vehicles and black SUVs. The voice-over described how a patient brought to the ER after ingesting insecticide had triggered a decontamination response and lockdown of the hospital. The picture switched to a breathless young female correspondent standing in front of the ER, describing in rapid-fire diction how local law enforcement and Homeland Security agents had descended on the hospital, only to be called off in less than an hour.

The talking-head news anchor appeared next. "Police found evidence at the victim's home that he had swallowed the insecticide in an apparent suicide attempt. He died early this morning. Hospital and government officials are justifying the lockdown and response as necessary to protect the public and their other patients." The screen switched to two men in white coats seated at a table across from the camera. One, a stout, bearded man with what looked like a permanent scowl, was identified as Dr. Jeremiah Hartman, Chief of the Medical Staff. The other, fiftyish, trim, tanned and ruggedly handsome, was Dr. Dennis King, Emergency

Department Director. He spoke in a confident, matter-of-fact voice. "Because the origin and route of contamination were unknown when the patient arrived, our on-duty emergency physician activated the hospital's anti-terrorism response protocol—out of an abundance of caution."

Marshall appeared beside her, partially dressed. "Abundance of covering their asses." He scoffed. "Whoever overreacted has hell to pay this morning, I'll bet."

Bridget nodded. "In my experience, ER docs are all wired to shoot, ready, aim."

CHAPTER TWENTY-FIVE

Thanks to Dennis King picking up his scheduled ER shift, Zack attended the memorial service for Walter Knowles a week after his death. Sitting near the back of the non-denominational hall, he thought it a sad affair, albeit billed as a celebration of Walt's life—a life shrouded in mystery, even in death. Zack saw no relatives in attendance, and none were named by friends who spoke in euphemisms about the price Walt had paid to pursue his true identity. Others described his quiet yet ardent support of the LGBT community, and his substantial financial contributions to political action committees and candidates who espoused diversity. Zack had never considered Walt a wealthy man. He had never seen him flout money in the ways that Zack and many physicians considered their right and privilege. He dressed humbly, never talked about his house, his car, foreign travel, or his stock portfolio. In truth, he seldom talked at all except for the business of the ER. Inscrutable unto death, but apparently with a full life well-known and respected among his own community.

Walt's partner, Roland Edwards, stepped to the podium. Younger than Walt by at least ten years, he spoke in a strong, passionate voice about their long-time companionship, about Walt's loyalty and fidelity—not only to his partner, but to anyone in whom he saw no guile. "Walter could never abide a bully. He'd been bullied plenty in his early years, most of all by an ignorant family that disowned him, and by a so-called faith community that reviled him."

The man went on to describe poignant vignettes of his life with Walter Knowles, whom he described as a compassionate and upright man who had withstood adversity to become secure in his own skin. An uncomfortable pause as the man started to break down. He steeled himself, looked out at the audience, scanned the faces of the ER staff in attendance, then locked his gaze on Zack. "They tell us that Walter committed suicide. I say, 'bullshit.'" He gazed upward, then focused back on Zack. "No one. No one ever loved life or hated death more than my Walter." Another pause to gather strength. "I don't know what happened to Walter that day, but I believe in my heart he did not take his own life. The man I knew and loved was incapable of doing that to himself." He focused on Zack a third time. "Someday truth will come out. I swear on his beloved memory I will not rest until it does."

As the audience stood and applauded, the man broke down and had to be helped from the podium. From the front of the room a piano played, and someone started singing "We Shall Overcome." Most of the audience joined. Shaken, Zack looked around and saw several faces staring at him. He half-nodded, then slipped out of the hall.

CHAPTER TWENTY-SIX

Across the region from the Knowles memorial service, in the board room of Desmond, Markle, and Larsen, LLP, Attorneys-at-Law, Bridget pleaded with her two partners. "I've sworn off ER docs, *and* Roger Meadows."

James Desmond, the managing senior partner, stroked a frizzy white beard. "A major client brings us a high-profile case, we don't field a rookie. You're our go-to for emergency medicine cases. And, personal issues understood, you have the best record of anyone in the area against Roger Meadows."

"I question high-profile," Bridget said. "Another ER doc misses a heart attack. Negligence or not, Roger will bludgeon the guy on the stand until the jury strings him up and gives the widow a nice sum for her troubles. That's after Roger badgers us to force a settlement. You know this 'major client' insurance company always pushes to settle, right?"

Andrew Markle, the junior name partner, pointed to documents in front of Bridget. "Recognize the hospital?"

Bridget followed his finger to a spot on the top page. "Yikes," she said. "I skipped over that. It was in the news after some doc locked it down for fear of terrorism, right?"

"An ER doc," Andrew said. "Guess who."

She read the answer in his eyes. "The defendant, one Dr. Zack

Winston. Damn." *This case will get messy.* Bridget folded her hands over the documents. "I'll stipulate potential high profile. Still . . ."

Neither of her colleagues spoke.

When the silence became unbearable, she pursed her lips. "Yeah, all right. I've got it."

CHAPTER TWENTY-SEVEN

The week after Walter Knowles' funeral, Zack rode a crowded Metro Red Line train to McPherson Square in northwest DC. A block from the station, on I Street, he found the eight-story ash-gray edifice with *Franklin Tower* in gold leaf on its facade. A half-hour early for his appointment, he walked around the block in the late fall chill to calm his nerves. The last remnants of falling leaves crunched under his feet on the sidewalk. Passing a coffee shop, he savored the aroma, and regretted omitting his morning coffee and smoothie. He had not wanted to fill either his churning stomach or nervous bladder, for fear of having to excuse himself during the consultation.

After three circuits of the block, he approached the building entrance ten minutes before the scheduled appointment time. *Close enough.* He located his assigned attorney's office on the fifth floor. Self-conscious, he walked into the lobby of Desmond, Markle, and Larsen, LLP. With time to spare, he found the men's room, emptied his bladder, then returned to sit and rock on the edge of a dark-green leather chair across from the receptionist.

The suite's interior design projected genteel openness. To the right of the unpretentious lobby, a glass-fronted conference room dominated the space. Hallways disappeared in either direction from the conference room, no doubt leading to various offices. Inside the conference room, three men in dark business suits occupied a table, animated as they talked and gestured. Zack felt under-dressed in casual khaki Dockers, forest-green Nike golf shirt, and dark blue casual Polo jacket.

Perhaps pitying his obvious anxiety, or from experience with other unsettled physicians who had occupied the same seat, the stoic receptionist offered him a cup of coffee. He declined. "I'm sorry for the wait," she said, "The partners are in conference. Shouldn't be too much longer." He changed his mind and accepted the coffee. The brew, dark and strong, stimulated his rattled nerves, so he asked the receptionist for a glass of ice water. The ice water's cooling effect was more imagined than real, but Zack managed to calm himself.

A statuesque woman about his age glided toward him. A tailored Bordeaux-red business suit over a modest aqua blouse complemented her shoulder-length wavy blond hair and fair, lucent complexion. He pegged her as the associate to one of the distinguished men in the conference room.

The woman came up to him and held out her hand. "Doctor Winston? Sorry to keep you waiting. I'm Bridget Larsen."

Zack stood, hoping his mouth did not gape too widely. They were about the same height, and he took immediate note of the ice-green shimmer in her eyes. Despite himself, he blurted. "You're—?"

"Your defense attorney." She smiled. "Did you expect someone different?"

He could not find his voice. She shook his hand with a firm grip, then led him past the conference room where the three men continued to converse, to the end of the hallway. She directed him to a glass-fronted office furnished with a large oak desk with matching chairs, a brown leather couch, and a four-place conference table. A young man wearing a simple gray suit stood to greet him.

"This is Lance, my paralegal."

Zack shook hands with Lance, who guided him to a chair in front of Bridget's desk while he took the chair next to Zack. Bridget slipped into an executive chair behind the desk. "Okay," she said. "Let's get to it."

Lance opened a legal pad, ready to take notes. While Bridget shuffled through the folder on her desk, Zack examined the two framed certificates on the wall behind her: Stanford University, BA (Classical), *Summa Cum Laude*; Harvard Law, JD, *Summa Cum Laude*; both awarded to Bridget Diane Larsen. On a side wall, three framed certificates from marathon races, two from the Marine Corps Marathon in DC, and one from the New York City Marathon.

She's a runner.

Bridget studied him over the top of her Persian blue-framed reading glasses. "I finished two years of medical school before I decided my true calling was the law. That plus eighteen years of defending against malpractice suits makes me familiar with medical terminology and the basics of anatomy, physiology, and such."

Message received. Don't talk down to her. He nodded. "Where did you attend med school?"

She gestured toward the undergraduate degree on the wall. "Stanford."

Impressive. "I'm from The City."

"I grew up in Santa Rosa."

"How did you get from Stanford to Harvard? Stanford's law school is one of the best."

Bridget leaned back and laughed, a good-natured chuckle. "You get accepted to Harvard Law, you go to Harvard Law. Otherwise you are certifiably insane. Plus, I was engaged to a doctor who got a residency at Brigham and Women's."

"Anyone I know?" Her physician husband could be a local practitioner.

"No wedding," she said. "Two big egos with grandiose career ambitions. It would never have worked." She held up the hand with the wedding ring. "I married a prosecutor instead." For a second she looked away, then shuffled through the files on her desk. "I see from your CV that you didn't stray far from the bay area; med school and residency at UCSF—no small feat—emergency medicine practice in San Bruno. How did you get to the east coast?"

He shrugged. "Post-divorce life redirection, by way of the US Navy."

Bridget nodded. "Oh, yeah, I read that." She looked up from the documents. "By the time we're done with this, I'll have your professional life memorized." She flashed a smile. "I will also know details of your personal life, but only those relevant to our case."

Zack decided he liked this Bridget Larsen, even as he buried his typical habit of predicting, within five minutes of meeting any attractive woman, the relative odds of an intimate relationship. (In this case, zero.) "Whatever it takes to win."

Their eyes met and Zack had an uncanny sense that she'd read his thoughts. He switched up. "I see you're a runner. Marathons, no less."

Bridget smiled. "Keeps me sane."

"I know what you mean. I'm also a runner."

She nodded. "Well, let's hope we can both channel our energies to get you across the finish line in one piece."

CHAPTER TWENTY-EIGHT

Bridget leaned forward in her chair. "Let's get down to business. Before we discuss your case, a couple of ground rules."

Zack sank into his chair like a child about to be lectured.

"My job is to defend you in front of a jury, not your medical peers. Some jurors might think doctors make too much money. Some may remember bad experiences they believe resulted from medical negligence. I'll do my best to weed those out during jury selection, but I can't guarantee complete success." Her emerald eyes bored into him. "You're up against a compelling plaintiff, a nurse who lost her husband in the prime of his life. Jurors will have more empathy for the grieving widow than the rich single doctor. You have two strikes against you before you walk into the court room—regardless of the facts. Roger Meadows, arguably the best plaintiff's attorney in town, will try to strike you out looking."

Zack appreciated the baseball analogy, but not the message. He scowled.

Bridget continued. "Roger will try to force a settlement, to convince you and me that you can't win if we go to trial. He will pound you until you believe losing is inevitable."

Zack looked down. "I'm getting the picture."

"Here's the hard inside slider."

Another baseball metaphor. *Does she know I'm a fan?*

"Your insurance company is at risk for the five-million payout, and they don't have a professional reputation to protect. They *will* recommend settlement. I've never had a case with that company where they opted for trial. They've already budgeted the payout, and it's less than five mil."

"Great."

"I won't entertain any settlement recommendation if I believe we have a credible chance of convincing the jury to find in your favor."

"I appreciate that."

Her voice turned stern. "You must promise me some things, Doc. First, I'm the lawyer and you're not. You can question anything I say or recommend, but do so knowing that I have training and experience you don't. Most important, you must be completely honest with me. Tell me everything that might pertain to your case, even if you're not sure it's relevant. Always answer my questions truthfully and fully. Withhold nothing. Clear?"

"Yes, ma'am." He thought about the copies of Barnett's ER records locked in his desk at home. "You've had issues with other physician clients?"

Bridget chuckled. "Indeed. In my experience arrogant physicians always lose in court."

Zack forced a smile. "I promise to behave."

She squinted at him. "If Roger can't beat you with facts, he will try to impugn your character. I can fight that only if I know the dirt before he slings it. That includes the most embarrassing personal information that could be used in court to discredit your character, ability, or trustworthiness."

A brief reflection of his departure from Japan wafted across Zack's mind. He wanted to crawl under her ornate oriental rug and hide. "I understand."

Bridget's expression softened and she leaned back. "For openers, with whom have you discussed this case before now?"

Straight in, no waiting. Zack squirmed in his chair. "Our ER group director, Dennis King. He's the one who contacted the insurance company that retained you."

She tilted her head. "What did you discuss, and when?"

"The next day, I told him about the case." He straightened his posture. "One other time, when I got the notice letter."

Bridget folded her hands on her desk. "Did you discuss the case in detail?"

Zack shook his head. "Not blow-by-blow. Just an overview."

She leaned her chin on tented fingers. "Were these two occasions the only times you discussed the case with him?"

Damn, I'd hate to face her from the witness stand. "No. I mean yes."

Bridget wrote some notes on her legal pad, then looked up at him. "Any other discussions of this case?"

"I reviewed the EKGs with Dr. Sevati Prakash, chief cardiologist on our staff; but I redacted Carl Barnett's personal information."

Bridget frowned. "All the EKGs?"

"Yes."

She scribbled another note on her pad. "Any chance that doctor might figure out the patient from what you shared? I imagine you don't get many similar cases."

"I suppose she could. But that's not her way. She was very helpful."

"Oh?" Her eyebrows peaked. "How so?"

Zack summarized his conversation with Sevati. "She said it wasn't negligence."

Bridget addressed Lance. "Put her down as a possible witness for us."

The paralegal asked for the correct spelling of Sevati's full name, and Zack gave it to him. Bridget cleared her throat and tilted her head to scrutinize him again over her reading glasses. Her eyes narrowed. "Who else have you discussed the case with?"

Zack squirmed. "Just my girlfriend. Well, my ex-girlfriend."

Bridget scowled. "*Ex*-girlfriend?"

"We're not a thing anymore, but I talk to her sometimes. We're still friends."

Bridget raised her eyebrows. "Name?"

"Angela Moretti. She's a lawyer."

"Not familiar. Where does she practice?"

"Southeast DC, solo practice. Low-fee and pro-bono work."

Bridget sighed. "What did you tell her about this case."

"Everything."

Stern, parental voice. "No more of that."

"Okay. Sure." *We both know I'll ignore that advice.*

Bridget put down her pen, took off her reading glasses, and focused on him. "You mentioned earlier that you spent time in the navy?"

Zack didn't want to talk about the navy, or Noelle. "Right."

"'Loose lips sink ships.' Are you familiar with that saying?"

"Yes."

"In this case, loose lips sink defendants. You cannot—must not—discuss this case with anyone except me. Any other conversation is discoverable by the plaintiff. I guarantee you Roger Meadows will discover it. He'll be all over Miss, uh—" She glanced at her notes. "—Angela as soon as he learns of her existence." She leaned forward and re-engaged his eyes. "No more conversations with her about this case. Am I clear?"

"Yes, ma'am."

"No more disclosures of any kind to Doctor King, either."

"Understood."

"Okay." She looked at the folder in his lap. "Have you made any notes, personal memos, or other records, in writing or digital, about this case?"

Zack slumped back in his chair, folded his arms. "I did an on-line literature search about coronary artery spasm and made some notes."

She held out her hand in a beckoning gesture. He slipped the notes out of the folder and handed them to her. She scanned them briefly, handed them to Lance, then nodded toward the folder still on Zack's lap. "Anything else in there?"

Zack could answer her exact question truthfully. He sucked in his cheeks. "No." He held the open folder in front of him so she could see it was empty.

Bridget smirked. "So much for the introduction and ground rules. Let's take five and then talk about the facts of the case. You'll find the men's room down the hall to your left, and Lance can get you whatever you need for refreshment. When you get back, we'll convene at my conference table so we can both review the documents." She winked at him. "Cozier that way."

Zack rushed to the men's room.

CHAPTER TWENTY-NINE

When Zack left the room, Bridget spoke to her associate. "What's he hiding?" Lance shrugged, a quizzical look on his face. "When you question a witness, or a client," she said, "pay as much attention to body language as to what they say. Did you see how he got defensive when I asked him if he had any other documents? He held up that empty folder like a shield."

Lance shook his head. "Totally missed that."

"Consider it a lesson learned." She rested her chin on her hand. "What are the odds he'll still discuss this case with his lawyer girlfriend?"

Lance chortled. "A hundred percent, unless the 'ex' means complete splitsville."

Bridget raised a hand and glanced toward the door to warn him of Zack's return from the restroom.

Her new client took a seat next to her at the conference table, where they could review the documents together. She kept the folder closed, turned to face him. "Before we dig into these documents, I need to ask a question."

"Shoot," he said.

"Were you the emergency physician who locked down Bethesda Metro Hospital a couple of weeks ago for fear of a terrorist attack?"

Zack stiffened, leaned away from her, folded his arms. "With good reason."

She put out a hand to reassure him. "No judgment here. I'm asking because Roger Meadows may try to exploit it."

He cocked his head but said nothing.

Bridget pressed. "What can you tell me about that incident? Stick to what I need to know to defend you if Roger attacks."

Zack rubbed his face then summarized the case of Walter Knowles and his decision to lock down the hospital. "Since we didn't know the origin or intent of the poisoning, it seemed prudent to shut down the hospital. Turned out he ingested the insecticide. Suicide, they say." He sat back, face grim.

Bridget tented her fingers in front of her, shook her head. "Thank you for the spin-doctor version, Dr. Winston. Try that on cross-examination and Roger Meadows will feed your carcass to the crows." His face fell and he reeled back. She proffered a motherly smile. "Fortunately, we have time to rehearse an honest answer, where you will tell the jury your actual thoughts and feelings at the time." She put on her glasses and opened the folder in front of them. "Let's move on."

For the next hour, they discussed details of the two encounters with Carl Barnett, starting with Zack's verbal narrative, then reviewing the medical records. Bridget asked probing clinical questions in anticipation of Roger Meadows' efforts to establish negligence and causation. Zack framed his laconic answers with excessive care, which made him appear to obfuscate. She closed the file, doffed her glasses, and turned to face him.

"You could be a self-destructive witness, Doc. You sure as hell don't volunteer anything. Made me drag it out of you. That could work in cross-examination, but you weigh every damned word before you answer. Do that in front of a jury and Roger Meadows will convince them you're hiding the truth." She tilted her head. "You're not hiding anything, right?"

He flushed. "No, ma'am."

"Cut the 'ma'am' stuff. This isn't the navy and I'm not your superior officer; I'm not your mother either. Call me Bridget—never Bridge. Only my friends can do that. I hope I may call you Zack. We're going to spend a lot of time together over the next eighteen months or so, and formality gets in the way."

"Eighteen months?"

"On average, that's how long it takes for a malpractice suit to get to trial once it's filed."

His face fell. "Then call me Zack."

"I'll tell you straight, Zack. This will be tough. I hope you're up to a prolonged, pitched battle."

He shrugged. "Not like I have a choice."

"You need to toughen up before you square off with Meadows or testify for a jury. If you show a glimmer of self-doubt or dishonesty, you go down in flames."

Zack looked at the table. "I understand."

She waved a dismissive hand. "Yeah, well, right now I see a man drowning in self-doubt. If we were in front of a jury today, I might not call you to the stand. Roger would gut you and leave your stinking entrails to rot."

Zack looked stricken. *Good.*

Maybe I got through that phony facade.

"You're not in front of a jury now, and you won't be for at least a year. We'll submit to a deposition, but that doesn't involve a jury. You have time to pull yourself together and trust the man I see in front of me: a competent, caring, emergency physician who did his absolute best for this patient."

"I appreciate that, ma— Bridget."

"Don't appreciate it, Zack, believe it. If you need help with that, get help; get it now."

"Thanks."

I should have been a coach, Bridget thought. "Thank me after we win." She closed the folder. "After they file the actual suit, we'll reconvene and talk strategy. In the meanwhile, call me anytime if you want to discuss the case, or to talk about how you feel about it. Remember, I'm the only one—other than a shrink or counselor bound by patient-doctor privilege—with whom you may discuss it. If you find yourself wanting to call your Angela Manicotti, call me instead."

"Moretti, Angela Moretti. Yes, I understand."

"Right. Don't discuss this case with her ever again." She rose from her chair. "Go home, have a drink, socialize, do whatever you must to put this thing out of your mind."

He stood and shook her hand. "Thanks, Bridget. I very much appreciate what we've done today."

"It's what I do." She's escorted him to the door.

Before leaving, he turned to her. "You're not like any lawyer I've ever met. Not like those TV lawyers either."

And you're no Doug Ross. "I take that as a compliment. Take care of yourself, Zack. We've got a fight ahead. You need to get ready for it if you want to win."

He turned and left the office. Bridget watched him stride down the hall. *Maybe his charming vulnerability can become a strength.*

CHAPTER THIRTY

Noelle surprised Zack in the elevator lobby. She spoke in a flippant, flirtatious voice. "She seems nice."

Zack shook his head. "Yeah? Why I am sweating like I've just been interrogated by the KGB?" He walked out of the building.

Noelle followed. "Pretty too; in a blond, pale sort of way."

"I hadn't noticed."

Noelle snorted. "Yeah, Zack. You never notice."

"Jealous?"

"Uh, no. What good would jealousy do *me*?"

"Right. Okay, she's pretty and smart, and . . ."

"On to you?" She paused, letting her words take root. "The lady saw right through you, Zack. Why did you lie about the medical record copies?"

Frustration flared. "I have no idea."

"I do. You always hide something so the woman doesn't get power over you."

Zack stopped in his tracks, looked at her with burning eyes. "Not always. I let you in. Still feel the hurt."

Noelle tilted her head, eyes soft. "Aye, sailor. That's the risk of total trust and vulnerability. Sometimes it works out. You should try it again."

"Never." He started walking, trying to outpace her. "I'm done with this conversation." When he turned the corner toward the Metro station, Noelle did not follow.

Z ack spent the rest of the homeward Metro journey thinking not about Bridget Larsen but about Noelle; how they had reprised their Hong Kong liaison in romantic ports throughout the Western Pacific. As the aircraft carrier wended its way south to a military exercise with the Australian armed forces, the young lovers had dined and danced in Manila's Makati night club district, ridden bikes and engaged with friendly Vietnamese citizens along China Beach in Da Nang, swum in warm waters in Pattaya Beach, Thailand, and drank original Singapore Slings at the historic Long Bar at Raffles Hotel. Except when required by duty to remain overnight on the ship, in each port they booked themselves into the best room in the finest hotel they could mutually afford.

After the US/Australian war games, the ship made a port visit to the gold coast resort town of Cairns. Zack and Noelle booked an excursion to the great barrier reef, where they enjoyed sightseeing, snorkeling, and sumptuous food. The next day, they stayed abed in their room at the Hilton Hotel until evening, then joined a crowd of Australian revelers watching a rugby tournament at a local pub. Later, they joined a group of fellow American sailors at a posh disco near the beach. They returned to their hotel at three a.m., too tired and drunk to do anything but crash.

For an instant, Zack's mind had harbored a thought of deserting the navy and living in this laid-back Aussie resort with this beautiful, fascinating woman, this soul mate who had soared into his life when he least expected.

W hen the ship returned to Yokosuka, Japan, the air wing disembarked to nearby Atsugi Naval Air Station. After taking a day to rest up and do laundry, Zack and Noelle headed south on the bullet train to Kyoto, where they toured ancient shrines, shopped, and drank sake with modern-day geishas. They continued to Hiroshima, where they toured Peace Park, conversed with Japanese children eager to practice English, and stood in awed silence as they viewed the moving exhibits in the Peace Memorial Museum. Zack noticed a single tear running down Noelle's cheek before she quickly wiped it away.

From Hiroshima, they took a ferry to Miyajima Island, where they stayed two nights in a traditional Japanese ryokan. They made love and slept in futons on the tatami matted floor, bathed in the hot spring onsen, and enjoyed elegant multi-course kaiseki dinners in their room—both of them finding it awkward to eat while sitting cross-legged on the floor.

The private in-room dinners, accompanied by fine sake and wine, gave them the opportunity to explore each other's lives to the same level of intimacy they'd enjoyed with their bodies. Youngest of five children of an African American father and white Canadian mother, Noelle had grown up in modest circumstances in Detroit where her father labored on the Ford assembly line. She attended public schools, worked part-time in high school to earn spending money that her parents could not afford to give her, and then worked almost full-time while earning an associate degree in pre-engineering at a local community college. Her outstanding grades earned her admission to the Wayne State University College of Engineering, from which she graduated *Magna cum Laude* with a degree in engineering technology. The day after graduation, her life-long fascination with airplanes led her to a US Navy recruiting office. Two months later, she kissed her parents and siblings farewell and moved to Pensacola, Florida to begin her career as a naval aviator.

Zack told Noelle about growing up in San Francisco as one of two children, graduating from the University of San Francisco, and medical school and residency at the University of California in San Francisco. He went on to describe his early emergency medicine career and his blighted first marriage, complete with details of his wife's infidelity, their divorce, and his estrangement from his two daughters.

Noelle reached across the table to touch him, almost falling over from her squat on the tatami mat. "I can't imagine how all that felt."

Zack didn't want to relive that past. "Let's go for a walk."

Twenty minutes later, they strolled through the magnific Itsukushima shrine with its white walls and carmine arches highlighted against the night sky. From the porch they gazed at the brilliantly lit red orange torii gate out in the bay, its reflection shimmering in the crystal blue water. A feeling of immense peace and confidence washed over Zack. His heart swelled. On pure instinct, with no premeditation or plan, he turned to Noelle and took her hand.

"Marry me?"

She smiled. "Of course."

CHAPTER THIRTY-ONE

The day after his meeting with Bridget Larsen, Zack showed up for his day shift with renewed confidence. He had rehashed in his head the conversation with his new defense attorney, and decided he liked what he'd seen and heard. She impressed him, not only with her legal expertise and strategic perspective, but also with her fund of practical clinical knowledge; most important, her empathy. Although uncomfortable at the time, he appreciated her straight, no-bullshit talk. By the time he'd gone to bed, sober and relaxed, he'd decided that he and Bridget Larsen would be perfect battle buddies. Janice Barnett and that Meadows fellow would be no match for their combined medical/legal juggernaut. Relaxed in bed, he'd thought about Noelle's teasing description of Bridget's physical appeal. Zack did find her attractive, albeit out of bounds. He drifted toward sleep with the notion that after they won, Bridget and he might remain friends. Noelle had blessed that idea, right?

When Zack walked into the ER workstation after changing clothes in the bunker, head nurse Monica Harris approached him. "Dr. Wolfe asked that you call him when you get a chance, or meet him in his office."

Path report on Knowles, Zack thought. He scanned the two charts of patients waiting to be seen. "Send the ankle for an X-ray," he said, "and get a urine and pregnancy test on the woman with pelvic pain. Tell Dr. Wolfe I'm on my way to his office. I'll be back soon." He hustled to the pathology department, located in a separate first-floor wing of the hospital, where he found Eric Wolfe at his desk.

Stone-faced, Eric handed Zack several sheets of paper. "Post-mortem tissue and fluid labs on Knowles."

Zack scanned the pages, handed them back to Eric. "No surprises. Stomach contents positive for parathion, as expected."

Eric shook his head. "Look again, ER Doc; and read the whole report for a change."

Quizzical, Zack did so. When he got to the second page, he frowned, raised his eyebrows, then stared at Eric. "Hair follicles positive for opioids? That doesn't compute. His emergency tox screen on arrival was negative. This must be a false positive."

"Not if he took the opioids more than five days before his fatal overdose. Takes that long for them to get into the hair."

"Not relevant. His parathion ingestion was acute."

Eric shook his head. "Please, Zack, quit pontificating and keep reading."

Zack read the entire report, then looked up, still puzzled. "Tramadol in his urine? What's that about?"

"Post-mortem exams are more comprehensive than your standard urine tox screens. Those test only for common drugs of abuse, not all opiates. Tramadol isn't in the routine screen."

Zack scratched his head. "You're saying that Walter Knowles overdosed on both parathion and Tramadol."

"Bingo. Give that man a gold star." Eric grinned. "I'm also saying he was using oxy or a similar narcotic up to at least five days before the final event."

On reflex, Zack scanned the report's header to confirm it was on Walter Knowles. It was. He shook his head and handed the report to Eric. "That makes no sense. No damn sense at all." He pointed to the report. "This is not the Walter Knowles we all knew." *Not that any of us really knew him.* "He never showed any signs of opioid abuse."

"The tests don't lie," Eric said. "Humans do that."

When Zack returned to the ER, three new patients waited to be seen. The first two were minor. The third one caught his eye. The nurses had put the patient in the private exam room often used for complaints of sexually transmitted diseases. Zack's attention was drawn to the chief complaint, a verbatim description of the patient's reason for coming to the ER: *Will speak only to the doctor.* This happened from time to time, and usually involved an embarrassed patient, sometimes with unusual presentations. ER physicians' social networks sometimes featured these clinical outliers—in the name of education and information-sharing, not mockery. Zack's only contribution had been an x-ray of an old-fashioned Coca-Cola bottle trapped in a man's rectum.

Curiosity got the better of him, and he went to see this patient before the others. A fiftyish thin but fit male sat on the edge of the exam table, fully clothed. The exam gown he'd been given rested on his lap. Zack recognized the man but took a few seconds to place him. Roland Edwards, Walter Knowles' former partner; the man who had locked his hostile gaze on Zack at the memorial service when he swore that Walt would never commit suicide.

The two men regarded each other. Zack spoke first. "I'm Dr.—"

"Winston. I know who you are." Roland's eyes seemed supplicant, not angry. "You tried to save Walter's life."

"I remember you as well," Zack said. "I am sorry for your loss. Walter was a special member of our team." The man returned a nearly imperceptible nod. Zack cleared his throat. "What brings you to the ER, Mr. Edwards?"

A wistful look crossed Roland's face. "You."

Zack tried to remain professional. "What can I do for you?"

Roland's face hardened. "Tell the truth."

Zack tilted his head, folded his arms. "I don't follow. Are you having symptoms?"

The man glowered at him, leaned forward on the exam table. Zack felt threatened. Instinctively, he made sure he was between the patient and the door so he could escape if attacked. Then Edwards relaxed his posture, spoke in a calm voice. "I'm not sick. I came to talk to you about Walter."

Zack shook his head. "We can do that, but right now I have other patients to see. If you're not sick or don't need to be treated, I'll have to ask you to leave. We can arrange to talk at another time."

Roland stiffened. He begged. "Now. I don't want to put it off. At least give me the time you would if I had a rare STD."

Zack wondered what the man had to say. He thought about the toxicology results he'd discussed with Eric. Maybe Roland Edwards knew something important. "Shoot. You've got five minutes."

"Walter could not have committed suicide. His mother killed herself when he was ten years old. Narcotic overdose. He found her. Left him with a terrible emotional scar. He would never do what his mother did."

Zack sighed. "I understand. However, suicide rates are higher in adult children of suicides. They learn it's a powerful way to stop their psychic pain."

Roland shook his head. "Walter wouldn't do that to me. He would never subject me to the same pain he suffered." He choked for a second. "He loved me too much to do that."

Zack walked his mind back a few paces. "Okay. I'll accept that." He paused. "Do you have any knowledge or ideas about what happened? The circumstances of his death were unusual and dramatic. Parathion is not easy to procure. Where did he get it? How or why did he drink it? Surely you understand why the police and coroner found suicide as the most plausible cause."

Roland's voice pleaded. "I don't know. That's why I needed to see you. I need your help to figure it out."

"Why me?"

"I know how hard you tried to save his life. Other doctors would have given up. 'Gay guy kills himself, big deal.' I have to believe you cared about him to do all you did. I believe you still care." He looked into Zack's eyes with the same fury he had at the memorial service. "I know Walter didn't kill himself." His eyes narrowed. "You know it too."

Zack contemplated those last words for a few seconds. He had locked down the hospital because the thought of Walter Knowles deliberately ingesting parathion never crossed his mind. Zack had been perplexed when Jerry Hartman relayed the easy conclusion after the police investigated Walter's apartment. To Zack, a terrorist attack seemed more likely than a Walter Knowles suicide.

He narrowed his eyes at Roland. "If you're that certain, why haven't you gone to the police with it?"

"I did. As far as they're concerned the case is closed unless new evidence surfaces." He spread his hands, as if in prayer. "I was hoping you could help me find that."

Zack sighed, looked at the ceiling, thinking again of the toxicology report. "Did Walter use drugs? Opioids?"

Roland scowled, folded his arms, crossed his legs. "Never."

"Can you be sure?"

Roland stiffened and huffed. "We shared lives for thirty years. I'm damned sure, Dr. Winston."

Zack raised a supplicant hand. "I believe you." He tugged on his ear. "I don't know if I can help you. I'd like to, but I don't have a smoking gun for you." He looked at his watch. "I do have other patients to see."

Roland deflated like a man-sized balloon. Zack started to leave. "Wait," Roland said. "There's some stuff, in retrospect, that might help. For the last few months, he wasn't altogether himself—"

A nurse opened the door. "Dr. Winston, they need you in resus STAT."

Zack decided. "Be right there." He turned to Roland. "I'll do what I can. The whole thing doesn't make sense, hasn't since the time he arrived. I have to go now. Come back just after six when I get off duty. Wait for me in the lobby. We'll talk then."

Roland beamed. "Thanks, Dr. Winston. Thanks so much."

Zack turned and left the room. He hoped he hadn't made another bad decision.

CHAPTER THIRTY-TWO

When Zack entered the resus room, he paused at the sight of chartreuse, pink, and gray Nike running shoes—the same ones worn by the woman they had nearly killed with epinephrine a few months ago. His gaze swept from feet to face and recognized Melody Snyder. She wasn't sitting up on the gurney gasping for breath. She was on her back, not breathing at all, and her skin was turning blue. At the head of the bed, a nurse tried in vain to force air through a bag-valve-mask into Melody's lungs. He looked at Zack with desperate eyes. "I can't move any air. Total resistance."

As Zack prepared to intubate the patient, a paramedic spoke over the din. "She was running alone. Another runner found her down on the trail, gasping for breath. He called 911 and tried to do CPR. It took us five minutes to get to her on the trail. We found her unconscious with stridor; ventilation with bag-valve-mask didn't improve her. We tried LMA, no help. Attempted intubation but couldn't see the cords. Bagged her on the way in but couldn't move much air."

Standing behind her, Zack tilted the woman's head back. A nurse filled his outstretched left hand with a laryngoscope handle. He advanced the blade along the tongue, but her throat appeared as a glob of swollen, red tissue. "Get the cric tray ready." Advancing the blade further, he managed to lift a swollen epiglottis the size of a thumb. He shuddered when he saw the vocal cords, clamped shut like a rusty iron gate.

A nurse thrust an endotracheal tube into his right hand. He dropped it to the floor. He did not dare move his left hand for risk losing visualization of the cords. He held up his right hand. "Give me the fiberoptic. Quickly." It took a second or two before someone placed into his right hand a narrow black rubber fiber-optic cable with a light at the end. He passed the tip up to the cords, trying to find a pathway through the locked gates. Not even a slit. The vocal cords turned purple.

"That's two minutes, Doctor." The time that had passed without any attempts to move oxygen into the patient's lungs. Zack withdrew the equipment from the woman's throat and stepped back. "We need to do a cric."

He had reached the last resort in emergency airway management, the urgent need to establish a surgical airway to save a life. Zack had to cut through the patient's throat, open a hole in the cricothyroid membrane below the obstructed vocal cords, and pass a tube into her windpipe—through which they could deliver oxygen to her lungs. In his entire career he had never performed a cricothyrotomy, except on rubber dummies and human cadavers for practice.

He picked up a scalpel with a pointed blade, felt the front of the woman's neck for the dent below the epiglottis that localized the cricothyroid membrane, and made an incision through the skin. Huge difference between rubber dummies, cadavers, and real humans, dummies and cadavers didn't bleed like the gushing river that erupted around Zack's fingers. He grabbed a pile of 4 x 4 gauze pads from the table next to him, sopped up the pool of blood, and tried to stanch it with pressure. Feeling the target between his fingers, he attempted to stabilize it as he stabbed through a welling pool of blood to enter the cricothyroid membrane. His fingers slipped in the goo, and the blade passed alongside the trachea. More bleeding. Sweating profusely, Zack tried to stem the flow of blood. "Get the on-call trauma surgeon, STAT."

"Pulse ox is falling, now sixty."

Shit. This very nice woman is going to die. He stuck his finger into the gash he'd created in her throat, felt again for what he thought was the trachea and cricothyroid membrane, and stabbed blindly in that direction. The blade hit something hard, not the membrane, and glanced off to the side.

"She's coding," a nurse said.

CHAPTER THIRTY-THREE

Chantal's dark brown eyes avoided Janice's, as if the girl were blind. She looked like the thirteen-year-old whom Janice had found seven years ago, not at all like a young adult woman. Janice wanted Yolonda and the social worker out of the room, but they would not allow her alone with Chantal—for her safety more than the child's. Her own daughter a threat? What was this place?

Yolonda had finally agreed to let her see Chantal, but only under controlled circumstances at the Neurobehavioral Unit at the Kennedy Krieger Institute's main hospital. Janice had taken a rare day off from the ICU, dressed and coiffed herself with uncharacteristic care, and allocated an hour and a half for the drive from Potomac to Baltimore; ample time to arrive poised and ready for the 11 a.m. meeting. She hadn't counted on a traffic snarl escaping the national capital area, nor the near-impossible task of finding parking in the labyrinthine downtown campus of The Johns Hopkins University Medical Center where the institute was located. After outmaneuvering an aggressive Ford 4x4 for the lone spot in a high-rise parking garage, Janice had rushed down the stairs, bolted out the door, and jogged the block and a half to the institute. She arrived in the conference room at the stroke of eleven; flushed, sweating, hair disheveled, and nerves fragmented—not the cool professional presence she had intended.

After tense introductions and scripted seating arrangements, no one had spoken. Yolonda and the social worker remained out of Chantal's view, while

Janice sat in front of the girl, a bit to the side to avoid seeming confrontational. She used the silence to compose herself, ease her breathing, wipe the sweat from her brow, and somewhat fix her hair. Chantal had not responded to anything, all the while rocking back and forth in a rhythmic cadence. Janice pursed her lips, wondering what to do. Yolonda spoke into her ear. "You have to talk first. Elsewise she'll stay like that all day."

Jan leaned forward in her chair, attempted eye contact with her daughter. For a second, their eyes met, and Jan thought she saw a light turn on inside the girl. Then Chantal resumed her rocking, staring, silent cadence. "Chantal," Jan said with a smile. "I'm Janice." No reaction. What to say next? "I've known you your whole life, but I haven't gotten to see you much. It doesn't mean I don't care about you. It's just . . ." Words failed her. Chantal didn't notice.

Try a different approach. Jan inched her chair closer to Chantal. "Your name used to be Amanda." A "grumph" and shuffle from behind Chantal registered Yolonda's displeasure.

Regroup. "Chantal is such a pretty name. I'm glad Yolonda gave you that name. It suits you so much better." Palpable visual daggers from Yolonda warned her to shift gears again. Silence passed as Janice tried to think of something else to say. Meanwhile, Chantal rocked and stared. In her peripheral vision, Janice saw the social worker glance at her watch.

Janice moved to the edge of her chair, a foot from Chantal. The girl made eye contact and held her gaze. Janice sensed churning mental wheels behind her daughter's piercing eyes. "I hope you will let me be part of your life. Think of me as Aunt Jan." A swell of emotion engulfed her. "I love you." On raw instinct, she reached out and touched the girl's knee.

Chantal's sudden keening shriek pierced the air. Janice looked up to see the girl's fist a second before it smashed her face and knocked her off the chair. The next few seconds raced by in a painful blur. Chantal jumped on top of her, bit her ear so hard Janice thought it would come off. She felt Yolonda and the social worker seize Chantal and drag her away. Jan looked up just in time to see her daughter's parting face, the youthful innocence transformed into a mask of primal hate.

In the Johns Hopkins Medical Center's ER, Janice threatened to sign out against medical advice if the physicians didn't agree to put dressings on her wounds and discharge her instead of calling in a plastic surgeon. She could get definitive care at Bethesda Metro, where she knew the staff. After telephone consultations with Dennis King and Jerry Hartman, the Hopkins ER doc agreed to a compromise. He washed out the gaping bite wound on her left ear lobe and packed it with gauze. "I don't see any cartilage involvement," he said. "I hope you have a good plastics guy at Bethesda."

She scoffed. "One of our top product lines."

Before she left the ER, Janice stopped in the rest room. The humiliated face in the mirror shocked her—bulky dressing over her left ear, hair disheveled and blood-stained, a purple and blue bruise on her right cheek; a spectral witch, not the Nightingale-like mother she'd tried to portray when meeting her daughter for the first time in thirteen years. A sudden gush of tears flooded her face.

Twenty minutes later, reposed and cleaned up as best she could, Janice walked out the ER doors. Yolonda waited for her, hands on hips, anger and empathy battling for control of her face. "Told you it was a bad idea," Yolonda said. Her posture relaxed. "Sorry that happened. She didn't mean nothing by it."

Jan recalled the hatred on Chantal's face when she attacked her. "Maybe I deserved it."

Yolonda shook her head. "No one deserves that, Mrs. B." She hesitated. "I respect you for trying."

Janice set her jaw, looked Yolonda in the eye. "I'm not giving up."

Yolonda smiled. "Good."

"I'll be in touch."

"We'll be waiting."

CHAPTER THIRTY-FOUR

Stuck in commuter traffic on I-95 between Baltimore and Washington, Janice rehashed Chantal's surprise attack. What had triggered it? Because Janice had touched her? Said the "love" word? A shiver ran through her. The girl's hate-filled eyes had scared her more than the shock and pain of the assault. Janice knew those eyes. Staff Sergeant Tyrone Jackson's climactic grimace while two white soldiers pinned her to the ground. Wicked eyes that still evoked naked terror in her nightmares. Vicious eyes she saw again when Tyrone's child assaulted her mother.

A violent shudder overtook Jan's body, and she feared she'd lose control of the car. Hyperventilating, she pulled into a rest area, parked, shut off the car, and cranked the seat back to full recline. She could not settle herself down, could not slow her breathing, could not stop the endless loop of upsetting images storming her mind.

Tyrone had been the leader. Took his turn first; and last. When he had finished, he straddled her, pressed a bayonet against her throat, and swore that he would kill her if she ever revealed what had happened. When she later had to reveal her pregnancy to Carl, she prayed it was his child, or at least white. Fundamentalist Carl demanded they get married at once.

After six heart-sapping months, she gave birth to a biracial girl. Carl was furious, but she withheld the truth. Tyrone could kill her—anytime, anywhere. She fabricated a story of premarital infidelity, begged Carl to forgive her, implored him to let her keep the baby, promised to care for her by herself. When they got home from the hospital, Carl took the baby away, returned alone. Refused to answer Jan's desperate pleas. He never touched her again, unless to slap her face; or worse.

She stayed with Carl only because she could use him to someday reunite with her child; her only child.

Janice had named the baby girl Amanda. She'd started searching for her at once. After ten futile years, she'd found her by happenstance when she volunteered at the Kennedy Krieger Institute. Someone had changed the girl's name to Chantal, but Janice knew her daughter by that singular instinct a mother feels when close to flesh of her flesh.

As the sun set, a chill seeped into the Mercedes. In the gathering dusk, Janice chided herself. How stupid to let Carl discover her secret support of Yolonda and Chantal. *What kind of idiot am I?* How hard would it have been to lock up or destroy the incriminating bank statements from her personal account?

She repositioned the seat, started the car, and headed out of the rest area. That secret phase of her existence had ended for good when Carl died. She would find a way to be in Chantal's life—if she could get the money. Why must she rely on damned men to get it done?

Back on the road, Janice called Roger Meadows. "You need to speed this up. It can't wait a year."

After a pause, Meadows said, "I do have friends in court. I'll see what I can do."

"Don't see, do." Janice pulled into the fast lane. "I have friends in court too."

CHAPTER THIRTY-FIVE

Zack stood outside the quiet room for a full minute before he forced himself to enter. Never had he felt so defeated and useless. What could he say to Melody Snyder's husband? He tapped on the door, then eased through it. He recognized Douglas Snyder from the previous encounter, when Zack had saved Melody's life. The young executive rose from the couch and approached him.

"Dr. Winston. Thank God you were here." Zack stood in the doorway, paralyzed. The man's expression morphed from relief to fear. "Doctor?"

Zack shook his head.

The man's jaw dropped, eyes gaped, body slumped. "Not. . .?"

Zack motioned Snyder to resume his seat on the couch, then sat next him in the side chair. "I am so sorry." His voice cracked.

The husband held up a hand, turned away as if to avoid an avalanche. "No. God, no. Please, don't say it."

"I have to tell you, Mr. Snyder. She's gone."

Snyder's face broke into disbelief. "How? You— You saved her before. Why—?"

Zack bit his cheek so hard he felt the metallic taste of blood. "We tried. We did all we could."

The man broke into tears.

Zack choked back the moisture in his own eyes. "She must have been down for some time before anyone found her. She arrived with complete airway blockage, from swelling. We couldn't restore her airway before she stopped breathing. There was so much blood . . ." Zack's voice faded to silence.

The two men looked at each other, neither able to speak. Zack moved to the couch, put his arms around Doug, and hugged him.

Zack turned toward a gentle tap on his shoulder. Monica Harris regarded him with kind, maternal eyes. "I'll take it from here. Dr. King is waiting for you in the ER." She pulled Zack to his feet, guided him to the door.

He opened the door, stopped, and returned to where Doug Snyder sat with head in hands. The man looked up, puzzled.

"I should have gotten that tube into her throat."

Doug Snyder stood and stared at Zack with wide, astonished eyes. He pursed his lips, blew snorts of air from moist nostrils, advanced on Zack like an attacking lion then abruptly stopped, plopped back onto the couch, and buried his head in the upholstery.

Zack reached out toward him, but Monica grasped his shoulder. "You need to go, Zack." It was the first time in nine years working together that she had called him by his first name.

Doug Snyder sobbed into the couch. Empty inside, Zack left the room.

CHAPTER THIRTY-SIX

Zack took ten minutes to compose himself in the men's room. Although his heart dragged behind him, he marched back into the ER to start seeing the new patients in the main treatment area. When Monica saw Zack head toward a patient cubicle, she raised a hand and pointed toward the rear of the department. "Bunker."

Racked by a new sense of dread, Zack did an about-face and went to the bunker. Dennis King and Jerry Hartman sat in the only two chairs, facing each other. Their conversation stopped when Zack entered. Dennis motioned toward the bed. "Sit down, Zack." His voice conveyed concern. Jerry said nothing, his face inscrutable. Zack sat.

"Tell us what happened," Dennis said.

Zack noticed a printed record in both physicians' hands, no doubt the chronicle of his attempt to resuscitate Melody Snyder. He nodded at the one in Dennis' hand. "You have the documentation there. What do you need from me?"

Hartman spoke up. "Everything, in your own words, from the beginning."

In a steady voice, Zack described his evaluation and treatment with as much detail as he could recall. When he finished, the three of them sat in silence, each assimilating what had occurred.

Dennis spoke first. "You're certain she had complete airway obstruction on arrival? No chance of securing a non-surgical airway?"

124

Zack shook his head. "I tried. Maybe for too long before resorting to cric."

Hartman looked at the document, then at Zack. "How many crics have you done?"

Zack raised his hands in a motion of surrender. "None."

Hartman frowned. "Might you have called sooner for the trauma surgeon?"

"In retrospect, yes." He tried to clarify. "We know how to do crics. Practiced many times."

"Not on dying humans," Hartman said.

"If I had doubted my ability, I would have called for Trauma sooner. Even so, she was crashing and needed immediate action. We couldn't wait for the surgeon. I had to proceed."

Dennis said, "Did you consider doing a needle cric instead of an open approach?"

"I didn't think it would be sufficient," Zack said. "She was already severely hypoxic. She needed a tube, not a needle."

Dennis shrugged at Jerry Hartman. "Sounds right."

Hartman nodded. "Yeah." He looked at Zack. "The surgeon explored the wound. Of course, post-mortem she didn't bleed. You missed the trachea. Created a false passage through the surrounding tissue."

Zack buried his face in his hands.

They let him be for a few minutes, then Dennis spoke. "I'm taking you off duty. Paula Cho will cover the rest of your shift. Plan to take off the rest of the week. We'll arrange coverage for your other shifts."

Zack looked up. "You're suspending me?"

Dennis raised a hand. "Not at all. This case has affected you, especially after the Barnett and Knowles cases. You've had too much stress in the past few months, Zack. Time off will do you good."

"I'll die of stagnation."

"You won't. I want you talk to someone professionally, one of the shrinks on our staff; or someone else if you prefer. Don't try to deal with this on your own."

Zack waved his hand as if shooing a fly. "I understand."

Jerry Hartman cleared his throat to get Zack's attention. He spoke in a matter-of-fact tone. "The medical staff will have concerns about your ability to practice, not necessarily from a competence perspective but because of the emotional trauma. Plus, you have the Barnett case in probable litigation. If Snyder files suit, that's two. You can't afford a third strike." Zack started to protest, but Hartman cut him off. "I'm not saying 'negligence,' but we need to protect you from legal action. I'm recommending a plan of supervision when you return to duty. Dennis or another of your colleagues will review every patient encounter within twenty-four hours."

Zack stared from one to the other. "I gather you two decided all this before I walked into the room. Any chance I change it?"

"Nope," Dennis said. "No chance."

Paula Cho stuck her head into the room. She looked at Zack with pity. "I'm here."

Zack tried to smile. "Thanks, Paula. I owe you." She hurried toward the treatment area, closing the door behind her.

Dennis and Jerry rose to leave. "This is for your own protection," Dennis said. "Go home, have a drink, get—"

Zack raised a hand. "Don't say it. Please."

Dennis shrugged and led Jerry out of the room. Jerry clapped Zack on the shoulder as he left.

Zack sat on the edge of the bed and buried his face in his hands.

CHAPTER THIRTY-SEVEN

Zack remained in the bunker for almost a half-hour after Dennis and Jerry left, to absorb all that had happened and to be sure the Snyders would not be around the ER when he returned. Melody Snyder was already gone. Zack wanted to avoid Douglas Snyder. No more emotional turmoil.

When he finally emerged from the bunker, the ER had returned to normal operations. Paula Cho was seeing and managing patients with her usual alacrity and expertise. As he sat in the work area to complete his documentation on the Snyder case, Zack wondered if Paula had ever suffered crises like Carl Barnett and Melody Snyder. Or Walter Knowles. How did she handle it? He'd never seen her out of sorts, distressed, or even mildly irritated. *Must be nice.*

Thirty minutes later, he headed home to begin his forced vacation. Irritated and despondent as he was, he could blame neither Dennis nor Jerry for taking the steps they did. He'd never aspired to a leadership position, but in their place he would have done the same, if not something more severe.

When he opened the door to his apartment and stepped in, he half-expected to see Noelle waiting for him. Would she still think of him as "BAFERD"?

She wasn't there. No sign of her since she had teased him about his attraction to Bridget Larsen. *Was that just yesterday?*

Exhausted to the marrow, Zack dropped his backpack in the study, pulled a Devil's Backbone Eight Point IPA from the fridge, and slumped to the couch. He surfed Netflix looking for a movie or TV show. Nothing appealed to him. He finished the beer, lay down on the couch, and stared at the ceiling, wishing his mind to go blank.

He awoke in the dark to the sound of his phone. Caller ID indicated the ER. *What now?*

"Dr. Winston, this is Alicia from triage. There's a Roland Edwards here. Says he was supposed to meet with you after your shift."

Damn. He'd forgotten all about Roland after the tragedy of Melody Snyder. "Thanks," he said. "Please put him on."

"Hello?" Roland's voice sounded more dismayed than angry. "They say you went home early."

"I did, and I am so sorry. We had a terrible case after I saw you. To be honest, I forgot our meeting."

After a pause, Roland replied in a subdued voice. "I understand. Don't know how you guys do what you do."

Zack looked at his watch. Seven p.m. "I still want to hear what you have, Mr. Edwards, but can't be tonight. Tomorrow?" He frowned. "Turns out I have the day off."

"Sure." They arranged a breakfast meeting for nine a.m. at Tastee Diner in Bethesda. Zack apologized again.

Roland's voice sounded grave. "It's okay. I just hope you can help me clear Walter's name."

CHAPTER THIRTY-EIGHT

After a restless night, Zack rose early for a run. The morning air had a nip to it. *Winter is coming.* Soon the Capitol Crescent Trail would be snowbound. Zack would have to use the apartment building's gym, where Noelle never showed.

He ran at a brisk pace, relishing the biting air in his lungs and the muscle-generated warmth in his legs. When he reached that certain corner on the trail, he saw her. His heart leapt. She joined him and matched his pace. They ran in comfortable silence, their communication non-verbal. Zack felt her love and support with each step. She stayed with him after the turnaround, back to their meeting spot where she stopped, serious. "Pay close attention to Roland Edwards," she said. "The 'why,' not the 'how.'" He nodded, continued running. Her voice called after him. "You're still a BAFERD, Zack Winston."

Zack and Roland ate in silence at the noisy Tastee Diner in downtown Bethesda. After exchanging pleasantries and a few opening remarks, neither was comfortable discussing Walter Knowles while waitstaff whirled around them.

Once they had finished eating and the waiter had cleared the dishes and refilled their coffee mugs, Roland scowled, put down his mug, and focused on Zack. "Walter did not kill himself."

"You've said that. I've told you I have my own doubts about it."

"Something was going on with him. Something I don't understand, but it worried me."

"Worried how?" Zack remembered Noelle's advice. "Why?"

"We were together for thirty years, shared everything. No secrets. No disloyalties." He took a swallow of coffee. "Sometime in the last year, that changed. He became distant." Another sip of coffee. "Sometimes he'd get a phone call and take it outside. We'd never cared what either of us overheard. Suddenly there was something he didn't want me to know."

Zack squinted. "Did you talk to him about it?"

Roland shrugged. "Of course. He said I was mistaken, that I sounded paranoid." He gazed at the ceiling.

Zack tried to be gentle. "Go on."

Roland sighed. "He started going out for periods of time. No explanation. When I confronted him, he'd either make something up or say he needed to be alone. That was bullshit, and we both knew it. But he stuck to it."

Zack frowned. "I hate to say this, but what you describe sounds like a man having an affair."

Roland's face hardened; his voice snapped. "That would be impossible."

"Why?"

"It just would. Trust me on that."

Zack thought for a few seconds. The man had described the same behavior Zack had cajoled himself to ignore when Natalie, his first wife before Noelle, had cheated on him. If that was all Roland had on Walter Knowles, this conversation was a waste of time. He looked at Roland. "If what happened to Walter was something other than suicide, not triggered by remorse over an affair, you have to trust me with the truth. Otherwise I can't help you."

Roland stared into the distance for a few seconds before looking back at Zack. "We were never wealthy, but we did okay. Double income, no kids. He never cared about money, wasn't into . . . stuff. He enjoyed people, especially in our LGBT community; he loved having a cause." Roland looked away. "After he died, I discovered a new bank account he'd opened less than a year ago." He shook his head, as if still in disbelief. "The balance was just over a quarter-million dollars."

Zack's jaw dropped. The picture became clear. He leaned closer to Roland. "You know the answer. Walt was doing something illegal. Drugs?"

Tears came to Roland's eyes. His voice broke. "I do know. I know. It breaks my heart, but I know."

Zack would have sworn he felt a firm tap on his shoulder, but when he turned no one was there. He looked into Roland's eyes. "The big question is why."

As Roland Edwards wept, Zack considered possible explanations to tie Roland's information to what he knew about Walter's death— like he would use the process of differential diagnosis to link a patient's history, physical, lab, and x-ray findings to determine the most likely of several possible causes.

If Walt were engaged in criminal activity, the logical arena for a hospital worker would be dealing drugs. Why kill himself? Why leave a cryptic note with the one word, "Sorry"? Why choose parathion to cause a terrible death? Why not OD on a narcotic? Or use a gun? Or any of the more convenient suicidal methods that he'd seen in the ER? Before Walt, Zack had never seen an organophosphate poisoning—accidental or deliberate. It made no sense that Walt Knowles would use that substance to kill himself.

Why hadn't Roland gone to the police with his information? He claimed to have tried but got blown off by the authorities' need to tie up the package and turn the media and government attention elsewhere. Death by suicide, an easy out for everyone. Except the grieving partner.

Another thought crossed Zack's mind. "Roland, who gets the money now that Walter is dead?"

"I do." A slight smile crossed Roland's face. "I wondered when you'd come around to that question. It's why I can't go to the police. I was the last one to see Walter alive and the first to see him dead. You know where that will lead."

Zack nodded. "There is logic to it."

Roland puffed up, voice firm. "I didn't kill my partner, Dr. Winston. I didn't kill Walter."

Zack believed him.

They talked for another ten minutes, but Roland had no more facts to reveal. He reminisced about happy times that he and Walter shared through their life together. He offered no clue why Walter had changed in the past year, no idea what would have motivated him to get involved in whatever he did; yet swore with absolute certainty that Walt had not killed himself, nor had Roland murdered him. Despite Zack's encouragement, Roland refused to go to the authorities.

"We're stuck then," Zack said. He motioned for the check. "Maybe something new will come up, a different clue to point us in the right direction. Sorry I couldn't help more."

Roland smiled. "It helps that you believe me."

Zack nodded. "I do. Let's agree that if either of us learns something new that might help, we'll get in touch."

"Okay." Roland tossed a twenty-dollar bill onto the check. "Thanks for listening, Dr. Winston, and for believing."

Zack matched Roland's twenty and rose to leave. *Hell of a tip, but so what?* "Anytime," he said, "and call me Zack."

B ack home, Zack sat on the couch, tented his fingers, and pondered. Uncertainty over Roland's revelations and whatever really happened to Walter Knowles displaced his grief and self-recrimination over Melody Snyder's death. The truth hid somewhere just below the surface. He had to find it.

His phone rang. "Zack, it's Bridget Larsen. Not good news. Roger Meadows filed the malpractice suit this morning. I don't know how, but he got the judge to expedite the process. He's already sent over written interrogatories, and he wants to depose you within the month."

"What the hell?"

"We can fight the rush. On the other hand, if we get our case together, we might spare you months of uncertainty and mental anguish. Can you come to my office today? We can start through the interrogatories and talk strategy. I need to get back to Roger in a day, either to cooperate or stonewall him, whichever is to your advantage."

"Turns out I have unscheduled time off." He summarized the Melody Snyder case and its aftermath.

"Damn. I'm sorry, Zack."

"I can shower, dress, and be at your office in an hour."

"Okay. Do us both a favor. Put on your BAFERD face."

How does she know that term?

CHAPTER THIRTY-NINE

Zack took a seat at the conference table in Bridget's office. She sat beside him and dropped a short pile of documents in front of him.

"Your copies." Bridget set an identical pile in front of herself. Her brow furrowed. "Roger had to pull heavy strings to get this case expedited." She looked him in the eye. "Any notion why Mrs. Barnett would pressure him to do that?"

Zack shook his head. "No clue."

She held eye contact for a few seconds then shrugged. "Okay. Let's get to work. Did you bring the documents I mentioned?"

"I did." Zack pulled them from his briefcase, handed each to her in turn: "Updated CV. Original medical degree and medical school transcripts. Residency certificate. Original board certification and recertification certificates. Licenses to practice medicine in Maryland, the District of Columbia, and Virginia. Continuing medical education documentation for the past ten years." He stopped, looked at her, irritated. "Some early ones may be missing. The licensing boards require only the most recent three years."

Bridget cast a sardonic smile. "Lawyers."

Zack produced the last documents, the ones that worried him, and held them toward her. "Military service record and DD-214 verifying honorable separation from the United States Navy."

She gripped the folder without taking it; looked into his eyes instead. "Anything there we need to talk about?"

Zack glanced away. "No."

Before putting those documents into his briefcase, he had scrutinized every page with a single purpose: Find the dirt. He had paid closest attention to the annual performance evaluations from his reporting-senior naval officers. All described him as a skilled professional medical officer with consistently superior performance, recommended for early promotion and positions of increasing responsibility. Searching for "coded" faint-praise language, he found no subtle suggestions of misconduct or incompetence. Zack had mouthed a virtual "thanks" to Ed Walsh, his former navy boss, wherever he was. *Should be surgeon general of the navy by now.*

"Okay," Bridget said as she dropped the file onto her pile. "Anything else?"

"No." Zack had left his copies of Barnett's records at home—again.

Bridget's piercing gaze disturbed him, as if she could see into his soul. With an almost imperceptible tilt of her head, she handed Zack a sheaf of printed papers and a thumb drive. "These are interrogatories for you. It's the first phase of discovery. Copies are on the thumb drive. Your homework is to answer them as completely—and honestly—as possible. Save them to the thumb drive, then either bring it or have it delivered to me tomorrow. That's a short deadline, but we need to move quickly if we're going to beat Roger."

Zack leafed through the pages. Most of the questions seemed simple, straightforward, boilerplate, until he got to the last page. Two questions grabbed at his throat.

Has Zachary Winston, MD, ever been formally reprimanded, censured, disciplined, or counseled, including but not limited to suspension or limitation of clinical privileges, or placed under supervision of clinical activities for practice of medicine below the standard of care?

He sucked in his lower lip. He could truthfully answer no. *Never* formally *reprimanded or disciplined.*

Has Zachary Winston, MD, ever been found to be impaired by drugs, alcohol, mental instability, or emotional disorder while practicing medicine in a clinical setting?

Another no. His copy of a blood alcohol test below the legal intoxication level in Japan could prove that.

Bridget leaned over to see what had caught his attention. "Something of concern?"

Startled, he closed the document. "Uh, they got my name wrong. I've never been Zachary. My parents named me Zack."

She gave him a doubtful look. "Hmm. It's that way on the filing and other documents too. I'll get Roger's office to correct them. Won't matter in the grand scheme, but good that you caught the mistake on the last document you read."

Those piercing eyes again, and an intimidating smile. *She misses nothing.* He looked down at the table.

"Need a break, Zack? Cup of coffee? Water?"

He raised his hands in "no" gesture. "I'm fine, thanks."

She shrugged. "Do you know an emergency physician by the name of Julian Schwartz?"

"Everyone in emergency medicine knows of Dr. Schwartz. Stellar reputation. Past President of the American College of Emergency Physicians *and* the American Board of Emergency Medicine. Respected academic out of UCLA. I've never met him, but I've heard him speak."

Bridget smirked. "You'll get to meet him. He's the plaintiff's expert witness."

Zack felt as if the chair had collapsed beneath him. "Shit."

"They weren't going to pick a dumbass. Roger's been in hyperdrive building this case. He shot me a copy of Dr. Schwartz's written report." She pushed a document toward him. "Not favorable, but that's expected. Don't go ballistic when you read it. Don't make it personal."

Zack had seen Julian Schwartz present at national emergency medicine conferences. A dominant personality, he conducted himself with an air of superiority and complete confidence. Pity the physician who dared to challenge this titan's erudite opinions. An arrogant academic, he emoted with absolute certainty, no matter if he was right or wrong. Zack opened the folder, pictured Schwartz's style, and imagined his cocky voice as he read the report, which was much shorter than he'd expected. After a superficial summary of Zack's evaluation and treatment of Carl Barnett on his first visit, the esteemed consultant rendered his expert opinion. The key words popped off the page and pierced Zack's heart.

Ignored important facts . . . EKG findings consistent with acute myocardial ischemia . . . erred in discharging the patient . . . below the standard of care . . . negligence . . . caused irreversible cardiac arrest and wrongful death.

Drowning in a flood of anger and remorse, Zack re-read the report twice to get past the shock of the words. He glowered at Bridget. "He's full of shit. He oversimplifies the patient's history and findings. Doesn't mention the negative HEART score. Ignores that the pain resolved without treatment." He flung the document onto the table. "Those EKGs were normal. If he were one of my interns, I'd rip him a new one."

Bridget sat back. "That's the spirit. I always try to discredit the plaintiff's expert." She glanced away. "Didn't work in my last ER case." She turned to Zack. "Schwartz may be unimpeachable."

Zack nodded. "Yeah. He's always certain, even when dead wrong. Dominant personality."

"We need an expert to help us rip Schwartz that new one." She smiled. "Got anyone in mind."

"Dennis King could do it."

"Your boss? Non-starter. As head of your group, he's also a defendant. We need someone completely detached."

Zack thought for a minute. "I may know the right person. Hates my guts, but honest and objective to a fault. She'd probably be willing to help."

Bridget scoffed. "She? Any past relationship there?"

Flushed, he looked at the table. "Yeah. Another non-starter, huh?"

"No kidding. Find us a *guy* who hates your guts, Zack, and not some former girlfriend's boyfriend or husband. Professional relationship only. Hating your guts will add to his credibility. Surely you can find someone who matches our need." She stood. "That's all for today." She held the door for him. "Don't forget your homework, Doctor."

Zack understood he'd been summarily dismissed.

CHAPTER FORTY

As soon as Zack Winston left, Bridget returned to her desk, spun her chair around, and gazed out her fifth-floor office window. Nothing to see except the opposite building and the constant flow of one-way traffic on I Street. She didn't care about the view. She worried about the warning flares inside her head. Five minutes of deep breaths and precious silence assuaged her annoyance with Zack Winston and enabled her to concentrate.

The question was not *what* her client was hiding, but *why*. Something about his naval career that he didn't want anyone to know, even after her clear admonition that she required absolute honesty. Further, what about that self-serving suggestion of some woman doctor from a prior relationship as his expert witness? Did Zack Winston want to win this suit? Did he care a rip about his career or reputation? Or was this some novel narcissistic adventure drama featuring Bridget as his supporting actress?

I should bail on this one now. No good would come of this case. As she turned back to her desk, a strange internal voice prompted her. Why not sign on to Zack's mad adventure; see where it goes? Something about the man intrigued her. Charming vulnerability or vulnerable narcissism? She shrugged. *Could be fun. I get paid either way.*

If she did continue to represent Zack Winston, he wasn't the only one with homework to do. She picked up the office intercom. "Please contact Dominic. I need to speak to him at first opportunity."

The firm's private investigator called within five minutes. "Dom, I need you to find all you can on a Dr. Zack Winston, ER doc at Bethesda Metro. First name is Zack, Z-a-c-k, not Zachary. Former navy doc. That's the time period of primary interest. Also, see what you can find on a Carl or Janice Barnett. That would be the late Carl Barnett and his surviving spouse." She stopped to listen. "Of course, your usual fee. I need Winston soonest, Barnetts within a month." She paused a beat. "And, Dom, try to stay within at least the outer limits of the law this time."

She chuckled at his response, hung up, and punched the intercom again. "Roger Meadows, please, and don't take 'he's in conference' as an answer."

Forty-five minutes later, Roger Meadows called her back. "Sorry, Bridge. I was—"

"In conference, yeah, yeah." She frowned, knowing that he knew how much she hated his calling her 'Bridge.' "Thanks for calling back. I'll be brief."

"All yours, Bridge."

She knotted the hand not holding the phone into a tight fist. The other hand squeezed the handset so hard the plastic seemed to bend. "What's with the rush on the Barnett suit?"

"Rush? What do you mean?"

Such a vile creature. "You know damn well. Why did you pull strings to get it expedited?"

His voice reeked of conceit. "I'm doing your client a favor. Sooner we get to settlement, sooner he can have his life back."

Bridget could dish it out too. "I smell a rat, Rog, and it stinks like you."

Roger responded with feigned hurt. "Come now, Bridge, no need to sling mud. I'm doing what my client wants. If you need the reason, ask her."

"I will when I have her on the stand under oath."

He scoffed. "This case will never get to trial. You know that. I hope you're talking settlement numbers with your client and his carrier."

Bridget huffed. "We agree to a preliminary deposition within the month, but I'm giving you the chance now to disclose anything we haven't seen or won't see before you question my client."

Derisive laugh. "Whatever makes you think I'd do that, especially on a case that's already in the bag?" His voice turned smug. "Your client will be my best witness."

"You've tried to pull that crap in the past. I won't stand for it. Any funny business in depo and we walk."

He snorted. "That would not be a wise move on your part, Bridge."

"Fair warning, Rog."

He seemed offended. "I wouldn't do that to you. You and I go back a long way. We had some pleasant times together."

The leer in his voice infuriated her. She hung up without responding, then spun her chair around to look back out the window. *Zack Winston's not the only one hiding something from me.*

CHAPTER FORTY-ONE

When Zack got off the elevator after meeting with Bridget, his heart swelled when he saw Noelle waiting for him. He did a double take when he moved closer. She leaned her back against the corner of the small lobby, arms crossed, one foot braced on the wall, eyes glaring—a posture and expression he'd seldom seen from her.

She spoke in a sharp voice. "You sure managed to put her off."

He walked past her, through the outer door, onto the sidewalk. She followed. "Why did you do that, Zack? Why alienate the one living person on this earth who can get you out of this mess?" Zack kept walking. He didn't answer, because he didn't know the answer.

Noelle was not done. "Still hiding that medical record copy? Not admitting you have it? Why do you lie to her?"

Zack didn't know the answer to that question either. He continued to walk, despite knowing she wasn't about to let up.

"What's with the secrecy about the navy, Zack? Why do you hide that? Why bury the truth about us?"

That last question struck a heavy blow to Zack's chest. He wheeled around, shouted in her face. "I don't fucking know!"

The crowd on the sidewalk had suddenly gone quiet. People stared at him as if he were a crazy man. "Sorry," he said to those closest to him. "Sorry." He turned and walked away.

Noelle stayed with him, but now her voice was calm, soft. "You need to figure it out, Zack. You need to figure out why you do shit that hurts you. If not, you will lose everything, including me."

Zack stopped walking, struggling to control the flood of emotion inside him. He spoke in a whisper. "I know. I know."

"Then do it," Noelle said. "Start by forgiving yourself. What happened to me was never your fault. Get past it. Be the man I loved and married."

Zack nodded, not feeling as resolute as he wished, but with a slight sense of renewed determination. He started walking again, a slow positive stride.

"Uh, Zack," Noelle said. "You passed your Metro station two blocks back."

CHAPTER FORTY-TWO

Chagrined, annoyed with himself, and torn by Noelle's displeasure, Zack rode the Metro in silence to Bethesda. His mind reminisced on their idyllic days.

Six months after their first night together in Hong Kong, two months after their romantic betrothal in Miyajima, Zack and Noelle stole away on a warm Saturday evening for the short train ride from Atsugi to Tokyo. They dined at an upscale teppanyaki restaurant in the heart of the bustling Roppongi nightlife district. A skilled chef butterflied shrimp on the hibachi grill in front of their table of eight customers, the rest of whom were Japanese. Zack raised his sake glass in a toast to Noelle. As on their first night together and many nights since, they clinked glasses and gazed into each other's eyes.

"To our engagement," Zack said.

"To our happiness," Noelle said.

"Kampai," they said together, and each swallowed the sake in one gulp.

An older Japanese gentleman sitting next to Zack turned to him.

"Excuse me," the man said in near-perfect English. "My name is Haruki. I apologize for my forwardness, but did I hear you are engaged?"

"Yes," Zack replied. "As of two months ago."

Haruki spoke in Japanese to the chef, who then gave directions to the server. She left, then returned with a bottle of sake and nine glasses. Haruki stood and addressed Zack and Noelle, "Please allow a congratulatory toast. This is Juyondai sake, best in Japan. Hard to find. Most fitting for such special occasion. Can you please say your names?"

"That is very sweet of you," Noelle said. "He's Zack. I'm Noelle."

When all the glasses were full, Haruki made an upward motion with his hand, and all the Japanese at the table stood. The chef paused his cooking and took up a glass as well. Haruki grinned and spoke loudly in Japanese to anyone in earshot, gesturing toward Zack and Noelle. Others in the restaurant stood and raised glasses. Zack and Noelle rose and bowed toward Haruki. He bowed, then raised his glass. "To Zack and Noelle, our American friends, *kon'yaku omedeto*, congratulations on your engagement." The others in the restaurant raised their glasses and chimed together, *"Kon'yaku omedeto!"* Much bowing followed, first the Japanese, then Zack and Noelle, then the Japanese again, and so on, until Zack whispered in her ear. "You can never outbow the Japanese." They took their seats.

The chef resumed cooking and the restaurant returned to its normal milieu. Zack tasted the sake, amazed at its easy drinkability. The fruity, delicate liquid flowed down his throat like nectar. *"Arigato gozaimashita,"* he said to Haruki. "This sake is amazing."

"It is my pleasure. Please keep the bottle as a token of the affection between our people and yours."

Speechless, Zack bowed to him.

On the train back to Atsugi, Zack made the decision to stay in the navy for another tour of duty, to which Noelle gleefully agreed.

Because of the time zone difference between Japan and the US, Zack had to wait until Monday night to call his navy detailer to request a follow-on assignment. He offered to continue his commission if he could remain in Japan. Since Noelle had another year with the air wing, Zack requested collocation as married officers to duty in the same geographical location. He asked to be assigned as an emergency physician to the naval hospital in Yokosuka, thirty miles from the naval air station in Atsugi.

"You can't request collocation until you're married," the detailer said.

Zack and Noelle planned a traditional wedding with family and friends in Michigan after the deployment that would begin in three weeks. "The wedding won't happen for six months or more," Zack said.

"Then I have to assign you as a single officer. I've got another ER doc penciled in for that Yokosuka billet, someone senior to you. Plus, I need to consult with your emergency medicine specialty leader. He may need you somewhere else."

Zack's heart sank. "If that's the case, I'll quit active duty."

"Your choice. Understand that you can't stay in Japan as an unmarried civilian, so you solve nothing by getting out while your fiancée still has a commitment." Zack could hear the man typing. "I might have an ER position in Okinawa. I won't know for another month or two."

Zack retorted. "Okinawa may be in Japan, but that's like saying New York and Omaha are in the US—nowhere close. How about I extend for another year in the air wing?"

"Sorry, that's promised to the top graduate of the current flight surgery class. You know how that works."

"But I'm senior to that guy."

"Woman. Not gonna happen, Lieutenant Commander. Sorry."

Zack's brain lit up. "Tell you what, Commander. Let's leave it there for now. I'll get back to you in a couple of weeks."

"Okay," the detailer said, "But don't put it off for long. You might find yourself with the Marines in Afghanistan."

"Not gonna happen, Commander. I will be in Japan with my wife."

Two weeks later, on a balmy Saturday morning in April, Zack and Noelle wed in the Atsugi naval air station chapel, without the presence of family or friends other than their air wing shipmates. *USS Kitty Hawk* would deploy the following Monday. The Winstons would spend their honeymoon living in separate quarters on the ship, accompanied by five thousand other sailors—with intermittent conjugal soirees in some of the most romantic foreign ports in the world.

A week after they embarked, Zack received an e-mail from his detailer. Attached were his follow-on orders to report in July as an emergency physician to US Naval Hospital, Yokosuka, Japan.

CHAPTER FORTY-THREE

Zack got off the Metro at Bethesda Station and strolled to his apartment, lost in his memories. He thought about his earlier tiff with Noelle outside Bridget's office. He had no clue why he withheld information from Bridget, nor did he want to ponder it. He had enough external battles to wage. No sense in dragging his inner self into a wild-goose chase. A fine bottle of Chianti and leftover pepperoni and sausage pizza awaited him at home. That would do him just fine.

His phone rang as he poured a glass of the chianti. *Ange.*

Her voice bubbled. "You'll never guess what I just did."

Surprised and intrigued, he put off pressing the "Start" button to microwave the pizza. "No clue. You sound happy."

"I am, and I hope you will be too."

Intrigued, Zack took a sip of wine. "Shoot."

She paused, all at once uncertain, then spoke in a rush of words. "I joined your defense team."

He almost choked on his wine. "You did what?"

"As of tomorrow, I am an associate attorney at Desmond, Markle, and Larsen, assigned to Ms. Bridget Larsen."

Zack put down the glass. "What the heck, Ange? What about your practice?"

A rush of air into the phone. "Defunct. Belly up. Could not cut it alone after Keisha left." Her voice turned sour. "Haven't paid the office rent for three months. They threatened me with eviction, so I decided to shut it down."

"Yeah, but, why Bridget?"

"First, she's the best tort defense attorney in town." She paused. "Second, as I told her, you're getting the shaft and I want to help you."

Zack took a deep breath. "Bridget bought that?"

"With some reluctance. I had to assure her we're no longer a thing, just friends." That caused a slight pang in Zack's chest, even though he accepted it as fact. Ange continued. "She said that as a member of your legal team Roger Meadows can't call me as a witness to tell what I know. We can protect those conversations under attorney-client privilege."

"What you know? I don't get it."

"What you told me about the case, and what I know about you."

Zack ran his fingers through his hair. "I'm not following any of this, but it seems good."

"You bet it is. You have another fighter on your side."

Zack was at a loss for words.

"Listen," Ange said. "We can talk in person if you want. Have you had dinner yet?"

Zack looked at the microwave and its cold pizza inhabitant. "Not really. Just opened a bottle of wine."

"Cork the bottle and meet me half-way. I'm still in DC near Bridget's office."

"I just came from there."

"Up to you," she said. "Just friends meeting for dinner. Several restaurant options around here."

"Okay," Zack said. "See you in about thirty."

Five minutes later, he strode out of his apartment building toward the Metro.

CHAPTER FORTY-FOUR

*R**oger Meadows is a ferret.*
Such was Zack's reaction when Janice's attorney entered the Cooper Meadows conference room. Zack, Bridget, and Ange had waited for thirty uncomfortable minutes past the scheduled time for the deposition. Other than nervous small talk, they had sat in silence—as if they feared the room was bugged.

Meadows slunk into the room and oiled his way around the large conference table. He was shorter in stature than Zack's female companions. He wore a tailored charcoal suit, white shirt with gray tie. His pallid, puggish face and black horn-rimmed glasses gave him a polecat appearance. Inch-long curls of body hair protruded from his starched shirt collar and cuffs. *A ferret.*

With a hungry grin, Meadows offered Zack a hand. "Doctor Winston, I'm Roger Meadows. Thank you for coming."

Zack shook his hand with a vise-like grip he seldom inflicted on other men. "No problem."

Meadows gave Bridget a fraternal hug. She bent at the waist to accommodate him but remained stiff. She introduced Ange. "My associate, Angela Moretti."

"Welcome," Meadows said. Stiff as pipe, Ange shook his hand.

He turned to introduce the person behind him. "My associate, Ms. Keisha Rollins."

Zack recognized Keisha as Ange's friend and former law office partner. She and Ange exchanged handshakes as if they'd never met. Zack followed suit. "Pleased to meet you, Ms. Rollins."

The ferret motioned for Zack to sit in front of a video camera as he took the opposite seat. "Shall we begin?" Zack was sure he saw a pair of needle-like pointed incisors in the man's mouth.

After a half-hour of banal exchanges about Zack's professional history and credentials, Meadows changed his expression, leaned forward with piercing eyes that Zack could swear were red.

"Doctor, on July thirteenth of last year were you on duty in the emergency department of Bethesda Metro Hospital around four p.m.?"

"Yes."

"Did you evaluate a patient by the name of Carl Barnett?"

"Yes."

Meadows smirked, then passed a file across the table. Zack acknowledged the ER record from Carl's first visit.

"Please describe that encounter. Feel free to refer to the record if you need to refresh your memory."

"That won't be necessary." The sarcasm in his own voice surprised Zack. Bridget touched his arm in a pre-agreed warning gesture. He cleared his throat then described in detail his first encounter with Carl Barnett, making a show of dumbing it down for the non-medical folks across the table—until Bridget touched his arm again.

The ferret raised a hand to interrupt Zack's monologue. "What was your assessment of Mr. Barnett at that time?"

"I would first like to add that over the course of this evaluation his chest pain resolved without treatment."

Meadows turned stern. "Answer the question I asked, Doctor." He pronounced the word "doctor" with the same inflection that one might say "filthy worm."

"Mister Barnett did not meet evidence-based criteria for acute coronary syndrome."

Meadows feigned frustration. "You did not believe Carl Barnett was at risk for a heart attack, even one severe enough to kill him?"

Bridget interrupted, looked at her watch. "He's answered that. Please move on."

Roger flashed a wicked stare at Bridget. "Very well." He glared at Zack. "Carl Barnett died the next day, didn't he?" Bridget tapped softly on the table, twice—their pre-arranged signal that the ferret was about to get vicious, but Zack should not react in kind.

Zack kept his voice steady. "Mister Barnett arrived by ambulance after suffering an apparent cardiac arrest at home. We could not resuscitate him because his status on arrival was incompatible with life."

Meadows snorted. "He died." It was not a question.

"Yes, sir."

"From cardiac arrest." Another snort.

"Yes, sir."

"Can you be more precise, Doctor? And please don't talk down to us like you did before. We may not have your degree, but we do understand medical terminology."

Bridget fixed her gaze on Meadows. "I won't allow you to badger my client, Roger."

"Well, if we're going to be sensitive—"

"For the record, I object," Bridget said. "Stop it or we walk." She turned to Zack. "You can answer the question."

He described the attempted resuscitation of Carl Barnett in full clinical detail, without explaining the medical terms.

Meadows scowled. "Would you agree, Doctor, that the only opportunity to spare Carl Barnett from untimely death would have been to diagnose his cardiac disease when you saw him the previous day?"

Bridget interjected. "Object to that. Presumes facts not in evidence." She nodded at Zack to answer.

"As I stated earlier, on the first day he demonstrated no criteria for cardiac disease. There is no evidence that links the two events."

Meadows studied his notes. Ange and Keisha glanced at each other across the table, expressionless.

"Did you review the autopsy report on Mr. Barnett?" Meadows said.

"Yes."

"Please summarize the pertinent findings for us."

"He had clean coronaries. No evidence of pre-existing heart disease. No myocardial infarction."

"Cause of death?"

"The pathologist listed it as 'cardiac arrhythmia.'"

"In other words," Meadows' eyes narrowed, and the corners of his mouth twisted slightly upwards as he read aloud from his notes. "An abnormality or perturbation in the normal activation sequence of the myocardium." He scowled at Bridget. "Direct quote from the Cleveland Clinic Center for Continuing Education." Bridget did not react.

Zack answered. "That would be one definition."

Meadows feigned surprise. "Are there other definitions?"

Zack sensed a trap. "Not really."

Meadows ran a hand through his sparse, thin hair. "A cardiac arrhythmia is an abnormal electrical impulse in the heart's beating mechanism, correct?"

"Yes."

"Can one suffer an arrhythmia with, how did you put it?" He made a show of consulting his notes. "Clean coronaries?"

"Yes."

He tilted his head. "Really? What might cause that to happen?"

Zack had no clue where this line of questioning was headed.

"Answer the question, please, Doctor." This time he said "doctor" with the same inflection as one might say "viper."

"Tone, Roger," Bridget said. Meadows ignored her.

Zack glared at him. "Coronary artery spasm, for one."

Meadows leaned forward. "Describe that please."

Zack summarized what he knew about coronary artery spasm.

"To be clear, Doctor, coronary artery spasm can cause acute chest pain and sudden death."

"Chest pain, yes. Sudden death, rare."

"Sudden death does happen, right?"

"Yes."

"Could Carl Barnett have suffered coronary artery spasm the first time you saw him?" Bridget moved beside Zack, but she neither objected nor signaled to him.

Zack leaned back in his chair. "Not likely, based on the criteria I've described." The ferret eyed Zack's neck and the underlying jugular vein and carotid artery. Zack signaled to Bridget that he needed a break. She started to speak, but Meadows talked over her.

"What are the specific EKG findings in acute cardiac ischemia? Doctor?" This time "Doctor" sounded like "dirty rat."

Weary, Zack sighed. "ST segment elevation greater than two millimeters in at least two contiguous leads."

The ferret leered like an animal smelling blood. He pulled an EKG caliper from his coat pocket. The room felt hot and fusty. Zack wanted out of there. He needed fresh air, but Bridget didn't move or say anything. Meadows tossed the caliper across the table. "Doctor Winston, please refer to the document I handed you earlier, the one you stipulated is a true copy of the emergency department medical record from Carl Barnett's first visit."

Her faced lined with worry, Bridget handed Zack the record.

Meadows wet his lips. "Please turn to the first EKG tracing and measure the ST segments."

Same tracing Zack remembered from his prior review. "The ST segments measure less than two millimeters elevation."

"Not outside the limits, correct?"

Zack looked from the record to Roger Meadows. When their eyes met, a sudden chill ran through Zack's body—despite the warm room. "Correct. Normal EKG."

The ferret bared his teeth. "Now, Doctor, do the same measurement on the next EKG tracing, the one performed an hour after the first one."

When Zack turned the page to that tracing, his heart exploded. He did not recognize the EKG. Had never seen it before. He gawked at Bridget, who looked back with puzzled eyes. He glanced at Ange, whose eyes widened in fright at his expression.

"We're waiting, Doctor," Meadows said in a sneering, sing-song voice.

Zack's voice trembled. "This isn't the right EKG."

Meadows feigned surprise. "What?"

"This isn't the right EKG. I've never seen this one. It's not the one I saw on that day, and it's not the one I reviewed to prepare for this deposition." Hearing that, Ange scrambled through their copies of the record.

Meadows' voice dripped with disgust. "Really, Doctor Winston? *Now* you challenge the validity of this record? Read the label on that tracing. Does it not identify the patient as Carl Barnett, and the date and time of the tracing consistent with the date and time you saw him?"

"It can't be the same EKG."

"Can't be?" He gestured at Bridget. "Did your lawyer not explain chain of custody to you?"

Shaken and nonplussed, Zack couldn't answer.

"Can we take a break, please," Bridget said. "Clearly my client is upset."

Roger Meadows glowered at her. "He has to answer my question first." He turned to Zack. "Tell me what you see on that EKG, Doctor."

Zack looked to Bridget for guidance. She shrugged and spread her hands. "Go ahead and answer. We're going to protest this anyway."

Fury rose from his chest and seared his brain. Ange was trying to get his attention, but he ignored her and glowered at the ferret. He tossed the EKG caliper across the table. "I don't need your damned caliper. The ST segments in the precordial leads are elevated, over two millimeters." He slammed his fist on the table. "But that's not the right goddamn EKG."

Unshaken, the ferret spoke in a sappy, condescending voice. "Thank you, Doctor. You may take your break now."

CHAPTER FORTY-FIVE

Zack and Ange bolted from the conference room as if escaping a tsunami. Keisha disappeared through another door like a sylph. Bridget held her ground to confront Roger Meadows.

Taking refuge in an alcove off the conference room, Zack and Ange found a couple of modern chrome and black vinyl uncomfortable chairs. Since they had arrived at the law offices of Cooper, Meadows, et. al., Zack had imagined himself on the set of a Hollywood legal drama. In contrast to the tasteful style and decor of Bridget's firm, this office suite reeked of arrogance. All the furnishings and decorations, including those in the conference room they had just escaped, seemed to exist for the sole purpose of intimidating any outsider who dared to enter. Zack found it quite effective.

The alcove had no door, and they sat a mere twenty feet from the conference room. Through the closed door, they heard Bridget's and Roger Meadows' verbal battle.

Zack caught his breath. "Where the hell did they get that bogus EKG?"

Expressionless, Ange handed him their copy of the medical records, turned to the page with the second EKG. She pursed her lips, silent while he scanned it.

"That's the right EKG," he said. "The one I saw on the first day." From the conference room, Bridget's voice waxed righteous.

Ange spoke in a whisper. "This document is stamped as a certified copy of the original record, same as the one Meadows handed us. I compared the two while you were testifying. The dates are different. Ours is stamped three days after his."

"Their version trumps ours?"

"Timewise, yes. Something is rotten; and you're in a world of hurt."

Zack rubbed his eyes. He spoke in a low, embarrassed tone. "I have an earlier copy, from the same day Barnett died."

Ange gasped. "You have another copy of the record?"

Zack nodded.

"Does Bridget know that?"

He shook his head. "Walt Knowles, the ER secretary, made a copy at my request the day of Barnett's code. Dennis King told me to destroy it, but I didn't. It's hidden in my apartment. Bridget doesn't know about it."

Ange slumped into her chair. "Oh, Zack . . ."

Bridget strode toward them from the conference room, her face crimson. "I got him to agree to a one-week recess so we can research the authenticity of that EKG." Her eyes probed Zack's. "Are you absolutely certain that's not the right EKG?"

"I'd stake my life on it."

Bridget's eyes narrowed. "You may have to do exactly that. Is it different from our copy?"

He nodded in Ange's direction. "We just looked at our copy. It's not the same EKG. I've never seen the one they showed us."

"Then what the hell?"

Ange told Bridget about the dates of the copies being different.

Bridget deflated. "His version predates ours?"

"By three days," Ange said. She cast a menacing glare at Zack. He shifted his feet and stared at the floor.

Bridget didn't notice. She spoke as if pondering aloud. "He'll claim to have the true version. He'll allege that ours is a fraud, altered to support Zack's version of the first-day assessment."

Zack could not make eye contact with Bridget or Ange. "I know what I saw that day. I would barter my soul with the devil before I'd accept the one he showed us."

Livid, Bridget pointed toward the conference room. "The devil in that room believes he already owns your soul. If we don't figure this out, you will have more than hell to pay."

Zack nodded, speechless. Ange's eyes bore into him.

"We have to go back on the record in there to officially recess until next week," Bridget said. "Don't answer any questions unless I tell you. Volunteer nothing, and for God's sake don't go into a rant."

"Yes, ma'am."

Ten minutes later, the trio climbed into Bridget's Range Rover in the parking structure adjacent to the Cooper Meadows building—Bridget driving, Zack in the right front seat, Ange in the back seat behind him. She had not spoken since Bridget came out of the conference room. As Bridget started the car, Ange kicked so hard at Zack's seatback that his head lurched forward.

He stayed Bridget's hand from shifting into reverse. "Before we move, I need to tell you something."

CHAPTER FORTY-SIX

Bridget said nothing when Zack told her about his private copies of the medical records. She slammed the Range Rover into reverse, swung it from the parking space, and bolted from the garage. No one spoke during the ten-minute drive back to her office. When he glanced sideways, Zack saw Bridget squeezing the steering wheel, eyes focused straight ahead, body tense, like a lioness about to strike. Her posture awoke the same puerile dread he used to feel just before his mother unleashed one of her demeaning tirades after he disappointed her.

In the lobby of the law offices, Bridget spoke to Ange. "Give Zack and me a few minutes alone. In fact, call it a day. You're free to leave." She turned and headed toward her office.

Ange whispered to Zack. "Be honest, damn it."

Bridget sat board-like behind the desk when he entered her office. "Close the door."

He did so and waited for further direction. Bridget stared at him, eyes smoldering. He took the chair across the desk. She folded her hands in front of herself, like a stern teacher about to put an errant student on detention. "I should fire you."

"I'm sorry. I—"

She held up her hand in a "stop" gesture. "You lied to me, Zack. You lied to me the same day I told you I require absolute honesty."

"I—"

Same hand gesture. "Don't make an excuse. Don't apologize. Don't rationalize." Her nostrils flared. "Don't. Say. Anything." She rotated her chair so her back was to him. Stared out the window. Stiff except for random deep breaths.

Zack sat in silence, examining his fingernails, wondering how to get a new lawyer. What effect would that have on his case?

Five minutes passed, and he was still looking at Bridget's back. *Does she know I'm still here? Should I leave?*

Bridget spun her chair around, faced him, eyes on fire. "Where is your copy of the records?"

"In a locked desk drawer in my apartment."

"Who else knows you have it?"

"No one. I let Dennis King believe I destroyed it, on his direction."

Bridget tilted her head. "Dr. King told you to destroy copies of the medical records?"

"Yeah. He said I shouldn't have them."

She stroked her chin. "Who gave the original records to the insurance carrier, the ones Meadows passed to us today?"

"Dennis did that, the day after the code arrest."

"Do you know when he did it? The death happened on a Friday, right? Late in the day?"

He sensed a thin opening in the black pall that enveloped him. "He might have waited until Monday."

Bridget leaned her chin on her left hand, a finger tapping on her cheek. "Is your copy of the records time-stamped?"

"I think so. I believe the copier in the ER is set to do that."

She stared past him. "Are you absolutely certain, beyond a glimmer of doubt, that the EKG in your private stash is not the one Roger showed you today?"

"No doubt. I referenced it in the notes I gave you when we first met."

She grimaced. "So, we have the earliest copy of the record—except its inadmissible because you violated chain of custody."

"Can't we get the actual original record?"

"Too late. We can't prove it hasn't been altered at any time since the event happened." She gazed at the wall behind Zack. "Let's suppose someone conspired to make it appear that Roger's copy, with a bogus EKG, is the true and valid version. Can you think of any way, besides your maverick copies, to find the original EKG? Assuming one does exist?"

He pondered for a bit, then it hit him. "Sevati!"

"Huh?"

"Sevati Prakash, the cardiologist. They run duplicate originals in cardiology."

"You think they would have the real EKG, and it would match our copy?"

"I sure as hell hope so."

Bridget leaned back in her chair, arms crossed, face stony. "Okay, Zack, here's my deal. I should fire you as a client, but I won't—not yet. We'll subpoena this Doctor Sevati for the original EKG. If we can prove it's identical to the one in our copy of the records, then we've got the plaintiff, and a person or persons unknown, on evidence tampering. Your case goes away. If we can implicate Roger Meadows in that conspiracy, we bring him down."

Wow. Straight for the throat.

"Who had access to the original record, Zack?"

"Walter Knowles, the ER secretary, made my copies. He always had access to the records." Zack looked askance. "He's dead now. The insecticide poisoning."

Bridget frowned. "That seems a bit coincidental."

Zack shrugged. "Walter was a strange duck." Mindful of Ange's advice, Zack strove for total honesty. "His death was ruled a suicide, but about a week later his partner came to me swearing Walter would not have done that."

"Not an unusual response from a loved one left behind by suicide, right?"

Zack nodded.

"Did the partner have any evidence to suggest foul play or some other cause."

Zack shook his head. "None."

"What was the partner's name?" Zack told her, and she wrote a note on her legal pad. "Back to the original record. Anyone else have access to it that day?"

"Jerry Hartman, the Barnetts' personal physician and director of the ICU. He was in the ER the day Barnett died, shortly after Walt made the copies for me." He told her about his confrontation with Hartman.

"Either of them could have altered the record before Doctor King got it?"

"It's possible. I didn't tell Dennis about Barnett until the next day, Saturday, but he'd already heard about it. I don't know when he picked up the original ER records."

"Would anyone else have the same opportunity?"

"Anyone who worked in the ER; Nurses, techs, quite a few people."

"What about Dr. King?"

Zack shook his head. "No way. He would have no motive. I trust him. He's always treated me well."

Bridget's eyes softened. "Without the valid original EKG, your case is shot. You will have no choice but to settle."

A wave of trepidation washed out any sense of relief in Zack. "I understand that." *My future depends on Sevati Prakash.*

"We have to move fast," Bridget said. "I agreed to resume the deposition on Wednesday, and I doubt Roger will let us postpone it. I'll subpoena the cardiologist on Monday. I sure as hell hope she's available."

"I can check."

Bridget half-rose from her chair. "Stay the hell away from her, Zack. Stay away from anyone connected with this case. Stay away from that hospital. Better yet, don't leave your apartment until I call you. I can't trust you anymore. You're too much of a liability, not only to me but to yourself."

Zack swallowed and forced a smile. "Thanks, ma'am. I needed that."

"Get out of my office."

CHAPTER FORTY-SEVEN

As soon as Zack left her office, Bridget called her private investigator. "Dominic, anything on Dr. Winston?"

A short pause. "Not of any substance. Everything I've found matches what you already know. I'm trying to hunt down contemporaries from his navy tour. Maybe someone knows something that's not in the official record. Wouldn't be the first time an officer resigned for reasons not officially documented."

"Keep looking," she said. "What about the Barnetts?"

Dominic whistled over the phone. "Mr. and Mrs. Got-It-All? They have more dirt under them than the capitol building. Still digging."

That piqued Bridget's interest. "Such as?"

"Don't know the whole story yet, but not long before he died Carl Barnett moved his personal assets into a trust that Janice couldn't touch. He'd been talking to a divorce attorney."

"Motive for conspiracy?"

"I'd almost bet on it. Janice has a separate bank account where she puts her nursing salary, plus Carl used to deposit some of his income there as well. Until he froze her out of his assets. Then that stopped."

Bridget shook her head. "Not seeing motive, Dom."

"That's where I'm digging. For years, Janice withdrew substantial sums of cash, a thousand or more every month. No idea where that money went. Yet. She's still doing it, but in lesser amounts since Carl cut her off."

Bridget blew into the phone. "Sounds like she needs a cash-flow transfusion. A hefty malpractice settlement, perhaps."

"What I'm thinking," Dominic said.

"Would help to know where those cash withdrawals went," Bridget said. "Keep digging."

"Will do."

Bridget paused before continuing. "I have an additional task for you."

"Shoot."

"A short time ago Bethesda Metro locked down for a feared chemical attack that turned out otherwise."

"Yeah, some guy poisoned himself with insecticide."

"Guy's name was Walter Knowles. He worked as ER secretary at that hospital. Partner is one Roland Edwards. I need everything you can find on those two, and anything about that hospital locking down. As much detail as you can get."

"On it, ma'am."

"Thanks. Yesterday would be great."

"Roger."

"Please don't say that word." Bridget hung up and stared out the window. *Something rotten indeed.*

CHAPTER FORTY-EIGHT

When he descended in the elevator from Bridget's office, Zack expected to find Noelle waiting for him. Ange was there instead. On her face, a mixed expression of rage and pity. "So?"

He felt like a little brother who'd just been paddled. "Still in the game."

Her eyes flared. "Really? I would fire your ass."

"Let's say I'm on probation."

Her eyebrows peaked.

Zack smiled. "We have a way to get a true copy of the original EKG—from our cardiologist at Metro."

Ange shook her head. "How do you do it, Zack?"

"Do what?"

"Always pull your butt out of the fire, especially the ones you light for yourself?"

"I don't know." The workday was ending, and people streamed off the elevators into the lobby. "Let's walk, okay?"

She shrugged. "Sure."

They strolled in silence a few blocks to Franklin Park, where they sat on a bench. People scurried past in all directions as rush hour reached full warble.

"Why did you lie to her, Zack?"

He shook his head. "If I knew the reason, I wouldn't have done it."

Ange rested her hand on his thigh. "Zack, I care for you. A lot. I'm going to tell you what you don't want to hear. Promise you won't hate me for it."

His deepest defenses buzzed in alarm. "I could never hate you."

She fixed her eyes on his. "You have a demon inside you. It wants to destroy you. It terrifies you, so you've built a wall around it. No one gets past that wall; not the people who love you, not even *you* can get through it."

Zack blew out all his breath. "Please, not the shrink stuff again."

"Call it what you want. It's the truth."

His mind swirled, his heart beat with irregular rhythm. He couldn't find his voice.

Ange tapped him on the chest. "Sometimes a part of whatever demon lives there gets out and takes a hunk out of you. Makes you do stupid things like lie to your attorney."

Zack concentrated on deep breaths, reverting to what his actual shrink had taught him to do when emotionally threatened. After a minute, he regained control. "Nice theory, but I don't have time for psych games. I've got to find that EKG."

Ange moved away, face flushed, voice scolding. "No, Zack. *You* don't have to find that EKG or anything else about your case." Her voice rose. "Do not force Bridget to bail on you. If that happens, you lose. You lose everything, including me."

Zack shut his eyes against the sensation of a looming storm. When he opened them, Ange sat rigid on the bench, arms folded across her chest.

"You're right," he said, "on all counts. Please tell me you'll stay my friend through this."

Ange scowled. "I'm still here, aren't I?"

They walked in silence to the garage where her car was parked. Halfway there, Ange squeezed his hand, and he squeezed back.

Inside the garage, he walked with her to the lower level reserved for members of the law firm. She let go of his hand to retrieve her keys and unlock the car. As she opened the door, he touched her arm.

"I don't suppose—"

She jerked away and fixed him with an angry gaze. "No, Zack, you don't."

Riding home on the Metro, Zack endured long delays as the Red Line operated on a single track between Friendship Heights and Bethesda. It took over an hour for what should have been a thirty-minute trip. He reflected on Ange's accusation of a locked inner demon. *So what? Nothing I can do about it. Two years of psychotherapy didn't give me a key.*

He willed his thoughts back to the near and present threat. "I hope to hell Noelle has that EKG," he said aloud. People looked at him as if he were daft. *Of course, I meant Sevati, not Noelle.*

CHAPTER FORTY-NINE

The next morning, Zack slept late as sensuous images of Noelle danced in his head. He dreamt of their unusual but romantic honeymoon the first two months of their deployment on *Kitty Hawk* as husband and wife—except for not living together. They made up for that in liberty ports, disappearing from their shipmates to spend days and nights in high-class hotels. In Zack's dream-memory, he and Noelle had returned to Manila's Peninsula Hotel from a golf outing hosted by the Philippine Navy. Sun-drenched, exhausted, and sated from the post-golf dinner and alcohol, they shared the shower then tumbled into bed.

Zack's phone ringing jolted him from the dream. Bridget's secretary. "Ms. Larsen wonders if you could come to her office this afternoon?"

He looked at the clock—just past ten a.m. *Talk about your slack-ass days.* The forced time off from ER duty, plus the daily long runs and self-imposed abstinence from alcohol, had turned Zack into a sleeping machine. At least his head was clear—most of the time.

"Sure. Why?"

"She received a document from the cardiologist. She needs you to review it with her."

That was quick. Thank you, Sevati. Zack's awake mind drew a curtain over the intimate memories of Noelle. He crawled out of bed, started coffee in the kitchen, and headed to the shower—silently promising Noelle a reprise at a place and time she would determine.

Around one in the afternoon, Zack arrived at Bridget's conference room to find her and Ange poring over documents. They stopped talking when he entered the room. Bridget wore a loose rose-colored sweater over a burgundy knit skirt. A single strand of pearls adorned her neckline. Ange wore a clinging pale-yellow blouse—complementing both her figure and her Mediterranean-dark complexion—over tailored navy-blue slacks. *She's put the steady income to favorable use.* His off-duty uniform of vintage jeans and a tired blue/white rugby shirt felt discordant as he took a seat across from them.

Bridget shot Zack a condescending look. "I hope you remembered to bring your unauthorized, useless copies of the ER records." A bit nonplussed at her attitude, he removed the copies from his briefcase and tossed them onto the table.

She pushed a paper to him, a copy of an EKG tracing. "From your cardiologist friend."

Zack scrutinized the tracing, including Sevati's written interpretation stating that the tracing did not indicate myocardial ischemia. He then compared this official version to the one contained in the copies he took the day of Carl Barnett's death, and to the certified medical records copies in Bridget's possession. "Without doubt, all three are the same EKG, the second one we performed on the day that he presented with chest pain."

Bridget laid those beside the one submitted by Roger Meadows. She beckoned Zack around the table to look over her shoulder. He paused for a second to admire the golden sheen of her hair. She shot him an annoyed glance. "Describe what you see."

She means the EKG, Stupid. "They are different EKGs. Not from the same person."

"How do you know?"

"The same way I know that your face is different from Ange's, or any other woman's. They are not the same."

Bridget huffed. "Not convincing, Doc. Show me. Pretend that in your analogy I'm blind and you trace my fingers over Ange's face and mine to appreciate the difference."

Zack liked the idea of tracing his fingers over Bridget's face, or Ange's. He shook off the thought. Using a pen to indicate specific areas, he explained the basic EKG, which area of the heart each line represented, and what constituted normal from abnormal. "It's a static two-dimensional representation of a three-dimensional, dynamic organ."

The corners of Bridget's mouth turned up a bit. "We covered that in sophomore year of med school, Doc, but thanks for the review." Zack flushed. He'd forgotten she'd spent two years in medical school before going into law.

"It's all new and interesting to me," Ange said, her rescue effort too obvious.

"Please continue," Bridget said.

He pointed out the technical differences between the two tracings. "No way these tracings recorded the same heart, not even at two separate points in time."

"I'll buy that," Bridget said. "Be prepared to do it again for Roger Meadows. He won't be as receptive as we two."

"Understood." He stepped away.

Bridget beckoned Ange to move closer, which took Zack out of the conversation. "Look here," she said, "at the labels on these two. This fine line on two sides of the label on the bogus tracing, but not on Zack's copy or ours."

"I see it," Ange said.

Bridget looked at Zack. "The EKG machine prints the patient information directly to the paper, right? They don't paste on a label before or after the tracing is performed?"

He crossed his arms. "Correct."

She turned back to Ange, "It looks like the original label was copied and pasted onto the Meadows version to cover the real patient data."

Ange leaned over to see better. "I agree."

Zack craned his neck to scrutinize the pages. "I see it too."

Bridget cocked her head. "At that distance? Good eyes, Doc." She addressed Ange. "Take all these and see if you can make a case for the second being a forgery. Get one of our IT geeks to help."

"Will do," Ange said. The two attorneys broke up their tete-a-tete.

Bridget stared across the table at Zack. "Who's your enemy, Zack?"

He remembered Noelle's admonition from what seemed like months ago. "Who, and why?"

"Right," Bridget said.

Zack shook his head. "I have no idea. Not Janice Barnett. She had neither the means nor opportunity. I hate to say it, but Walter Knowles had the best opportunity and the right skills. But why? I never had any run-ins with him."

All three lost themselves in thought. Ange broke the silence. "More immediate, how do we use this information?

"Discredit their expert," Zack said. "Refute the notion that I missed a no-brainer diagnosis. We have the official, real-time EKG. That trumps their later-dated copy. They have no case now, right?"

Bridget scoffed. "This information only works for removing the fraudulent EKG from evidence. Roger won't throw in the towel over it. He will say that even with a non-diagnostic EKG you exercised poor judgment in not admitting the patient."

Zack stiffened. "Poor judgment is not negligence."

"Right." She threw him a condescending smile. "If you can get the jury to buy that, you're home free."

Ange looked at Bridget. "You have doubts?"

"I know Roger Meadows. I believe he's aware of this discrepancy in his evidence, probably always knew it. If he is involved in whatever conspiracy exists to discredit you, Zack, he has a different plan. He had to know we'd discover the EKG subterfuge."

Zack's spirit deflated. "Are you saying this EKG shit is a red herring?"

Bridget shrugged. "I wouldn't put it past that weasel."

"Thanks for bursting my small bubble of hope."

She looked at him with some semblance of empathy, for the first time that day. "Not the only bubble we will burst today. Tell him, Ange."

Ange passed him a series of photos downloaded and printed from the

Internet. Jerry Hartman and Janice Barnett together at Society of Critical Care Medicine annual meeting social events over several years in different locations around the country.

"Do nurses often accompany physicians to national specialty conferences?" Bridget asked.

Recalling his own prior dalliances, albeit when single, Zack cringed. "It happens. Not prevalent, but ICU nurses might attend that conference."

Bridget frowned. "Have you ever seen Jerry Hartman and Janice Barnett together in a social setting?"

He thought for a few seconds. "Possible. The hospital hosts an annual gala event, and a picnic. I might have seen them at one or the other. I need to think about it."

"You do that, Doc," Bridget said with ice in her tone. "You think about it. Let me know if you come up with anything concrete."

Zack nodded, chagrined.

"Okay," Bridget said. "Let's summarize where we are and where we need to go. We resume the deposition next Wednesday; at which time we'll discredit Roger's bogus EKG and find out what else he has in his arsenal. Zack, you need to think hard about who besides Janice Barnett would have motive to discredit you. The more I see of this, the more I think she's a pawn in a larger game.

"Ange, as much as we might benefit from an affair between Hartman and Barnett, these photos alone prove nothing. Keep digging. Scour that website, crawl all over their Facebook, Twitter, Instagram, LinkedIn, and any other social media sites you can find. See if any of Carl Barnett's are still online. Download and copy anything that might be pertinent, even if it's only a gut feel on your part."

Bridget turned to Zack. "Is Hartman married?"

"He could be."

Bridget scoffed. "Could be celibate, or a eunuch. 'Could be' counts for nothing in court." She turned to Ange. "Chase down anything you can find on that, not just whether or not, but details; date and place of marriage, prior marriages, children, the whole lot. Also, dig for evidence that either Hartman or Janice have a history of philandering. The more dirt the better. Touch base with Dominic. See what he's found."

Ange made hasty notes, then nodded.

"That's it for today." Bridget stood and left the conference room.

CHAPTER FIFTY

Zack followed her into her office, stood in front of her desk. She looked up at him, stone-faced. "Yes? Did you need something?"

A fire rose inside him. "Respect, for one."

She arched her eyebrows. "Say what?"

"You treated me like shit in there."

Bridget groaned. "No time for hurt feelings. We have a tough climb to get you out of this mess, much of which is your own making." Her eyes remained stern. She placed her thumb and forefinger nearly together. "I'm this close to telling you to settle for whatever the plaintiff demands; not only because I think you may lose, but more so because I cannot abide a client who lies to me."

Zack spread his feet. "I get that you're pissed. I said I'm sorry."

"Pissed is right, and sorry doesn't cut it."

"I'm marginalized as we move forward?"

"Call it what you want. We have no choice. Thanks to your Sevati friend, we'll beat this bogus EKG. But we can't afford to give Roger any more ammunition to discredit you. He's after something else. It's what I'd do in his place. I would raise enough doubt about your competence and integrity that any jury in the world would consider it their duty to hang you." She thumbed through files on her desk, a non-subtle indication that she was done talking. "Lay low, Zack. We'll take it from here."

Zack exploded, banged his fist on her desk. "No. Now you listen to me, counselor. *My* life is on the line here. Not yours. Not Ange's. Not even Janice Barnett's and her mysterious co-conspirator. You may be the best damned lawyer in DC, but it's just your job. My case will end up as another number in your won or lost column. It's *my* career. I trust you to do your job, but I will *not* allow you to mother me. I will not put my head down and go to my room while you take over my fight."

Bridget stared at him, eyes wide, mouth agape. Then she nodded her head and clapped her hands in slow, rhythmic cadence. "Finally, a real emotion. We might win this thing after all."

He leaned on the desk, glared into her eyes. "Damned right, we will." He poked the desk with his finger. "As partners. I will participate in my own defense. Won't have it any other way."

She smiled. *Genuine.* "Well, okay." She stood and reached across the desk to shake his hand. "Let's do this."

CHAPTER FIFTY-ONE

The following morning, Zack went for a long run. He left his phone behind because he wanted no distractions, least of all if he happened onto Noelle.

She appeared at their usual spot on the trail, joined him, and broke their ritual of first running together in silence. "You've had quite the week."

"Quite." He picked up the pace. She matched him step for step.

"Ange is back in the picture." Her voice carried a taunting edge.

"Yeah. Just business."

Noelle laughed so hard she almost tripped. "You are such a liar, Zack Winston; most of all to yourself." He didn't stop running. She caught up to him. "You still have the hots for her."

Zack started to pant. He slowed his pace. "She reminds me of you."

She chortled. "When I was eighteen maybe."

He didn't answer. Not the conversation he'd wanted.

Noelle would not be silenced. "You need someone your own age. Your lawyer friend?"

Zack stopped as if he'd hit a wall. "'Friend' is accurate. She's my defense attorney, nothing more. My married defense attorney."

"Yeah. Of course." Noelle started running again. Zack ran after her. To his relief, she changed the subject. "What about your case?"

He thought about it, trying to connect loose ends. "One, Janice Barnett may have a financial motive for suing me. Two, she had similar motive to kill her husband. Three, she had help. Four, it's connected to Walter Knowles, who did not commit suicide, but I don't know what happened to him. Five, Jerry Hartman may be involved, although that seems out of character for him. He's bluff and bluster, but not a crook."

"Six," Noelle said, "whoever is driving it knows how to mess with your mind."

He stopped cold in his tracks. Noelle pulled up beside him. *She's right,* he thought. "Why me? Why am I the target?"

Noelle placed hands on hips. "Maybe you're not the victim. Maybe you're the agent."

"A cog in a larger machine?"

Her eyes sharpened. "Exactly."

"I have to figure this out." He turned to run home.

Noelle didn't move. She called after him. "One other thing, Zack." He stopped, walked back to where she stood. Her eyes turned soft, like in their honeymoon days. "At least two people are dead, and you don't know why. There may be more." She caressed his cheek. He flinched. She hadn't touched him since . . .?

He reached out, but of course couldn't touch her.

Her eyes turned serious. "Be careful, Zack. You may be in danger."

When he returned to his apartment, his phone blinked with a voice mail. Bridget. "Zack, we need to meet. Today. We have new information. Call me when you get this."

He punched *Reply*. At least she had called him herself instead of leaving it to her secretary.

CHAPTER FIFTY-TWO

When Zack arrived at Bridget's office suite, the receptionist directed him to a conference room where she and Ange conversed with a heavy-set man who looked like a Tony Soprano cosplayer. They stopped talking and stood when Zack entered the room. Bridget introduced the man as Dominic, her private investigator.

"Pleased to meet you, Doc." Dominic's beefy paw engulfed Zack's hand in a firm grasp. Unsure what to say, Zack nodded, eyeing the bulge under the man's faded brown jacket.

Bridget motioned for all to be seated. "We have three business days before the next deposition. New items to discuss." She gestured at Ange. "You start."

Ange cleared her throat. "I spoke to a reliable source last night who shared troubling information."

"Reliable source?" Zack said.

"Don't ask. Trust me."

He bristled. "What did your 'source' say?"

"Someone from Metro Hospital met with Roger Meadows in his office yesterday."

That got Zack's attention. "What? How?"

"No details because my source was not privy to the conversation. This person and Roger Meadows conversed behind closed doors for at least a half-hour."

Zack frowned. He remembered Keisha Rollins, Ange's former partner now an associate for Roger Meadows. "How did your 'source' know the visitor was from the hospital?"

"He wore a Metro Hospital badge. Meadows made him take it off as soon as he saw it."

"Your source couldn't read the name?"

"No."

"Did she mention the color of the badge?"

Ange frowned. "I never said my source was a 'she,' but the badge was green. My source said the exact words, 'green Metro Hospital badge.'"

Zack deflated. "Medical staff. The badges are color-coded according to roles, for security in case of a major event or disaster; green for medical staff, blue for nurses, purple for administrators, that sort of thing."

All fell silent until Zack voiced the unthinkable conclusion. "Jerry Hartman."

"We don't know that," Bridget said.

Zack turned to Ange. "Did your source describe the visitor? Heavyset man with a beard, perhaps?"

Ange shrugged. "Didn't say. I can ask."

He looked at Bridget. "Can Jerry Hartman testify against me?"

"He's not listed as a witness. If Roger calls him without first disclosing it to us, I can temporarily block him from testifying; but Roger can list him any time before the trial. Plenty opportunity left." She tented her fingers. "Any idea why he'd conspire with the plaintiff?"

Ange answered. "What about his affair with said plaintiff?"

Bridget brushed her off. "We don't know that for sure." She addressed Zack. "You've said Hartman has it out for you. Can he offer anything to Meadows that Roger couldn't get from his medical expert, in terms of standard of care?"

Zack shook his head. "He's an intensivist, not an emergency physician. I have no clue what he could offer to Meadows."

Bridget turned to Ange. "Did your 'source' say whether the

mysterious visitor brought anything with him? Anything he might have given to Roger?"

Ange shook her head. "Didn't say. I could ask."

"Let's hold off on that," Bridget said. "We need to be careful not to put your friend, I mean source, in jeopardy. She could be an asset as this moves forward."

Ange reiterated. "Never said it was a 'she.'"

Zack scowled. "C'mon, Ange. We know it's Keisha." Ange remained silent, but her eyes confirmed it.

Bridget laid her hands on the table. "She could get fired or worse for disclosing that to us. For now, we hold it tight. Ange, be very careful about communicating with Keisha. It's to our benefit that she keeps her current job. In fact, don't talk to her at all without consulting me first."

Ange nodded.

"Meanwhile, in other news . . ." Bridget looked at Dominic.

CHAPTER FIFTY-THREE

Three days later, Zack sat in front of the same video camera while he, Bridget, and Ange languished in the Cooper Meadows conference room waiting to resume his deposition. Once again, they were left to cool their heels and stoke Zack's anxiety, well past the appointed time. He looked at his watch, snorted.

"Don't let this get to you," Bridget said. "Remember our strategy. Don't go off script."

He cleared his throat, rattled off the checklist. "Discredit the EKG, deny coronary artery disease, accept remote possibility of coronary artery spasm, cite articles acknowledging the primacy of clinical judgment. Retrospective questioning of clinical judgment does not prove negligence. Ergo, no malpractice."

Bridget smiled. "By George, I think he's got it."

Ange chuckled.

The abrupt presence of the ferret's mousy secretary at the conference room door interrupted their mirth. "Ms. Larsen," she squeaked, "Mr. Meadows wishes to meet with you in his office before beginning the deposition."

Bridget's eyebrows scrunched and her face hardened as she rose and headed to the door. She glanced at Zack and Ange. "You two sit tight."

Zack looked at Ange, "Have you seen Keisha today?"

Ange put a finger to her lips in a shushing motion, then made an exaggerated show of looking around the room, pointing at the ceiling.

Zack frowned. *She seriously thinks this room could be bugged? What kind of melodrama have I gotten into?*

They sat in silence for fifteen minutes before Bridget returned. No mouse. No ferret. No Keisha. The grim expression on Bridget's face alarmed Zack as soon as she walked through the door.

"The hospital settled this morning," she said. "Without getting into the legal details of joint and several liability, the upshot is that Roger elected to let them go without paying anything. Last week, your physician group, EHA, won a summary judgment stating that they have no responsibility for your actions since you are an independent contractor and not an employee. We expected that." She pursed her lips and looked at him, her eyes soft. "You are now the sole defendant, Zack. If we lose, you're on the hook for the entire five million."

"What the hell? Why?"

Bridget shook her head. "It's the game, as I warned you on day one." She sat and turned her chair toward him, looked at him like a mother counseling a troubled child. "Roger offered us a settlement. Three and a half-million, *if* you accept it now before the deposition."

Zack felt like a category-five hurricane had made landfall on his head. His mind swirled in the raging storm, his thoughts ripped apart, his vision fogged. A minute passed before he cleared his brain and found his voice. "Why would we—? Why would I do that?"

She put a hand on his arm. "To walk away from this, right here, right now."

"With a permanent scar on my reputation? A scarlet 'M' burned onto my chest?"

She shook her head. "Not that dramatic. The settlement will stipulate that you do not admit fault."

A flush of rage overcame Zack. "No way, Bridget. Any payment, whether I admit fault or not, gets reported to the National Practitioner Data Bank, right?"

"Correct."

"Anytime I apply for clinical privileges, or for a medical license in another state, it comes up, right?"

"Yes, but you get to explain. It's not a career killer."

Zack could not believe what he was hearing. He rolled his chair away from Bridget and glowered at her. "No." From the corner of his eye, he glimpsed a slight nod of encouragement from Ange. *At least she's still on my side.*

Bridget sat in silence, letting Zack process. When he relaxed his posture, she spoke in a quiet voice. "Your insurance carrier will accept the settlement. They will pay three and a half-million to avoid a certain five-million loss if this goes to trial."

Zack's anger gave way to gushing sadness. "I can't believe you've turned on me, Bridget. I thought I could trust you to defend me."

She sighed. "I haven't turned on you, Zack. I'm obligated to present this settlement offer in an objective manner."

His hands knotted. "That's a crock."

"It's the process, Zack."

He hardened his face and stared into her eyes. "Are you telling me to settle? Right here, right now?"

Bridget didn't retreat from his angry advance. "I'm as perplexed as you are. It seems premature, unless he's afraid the real EKG will torpedo his case and he's trying to recover something for his client." She paused, contemplating. "That's not the Roger Meadows I know. My gut tells me he's got something else, something he's hiding until the best time to use it."

"What?"

"No idea. I hoped you might have a notion."

Zack shook his head, ignoring a tiny muted voice from deep within his brain. "To find out, we have to reject this offer, sit through the deposition, and go to trial where I'm on the hook for five mil?"

"Not personally on the hook, but yes. Unless they come back with another offer, or we think we can persuade the plaintiff to accept a different settlement. Not out of the question—depending on how much damage Roger does with whatever he has." A beat. "If he has anything."

"Russian roulette," Zack said, "with my reputation and career on the line."

"Except we don't know how many bullets he's put in the chamber."

Zack homed in on Bridget like a son trying to make a crucial life decision. "You're not going to tell me what to do, are you?"

"Not my place. As you said before, it's your life on the line."

He looked at Ange; she sat there, passive and inscrutable. What would Noelle say? In a flash, he turned back to Bridget. "Spin that cylinder. Bring on Roger Meadows. Let's see what he has."

CHAPTER FIFTY-FOUR

Fifteen minutes later, Zack was sworn in and faced the video camera. The ferret glared across the table at him. No sign of Keisha. A young associate introduced simply as "Steve" occupied the seat next to the ferret. Steve resembled a lynx.

"Doctor Winston," Meadows said, "during the prior deposition you interpreted this copy of an EKG." He handed it across the table. "You testified to your belief that this was not the same as the tracing from Carl Barnett that you viewed the day he presented with chest pain, correct?"

"Yes."

Meadows handed Zack a copy of the true EKG tracing. "Does this tracing, marked as plaintiff's exhibit ten, look familiar, Doctor?"

"Yes. It's a copy of the actual EKG from Carl Barnett on the day in question."

"Where did this one come from?"

"The backup copy of the original EKG on file in cardiology at Metro Hospital."

Meadows sneered as if about to rip into Zack with razor teeth. "Plaintiff stipulates that this is a true copy of the version on file in cardiology at Metro Hospital." He paused. Narrow eyes pierced Zack. "Can you please interpret this EKG, Doctor?"

Zack described the normal the EKG.

"That's different from the EKG you saw in the prior deposition?"

"Yes. That one showed significant ST elevation, consistent with cardiac ischemia."

"And this one does not, correct?"

"Correct."

Meadows studied his notes, then looked at Zack without expression. "Do you have a theory as to why two different EKGs got entered as evidence in this case?"

Bridget raised her hand. "Object. Calls for speculation." She turned to Zack. "You can answer."

"No."

Meadows scowled, spread his hands. "Well, clearly one is a forgery, right?"

"Same objection," Bridget said. "Doctor Winston will not say what you're trying to make him say, so move on, please."

Meadows scoffed at her. "My turn to object for the record. Defense counsel is coaching her client in order to derail my examination." He wheeled his attention on Zack. "You have to answer my question, in spite of your lawyer's interference."

Zack folded his hands on the table. "I wouldn't know."

"Isn't it possible, Doctor," Meadows said in the same tone as one might say "criminal," "that you or someone in your employ forged that non-diagnostic EKG?"

Zack fumed. He leaned forward, glowered at Roger Meadows. "No. That tracing was transmitted directly to the cardiology department in real time while it was recorded from the patient."

"No way it's a forgery?"

Bridget spoke with unbridled irritation. "He's answered that. Move on."

Meadows scoffed. "Very well. Let's all stipulate that the EKG in your hand is the true one, and none of us knows how the other one got into the record." He leered at Bridget. "Fair enough?"

Bridget crossed her arms, did not respond.

"Fair enough, Doctor?"

Zack saw Bridget nod. "Okay."

The ferret heaved a dramatic sigh. "Carl Barnett did not have coronary artery disease, did he?"

Annoyance raged inside Zack. "As I've said several times, no."

"Forgive me for being thorough, Doctor, but this is a key point, wouldn't you say?"

Bridget interjected; her voice sharp. "Speculation. Move on."

Meadows glanced back and forth between Bridget and Zack. "Do you two need a break? You both seem a bit snarky."

"I'm okay to continue," Zack said. He wanted this done.

Meadows shrugged. He shuffled through his notes before continuing. "Doctor Winston, please state the final factor a reasonable emergency physician uses to determine whether or not a specific patient is at risk for an acute cardiac event. What's your ultimate go-to for that decision?"

Zack looked at Bridget for any clue where the ferret was headed. She shrugged. Turning back to Meadows, he spoke in a voice more confident than he felt. "Clinical judgment."

Meadows smiled like a spider to a fly. "Can you elaborate on that?"

Zack paused to frame his answer. "No tests provide the definitive answer in terms of zero or one-hundred percent risk that a patient with chest pain will later suffer a cardiac event. We have algorithms and protocols for emergency department evaluation and disposition of chest pain, but none of them are definitive. In the end, you consider the total picture of the individual in front of you. You take into account all the objective data, like EKGs and lab results. You consider the patient's history, appearance, and physical examination. No hospital has capacity to admit everyone with chest pain, so you use your best clinical judgment; the sum total of all the data, plus your knowledge and experience. That's why we refer to the practice of medicine as both a science and an art."

Meadows yawned. "Thank you, Doctor. I get it." He leaned forward, his face grim. "Did you exercise proper clinical judgment when you sent Mr. Barnett home the first day, rather than admitting him or scheduling further diagnostic tests?"

"Yes."

Meadows leaned back, folded his arms. "Doctors make clinical judgments every day, right?"

Confused, Zack nodded.

"You have to verbalize your answer for the record."

Zack huffed. "Yes."

"Sometimes physicians make errors in judgment, right?"

Zack shifted in his chair. "Everyone has, at one time or another. No one is perfect."

Meadows uncrossed his arms, leaned forward. "How many wrong judgments can a clinician make before being considered incompetent?"

Bridget objected before Meadows could draw a breath. "Speculation, facts not in evidence, badgering—at a minimum." She narrowed her eyes. "Move on with a proper examination or we're done."

Roger wagged a finger at Bridget. "Ask and you shall receive."

Bridget cocked her head. Zack's breathing accelerated.

Meadows stood, a posture of dominance over Zack. "Doctor Winston, did you exercise proper judgment when you allowed a nurse to overdose a patient with epinephrine?"

Bridget objected, but Meadows ignored her. "Or when you locked down an entire hospital and forced staff to get naked in front of each other over a patient who simply committed suicide?"

Bridget jumped to her feet, pounded the table. "Object!" Meadows talked over her. "Or when you botched an emergency airway on a young woman—the same woman you almost killed earlier with epinephrine?"

Zack reeled from Meadows' fury. How did he know about those other cases? He started to respond, but Bridget grabbed his arm. "Don't answer." She pointed a finger at Meadows, straining to control her voice. "The only case in evidence here is the Barnett case. Stick to that one, or we're done."

Calm and in control, the ferret shrugged, tossed her a condescending smile. "Okay." He resumed his seat, shuffled his notes, stared at Zack in silence for some seconds before speaking. "Dr. Winston, was your judgment impaired when you saw Mr. Barnett the first day?"

The question confused Zack. "I— I don't understand."

"A few minutes ago, you said you used your, quotes, best clinical judgment, close quotes, in deciding Mr. Barnett's disposition. I'm asking if your clinical judgment was impaired at the time."

A tsunami of dread washed over Zack. "Doctor Winston, were you drunk when you saw Mr. Barnett?"

Bridget started to object, but Zack stopped her with a hand on her arm. His face flushed with anger. "Of course not."

Meadows remained calm, detached, his voice flat. "Under the influence of drugs?"

"No."

"Suffering from pathologic depression?"

Bridget stood and leaned over the table. "Object. You have no basis for this line of questioning. Lacks any foundation whatsoever. We're done here, Roger."

Meadows raised his hands in a "not so fast" gesture. "If counsel would refrain from disrupting my examination, I will show foundation."

"Make it quick, or we walk." Bridget resumed her seat, arms crossed, eyes on fire.

Roger Meadows glanced at his notes. "I don't believe you answered the last question, Doctor, with respect to suffering from pathological depression?"

"Not at all."

Meadows' voice reeked of condescension. "Thank you, Doctor." He cast Bridget a snide smile. "Almost done. Thank you for your patience."

From the pile of documents in front of him, Roger pulled out a sheaf of papers stapled together. "Tell me Doctor—and I remind you that you are under oath and subject to penalty should you perjure yourself—have you ever, in your entire medical career, civilian and military, evaluated and treated patients in the emergency department when you were drunk, under the influence of drugs, suffering from pathologic depression, or any other impairment?"

A vice squeezed Zack's head while his heart sank into his abdomen. He thought he would vomit. He glanced at Bridget and Ange, both of whom stared at him with wide eyes. He wanted to jump across the table and rip out the ferret's throat.

Meadows smiled; his voice turned saccharine. "Answer the question, please, Doctor."

He has me. From the earthquake raging inside Zack, a tiny voice spoke. "Yes."

Red-faced and shaken, Bridget leaped from her chair and yanked Zack out of his. "Don't say another word. We're leaving."

"No further questions," the ferret said.

As Bridget pushed Zack out the door, Ange in trail, Roger Meadows shouted at their backs, "The settlement offer is still on the table. But only for twenty-four hours."

CHAPTER FIFTY-FIVE

They drove in silence back to Bridget's office. Zack's chest felt constricted by tight metal bands. The auras radiating from Bridget and Ange made him feel like he'd been packed into an ice chest.

How the hell did that weasel find out about Japan? There's no trace of it in my record. His heart wasn't ready for the answer enfolded in the deep recesses of his brain.

Getting out of Bridget's car in the parking garage, he said, "If you're going to fire me, do it here and now so I don't have to go up to your office just to come back for my car."

"I'm not firing you." She walked away toward the elevator. Zack stood in place, dumbfounded. Ange passed him without a word or a look. Zack hustled to catch up, sidled into the elevator just as the doors closed. The elevator ride was icier than the car trip. When they reached the office suite, Ange said, "I need to find Keisha."

Bridget admonished her. "Not while she's at work." Ange nodded, glanced at Zack, and hurried away as if fleeing a demon. Zack followed Bridget into her office. She motioned him to the couch while she took a side chair—the first time they had used the soft furniture. It reminded Zack of his first visit to a psychiatrist. "I—"

Bridget held up her hand. Her secretary entered with two large glasses of ice water. "No calls," Bridget said to her.

Sipping ice water, Zack studied Bridget's body language. The chill had gone. She appeared neither angry nor upset; no emotion at all, like his past psychiatrist. She set down her water, and faced him, eyes piercing his. "Start from the beginning, the real beginning. Omit nothing."

Averting his gaze, Zack stared across the room to gather his thoughts and quell his emotions. Bridget didn't prod. She seemed content to let him process before speaking. With a heavy sigh, he gazed out the window and began the story that he'd previously shared only with his psychiatrist.

"After my first wife left me, I wanted a new life. I joined the navy as a flight surgeon, got assigned to a carrier air wing out of Atsugi, Japan. Deployed across the Western Pacific in the aircraft carrier, *USS Kitty Hawk*, based in Yokosuka. During my second deployment, I met a naval aviator, Noelle Robinson. I—" His voice choked as tears wet his eyes.

Bridget handed him a tissue from her purse. "You fell in love."

Zack nodded. He told Bridget about his torrid love affair with Noelle, their engagement and rushed marriage just before that last deployment. He stopped speaking, his mind reliving those happier days. Then, like a sudden thunderstorm, deeper memories crashed into his consciousness.

He shifted on the couch to face away from Bridget. Like a patient in analysis, he relived what happened to Noelle.

CHAPTER FIFTY-SIX

The sun had set over *Kitty Hawk*, transforming the South China Sea from a shimmering golden mirror to a pellucid sheet of deep blue glass. The ship plowed through the water on its return leg to home port in Japan. Inside, Zack sat in the back of the squadron ready room, watching Noelle and her fellow aviators brief for their night flights—the most dangerous of the risky operations in the life of a naval aviator.

After the brief, Zack and Noelle lingered in the ready room; their squadron mates allowing the newlyweds some private time together. Zack kissed her. "Fly safe, love."

"Always."

"Think of your next flight in ten days, on a jumbo jet with your husband at your side." They had booked reservations from Tokyo to Detroit to Traverse City, Michigan for their second, formal wedding amid family and friends at the Grand Traverse Resort.

"Ugh," Noelle said. "I don't want to think about fourteen hours crammed into an over-sized aluminum tube, even with my true love."

"Who happens to be a flight doc who gets you a supply of Ambien. You'll sleep all the way and arrive rested; a proper blushing bride."

She hugged him. "Gotta go. Slip the surly bonds and all."

"Fly safe."

Noelle frowned. "Quit saying that." She turned and left the ready room.

*Z*ack climbed the interior stairs up to Vultures' Row to watch Noelle's launch and landing. Aptly named, the balcony-like exterior catwalk on the next-to-highest level of the carrier's island provided an ideal venue for sailors to observe operations on the flight deck six levels below.

Zack watched Noelle's confident, professional stride as she walked to her jet. He waved as she climbed into the cockpit, but she did not look toward Vultures' Row. She knew he was there, but once she walked onto the flight deck, Noelle allowed nothing to occupy her mind except the immediate mission.

On her turn to launch, she taxied the Hornet onto the catapult. The flight-deck crew performed final checks then signaled with thumbs up. The Hornet made a slight forward bump as it went into tension on the catapult shuttle. Noelle throttled the jet up to full afterburner. A second later, the catapult hurled it forward and slingshot it off the deck in a stream of fire from the burner. Zack's heart raced, followed by a flush of relief and pride when the Hornet established a steady climb. Noelle took it out of afterburner and soared into the black night.

A sudden flash ignited in the area of Noelle's left engine; then another on the right. The aircraft position lights dove into rapid descent toward the water's surface. Zack's heart rose into his throat. Then he saw a smaller flash followed by a thin stream of light rising toward the sky. A second later, the soul-rending cacophony of combined explosion and massive water displacement shook the night. Noelle's jet had crashed into the sea.

For several heartbeats, Zack froze in disbelief—as did everyone who had seen the calamity. His turbulent mind guessed that the brief rising flash meant Noelle had ejected before the plane hit the water.

She might be okay.

He bolted from Vultures' Row—sailors jumping out of his path—and scurried down to the flight deck first-aid station. Two hospital corpsmen wearing head protection and flotation coats over their white jerseys acknowledged him with combined pity and horror.

Zack addressed the corpsman holding a radio. "What do we know?"

"She ejected, sir. Helo's on scene. They have visual on the pilot." The young man gulped.

"And—?"

The corpsman could not make eye contact. "They'll retrieve her and bring her here."

"Right," Zack said. From the bulkhead, he grabbed a float coat and cranial and put them on.

The door flew open. Marvin Gaines, the other air wing flight surgeon, burst into the room. "Zack, let me handle this."

Zack shook his head. "No. I'm more experienced." He swallowed hard. "I must do my job."

Marv looked as if he would argue, but one glare from Zack stopped him.

The air boss' voice boomed over the flight deck loudspeaker. "Man spot three, man spot three. Helo inbound with survivor."

Survivor!

CHAPTER FIFTY-SEVEN

Bridget asked if he needed a break or a glass of water. He waved her off and continued his story. . .

Zack and his colleagues watched the closed-circuit television as the lights and then the fuselage of the HH-60 rescue helicopter came into view, hovered over its landing spot, and gently set down. The corpsmen charged out of the battle dressing station, carrying a stretcher between them, and ran toward the helo. Zack and Marvin followed. All four bent under the still-turning rotors and approached the helicopter's open rear door. Assisted by the on-board rescue team, the corpsmen placed Noelle onto the stretcher and lowered her gently but swiftly onto the deck. Zack couldn't tell if she was alive or dead. Both her legs skewed at unnatural angles. Her flight helmet had cracked from crown to back. He shouted above the din. "Stabilize her neck."

A corpsman spoke in a loud voice. "I feel a weak pulse."

"Get her inside, now."

The team moved at a brisk walk from the helo to the battle-dressing station, one man on each corner of the stretcher. As they passed under a floodlight, Noelle's face looked pasty and pale, a stark departure from her usual velvet-brown complexion.

Major blood loss.

In the first-aid station, they got her onto a gurney while Zack shouted staccato orders. "Get her on O2, start two large bore IVs, keep her neck stable and remove the helmet." In the confined room, the smell of saltwater mixed with blood assailed his nostrils. "Cut off the damn wet flight suit and boots."

As his eyes adjusted to the glaring light in the room, the reality of Noelle's condition struck Zack like simultaneous blows to his chest and head. She looked already dead. "Vitals?"

"Pulse weak and thready at 150, BP 70 over palp, shallow respirations at ten. Unresponsive."

They removed her flight helmet. Dark blood dripped like thick oil from a jagged gash just behind her hairline. Shards of plastic from the helmet protruded from the wound. Zack leaned over and looked into her face. No expression, not even a grimace. "Noelle," he shouted, "can you hear me? It's Zack. Can you hear me?"

Her eyes stared ahead. No response. He pressed hard on the space between her eyebrows, testing her response to pain. Nothing.

The corpsmen, with Marv's help, had succeeded in starting the IVs and had undressed Noelle to her sports bra and Lycra shorts, reluctant to go further. Staring at her beautiful body, now pale and disfigured, Zack fought back the tears in his eyes. "Completely undress her, then cover her with blankets. She'll be hypothermic."

As soon as they cut off her bra, Zack noticed that with each shallow breath the front of her chest moved in the opposite direction as her torso. "Flail chest," he said. "I need to intubate her."

"I'm not feeling a pulse," a corpsman said.

"Keep feeling." Zack turned to Marvin and the other corpsman. "Squeeze those IV bags. Get that fluid in as fast as possible."

The door burst open, and Captain Rolando Cruz, the ship's senior medical officer, entered. Zack looked at him, desperate. "Help me intubate her, please, sir."

With the SMO's help, Zack passed an endotracheal tube into Noelle's throat, through her vocal cords and into her trachea. They hooked the end of the tube to an ambu bag and proceeded to force air into her lungs. This would accomplish two things: One, stabilize the flail chest so her lungs could expand; two, deliver enriched oxygen to her damaged brain. Only when he'd done the procedure did Zack realize his hands trembled and his breath came in irregular spurts.

Zack steeled himself, stepped back, assessed the situation, and summarized for the SMO. His voice quavered, his breathing in irregular gasps. "Major trauma. Don't know if her chute fully opened before she hit the water, but I think not. Injuries we know so far include open head injury with a Glasgow of three, flail chest, major blood loss, probably intra-abdominal, and compound long bone fractures of both lower extremities. Can't be sure about cervical spine until we get an x-ray and can't examine motor function because she's unconscious."

Tense seconds followed Zack's litany until the SMO spoke. "She's in the wrong place, Zack. Get her below. Surgeon is standing by in the OR."

Zack objected. "She won't survive the transport down, SMO. We need to get her stabilized here or it will be futile."

"Not your decision," the SMO said. He addressed the corpsmen. "Get her to the weapons elevator."

Zack ignored him, turned his attention to the corpsmen. "Vitals?"

"Still can't feel a pulse," the corpsman said. "No blood pressure."

"Keep squeezing those bags," Zack said.

The SMO stepped between him and Noelle. "Stand down, Zack. That's an order." He turned to the corpsmen. "Get moving to that elevator."

Zack bit his lower lip. His whole body shook. He started to challenge the SMO, then stepped back and watched as the corpsmen carried the love of his life out the door to the flight deck. He followed in trail as they hurried to the nearby weapons elevator, a simple cage that would carry her down two decks to the main medical department. The SMO clutched his arm. "You can join us in the OR."

He jerked away. "I'm not leaving her." The SMO looked into Zack's eyes, then motioned him to the elevator.

Over what Zack considered too many minutes, the elevator lumbered down a pitch-black shaft, stopping on the second deck, thirty feet from main medical. They hustled Noelle down the passageway, into the medical department, straight into the brightly lit operating room.

Zack stopped to change into scrubs and don a sterile gown. When he entered the OR, the ship's surgeon, Commander Amy Nelson, gowned and gloved, had just finished cleaning Noelle's abdomen with Betadine, while the anesthetist hooked the breathing tube to a mechanical ventilator.

Zack gasped when he noticed the distension that had developed in Noelle's abdomen, as if she were pregnant. *Internal hemorrhage.*

Amy looked at Zack. "Watch if you must, but don't touch. Best shot is to get in there, cross-clamp the aorta, and hope to hell we find something to fix. At least with your aggressive resuscitation we got some vitals. We have a chance, but it's slim."

A wave of nausea and dizziness overcame Zack. He reeled back, bracing himself against the metal bulkhead.

Amy reached out a gloved hand and the OR tech placed a scalpel into her grasp. When she cut through the skin, it did not bleed. Amy shook her head. She and Zack glanced at the monitor to verify that Noelle's blood pressure and pulse remained steady. They did not.

"Pulse rising, BP dropping," a corpsman said.

In seconds, Amy dissected through the thin fat layer and fascia of Noelle's abdomen to expose the peritoneum. When she pierced the membrane with the knife point, a jet of dark red blood spurted through the opening and struck Amy in the face. She ignored it. "Scissors." Someone placed a pair of Metzenbaum scissors into her hand. She sliced upward from the original hole, still spurting blood, toward the sternum—a desperate maneuver to gain high access to Noelle's abdominal aorta to clamp it and stop the bleeding inside her abdomen. Dark red blood poured through the incision, drenched the OR sheet, and dripped onto the floor.

"She's lost vitals," a corpsman said. "Monitor shows agonal rhythm."

Amy plunged her hand into the hole, trying to feel her way through the welling blood to what she hoped would be a still-pulsating aorta that she could compress with her fingers until she got a clamp onto it. "I have it."

From his vantage point opposite her in the room, Zack absorbed the entire scene. His beautiful wife lay naked under a blood-soaked sheet on a narrow table, her skin yellow-gray. Protruding from her throat, a tube connected to a ventilator. Her chest made a clacking sound as each forced inspiration caused the edges of her multiple broken ribs to rub against each other. Her abdomen gaped open, a well of blood engulfing the surgeon's hand. Both legs twisted at unnatural angles.

Most of all, she didn't move. Noelle had not moved, not a twitch, since they took her off the helo. Tears filled Zack's eyes as darkness invaded his soul. *Already dead.* A sob lodged in his throat. He choked it out.

"Please stop. Everyone, please stop."

Amy stared at him across Noelle's body, her face grim, questioning. Zack's voice came in a whisper. "Please. Stop." In slow motion, Amy withdrew her blood-soaked hand and stepped away from the table.

Zack looked at the anesthetist. "Stop ventilating her." Tears blurred his vision. "Everyone step back."

All did as he commanded.

Zack moved to the head of the table, unhooked the endotracheal tube from the machine, and held his ear to the tube's end. No sound, not a whiff of moving air. He put his mouth next to her ear. "Noelle, show us something. Squeeze my hand, babe. Blink." No response. He shone a light into her eyes. Her pupils were dilated and did not respond to the light. He listened over her chest. No respirations. No heartbeat.

Dead.

Zack lifted the stethoscope and stepped back. Through eyes streaming with tears, he inspected Noelle from head to toe and back. He visualized this same woman on their last night in Manila, alive, vivacious, full of joy.

The real Noelle bore no resemblance to the broken, dead body in front of him. After several seconds, he forced his gaze away from her to the other people in the room, surprised to see both the air wing commander and the ship's captain standing in the back of the OR, watching. The ship's chaplain stood with them.

Zack nodded to the chaplain. "Father, she needs you now. The rest of you, thanks for your help and support. When the chaps is done, I'd like some time alone with my wife."

Two corpsmen covered Noelle's body to the neck with a clean sheet. As the priest administered last rites, Zack's shipmates filed out in silence. Some stopped to grip his hand or pat him on the shoulder. When the chaplain had finished his rite, he hugged Zack and stepped away.

Alone with Noelle, the true joy of his life now deformed and lifeless, Zack knelt by her side. His knees slipped in her blood on the deck. He broke down, sobbed without constraint. Never in his life had he known such bottomless sorrow and boundless agony.

The immediate wave of grief slowly ebbed. Zack felt a presence beside him. The chaplain, his lips moving in silent prayer. Zack reached out. The priest grasped his hand and helped him to his feet. Zack had never learned to pray. He would leave that to the chaplain.

Covered in the white sheet, with dark coagulating blood seeping through it in the area of her abdomen, Noelle seemed asleep—her face at peace, oddly radiant. Zack leaned forward. He kissed her, softly, tenderly. His lips lingered on hers, as if expecting the familiar response. Feeling none, he drew back and whispered in her ear.

"Be at peace, my love. You are in my heart and soul. Always."

Zack rejoined the chaplain. "She's asleep. We can go now."

CHAPTER FIFTY-EIGHT

Bridget wiped the tears from her eyes and waited in sympathetic silence while Zack composed himself. He stared at the ceiling; his body deflated like a broken balloon. After some seconds, she rested her hand on top of his. He looked at her with soft, wistful eyes. Aware of her own heartbeat, she removed her hand. "Do you need a break?"

"No," Zack said. "Let's press on."

Bridget pulled a pack of tissues from her purse and offered it to him.

He took one tissue, dabbed his eyes, and turned toward her. "Thanks."

She touched his arm. "Take whatever time you need."

Zack put the tissue in his shirt pocket, swallowed, and joined his hands in his lap as he spoke. "Instead of traveling with Noelle from Tokyo to Detroit for our wedding, I carried an urn with her ashes. After the funeral, I told my navy detailer I didn't want to return to Japan, that he could send me anywhere else in the world. He refused. Said I could either execute my orders or face consequences for failure to comply."

"Ouch," Bridget said. "Harsh."

He scoffed. "I did as I was told, but I couldn't handle it without Noelle. I sank into depression, self-medicated with alcohol and opioids. I became a total jerk in the emergency department. I vented my anger on staff and patients, without filters." He paused. "Could I get more ice water?"

Bridget called her secretary, who brought a pitcher to refresh their glasses of ice water. She looked between Bridget and Zack with puzzled eyes, then left them alone.

Zack took a swig of water. "One morning, hungover or still drunk after a late-night binge, I evaluated a young female officer complaining of vague lower abdominal pain. I thought she was whiny. Noelle never whined, about anything. I berated the woman for being a wimp, told her that a strong woman warrior would suck it up and do her duty."

He gulped down the remaining ice water and looked away. "The next morning, our emergency department director, Ed Walsh, informed me that the woman had bled to death from a ruptured ectopic pregnancy." New tears filled his eyes. "She died because I minimized her complaint and failed to do a proper evaluation." Zack swallowed hard. "Ed removed me from patient care, sent me to a shrink, and facilitated an honorable separation from the navy—by way of alcohol rehab. Because I was willing to get help, he made sure that none of that appeared in my official record."

Zack's hand had migrated back to the armrest of the couch. Bridget reached out and held it. "Such a terrible burden you've carried over the years. Have you told anyone? Ange?"

He shook his head. "Just my shrink."

"Many men would crack under that burden. Your survival attests to your fortitude."

He smirked. "More like denial."

A familiar concept to Bridget. "That too."

She let go of his hand. They sat in silence, both lost in their own thoughts. Bridget reminded herself of her role as legal advocate, not shrink or personal counselor. *Friend?* Familiar emotions arose within her. She shoved them away, shifted in her chair, and reverted to her lawyer tone. "To be clear, when your boss in Japan sent you to alcohol rehab, you two made a deal that none of your misdeeds would appear in your official record?"

Zack nodded. "My fitness reports and clinical performance reviews all say I was a stellar officer and competent physician."

She furrowed her brow, recalling how Dominic had come up blank on Zack's navy history. "Any idea how Roger found out?"

He shook his head, a bit of flush in his cheeks. "When I first joined the group, I told Dennis King about the Japan thing; nothing about Noelle. I wanted to be honest. Wouldn't want some rumor or stray fact to blindside him." His voice trailed off. "One of us got blindsided all right."

Bridget lifted her chin. "What else did you tell him?"

"The rehab and the psychotherapy. I wanted to assure him my impairment was a thing of the past. I gave him contact information for my psychiatrist, and permission to contact her if he wished."

That surprised Bridget. "Your psychiatrist was a woman?"

"Is a woman."

"The one in Japan?"

"No, the shrink I started seeing after I moved here."

There is always more to his story. "Do you still see her?"

"Not for a few years. We agreed I could stop. I'm free to go back anytime. I think it's time. I'll call her tomorrow."

"Excellent plan," Bridget said. She thought for a moment, wondering if Zack could not see the obvious conclusion, or if his denial could be that powerful. She needed to challenge him. "Could Dennis King have been the visitor Keisha Rollins saw in Roger's office last week?"

Zack shook his head, spoke in a stern voice. "Dennis would never betray me. He's invested in me. He's honorable. I told him about my past in confidence. He swore to uphold that trust."

"*Et tu, Brute?*" Bridget chastised herself the instant she said that.

Zack flushed, pulled out his phone, flipped through some pages, then showed the screen to Bridget. "Our group's duty schedule. Dennis had duty in the ER that day."

"Could he have switched, or had someone stand in for a couple of hours while he visited Meadows?"

Zack glared at her, punched a speed-dial on his phone. "Monica, it's Doctor Winston. I may owe Doctor King a shift. Can you tell me if he was on duty last Wednesday?" He smiled at Bridget. "All day? Did he get relief for a meeting or anything?" His smile broadened. "Thanks, Monica." He clicked off the call and grinned. "Dennis King did not visit Roger Meadows that day. He never left the ER."

Bridget sighed. "We still don't know the mystery person." She bit her lip. "Not that it matters now."

His brow furrowed. "What are you saying?"

She leaned forward, trying to project both empathy and candor. "I'm telling you to take the deal. Accept Roger's settlement offer."

Zack did not flinch or hesitate. "No."

"If this goes to trial, Roger will rip you to shreds in front of a jury. He'll make you out as the most contemptible human being ever to practice medicine."

Zack crossed his arms and legs. "Screw Roger Meadows. I was not negligent in my care of Carl Barnett. I will not let a bully take me down or ruin my career."

She touched his arm. "Zack, listen to me. Put aside your anger. Consider reality. This case is no longer about alleged malpractice. Someone is out to destroy you, professionally and personally."

He moved away from her touch, set his jaw. "Screw them all."

Bridget moved to the edge of her chair, closer to him. "They will crucify you, Zack. Roger will turn a case you should have won into a Circus Maximus, starring you as the lone Christian devoured by the lions. He will get it to the media. By the time these people are finished with you, the entire region will think of you as a drunkard; an impaired physician who killed a prominent citizen in the prime of his life. You won't be able to get a job as an orderly."

Zack erupted in anger, stood and loomed over her, arms perched on her chair. "None of that is true." He looked her in the eye. "You're supposed to defend me, not sell me to the damned Romans."

She stared back at him. "I'm giving you my best legal advice." Her eyes glazed. "I'm talking to you as a friend, Zack. You've suffered more than enough in your life. You don't need this crap. Give Janice Barnett her filthy lucre and get on with your life."

He had softened at "friend," but then steeled himself. She wished she could get the words back.

"I did nothing wrong. I was not impaired when I treated Carl Barnett. If I don't fight this, I'll never live with myself." He fixed her eyes with a penetrating gaze. "You want me to get on with my life, then help me beat this. You want to be my friend, Bridget? Never again say the word 'settle' to me."

The office ambiance had turned dim at the shank of the evening. Bridget's lawyer mind implored her to cut this loser loose, but she could not fathom that. It took considerable effort to control her swirling emotions before she could speak. "Okay. Okay." She bit her lip. "Understand that you're taking on the fight of your life. You will have to do things that go against your nature. If we're going to win, we can't hold back. We go all in, fight to the finish, or we quit. Now."

Zack glowered into her eyes. "All. In."

I must be crazy to do this. "Okay. Go home and rest. You'll need it."

His anger dissipated. He touched her arm. "Thanks."

"Thank me when we win."

His eyes softened. "I'm thanking you now for being my friend."

She smiled, in spite of herself. "Sure."

When he shook her hand to leave, he held on. She blushed. "Thanks again," he said.

She pulled her hand out of his grip. "Enough. Get out of here."

He was halfway through her office door when a thought struck her. She called after him. "Zack, only one way we can win this."

He turned back, anxious. "How?"

"It never gets to trial."

CHAPTER FIFTY-NINE

In the lobby, Zack found Ange waiting. She smiled; her icy veneer had thawed.

"Keisha?" he said.

"Home. She called in sick today. Didn't want to risk giving anything away at the deposition." She looked at him with cautious eyes. "She confirmed that Meadows' visitor was Jerry Hartman, based on your description."

"That's a relief."

Ange looked puzzled.

He sighed. "Bridget thought it might have been Dennis King." When she looked confused, he said, "Long story."

She gestured toward the elevator. "Are we still your attorneys?"

He shrugged. "For the nonce."

She looked puzzled. "You're going to fight on, and Bridget supports that?"

"Yep. Our strategy is never going to trial. Don't know how she plans to pull that off."

"She'll figure it out. She always does." Ange hesitated, then smiled. "Wanna get a drink?"

Before he could answer, his phone buzzed. Dennis King. "Sorry," he said to Ange. Showed her the phone. "I need to—"

"Of course," she said.

Dennis sounded tired. "How went the deposition?"

"Terrible. I got my ass and one leg handed to me."

A pause. "Sorry to hear that. Are you okay?"

"I will be."

Another pause. "I hate to pile onto an already shitty day, but I need your help."

Zack furrowed his brow. "How?"

Dennis cleared his throat. "Paula Cho was admitted in pre-eclampsia today. Six weeks before her due date. She's out of service."

Zack's empathy was genuine. "Sorry to hear that."

Dennis blew into the phone. "I need to put you back on the schedule, Zack."

"But I thought—"

"Already cleared it with Jerry Hartman. You'll be on a plan of supervision; I need to review your charts within twenty-fours of each shift."

A wave of elation flowed through Zack. *Back in the saddle.* Plus, he owed Paula. "Sure. Okay."

"Good. You'll be on day shift tomorrow and the rest of the week. Can you do that?"

"Absolutely."

"Thanks, Zack."

Not like I have a choice. He told Ange about the call. "I gotta go home and get some rest."

Ange nodded. "I understand." She brushed her lips on his. "Good night, Zack."

He looked at her like a conflicted teenager. "Can I get a rain check on that drink?"

Ange smiled. "Ask me next time it rains."

CHAPTER SIXTY

Lounging in her sitting-room comfort chair, Janice Barnett poured a double dose of Maker's Mark over a single ice cube. Now five weeks since the attack by Chantal, she'd substituted bourbon for Percocet. She touched the healing scar on her ear lobe, confident that her lengthening hair covered it. *Well enough.*

Her phone buzzed. She'd been waiting for the call. "Well?"

"The idiot refuses to settle."

Janice snorted. "Told you. Heroes like him will charge into a roaring fire with a garden hose rather than look weak." She chortled. "Gotta admire that kind of courage."

"The guy is dense as concrete."

She set the whiskey glass on the side table, sat up on the edge of the chair. "How long till we get him into court, in front of a jury?"

A deep breath at the end of the phone. "Six months; maybe sooner, but no promises."

She blew into the phone. "I can't afford six months."

A short pause. "There might be another way."

She took a sip of the Makers. "How?"

"Strike where he's most vulnerable. His reputation."

Janice stood, paced the room, whiskey glass in one hand, phone in the other. "How? He didn't cave at the threat of his past coming out at trial."

"He believes he's put that behind him. Swears he's clean now."

Jan stopped pacing, smiled. "If it turns out he's not clean?"

"Bingo." A beat. "What if that revelation happens in a most public and humiliating way?"

"Do tell." She finished off the glass of whiskey, set it on the side table. "Where are you now?"

"Working."

She chortled. "Not."

"Busted. I'm turning into your neighborhood. I need some, uh, supply."

A lascivious smile crossed her face. "I'll flip on the porch light and unlock the door. Come to the bedroom."

CHAPTER SIXTY-ONE

Despite a sober but restless night, Zack arrived in the ER right on time for his 6 a.m. shift. With no patients in the ER, he seized the opportunity to catch breakfast in the hospital cafeteria. Sitting at an isolated corner table, his mind sorted through the hodgepodge of rampant dreams and awake worries he'd suffered during the night. Noelle, alive and dead. Ange back in his life. Bridget? *I'm talking to you as a friend.* Real or a dream? Zack couldn't say for sure.

As he took a last bite of bacon and finished off his egg-white vegetable omelet, Dennis King took a seat at the table. Zack hadn't seen him enter the room. "You look worse than crap," Dennis said. "Are you okay to see patients?"

"I'm fine," Zack said. "Restless night." He waved a hand. "I've had worse. No problem working."

Dennis shrugged. "If you say so. Appreciate you doing this."

Zack chuckled. "Glad to be back." Dennis appeared haggard. "You don't look so hot yourself," Zack said. "This is early for you."

"Medical staff executive committee meeting at seven-thirty. Gotta accommodate the surgeons' schedules, you know."

Zack scoffed. "The price of leadership. Better you than me."

Dennis and Zack looked at their watches at the same time. Seven-twenty. Dennis stood. "I don't have time now, but I need to talk to you today."

"You know where I'll be until six."

"I'll come by after the committee meeting. Maybe the ER won't be busy yet."

"I'm all atwitter." The joke failed. "Sorry, still waking up. Whenever is fine."

Dennis strode out of the cafeteria.

What's up with him?

Seconds later, Zack got summoned back to the ER. *Game on.* He took the tray and plates to the busing line. In a hurry to return to the department, he burst through the cafeteria door and collided with Janice Barnett. Their bodies bounced off each other like opposing tackles at the line of scrimmage. Embarrassed, Zack stepped aside to let her pass. "Sorry, ma'am. Didn't see you."

She stood in front of him, looked him up and down as if she were an inspecting officer. Then she lifted her head toward his face and made a show of sniffing his breath. "I hope you haven't been drinking on duty this early, Doctor." She said it loud enough that several people in the hallway turned and gawked.

Speechless, Zack walked away without answering. Those who witnessed the encounter avoided eye contact. He heard Janice snort behind him.

Back in the ER, Zack struggled to concentrate on patient care as his mind reeled from Janice's overt attack. Did she know about yesterday's deposition? Had she heard about his disgrace in Japan? He wondered at the coincidence of her sudden appearance in his path as he left the cafeteria. Did she know he was there? He had to put those thoughts out of his mind or they would consume him.

Concentrate on your patients.

He looked from the chart in his hand to the woman in front of him. "I'm sorry." he said. "Please tell me again when the pain in your abdomen started."

CHAPTER SIXTY-TWO

B y mid-shift Zack was back in the groove. He found tranquility in seeing and treating patients. It allowed him to put other thoughts and worries from his mind. He was in the middle of a pelvic exam on a woman with mid-cycle vaginal bleeding when he heard EMS on the radio.

"En route your facility with fifty-five-year-old male, apparent OD, time undetermined. Found unconscious. Initial vitals, BP eighty over fifty, pulse fifty, respirations ten and shallow. Airway patent. On scene we bagged him with hundred percent O2, started IV with normal saline, and administered two doses of Narcan. Patient regained consciousness for a minute, then crashed, with zero vitals. No response to more Narcan. Now CPR in progress. We found empty bottles of Percocet and Restoril on scene. ETA your location seven minutes."

Mixed opiate and benzodiazepine overdose. Badness.

Zack finished the pelvic exam, which was normal, reassured the woman that he didn't suspect anything serious, and ordered appropriate labs, including a pregnancy test despite the woman's protestations. After his disaster in Japan, he would never again chance missing an ectopic.

Back in the work area, he scanned the list of waiting patients for anyone needing immediate attention or who could be discharged prior to the EMS arrival. Two patients complaining of flu symptoms could wait. Another one, with a sprained ankle suffered the prior evening, he could meet and street. The triage nurse had obtained an ankle x-ray. Zack noted a tear-drop avulsion fracture off the distal end of the fibula at the ankle joint. He took a quick look at the patient, verified a swollen, discolored ankle with point tenderness over the injury site.

He showed the x-ray to the patient, a twenty-something athletic-looking male. "You've pulled off the ligament that connects your lower leg to your ankle. He pointed at one spot on the x-ray. This little chip is where part of the bone came off your fibula."

The man gasped. "My ankle is broken?"

Zack gave him a reassuring pat on the shoulder. "Not really. It amounts to a severe sprain, which should heal fine. Bad news, you're going to be in a cast and non-weight-bearing for a about a month, followed by some rehab to build it back to normal strength."

The man frowned. "I'm supposed to play in a club soccer tournament this weekend."

Zack shook his head. "Sorry. You're out of action for at least six weeks."

The man glared as if Zack had just told him he had to go to jail.

"We'll put a splint on it here, because the progressive swelling will make a rigid cast risky. I'll refer you to an orthopedist who specializes in sports medicine. He will see you in a couple of days and cast it when the swelling's reduced. You'll be back on the field as soon as it's safe."

The man winced at his swollen ankle, enveloped in an ice bag. "Can I get something for the pain?"

Zack thought about the inbound narcotic overdose patient. "Tylenol works just as well as narcotics, with less risk. Once we immobilize your ankle it will feel better. Keep it elevated and iced, no weight bearing whatsoever, and you won't need much pain medicine." The patient put his head in his hands, no doubt overwhelmed about the sudden demise of his amateur soccer career.

Hearing the ambulance arrive out front, Zack gave orders to the ER tech. "You know the drill, Ace. Splint, crutches, ice bags, non-weight-bearing instructions, referral to sports medicine ortho in five days." The young tech nodded. Zack didn't know his real name. He'd always called him, "Ace." In truth, Ace knew more about treating extremity injuries than Zack ever would.

Zack turned toward the resus room. "I'll finish the chart after I take care of this OD."

As soon as he entered the resuscitation room, Zack recognized the patient. Roland Edwards, Walter Knowles' partner. The nurses and medics had transferred Roland to the gurney. One medic performed chest compressions while a nurse took over squeezing the ambu bag. "Still no vitals," the medic said. Roland's skin had turned blue. The team had prepared to intubate the patient. A deep sense of impending doom washed over Zack. He froze. Anxious looks from the medical team shook him out of it, and he moved to the head of the bed to intubate Roland Edwards—already dead.

Thirty minutes later, after an uncomplicated intubation and ventilation, with no response whatsoever to their resuscitation efforts, Zack shook his head and called it off. "Time of death, 0840." He turned to the paramedics. "Did you bring in those two medications?"

"We found more," a medic said. He handed Zack a bag containing about a dozen pill bottles. Other than the Restoril, all were opioids issued to Walter Knowles before his death, prescribed by various physicians including every emergency physician on staff; five from Dennis King, two from Zack Winston.

Forged prescriptions.

"I'd guess he was dealing," the medic said.

Zack shrugged. He remembered Roland's earlier description of Walter's secret bank account, and his own protestation of innocence. "I didn't kill my partner, Dr. Winston. I didn't kill Walter."

Truth, or . . .?

haken, Zack returned to the workstation just as Dennis approached from the direction of the bunker. "Still the king of ODs," he said.

Zack was in no mood for joking. He gestured toward the resus room. "Roland Edwards. Walter Knowles' former partner. Percocet and Restoril, at a minimum. Medics found a cache of opioids, all written for Walter before he died. Two of them under my name, five under yours. Obviously forged."

Dennis raised his eyebrows, frowned. His eyes confronted Zack. "You never wrote a script for Walter?"

Zack flushed, angry. "You know damned well I'd never do that."

Dennis' eyes softened. He shook his head. "Neither would I." He gestured toward the resus room. "You never really know someone, do you?"

"Especially druggers," Zack said.

Five new patients waited to be seen. "Not a time to chat," Dennis said.

Zack shrugged. "Nope."

Dennis clapped his shoulder. "Hope it slows down for you. I'll check back later in the day."

"I'll be here."

CHAPTER SIXTY-THREE

As soon as Dennis left, Zack noted his phone's missed-call light flashing. Bridget, during the attempted resuscitation of Roland Edwards. He needed to tell her about Roland, but at the moment he felt overwhelmed. He would call her later when things let up.

He completed the ER record on Roland Edwards. Law enforcement and DEA would get involved, so he took meticulous care to note every detail. That documentation done, he worked through the other patients, all with minor complaints—from his perspective if not theirs: two adults with common colds, a child with an ear infection, an older woman with a recurrent urinary tract infection, and a young woman with a migraine history who had broken through her prophylactic medication.

He discharged the patients with colds, assuring them that they would get better in a week without treatment, whereas with pills it would take seven days. Then he attempted to reassure the crying child's mother that the ear infection was viral, not bacterial, and did not require antibiotics. Mom was not convinced, hostile even, so he discharged the child to their pediatrician's office across the street from the hospital. He started the migraine patient on an ergotamine drip. No new patients appeared, so he scurried back to the bunker to swig his health drink and assuage his thirst. He was about to call Bridget when a nurse poked her head into the room. "Chest pain in One."

Zack took the health drink with him to the workstation, albeit in violation of the rule against eating or drinking there. He was in no mood for administrative BS. The day had started out badly enough. He needed nourishment and hydration. After another large swig, he headed to Bed One.

The patient was a panicked twenty-three-year-old woman, hyperventilating at a respiratory rate near-thirty; blowing off too much carbon dioxide and causing her symptoms. Zack ordered IV Ativan to break her anxiety, while the nurses had her breathe into a paper bag to recirculate the CO2. The treatment calmed her to where they could get a good EKG. Abnormal, but not life-threatening. Zack turned to the patient. "How are you feeling?"

"I'm a little woozy. My heart keeps racing in my chest."

Zack explained that she had an abnormal but non-critical cardiac arrhythmia known as supraventricular tachycardia, a common occurrence in young women, especially those prone to anxiety attacks. At the mention of anxiety, her eyes went wide, her faced flushed, and she lurched forward. A crushing pain hit Zack's chest. For a second, he thought the woman had slugged him. The sensation passed. She was a few feet away from him, upset and angry, but she hadn't touched him.

He was about to reassure her when pain like a sledgehammer struck his sternum. The pain spread like lava to his left shoulder. His chest felt crushed in a vice. Lightheaded, he grabbed the edge of the patient's bed to steady myself.

Alarm crossed her face. "Doctor, are you okay?" She yelled past him. "Nurse! Something's wrong with the doctor!"

Woozy, Zack leaned on the bed with his left hand and clutched his chest with the right hand. He heard a rush of movement as two nurses appeared from nowhere on each side of him. "Doctor Winston, are you okay?"

Short of breath, dizzy, and nauseated, he couldn't speak, but managed to shake his head. *Most definitely not okay.* He squeezed his eyes tight against the pressure in his chest, which was now also in his neck and jaw. He thought he might choke.

Someone or something came up behind him. Strong arms lowered him to a sitting position, planted his butt into a wheelchair. As soon as he landed, the chair accelerated backwards, made a sharp turn, and drove straight to the resus room where nurses were cleaning up after the removal of Roland Edwards' body. He heard a nurse shout toward the workstation. "Call Doctor King."

They wheeled him to the side of the gurney. In the background he heard the hospital pager, "Doctor Dennis King, ER STAT. Doctor King to ER STAT."

Zack's head filled with dense fog. He fought to remain conscious— uncertain if the fog was from the severe chest pain or if the angel of death had come to fetch him. Strong arms lifted him onto the bed. He wanted to help, but he couldn't feel his arms or legs. Someone inserted a nasal cannula into his nostrils, and he welcomed the cool flow of oxygen into his lungs. Someone else cut off his scrub shirt, while yet another person poked his right arm with a needle to start an IV. He felt EKG leads being pasted to his bare chest, shoulders and ankles.

"What's going on?" Dennis King, from a distance.

A disembodied voice answered. "Acute chest pain. Near-syncope."

"Vitals?" Dennis again.

"BP ninety over fifty, pulse fifty."

Zack forced his voice to work. "Normal for me. Athlete."

Dennis' voice in his ear. "Any history of heart disease, risk factors? You know the list."

He could not find Dennis in the fog. "No. Healthy."

"Drinking, drugs?"

"No."

"Get that EKG done," Dennis said.

"Reasonable thought," Zack said, but then realized Dennis was not talking to him.

"Sinus brady on the monitor," Dennis said. "Shit. PVCs, multiple. Bring the defibrillator."

Dennis' voice in his ear. "Zack, how's your chest pain?"

Like I'm stabbed by a molten spear. "Nine of ten."

Someone's fingers stuffed an aspirin tab into his mouth. Whoever owned the fingers spoke in a loud, demanding voice. "Chew it, Doctor."

"Push two milligrams of morphine IV," Dennis said. "Watch his blood pressure and respirations."

Zack lapsed in and out of consciousness, until someone ripped something off his chest. The twelve EKG leads, he thought.

Dennis' voice, louder, excited. "ST elevation across the precordium. Call a STEMI."

With the morphine taking effect, Zack felt like he was floating over the ER, watching it all happen to someone else. He heard the overhead announcement, as if through radio static. "Code STEMI, ER. Code STEMI, ER."

"I need to take care of that STEMI," Zack said.

Then his heart rocketed out of his chest.

"Runs of V-Tach," someone said from way back in the fog.

"Paddles ready," Dennis, closer but muffled.

Darkness closed in around Zack. Only a small dim tunnel remained in the center of his vision. Then that light went out. Someone pounded his chest, but a bale of cotton absorbed the blow. His heart stopped.

A muted voice warbled in the distance. "V-Fib."

Zack's body sank into the bed, through the bed, through the floor, into the ground. Blackness surrounded him; bitter cold enveloped him.

Already dead.

A dim light appeared in the blackness, and Zack fell toward it headfirst. The light brightened. In its center, Noelle; beautiful, radiant Noelle, reached out to him. Their fingers touched.

Dennis' disembodied voice from miles above him. "Clear!"

A searing, powerful, agonizing electric volt shot through his chest. His body levitated, then flopped down like a melted plastic doll. His desperate brain searched through the frigid darkness.

Noelle was gone.

CHAPTER SIXTY-FOUR

"Zack." Dennis' voice through a wad of gauze. "Zack, can you hear me?"

"Please don't hit me again," Zack said. His chest felt on fire, his brain like charred mush.

A disembodied voice from somewhere behind and above him. "Sinus rhythm with PVCs."

Zack blinked his eyes. Dennis swayed into and out of focus. Three more blinks, and Zack saw Dennis clearly. Sevati Prakash appeared next to him. They turned away, but Zack could hear them talking. "Acute chest pain while on duty," Dennis said. "ST segment elevation in the precordial leads. He started flipping PVCs, with rapid progression to V-Tach and V-Fib. Shocked him once, returned to sinus rhythm, still with PVCs. He was down about thirty seconds."

"We need him in the cath lab." Sevati's face came into view. "Zack, can you hear me?" He nodded. "Does your chest hurt?"

"Like the proverbial elephant sat on me, then someone shocked me with a high voltage cable."

Sevati looked at someone else. "Six milligrams of morphine IV, slowly please." Back to Zack. "Acute coronary syndrome, Zack. I am taking you the cath lab, planning PTCA if we find an occlusion."

Zack shook his head. "No risk factors. Not even family history."

"That does not matter now."

Of course, she was right. The chest pain diminished as morphine-induced velvet euphoria surged through his brain. "Do what you must, Sevati. Clean it out." He closed his eyes, drifted into a pleasant void.

Noelle and he made passionate, unrestrained love, then lapsed into exhausted bliss. Zack wanted to die like this, in Noelle's embrace, their bodies and souls locked in perfect harmony, his senses effete, his heart full. If there were a heaven, it must be this ecstasy, forever joined with Noelle. Her golden voice whispered in his ear.

"Zack, can you wake up?" He did not want to wake up. He did not want this rapture to end. "Zack, wake up." If he did awaken, if he succumbed to full consciousness and restored sensation, then Noelle and he could do it again, lose themselves in each other's bodies and souls. He wanted that.

"Zack?" Noelle's sweet face close to his, the succulent scent of her. He opened his eyes. Sevati Prakash smiled at him. "Hi, Zack. Welcome back." Behind her, a bright light chased away his vision of Noelle.

Zack blinked and looked around. The surroundings seemed at once familiar and strange. He was in a hospital bed, but not in the ER. Confused, he looked at Sevati. "Where is Noelle?"

A puzzled look crossed Sevati's face. She touched his shoulder. "You are in CCU. Cath is done."

Zack's memory awakened and yanked him without compassion into harsh reality. He shut his eyes, eager to return to the dream. Gone. He willed his eyes to open and focused on Sevati. "Guess I'm alive."

She smiled; her voice tinged with empathy. "Alive and likely to remain so. Any chest pain now?"

"None." He forced a return smile. "Ready to run a marathon."

"Good news, no coronary occlusion. Your EKG has returned to normal. No MI either."

That seemed strange. "What the hell?"

"You have minimal coronary atherosclerosis for a man your age, no significant plaques; and great collaterals, a clear benefit of your fitness regimen."

He repeated, "What the hell?"

She shrugged. "We figure coronary artery spasm, quite significant given the ST elevation and subsequent arrhythmia. Had you been anywhere but the ER, you would be dead. Dennis King and your ER team saved your life."

Zack closed his eyes, taking time to process her words. He looked back at her, now fully alert. "I've never had anything remotely like this. Why now?"

Sevati shrugged. "I was going to ask you. I assume no illegal drugs, right?"

He scowled and shook his head. "Of course not."

"Any medications?"

"None."

"Caffeine?"

"My coffee intake has increased since I quit drinking, but—"

"Yes, far-fetched." She tilted her head. "We may never know for sure, but I wonder about stress. You have been hit hard with that lawsuit and the threat to your privileges."

How did she know about that? The irony of her statement caused a stir within him. Odd that he would suffer the very same pathology he allegedly missed in Carl Barnett. *Strange coincidence.*

"May be," he said, not convincing himself.

Sevati patted his shoulder. "We will give you a chance to get some rest. If you remain asymptomatic and your EKG and enzymes stay normal, I will send you home tomorrow. Dr. King plans to keep you off the ER schedule for two weeks. After that, we will re-evaluate and see if you are ready to return to work."

"No way," Zack said. "They need me on the schedule. I must pull my weight. If not, I guarantee I'll be more stressed than working, even the craziest shifts."

Her voice turned stern. "You must rest, Zack."

He tried to sit up, foiled by multiple IV lines and oxygen tubing. Frustrated, he stared at her. "I know myself. Down-time when I should be supporting my colleagues is the most stressful thing you can do to me."

Sevati folded her arms across her chest. "I will talk to Dennis; see what we can do."

CHAPTER SIXTY-FIVE

The next morning, Zack was like Gollum on an Elvish leash. He wanted to rip out his IV, tear the EKG leads off his chest, and bolt from the CCU wearing nothing but a hospital gown; no matter if his lily-white hairy butt-cheeks flashed the air.

How to torture a healthy human. Stick him or her into a closed hospital space with sick people.

The constant din of monitors beeping, nurses bustling, and patients croaking had kept him awake most of the night. In the next cubicle, someone died. Zack didn't know who, what gender, how old, or what from, but for thirty minutes he was forced to eavesdrop on a futile resuscitation as it unfolded on the other side of a thin wall. At one point, he almost got up to join the team; but just then they called it quits. His sleep-deprived thoughts regressed to the day he lost Carl Barnett. Except Carl arrived already dead. Somehow, Zack had made it to the elite already-dead-to-almost-died team. The person in the next cubicle hadn't been so lucky.

At seven a.m., he picked at the low-fat breakfast on the tray in front of him, ignoring the glass of tomato juice (or was it V-8?). He never ate breakfast without coffee. He started to push the tray away just as Jerry Hartman walked into the cubicle, Zack's chart in his hand.

"What are you doing here?" Zack hoped his voice did not sound as hostile as his thoughts. Then he remembered the change in Jerry's attitude toward him after their face-off in the ICU, where Walter Knowles lay already dead.

Jerry scowled. "As chief of the medical staff, I have a duty to check on any of our physicians who come into the hospital, especially someone who almost died."

Zack pushed the breakfast tray to the side, forcing Jerry to step back. "No worries. I'm fine."

Jerry held up the chart. "I hope so. According to this, you suffered unexplained coronary artery spasm. Any thoughts about why?"

"Clueless. I already went through it all with Sevati."

"As I noted from her usual obsessive-compulsive documentation. Any new clues overnight?"

"None."

Jerry cocked his head. "No drugs, including prescription medicine?"

"Damn straight. Never." *The next person who mentions drugs will get my fist in his eye hole.*

"Okay," he said. "Hope you feel better." Then he walked out. Zack's eyes followed him to the door.

What the hell was that about?

Ten minutes later, Sevati appeared in his cubicle with Zack's chart in her hand. *(That thing is getting a workout this morning.)* Something different about her. She seemed cool, reticent, detached; gave more eye contact to the chart than to him. Way out of character. "Something wrong, Sevati?"

"No, not at all." Her voice did not convince.

"Did you talk to Dennis?"

She averted her eyes. "I did. He has duty in the ER today. He'll be up to see you when he gets free."

"What did he say?"

Sevati wrote in the chart. Zack almost rationalized that she didn't hear him, but he knew better. She stared at the chart while she spoke. "I'll go ahead and discharge you, but you need to stay here until Dennis comes."

"What did he say?"

Sevati left before he finished the sentence.

Twenty minutes later, a nurse entered to take out his IV, disconnect the monitor, and allow him to get dressed. At the bedside, he found the clothes he had worn to the hospital before his last shift. Someone had retrieved them from the bunker where he had changed into scrubs, a lifetime ago. Zack pondered that he had spent twenty-four hours in the CCU after almost dying and had not a soul visit him; no one to bring a fresh set of clothes or to take him home when discharged. He thought about calling Ange; found his phone among his belongings. The flashing green light caught his attention. Three missed calls from Ange, two from Bridget. Text messages from both asking him to call as soon as possible.

He finished dressing, started to call Ange, but the nurse returned with discharge papers to sign. She handed him written follow-up instructions, but also felt compelled, or required, to read them aloud. "Rest today, eat a healthy diet, call Dr. Prakash if you have any symptoms. Call nine-one-one if serious or urgent symptoms."

He put the phone in his pocket. "Got it. Thanks."

"Doctor King called from the ER. He wants you to stop by there on your way out."

Zack thought he should put off returning those phone calls until he had more privacy at home. He thanked the nurse and the other staff on his way out of the CCU. He stopped in the men's room, where he stuffed the discharge instructions and other paperwork into the trash bin. Then he took the stairs down to the ER.

CHAPTER SIXTY-SIX

When Zack arrived in the ER, Dennis was finishing a laceration repair. "I'll meet you in the bunker as soon as I'm done, Zack."

Zack sensed the same distance and coolness he'd felt from Sevati. "Okay."

In the bunker, he found his sport-drink container. Someone must have retrieved it from the workstation and washed it out. A sudden pall of ennui wrapped around him. He didn't recall the last time he'd felt so tired and listless. Perhaps Sevati was right; some rest might benefit him. *Not two frigging weeks.* He'd filled the prior involuntary time off with activity related to the lawsuit. Now that he was in waiting mode on that, he could not fathom so much idle time. What would he do with himself? Obsess over what had caused his near-death a day ago? *No way.*

He leaned back in the desk chair and closed his eyes. Just as he dozed off, Dennis entered the bunker. Zack started to get up, but Dennis motioned him to stay seated. "Full code on the way in. I'm sorry, but I have to make this brief."

Zack searched his mentor's eyes. "I assume it's about Sevati's recommendation for two weeks off."

Dennis remained standing, arms folded, face stern. "More serious."

His posture alarmed Zack more than the words. "Say it, Dennis."

"I'm taking you off the schedule, indefinitely."

Zack erupted from the chair. "What?"

Dennis held his ground. "Pending an investigation into your fitness to continue practicing emergency medicine in this hospital; or anywhere for that matter."

A new pain ignited inside Zack's chest. "What are you saying?"

"When the ER tech picked up your clothes to take to the CCU this morning, he found an empty packet of white powder." His eyes bore into Zack. "Sure looks like cocaine."

Zack's chest and head burst. "Ridiculous. I've never done illegal drugs in my life."

Dennis remained impassive. "I'm telling you what we found, Zack. I sent it to the lab for verification. We're also running a tox screen on the CCU blood samples saved from yesterday."

Zack smiled with relief. He spoke in a firm, confident voice. "Good. I guarantee it will be negative."

The sound of an approaching siren filtered into the room. Dennis stepped toward the door. "How do you explain the used packet in your jeans, Zack?"

Zack glowered at him. "I don't, because it's not mine. I have no idea where it came from."

Dennis opened the door to leave, then turned to face Zack. "We need to figure this out. Cocaine use would explain your episode of coronary spasm yesterday; and you do have a past history of substance abuse."

Zack flushed with rage. "You know me better than that."

Dennis offered a small smile. "Maybe, but I have to think about the larger issues."

"This is bullshit."

"I hope so, but it looks bad. For now, I need you to go home and stay home. We'll figure out how to cover the rest of your shifts for the month."

Before Zack could reply, Dennis was out the door. Zack heard the onrushing crisis blast into the ER. Thunderstruck, he stood in the middle of the room. One by one, he turned out the pockets of his jeans. Along the seam of the right pocket, he found what appeared to be white powder residue. He got some of it on his finger and tasted it like a TV detective. Zack had no idea how cocaine was supposed to taste, but he felt an unnerving numbness on his tongue.

He stuffed the sport-drink bottle into his briefcase and bolted from the room. When he passed the treatment area and the resuscitation room, everyone was engaged in patient care. He needed to get out of the place before it suffocated him. In his haste, he ran square into Monica Harris returning from the quiet room.

"Are you okay, Doctor Winston? You look like you're being chased by a white walker."

"Worse," he said. "Whatever's chasing me isn't dead already."

CHAPTER SIXTY-SEVEN

Zack found his Lexus where he'd left it in the physicians' parking lot two days before. He drove home on autopilot, oblivious to the surroundings or how the car responded to traffic. His mind could process nothing beyond the meeting with Dennis. Replay after replay turned in his brain, and yet the scene remained unreal—as if he were watching it happen to someone else in a reality TV show. From somewhere deep below consciousness, a simple truth struggled to be heard over the din of his internal struggle. Its cries died before they could reach his distraught mind; itself a haze, a jumble, a mishmash, a swirling cacophony of unintelligible, racing half-thoughts. If Zack remained much longer in this state, he would surely lose what remained of his sanity.

Entering his apartment, he searched for Noelle. Not there. Had she disappeared for good when he returned from the already dead? Anxious, he wandered through each room. Surrounded by his familiar world of things, his mind cleared a bit—enough to lift him from the chaotic quagmire and to formulate a logical thought.

Ten a.m. on a weekday morning. Healthy individuals will be at work. He needed to call Ange and Bridget. *Start with Ange.*

Digging his phone from the briefcase, he reckoned she would be furious with him for not telling her he was in CCU. He would claim he did not have access to his phone. True, but he could have asked for it. He would accept her wrath because he needed to talk to someone who still had her wits, before he completely lost his. He started to press the speed dial for Ange's number, but in the final second punched Bridget's private line instead.

She picked up right away. "Zack? What the hell? Where have you been?"

The sound of her concerned voice injected calm, as if he had reached through from the upside down and touched a real person. He could not find his own voice.

"Zack? Hello?"

He swallowed hard. "I need to talk to you, in person. Ange too."

"Are you all right? You sound terrified."

"I am terrified. Scared to actual death."

A pause, during which he sensed her mind churning. "We need to talk to you as well. In private. Can you come to my office?"

Thinking about that question lifted another layer of fog from Zack's brain. "I shouldn't drive. I'll take the Metro."

Bridget paused. "Not sure about that. You don't sound well at all."

His voice quivered. "I'm not. It's urgent that we talk."

After a few seconds, Bridget spoke in a slow, steady voice. "Okay, but you're not driving or taking the Metro. We'll come to you."

He sighed in relief. "Better plan."

"Can we find a private place to talk at the hospital?"

Zack cleared his throat. "Not the hospital. Home."

"You're at home? Are you ill?"

His voice faltered. "I'm totally fucked, Bridge."

CHAPTER SIXTY-EIGHT

Bridget and Ange both reacted with alarm when they saw Zack. The three sat around the coffee table in his living room, Ange and Bridget on the sofa, Zack in a side chair. He told them about his crash in the ER and stay in the CCU.

"You almost died, and you didn't call me, or Bridget?" Ange, as predicted, was furious. Bridget seemed more worried than angry, although traces of both emotions showed in her face.

"I didn't have access to a phone in the CCU." Even to him, his voice sounded defensive.

"Bullpucky," Ange said. "You could have sent word via the nurses, or Dr. King."

"Guilty, your honor." He spoke with edgy sarcasm. "Try coming back from dead yourself sometime, then you can criticize."

Bridget raised a hand. "Please, don't fight, kids. Work it out later if you must." She cast curious eyes on Zack. "Why did you want to talk to us in person? Did something else happen?"

His addled mind had cleared since the phone call with Bridget. Stifling his emotions, he recited a coherent chronology of the events after his admission to CCU; starting with the first encounter with Sevati, how her attitude changed overnight, Jerry Hartman's visit, the shattering conversation with Dennis, and his own examination of his jeans pocket.

"Are those the same jeans?" Bridget asked, pointing.

"Yeah." He started to pull out the pocket.

Bridget raised a hand. "Stop. Take them off and give them to us. Right now."

He went into the bedroom and did as directed, changing into a pair of Adidas running pants. Back in the living room, he handed the jeans to Bridget.

"Do you have a plastic bag; a garbage bag, perhaps?"

Once the jeans were quarantined in a black plastic bag, Zack returned to his seat and handed the bag to Bridget. "That's the whole story. I swear I've never done street drugs, and for sure I didn't have cocaine on me when I showed up for my shift." His eyes passed from Bridget to Ange and back. "I hope you believe that."

"Of course," Bridget said.

Ange shrugged. "Yeah. Sure."

"So?" He raised his hands in a gesture of helplessness.

"Someone planted what looks like cocaine, or actual cocaine, in your jeans," Bridget said. "You get that, right?"

Zack's body relaxed. "Seems like."

Bridget addressed him with a courtroom voice. "Who has access to that room?"

He'd already thought about it. "Everyone in the ER, and Lord knows who else. It has no lock. When the ER is busy, anyone could go in there undetected."

Her eyes narrowed. "Did you see anyone around there during your shift?"

Zack shook his head. "Just Dennis, but he's in and out of there all the time."

"Maybe he saw someone," Ange said.

"I could ask him, but we're not on speaking terms right now."

Bridget wrinkled her brow. "Does Janice Barnett ever go in there?"

Zack shook his head again. "Doubt it. She's seldom in the ER, and then only to transfer a patient to ICU."

Bridget stroked her chin. "Janice would benefit from your disgrace as a drug user. It would force you to settle the case. Let's assume that somehow she managed to sneak in and plant the packet or conspired with a third party to do so."

Zack shrugged.

"What I don't get," Bridget said, "if you did not use cocaine during your shift, what caused your convenient episode of acute coronary syndrome, or spasm, or whatever it was?"

Ange interjected. "Are you suggesting someone caused Zack to have the chest pain, to make a case for him using coke on duty?"

Bridget nodded. "That would make it hard to claim the coke was planted but never used."

For the first time since they arrived, Zack smiled. "The tox screen will blow that out of the water. It's bound to be negative."

Bridget scoffed. "Like Carl Barnett's first EKG?"

CHAPTER SIXTY-NINE

Zack took a break to make and distribute coffee. The three of them sat in silence for the next several minutes, each lost in private thought. Aware that both women had tried several times to reach him while in the hospital, and recalling that Bridget had mentioned meeting in private, Zack wondered what else he was about to learn that might accelerate his current death spiral. He didn't want to ask, because he didn't know if he could handle any more crises. He remained quiet, thinking about who might have planted the cocaine, and what had made his heart stop. His clinician mind refused to function on the latter, and his penchant for denial blocked any ideas on the former.

Just as the silence became unbearable, Bridget looked at him. "What if this is not about you, Zack?"

Taken aback, Zack fumbled for words. "Not about me? I almost died."

"Yet you did not," she said. "Dennis King saved your life."

Zack frowned, shied away from her. "What are you saying?"

She scrunched her face. "Not sure; but someone is making a lot of effort and accepting considerable risk to destroy your career. That seems excessive if the only payout is Janice Barnett winning her lawsuit—especially since Roger Meadows has already set you up to lose."

Zack shook his head. "I'm not following."

"Maybe you will after we fill you in on our discovery. Ange?"

Ange pulled a file folder from her briefcase. "While you battled death and disgrace, I conducted research, with the help of our firm's private investigator."

Zack scoffed. "I've met Dominic Soprano."

Ange stifled a smile. "This is serious, and Dominic happens to be one of the best investigators in the area."

Zack waved her off. "Whatever. What did you find?"

Annoyed, Ange turned to face him, started to pull documents from the folder on her lap. She glanced at Bridget, who nodded. "Okay," Ange said, "here's what we know." A beat. "First, someone forged that EKG that Meadows presented in the first deposition."

Zack yawned. In retrospect, that event seemed from another lifetime. "So?"

Ange continued. "Our IT guys confirmed the forgery. They also found, by comparing it to your copy, that the forgery was made on the same copy machine as all the other record copies you saved after Carl Barnett's death."

"Walter Knowles made those copies," Zack said. "But other people use that machine. It doesn't mean that Walter made the forgery."

Ange smiled. "Except, each person who uses the machine has to enter a unique code to operate it. That code appears in the header for each copy." She paused, seeming to enjoy the drama. "Same code appears on your copies of the ER records and on the bogus EKG. Walter Knowles made both."

Zack waved his arms in exasperation. "That makes no sense. Why would Walter—?" He stopped in mid-thought, remembering his meeting with Roland Edwards soon after Walter's death. He looked from Ange to Bridget, then told them what he'd learned about Walter's secret bank account. "Well beyond what he would earn as an ER secretary."

"Drug money?" Ange asked.

"Not necessarily," Bridget said. "Could have been payoff money for forging that EKG, which would be a criminal act."

"That would mean someone's desperate to frame me," Zack said.

"Yet Roger was happy to drop it when we came up with the original," Bridget said. "Doesn't compute."

"Had to be drugs," Zack said. Bridget raised an eyebrow. He described Roland Edwards' overdose death, and the discovery of prescription opioids written for Walter.

Ange scowled. "Doesn't that cast suspicion on each of their deaths, Walter's and Roland's?"

Zack shrugged. "I don't know."

Bridget took a deep breath, seemed to be pondering something, but did not speak.

Zack turned to Ange. "What else did you and Mr. Soprano discover?"

Ange glanced at Bridget, who seemed to awaken from a fugue. "A lot about Janice and Carl Barnett, and an illegitimate child." She went on to describe how shortly before his death Carl Barnett had sheltered his assets from his wife, then about her discovery of Chantal Davis, nee Amanda Barnett, and how Janice's monthly payments to Yolonda Davis had diminished after Carl died.

Zack rubbed his forehead. "Janice was carrying a love child when she married Carl, and that child was not altogether white?"

Ange nodded in affirmation. "We surmise that he made Janice give up the child when he realized it wasn't his. Sometime later she found her daughter and started to support her in secret from Carl."

Bridget summed it up. "We think he discovered that and sequestered his assets. We also know that he'd paid several visits to a divorce lawyer. He planned to cut Janice off from his fortune and divorce her."

Zack blew out a breath. "Well, that would give her plenty of motive to go after a big malpractice settlement."

"And to murder her husband," Ange said.

"How?" Zack said. "She may have had motive, but we found nothing to suggest a method."

Bridget cleared her throat. "You didn't do a tox screen on Carl, right?"

"I saw no reason for one. As for the first day, you don't run toxicology on everyone with non-cardiac chest pain. The second day, it would have been futile. He arrived already dead. A tox screen would not have yielded any useful clinical information."

"Got it," Bridget said. "No tox screen, ergo no evidence that he was or was not poisoned."

Zack buried his head in his hands. This discussion was leading nowhere. He stared at Ange. "Is that all you have?"

She blushed. "Up to now. We're still looking for concrete evidence of an affair between Janice Barnett and Jerry Hartman."

Zack didn't think that Hartman would have an affair with Janice, or that he would be involved in criminal activity. He described his earlier interaction with Jerry during the treatment of Walter Knowles. Once Zack stood up to him, Jerry's attitude changed to one of professional trust. When Jerry had visited Zack in the CCU earlier in the day, he seemed more concerned than critical.

"Even if there is an affair, I don't see Jerry risking his career to support her."

"Speaking of Knowles and his partner," Bridget said, "Dominic has found nothing on either of them. He speculates that information may have been buried with them." She locked eyes with Zack. "This is no longer about a malpractice case. If whoever is behind this manipulates that tox screen, if it comes back positive, you will face criminal charges for substance abuse on duty. Even if Janice wins and gets her award, those consequences pale compared to what will happen if you can't refute the cocaine evidence."

Zack's eyes turned dark; his face slackened. "What are you saying?"

"Take the settlement offer so you can redirect your efforts toward criminal defense."

Zack blustered. "No damn way." He crossed his arms and glared at her.

Bridget looked at Ange, seeking support. Ange shook her head, did not speak. Bridget reached across and touched Zack's arm. He flinched away. "Zack," she said, "I'm telling you as a friend. You can fight only so many battles at once. Settle the malpractice suit. I'll hook you up with a top-notch criminal defense lawyer."

He wheeled around, brought his face close to hers, his eyes on fire. "I told you never to say that word again."

Silence ensued, broken only by the sound of Zack's heavy breathing. Again, Bridget looked to Ange for help, but got a slight shake of the head in return. She looked back at Zack. "Then I can't help you any longer. I can't take a chance on being caught up in a criminal situation." She stared at the floor. "I'll help you find a defense lawyer, criminal or malpractice. But I can't risk my own professional life supporting a Quixotic charge with no chance of success."

Zack exploded from his chair. "Your career! You're worried about your career, Bridget? Sacrifice me to cover your own ass?" He brought his glowering face inches from hers. His voice quaked when he spoke. "You have a lot of damned nerve calling yourself my friend. I'm no expert on relationships, as you well know, but I can tell you true friends don't do what you're doing."

She shrank away. "Zack, I—"

He held up a hand, stepped back, pointed to the door. "Get out."

CHAPTER SEVENTY

As soon as Bridget and Ange left his apartment, Zack rushed to the bathroom, threw off his clothes, and got into the shower. He turned the cold water full blast to quell his rage. Didn't help. He tried hot water, then lukewarm as he scrubbed himself almost raw. His hands shook, and he dropped the soap several times. Zack could not wash away the anger raging inside him. Anger at Bridget, anger at Ange, at Carl and Janice Barnett, Jerry Hartman, and most of all Dennis King. Was there no one Zack could trust? Anyone in whom he could confide? Ange had not joined in Bridget's entreaty, but she had damn sure gotten out of his apartment as soon as he dismissed Bridget. Maybe someday he could trust Ange again. But Bridget? She had abandoned him when he needed her most. In the process, she had broken his heart.

Friend, my ass.

He got out of the shower and toweled down. He did have someone, if he could find her.

Five minutes later, he burst from his apartment in running attire. Ignoring the elevator, he ran down the stairs and out into the fresh air, sprinting to the Capital Crescent Trail. Once there, he accelerated as if a demon bore down on him. Within two minutes, he was forced to stop;

panting, out of breath, dizzy from the exertion. His clinical mind noted the absence of chest pain. *So much for exercise stress testing.*

Sitting by the side of the trail, he forced himself to slow his breathing, relax, let the fresh air chase the panic from his lungs. After a few minutes, his respirations slowed and he felt calmer. Turning south, he jogged at a reasonable place to the special bend in the trail.

Noelle waited for him there.

She smiled when he approached. "Death by running, Doc? Not the best solution for the matters at hand."

Zack laughed, in spite of himself. Noelle joined him as he continued to jog. She listened with quiet patience as he reviewed all that had happened since he last saw her, halfway between earth and heaven. She said nothing as he summarized what he'd just laid out in detail, what she for sure already knew.

"So here I am," he said, "without legal support, facing a malpractice suit I'm sure to lose, maybe lose my license—or worse—for trumped up cocaine use on duty. On top of that, I'm linked into suspicious deaths: Carl Barnett, Walter Knowles, Roland Edwards. Maybe Melody Snyder. I wish to hell Dennis hadn't put those paddles to my chest when I went into V-fib."

Noelle scoffed. "No, you don't. You would have shocked yourself if no one else did." She was right. No matter the appeal of forever being with her in some sort of afterlife, he was not ready to slip the surly bonds of earth on a one-way flight.

They jogged together in silence. Zack savored the endorphins of running, and Noelle's presence beside him. They ran all the way to the Lincoln Memorial, where Zack stopped on the steps to gaze at Mr. Lincoln, the tourists, and a few locals traversing up and down those many steps; people of all ages and colors, as diverse as America itself. He turned around to admire the sunlit sheen of the Reflecting Pool, then raised his gaze to the World War II Memorial, the Washington Monument, and the United States Capitol in the distance. Zack felt small in the presence of such history and grandeur, in the midst of people whose lives may have been as complicated as his, or worse. He was one of many individuals tossed but not drowned in a sea of troubles, small but never powerless. Recalling the details of his life, the challenges and triumphs, he vowed to fight; fight and win against whatever or whoever sought to destroy him.

Behind him, Noelle whispered. "Don't quit on Bridget. She cares about you. Let her do what's right."

He wheeled on her. "She quit on me."

"No, she didn't. You threw her out. Get her back. She's your only hope."

She speaks the truth.

"How?"

"Let yourself be vulnerable for once. Trust her, even if you can't see the whole picture."

Zack thought about that for a minute. "Okay," he said. "But I need you on my wing. My career, my whole life is at stake. I'm outnumbered and outgunned, but I will win. Watch my six, and—most important—don't let me beat myself." He stifled a sob. "I love you. Still. With all my heart and soul."

She flashed that same smile that had captivated him when they first met. "Always."

Zack became aware of a presence near him. He looked around to see an older woman staring at him. She probably thought him a crazy man, talking to no one in sight. The woman's deep brown eyes penetrated to his soul. "I don't know who you're talkin' to, mister. But I got a feelin' she's right there by your side."

"She is," he said.

Without warning, the woman hugged his sweaty body. "You be strong now." When Zack turned around, Noelle had gone.

The sun was setting, and Zack didn't want to run the ten miles home. He caught the Metro to Bethesda then walked to his apartment building. When he got off the elevator, he saw a familiar figure leaning against the wall by his door.

Bridget.

"We need to talk," she said.

CHAPTER SEVENTY-ONE

Zack had never seen Bridget look so vulnerable. She sat on the couch, same spot as before, hands clasped in her lap. She hadn't spoken after her brief words in the hallway.

"Drink?" he asked.

She raised a hand to decline but changed her mind. "Okay. Whatever you have handy."

"Red wine? Scotch?"

She thought for a second before replying. "Scotch, but not too much. I have to drive home."

Zack poured two Glencairn whisky glasses of Laphroaig, neat. He handed one to her. "Hope you don't mind peaty."

Bridget smiled. "Tastes like a burning hospital, right? My favorite, actually. Could use a single rock, though."

Zack's turn to smile. *Lady knows her scotch.* He pulled two ice cubes from the freezer and dropped one into each glass. He sat in the chair next to her and raised his glass. "Cheers."

She tapped her glass to his, exchanging a moment of eye contact.

They sipped in silence for a minute before Zack turned to her. "Does this mean you're still my lawyer?"

Bridget stared across the room, then glanced back at him. "It means I'm your friend. Believe it or don't, I am." She looked away. "Whether I remain your lawyer depends on . . . a number of things."

Puzzled, Zack took another sip of scotch. "I don't understand."

She put down her glass, turned in her seat to face him. "I need to tell you something that I am not supposed to know. In doing so, I'm putting my career on the line. If discovered, I could be disbarred."

Zack touched her knee. "Then don't tell me. Nothing is worth that risk. I'll settle the malpractice case, get a criminal defense attorney, whatever you suggest, before I will let you risk your career for me."

She shook her head. "It's not that simple. You need to know what I know. Otherwise I won't be able to live with myself."

Zack raised his eyebrows. "Whatever it is, you can't take a bullet for me. I'm not worth it."

Bridget tilted her head, half-smiled. "Yeah, you are. It would be easier if I didn't believe in you." She touched his hand. "You've been set up, Zack." She rubbed her face with her hands. "As for me, I'd rather serve justice than my own career."

Zack noted her empty glass. He rose, retrieved two ice cubes from the freezer, and poured each another glass of Laphroaig with one rock. "Okay," he said. "Spill it."

She took a sip, set down the glass, and looked him in the eye. "The US Attorney for Eastern Virginia, my husband, is investigating a clandestine operation that obtains and distributes prescription opiates to drug dealers across the region." She sighed. "He referred to it sometime in the past. No details, of course."

"And that's related to my case?"

Bridget pursed her lips, stared into the distance. "The other day, while you were out of touch in the hospital and Marshall was out of town, I got home and found a light on in his office. Thinking he'd come back a day early, I checked the office. He wasn't home; but, I, uh, might have seen a document on his desk."

"You mean . . .?"

She nodded. "Janice Barnett may have murdered her husband for a malpractice award to fund her child's support, but someone else is using her for a different purpose."

Something in that statement didn't make sense. "Janice is involved in a drug conspiracy?"

Bridget shook her head. "Maybe not. She could have been duped."

"By whom? Jerry Hartman?" He shook his head with vigor. "That does not compute, Bridge." He did a double take. "I mean, Bridget."

She smiled. "Please, Zack, we're beyond formality." She finished her glass, set it down. Zack gestured toward the Laphroaig bottle. She waved him off.

"I still don't get the connection," Zack said.

Bridget wrung her hands, stared at the floor. "Walter Knowles' name was on the documents."

Zack stared across the room. "That just confirms what we'd already suspected."

"There's more." She looked at Zack with earnest, worried eyes. "Something more threatening." She took a deep breath. "The organization has another line of work, murder-for-hire. They specialize in making assassinations and murder look like natural or self-inflicted deaths."

Zack reeled. "Not only Carl Barnett, but Walter Knowles, Roland Edwards, and . . ."

She moved closer to him. "Almost Zack Winston."

Before he could react, her phone rang. "Ange," she mouthed to Zack as she answered.

CHAPTER SEVENTY-TWO

When Bridget clicked off the call, Zack had not moved. His expression remained stunned. She wondered how much more bad news he could handle. "Ange has concluded that Janice Barnett is not having an affair with Jerry Hartman."

Zack shrugged. "Good news, I guess."

"We knew that already. Never made sense, especially with what we know now." She looked at her watch. Eight-thirty. Marshall was still out of town and Justin was staying overnight with a friend. No need to rush home. "I'll take that other drink now. Less scotch and two rocks."

Zack poured their drinks—his a double with a single rock. Bridget took a sip and faced him. "There's more I have to tell you."

He looked like a whipped puppy but forced a smile. "Can't wait."

"The easy part, Janice is having an affair. We don't know with whom but appears to be someone complicit in the scheme to eliminate Carl."

"And the hard part?"

"The murder-for-hire scheme, and probably the drug distribution operation as well, is run by a physician, known only as *El Medico Asesino*."

Grim faced, Zack translated. "Dr. Assassin."

"*De veras.*"

His face lightened. "*Hablas espanol?*"

"*Un poquito.*"

"Where did you learn to speak Spanish?"

"Probably same as you. California high school."

"Nah. None of us got fluent in high school Spanish."

"Right," she said. "My first fiancé, the physician, was from Argentina. I learned Spanish to converse with his family. It came surprisingly easy to me." She smiled. "How about you?"

"When I decided to become a doctor, I didn't want to major in science like the other pre-meds. Figured it was my last chance to do something different, so in college I majored in Spanish. Came in handy throughout my career." He grinned. "Plus, I'm a language nerd. *Nihongo o hanashimasu.*"

Bridget guessed. "Korean?"

He chided her playfully. "Uh, Japanese? Where I was stationed in the navy?"

She laughed. "Of course. I'm supposed to know that, aren't I?" *Maybe didn't need the third scotch. Getting a tad giddy here.*

"I learned only enough Japanese to get into trouble. Very difficult language."

"Got to admire the effort," she said. "I do know one Japanese word." She raised her glass. "*Kampai.*" They clinked glasses. This time each maintained eye contact, after which an uncomfortable silence descended on them.

Zack finished his drink, put down the glass, and looked at her with renewed gravity. "What do we do now?"

A familiar flush arose in her neck and upper chest. She tried to cover it by looking at her watch. "I need to get home."

He smiled. "I meant about the information you shared."

She smiled, embarrassed. "Right. Sorry." She glanced at her empty glass.

Zack leaned forward in his chair. "We go to the authorities, right? Tell what we know?"

Bridget shook her head. "We don't know shit, Zack. None of what we surmise has any hard evidence to support it. Maybe we have motive with

Janice, but no weapon. How did Carl Barnett die? Poison? What poison? How and when administered?" She paused while Zack pondered the questions.

"No clue," he said.

She continued. "With Knowles and Edwards, we may know the 'how,' but we can only guess at the 'why,' much less the 'who.'

"So we can't act?" Zack's face turned florid. "Then why the hell did you share it with me?"

A pang shot through her chest. "Because your life may be in danger, Zack. Whoever tried to kill you, for whatever reason, may try again." She touched his arm. "I came her to warn you to be careful."

Zack cocked his head. "Really? Is that the only reason?"

She didn't know what he meant by that. "Also, to say that I will continue to represent you. And to convince you to settle the lawsuit; and to help you in case you do get hit with criminal charges." A tear came to her eye. She hoped Zack didn't see it.

Zack's face relaxed, but he didn't speak. Bridget thought she saw a tear in his eye, which he quickly wiped away. When he spoke, his tone was firm. "Then you'd better hang on for a rough ride, because I swear, we are going to beat this. All of it." The steel in his eyes matched the stony set of his face.

"I hope you have an idea how."

He rocked back and forth, pondering. "I'm working on it. I might have a plan."

"When you formulate it, let me know." She waved a hand. "Sorry, I didn't mean to sound sarcastic. I'm with you, Zack. All the way. I've already jeopardized my career. What's a rough ride going to do to me?"

He reached out to shake her hand. "Deal." They shook. Bridget couldn't tell which of them held on longer than normal.

"With that," she said. "I need to get home." She rose and walked toward the door. The room seemed to tilt a bit. "We can talk more tomorrow."

"Right," he said. "I'll give you a call."

"Good." She stopped halfway to the door—her feet immobile. "And, uh, thanks for the drinks."

"Any time." He placed his hand on the small of her back to guide her out the door.

As he started to open it for her, she wheeled and faced him. She felt lightheaded. Tears moistened her eyes. She blurted. "My damned husband is in Richmond tonight sleeping with another woman."

He moved into her space, took her in his arms, warm, affectionate. He hugged her tightly. She hugged him back, harder. She looked at him, tears running down her face. "Thanks," she said. "I really needed that." She rested her spinning head on his shoulder. When the rotation stopped, she pulled away. He let go. "Okay," she said. "Gotta go."

He held her hand. "Will you be okay?"

She rose from whatever trance had seized her. "I'm fine. Thanks." She let go of his hand and started out the door, then turned back, posture rigid. "This—" She gestured between them with her hand. "Never happened."

Zack smiled. "What never happened, Bridge?"

CHAPTER SEVENTY-THREE

Z ack walked Bridget to the elevator, concerned whether she should attempt the drive from Bethesda to Alexandria. She reached for the elevator button, but her trembling finger missed it. Zack grasped her arm with one hand, pulled out his phone with the other. "I'm calling you an Uber."

Bridget punched the "Down" button. "That's sweet, Zack, but I'm fine."

He held out his hand. "Keys."

At first, she frowned at him, then her face softened. She pursed her lips, reached into her purse, pulled out her key fob, detached the car key, and handed it to him. A troubled smile crossed her face. "Whatever you say, Doctor."

He pocketed the key, summoned an Uber three minutes away, and rode the elevator with her to the front lobby. The car arrived a minute early. "I'll bring your car to your office tomorrow then take the Metro home."

She smiled. "Thanks, Zack. That's very kind of you." She sighed. "We have a lot of work to do."

Zack nodded. "Yup." He caught her eye. "We're going to win." She turned to leave. He caught her arm, pulled her to him in an awkward hug. "Thanks," he said.

"Be safe," she said.

Heading back to his apartment, Zack's heart raced. When he opened the door, Noelle sat on the sofa where Bridget had been. Her face beamed. "Strong work, BAFERD."

CHAPTER SEVENTY-FOUR

Zack was back in that deathly OR with Noelle, kneeling at her side, the knees of his thin scrub pants soaked with her blood.

A stream of sunlight over his face pulled him into the reality of his bedroom; his legs damp with sweat, not blood. Sheets twisted. Another night terror.

He should have died when his heart stopped in the ER; no more nightmares, no mourning a past life, no more living hell. But for Dennis King's intervention, he might be with Noelle, now and for all eternity. Such was not to be. Resolute, he rolled out of bed, went to the bathroom, rinsed his face with cold water, then headed to the kitchen to make coffee. The sight of two empty Glencairn glasses stopped him. *Bridget. Bridge.*

His phone rang. Dennis King.

"Hello?" As if Zack didn't know who it was.

"It's Dennis, Zack." As if he didn't know that Zack knew.

"What's up?"

"Your tox screen came back."

Zack's heart filled his stomach. "That was quick."

"Just the preliminary. We'll get the final in a couple of days." Dennis paused, too long. "It's positive for cocaine, Zack."

The bolt that struck Zack's chest made the electric shock of semi-conscious defibrillation seem like a minor jolt from a cattle prod.

"That's . . . impossible."

Dennis scoffed. "I'm sorry. You know as well as I that the test is reliable."

Zack paced the room, free arm flailing like a lawyer rebutting a hostile witness. "Not this one. Dennis, I swear to you I have never used cocaine or any illicit drug in my life."

The phone went silent, except for Dennis breathing. He spoke in a distant voice. "I want to believe you, Zack, but . . . I must consider all the evidence. It's compelling."

A surge of rage rushed from Zack's gut to his brain. "Dennis, you know me. You know I didn't use cocaine on duty; not during that shift, not ever."

Dennis blew into the phone. "Cocaine would explain your episode of coronary spasm, as well as your quick recovery within the time the drug would metabolize." He paused. "I want to believe you, Zack. I hope we can still beat this. You need to give me an alternative explanation, not only for this lab result but for the packet in your jeans."

Zack's fist clenched; knuckles whitened. "Give me time and I will." *When I figure out how.*

"That I can do. You'll stay off the schedule, but I'll sit on this prelim until we get verification. Then you and I will talk—whatever the final lab result."

Nothing more to say. "Thanks. I appreciate that." He started to end to call, then caught himself. "Can you send me a copy of that tox screen?"

Dennis hesitated for a second. "Okay. Sure. I'll email it to you."

"Thanks."

"I'll be in touch." Dennis cut off the call before Zack could respond.

Zack threw the phone onto the couch. His heart raced; his breath came in irregular puffs. He felt lightheaded. Panic attack. *No shit. Who wouldn't panic over this?* For a full twenty minutes, he beat a path from bedroom to living room to kitchen to bedroom, round and round. On about the fiftieth circuit, he detoured to the bathroom, stepped out of his nightclothes, and took a shower—setting the water as hot as he could stand.

Ten minutes later, he emerged from the steam like a samurai from an *onsen*, ready for battle. No more hyperventilating. He put on clean Dockers and a golf shirt, returned to his study, and opened his e-mail. Nothing from Dennis. He should have sent that copy of the tox report by now.

Zack recalled that he had been scheduled to work today. He reasoned that Dennis was covering his shift. A true emergency or busy ER may have precluded him from copying and sending the report. Zack commanded himself to chill. He had no reason to doubt Dennis' word.

When he returned to the bedroom, Zack's phone blinked with a voice mail. Ange had called when he was in the shower. "Hey, Zack. Just checking in to see if you're okay and if you're coming to the office today. We have some new information to share."

Zack pocketed his phone. In the living room, he grabbed Bridget's Range Rover key and strode out the door. The empty whisky glasses remained on the table.

CHAPTER SEVENTY-FIVE

Zack found Bridget in the conference room, huddled with Ange and stoic Dominic. Bridget smiled when she saw him. She waved him into the room.

"I got a call from Dennis King just before I came here," Zack said. When he disclosed the positive toxicology screen, Bridget scoffed. "What a surprise." She shrugged. "One more mountain to cross. We'll get there, Zack." She turned to Ange. "Bring Zack up to date on what you called me about last night."

Zack understood the cue. He was to play it as if he and Bridget had not reconvened in his apartment after the first meeting of the three of them. He figured that Ange did not know about Bridget's discovery in her husband's office. Now he felt uneasy, not only about his one-on-one with Bridget, but also at not knowing which of the four people around the table, if any, possessed all the relevant information.

Ange explained her discovery of evidence that Janice Barnett and Jerry Hartman could not be having an affair.

"I never believed it in the first place," Zack said. "They may be tight professionally, but they're not the type to fool around off duty."

Dominic scoffed. "No such thing, Doc. In my experience it's the ones you least expect that are getting it on in private."

Ange cleared her throat. "She's having an affair with someone. If not Hartman, who?"

Bridget nodded at Dominic. "That's number one on Dominic's to-do list." She paused. "Anything else to share with us, Dom?"

When Dominic was done, Bridget summarized what they knew, then leaned back in her chair. "Early this morning, I reminded myself, as I'm reminding you all, that our objective is to win or kibosh this malpractice claim. We know it's not a straightforward 'duty-negligence-harm-causation' scenario. Something else is driving it, from which Janice Barnett and others stand to gain. That something is probably criminal. However, we are neither prosecutors nor law enforcement officials. We cannot conduct a criminal investigation. That would not only jeopardize a real prosecutor's case, but—more importantly—put Zack in danger. Maybe others as well."

Zack voiced what he'd been thinking all morning. "Maybe I should settle the malpractice case, clear the way for the authorities to investigate the underlying whatever."

Bridget shook her head. "Yesterday I would have agreed with you, but I've had a night to think about it. We've seen only the top of the beehive. Most of what we think we know is conjecture. No evidence. There may be more under the surface, for which someone is playing a high-stakes game to get the malpractice money, and/or to discredit you—or worse."

"Settling the case may not be the end of it?"

"Right," Bridget said. She paused. "We need to put those dogs onto a different scent."

"Flush them out?"

"Make them think we know more than we do. If they fear exposure, they will drop the malpractice claim and redirect their efforts before they'll risk getting caught. Then if we can kill the cocaine ruse Zack lives to fight another day."

"What else do we need?" Ange asked.

"The murder weapon," Bridget said. "And a clear motive and opportunity."

They sat in silence for a few minutes, pondering. Similar to dealing with seemingly unrelated clinical data points in a difficult case, Zack connected the dots. He smacked the table. "I know how we do this. Ange, how close are you to Keisha?"

Ange's face lit up. She got the message. She wrapped her fingers together. "Close enough to share everything we know."

"Close enough for her to risk the job that enables her to support her family?"

Ange frowned, shook her head. "Probably not."

Bridget smiled at Ange. "She doesn't need to worry about that. I know a firm that would take her in a heartbeat, without forcing her to sell her soul."

Zack wrote furiously on the legal pad in front of Ange. "Here's your list. See what you can get."

Ange nodded, smiled. "Got it."

Zack looked from Bridget to Ange and back. "Since I'm still credentialed at Metro Hospital, I have access to the electronic medical record. I can VPN into that from a remote location. Could get useful information from that."

Bridget tented her fingers under her chin, rocked back and forth in her chair. Then she leaned forward. "I don't know. None of this is ethical."

Zack scoffed. "Neither is what Roger Meadows has done." He folded his hands on the table in front of him. "I learned from my navy experience that to win the fight, you plan to swiftly defeat your enemy with overwhelming force. Up to now, Meadows and company have been a step ahead of us. It's time to hit 'em hard." He stared Bridget in the eye. "Ethics be damned."

Stone-faced, Bridget looked at Ange. "You agree to that?"

Ange looked determined. "Damn right."

Bridget sat back, looked at the ceiling, then gazed at the office suite outside the glass-enclosed conference room. She looked back inside, a mask of inevitability on her face. "'No more ER docs,' I said." She shook her head at Zack, the corners of her mouth slightly curled. "You are definitely my last. My last ER doc. Probably my last defendant." She tapped the table. "All in."

CHAPTER SEVENTY-SIX

Bridget glanced at the ceiling. *Why am I risking my career here? Because I need this win as much as he does. Why?*

She nodded at Ange then tilted her head toward the door.

Ange got the message. "I'll go call Keisha, see if she's free for a girls' lunch."

"Be careful," Bridget said. "Do not put either one of you in jeopardy." Ange cast her a curious look, then another one at Zack. She left the room. On cue, Dominic followed her. Bridget felt like she and Zack were in a fishbowl. "Let's go to my office."

When they got there, she sat behind her desk, motioned Zack to one of the client chairs across from it.

"I have your key," Zack said. He glanced around to be sure no one was in position to see through the glass front of Bridget's office, then handed her the key. "Nice vehicle."

She scoffed. "Says the man who drives a top-end Lexus."

A concerned look crossed his face. "Are you okay?"

She waved a hand at him. "I am so far over the line on this that I may never practice law again."

"Then why—?"

She raised her hand. "Various reasons. Some of which I don't understand."

He took a deep breath, looked her in the eye. "How much further are you willing to go?"

"What do you mean?"

"Something I can't ask you to do."

She stared at him, nodded her head, pursed her lips, closed then opened her eyes. "No, you can't, but it doesn't matter." She patted the briefcase on her desk. "I've already done it."

CHAPTER SEVENTY-SEVEN

Zack stared at Bridget. *Why would she put herself at risk for me?*
She read his face, shrugged. "I said 'all in.' I meant it."

He shook his head. "Hell of a risk, Bridge. I wish I hadn't mentioned it."

"You didn't need to. My idea, my responsibility."

Zack frowned. "I don't want you to do anything irrevocable on my account."

Bridget smiled. "Not just on your account." She gestured around her office. "I've done this job for almost twenty years. I'm forty-five years old. Call it mid-life crisis or whatever, I'm ready for a change."

"Your call, counselor. We're both out on a limb here."

She sat straight in her chair, looked toward the door. A clear sign that the conversation needed to shift. "You can do your work from here. I suspect we have a better firewall than your home system. I'll find you a desk and computer."

Ten minutes later, Zack sat in an associate's cubicle, logged into one of the firm's computers. First, he checked his personal e-mail for a message from Dennis with the toxicology report. Nothing. *ER must be unusually busy today.*

He opened a new browser page and navigated to the Bethesda Metro Hospital physicians' site and logged into it, pleased that he still had access. It took a few minutes for him to remember how to get into the hospital's virtual private network. Unlike attending physicians in other specialties, ER docs didn't often use the remote feature of the electronic health record system. Zack remembered only one other time he had used it from home, a year or two ago to check on an interesting patient he'd turned over at change of shift.

He found the on-line instructions and navigated the VPN log-in process, which required a password change because too much time had elapsed since his last usage. He thought for a minute, then entered *E1M3dico@sesino!* Once in the system, he considered that he was about to commit what HIPAA defined as a criminal act.

What's another criminal charge at this stage?

Zack searched the directory and found the listing for Carl Barnett. With a deliberate hand, he clicked on the icon to access Carl's medical records. He began with the first ER visit when he evaluated Barnett for chest pain. The record contained a synopsis of that visit, along with Zack's detailed documentation of the findings, conclusion, and discharge. He pulled up the serial EKGs, which to his surprise were identical to the ones in his original copies of the record. He reasoned that the version in the EHR was the same as the one in cardiology, not the paper copy that someone had altered; or perhaps someone had revised the record again after Sevati gave him the true version. *Flotsam out to sea.* He wished he had such a simple problem to solve now.

Next, he studied the record from his failed resuscitation of Carl Barnett the next day. Nothing unusual there. He delved deeper into the EHR to search Carl's past medical history. Again, nothing remarkable. Other than some executive physicals, he'd had no other medical events, no indications of a man destined to die an untimely death. To be thorough, Zack reviewed all of Barnett's lab, x-ray, and pharmacy records. Nothing.

Before he moved on to search Janice Barnett's record, he checked his e-mail again. Still nothing from Dennis. Impatient, he decided to review his own record from the recent near-death and CCU admission. Nothing spectacular there, although he was impressed with Sevati's detailed, articulate summary, which made no mention of cocaine as a possible etiology for Zack's suspected acute coronary spasm. He pulled up the lab results and clicked on *Toxicology Screen*. When the page came up, his heart stuttered, and his breath quickened. He read the single line of text several times to be sure he was not fooling himself.

Negative for all drugs tested.

He grabbed his phone and called Dennis. It went to voice mail without ringing. Dennis would still be on duty in the ER, maybe couldn't answer. Zack left a message, "Dennis, it's Zack. I never got an email with the tox screen results. Please send it at your earliest opportunity or call me."

Zack printed a copy of the toxicology report. Staring at the black text on white paper made it more real—and disconcerting. *Negative for all drugs tested.*

What the hell?

He moved on to review Janice Barnett's record. It took a few seconds to navigate to it. No surprise, her attending physician was also Jerry Hartman. *Birds of a feather.* While her record contained more information than Carl's, Zack didn't find much of interest or significance. Her reproductive history listed one miscarriage in her late teens, and one live birth. *We know about that one.* She'd had one admission for pneumonia five years ago, and a history of migraines since her mid-twenties. She overdid the narcotics a bit from time to time, but no signs of any chronic or current opioid abuse. Zack started a thorough review of her pharmacy history.

His phone buzzed, a text message from Dennis King. *ER slammed. Can't talk. Hospital counsel says not to send tox report. Sry.*

Hospital counsel? He asked the frigging attorney? The most risk-averse guy on the planet? Of course, the lawyer would tell Dennis not to share that report with Zack. *What a stupid move.* Unless Dennis did it on purpose to generate an excuse not to share it. Why would he do that? More important, why did he tell Zack it was positive for cocaine, with the negative result documented in the EHR? He resolved to confront Dennis once his shift was done.

Zack returned to the EHR to review Janice's pharmacy record. Over the years, she'd had multiple prescriptions for narcotics, mostly to treat her migraines. The frequency of opioid prescriptions declined after Jerry started her on ergotamine. That made sense.

He was about to click off when he noticed an interruption in the regular pattern of ergotamine refills. He double-checked the dates. She got her usual monthly prescription a week before Carl's chest pain episode; and an extra one, out of sequence, the day after he died. Scrolling the remainder of her medication history, Zack found another extra prescription the day before his near-death in the ER. He clicked through to the details of the individual prescriptions. Like sunlight dispersing heavy clouds, the chaos in his life turned crystal clear.

Zack stared at the computer screen as he processed the information in front of him. He didn't want to believe it. He searched his brain for another explanation, but the more he pondered, the better the pieces fit. He squeezed his eyes shut, rubbed his face with his hands, then looked back at the computer screen. The vision of naked truth seized his breath and constricted his chest. He reached out to shut off the computer, to wipe the image from his brain. At the last minute, he printed it instead.

When he entered Bridget's office without knocking, her face erupted in shock at his appearance. "Zack. What's wrong.?"

He handed her the printout. "I found the murder weapon."

CHAPTER SEVENTY-EIGHT

In his haste to catch Dennis before the end of his ER shift, Zack eschewed the Metro and borrowed Bridget's Range Rover. Wary, she passed him the key. "I'll Uber home," she said. "Bring it back in one piece. You too. In one piece. Please."

To his dismay, he encountered stop-and-go traffic heading north on Wisconsin Avenue. By the time he broke loose onto Old Georgetown Road, he sped the rest of the way to the hospital and arrived at 6:15. Too late? Maybe not. Night had fallen. He pulled the Rover into the physician parking lot and drove slowly up and down the rows searching for Dennis' Jaguar. He turned the final corner and spotted it near the end of the row.

He's still here. Zack started to maneuver into an empty space when the Jaguar's taillights blinked on, then the backup lights. Dennis was already in his car. He backed out of the space, maneuvered in the opposite direction from where Zack had stopped, and headed for the exit.

Zack was half-way out of the Range Rover, intending to catch Dennis before he left, but he was too far away. He jumped back into the SUV, started it up, and hurried from the space he'd half-way entered. He would follow Dennis home, confront him there. *More private anyway.* He departed the lot a few car lengths behind the Jaguar, then settled in behind it to follow at a discreet distance. Zack figured Dennis wouldn't pay particular heed to another SUV on the road. There were so many in the National Capitol Area.

To Zack's surprise, instead of continuing on Old Georgetown Road toward Dennis' Rockville home, the Jag turned left onto Greentree Road. Was Zack following the wrong car? He ran the red light to turn onto Greentree, then risked moving closer to the Jag so he could check the license plate. ERDOC1. Dennis' car, but not headed home.

Zack followed and almost lost Dennis as he made a series of abrupt turns before settling onto Bradley Boulevard. Minutes later, he made a right turn onto River Road. A few miles later, the Jag turned into an exclusive neighborhood in Potomac. Zack followed, but decelerated to drop further behind to avoid being spotted. He lost sight of the Jag. The short bending road ended at a T-intersection. The Rover's GPS indicated that the crossing street was a continuous circle. Zack looked left and right, but saw no taillights. He turned left and accelerated, figuring he would either catch up to the Jag from behind or, if Dennis had gone the opposite direction, encounter it from the front. Either way, Dennis would not recognize the Range Rover.

He completed the full circle and arrived back at the original cross street. No sign of the Jag. Dennis must have turned into one of the dozen or so mansions along the circle. Zack slowed the Rover to a crawl, looking left and right, searching. Nothing. Could Dennis have driven out of the neighborhood while Zack circled? Why? Perhaps Zack had missed the Jag in one of the driveways. He made a Y-turn and reversed course, again driving at slow pace, looking left and right into each driveway. He'd almost completed the full circle when he saw the Jaguar's nose jutting out from behind a tree inside a circular drive. It was parked under a portico in front of a mansion. *What the—?*

Worried that someone had seen him driving twice around the circle like a criminal scoping it out, Zack drove past the manse's driveway, turned back onto the cross street, then stopped at the side of the road. He pulled out his phone and called Bridget. "Can you get hold of Dominic? Need an address lookup and some photos."

As he drove away, Zack had a new thought; a memory from a long-ago conversation with his mentor. He pulled to the side of the road to do a search on his phone. He found Dennis King's bio on a physician information website. Where did he attend medical school? *Universidad Autonoma de Guadalajara*—a common alternative pathway to a legitimate MD degree for qualified applicants not accepted to US medical schools.

CHAPTER SEVENTY-NINE

Two days later, Bridget, Ange, Dennis King, and Zack waited in Bridget's conference room for the arrival of Janice Barnett and Roger Meadows.

Zack and his two attorneys had conceived a strategy that carried significant risk to the individuals and the firm. Once Bridget got a reluctant green light from her partners, she called Roger Meadows to report that Dr. Winston had agreed to discuss settlement on two conditions: first, it had to happen within forty-eight hours; second, all interested parties must be present. Roger agreed. Zack had requested that Dennis attend the meeting as his mentor and supervisor, and to function as an emergency medicine expert if needed. Neither of them mentioned the toxicology screen.

Bridget looked at her watch. She had insisted they not resort to the make-them-wait game Meadows played on his turf. "We don't need to show we're in control."

The first score went to the opposition, because Zack's team now waited on its home field.

Thirty minutes after the scheduled time, the plaintiff's team arrived in the front lobby. From his position in the glass-enclosed conference room, Zack watched as they shed raincoats and parked umbrellas. Surprised, Zack glanced at Bridget, but she remained stone-faced. A receptionist escorted four people to the conference room: Roger, Janice, Keisha, and—Jerry Hartman.

They stood when the visitors entered the room. Awkward handshakes and formal, albeit not pleasant, greetings passed all around. The ferret offered lame excuses about slow traffic due to the cold mid-December rain. Formalities complete, the four took seats on the opposite side of the conference table from Zack and his colleagues. Unlike Zack's depositions, there were no cameras in the room.

Once all were seated, Bridget began the meeting. "Thank you for coming over here. Apologies for the weather."

"No problem," Roger Meadows said. "Doctor Hartman is a last-minute addition, but we assumed you wouldn't mind. He agreed to join us after we learned Doctor King would be here on your side."

Bridget looked at him, expressionless. "We welcome Doctor Hartman to the discussion."

"Thank you," Meadows said. "Let's begin."

"To be clear," Bridget said, "this is a conference to discuss possible settlement of the case. Unlike a deposition, it is off the record in hopes of enabling honest, productive dialogue. All are welcome to take notes, but there will be no formal documentation of the meeting. Whatever notes we take or discussion we have will not be discoverable should this litigation continue to further depositions and/or trial. Also, standard rules of evidence do not apply. That means, among other things, that Mr. Meadows and I won't enter objections for the record. Does everyone understand the ground rules?"

Heads nodded all around.

"Doctor Winston asked for this meeting," Bridget said, "so I would like him to open the discussion."

Zack cleared his throat and faced Janice Barnett, who—by design or coincidence—sat directly across the table from him. "Mrs, Barnett, Janice, I am deeply sorry for your loss. I assure you we did everything in our power to save Carl when he arrived in cardiac arrest."

Janice stared at him, implacable, more like a statue than a human being—except for angry eyes that bore into him. He glanced away for a second, then re-established eye contact. "As for Carl's visit the previous day, I've scrutinized my evaluation and care from all conceivable angles. I'm convinced beyond any doubt I was not negligent."

Janice fixed Zack with an icy stare. "Not convinced."

"Regardless," Zack said, "this process over the last year has sapped me. I'm ready to get it done. Today. That's why I asked Ms. Larsen to call the meeting. I hope we can end this now, and all get on with our lives."

Janice cast a fleeting glance at Dennis, who sat to Zack's left, before she turned to Roger Meadows as if to cue him.

Meadows shuffled a pile of documents in front of him, removed his glasses, and glared at Bridget. "You are wasting everyone's time here, counsel. Why on earth would my client settle now when she can count on a full award at trial?"

Bridget spoke in a matter-of-fact voice. "We have a different opinion. We're prepared to go to trial, where we expect full exoneration of my client."

Meadows threw up his hands. "What have you been smoking, *Bridge*?" He leaned forward, sneering. "Or have you and your client been snorting coke together?"

Bridget glared at him. "This discussion may be off the record, *Rog*, but I expect you to keep it civil. Any more abusive comments and I will have you removed."

Both attorneys remained locked in their aggressive postures, like two gunslingers about to draw. To Zack's surprise, the ferret blinked first. "Fine. Your turf, your rules. Do try to keep it within the realm of reality. Don't try to bluff us with bogus proclamations of certain victory."

"Back at you," Bridget said.

An uncomfortable silence descended over the room, during which Zack witnessed brief eye contact between Jan and Dennis, and on the opposite end of the table, between Ange and Keisha. Jerry Hartman stared at the ceiling.

Bridget broke the silence. "At the time of Doctor Winston's last deposition, you offered to settle for three-and-half million."

Meadows laughed. "That fell off the table twenty-four hours after the deposition, as advertised. In the interim, your client almost killed himself with cocaine while on duty in the emergency department. He's an impaired physician whose fitness to practice medicine is in serious doubt. When that information comes out at trial, the jury will find for Mrs. Barnett."

"Is that so?" Bridget said. She turned to Zack. "Doc, did you take cocaine on duty in the ER? Ever?"

"Never."

She turned back to Roger. "Whatever would give you that idea?"

Meadows hesitated, calculating. "It's in his medical record."

"Really? How would you know that?"

For the first time in this long ordeal, Zack saw Roger Meadows on his heels.

Meadows spoke in an uncharacteristic waning voice. "From a reliable source. I'm in process of obtaining copies by way of discovery." He tried to regain the objective. "I suggest you do the same, counselor. You will find the evidence quite damning."

Bridget reached into her file folder and pulled out a sheaf of papers. She tossed them across the table at Roger. "Is this the record you mean?"

Meadows skimmed the documents. Janice and Jerry both looked. Zack sensed Dennis craning to see it too.

"It might be," Roger said. "I can't be sure this is a valid copy."

"It is," Bridget said. "We have the original, certified, which we will produce at trial if needed." All eyes turned to Bridget. "Please look at the toxicology report there, Roger. I believe it's the last page in the document."

All eyes shifted to Roger as he shuffled to the back of the stack. Janice and Jerry inched closer for better visibility. Dennis moved to the edge of his chair.

"It's negative for cocaine, isn't it?" Bridget said. "Or any other drug."

As if on involuntary reflex, Janice and Roger both cast not-so-furtive glances at each other, then at Dennis. Jerry Hartman stared ahead, making no effort to conceal his displeasure. Dennis remained stiff, avoiding eye contact. Meadows shrugged, pushed the document back across the table to Bridget. "We will reserve judgment until we see the original record, if it exists in an unaltered state."

"I assure you it does," Bridget said. "But let's move on. In light of this new information, what are you prepared to offer my client by way of settlement?"

"I need to confer with my client."

"Fine. We'll give you the room. How much time do you need?"

Roger looked at Janice. "Ten minutes?"

She nodded.

As Bridget, Zack, Ange, and Dennis left the room, Bridget paused at the door to address Roger. "Oh, I almost forgot to mention this." She walked back into the room, and—taking full advantage of her height—leaned across the table over Roger and Janice. "If either of you, or your 'source' obtained a copy of Doctor Winston's medical record without authorization, that would constitute a HIPAA violation. As you know, willful violations carry severe civil and criminal penalties."

Roger and Janice stared back in silence.

"Okay," Bridget said, "we'll leave you to it. Have a nice chat."

CHAPTER EIGHTY

While Dennis bolted to the rest room, Bridget, Ange, and Zack huddled in Bridget's office.

"So far, so good," Zack said.

"You're doing great," Bridget said. "Just keep to the script."

Through the glass, Zack saw Dennis leave the rest room and wander toward the lobby. He gestured in that direction. "Did you all catch his eye contact with Janice?"

"I did," Bridget said.

"I'm going out there."

Bridget touched his arm. "Be careful."

Zack walked up to Dennis in the lobby. "I appreciate your being here, Boss. Means a lot to have you at my side."

"Hope it helps." Dennis' eyes focused past Zack.

"Did you ever find out why that initial tox screen was reported as positive?"

Dennis shrugged. "Lab error. Preliminary results got transposed between you and another patient. It happens. That's why we wait for validation."

"In this case, to our advantage."

Dennis looked Zack in the face. "Doesn't mitigate what was found in your jeans. Regardless of how this case turns out, we need to deal with that."

That sounded like a threat. Zack gave him a hard stare. "Maybe we'll find an answer for that too." He saw Roger Meadows standing at the door of the conference room. Ange and Bridget walked in that direction. "They're ready for us." He clapped Dennis on the shoulder. "Thanks again, friend."

Jerry Hartman walked past them, on his way from the rest room. He avoided eye contact.

O nce they had resumed their seats, all eyes turned to Roger Meadows. "Three million," he said.

Bridget guffawed and pitched forward, as if about to blow her lunch. Recovering, she smiled. "Get serious. No way."

Meadows leered at her. "We can sit here and negotiate all day, at the end of which we'll walk away with a three-million-dollar settlement. Winston said he's ready to settle. Let's do it now so we can all beat the traffic home." He waved a dismissive hand at Zack. "Not his money anyway."

Bridget rested her chin on her hands, stared across at the table at Janice, Roger, and Jerry in sequence, then fixed her gaze on Roger. She spoke in a quiet, confident voice. "No."

Meadows threw up his hands. "You not only waste our time, but you insult us with your attitude. Make a reasonable counteroffer or we leave."

With chin still resting on her hands, Bridget paused for full effect, then batted her eyelids at Roger. "We think you should drop the suit entirely."

Meadows slammed his hand on the table. "Ridiculous." He turned to Janice. "Let's go, Jan." They both stood. Roger glowered at Zack. "We'll see you in court."

Bridget blocked their path to the door. Wearing heels, she stood a foot taller than either of them. "I insist that you sit down and listen to why dropping the suit will be in your own best interests."

Meadows scoffed. "Why the hell should we do that?"

"Because this case will never go to trial, no matter what you do. Instead, your client will face criminal charges."

Janice uttered a slight gasp. Meadows stood his ground. "That's a bold statement."

"Sit down," Bridget said. "You'll understand when we're done."

CHAPTER EIGHTY-ONE

The ferret looked ready to rip Bridget to shreds with razor teeth. After glaring at Bridget for a few seconds, he led his client back to their respective seats at the conference table.

Roger crossed his arms. "Off the record, non-discoverable, correct?"

Bridget returned to her seat. "As we said at the beginning."

"Proceed."

Bridget tossed her head, hair billowing around her neckline. "We reserve the option to enter any of this material into evidence should we fail to reach an agreement today."

Roger scowled. "Get on with it."

Ange produced several documents from a thick file folder. Bridget passed them across the table to Roger. Janice scanned the documents and gasped. Zack wished Dominic Soprano were in the room so he could hug him.

"Where did you get these?" Janice said, her voice harsh, eyes threatening.

Roger extended a hand to settle her. He glared at Bridget, "I assume you can show cause for invading my client's personal financial records?"

Bridget nodded. "As you will see."

A tense chill infused the room. Roger Meadows and Janice Barnett looked like cornered, dangerous animals. "I need to confer with my client," the ferret said.

"Five minutes," Bridget said. She gestured, and her team vacated the room to the adjoining lobby. Dennis rushed to the bathroom. Through the glass, Bridget, Ange, and Zack watched Roger and Janice conversing feverishly. Jerry occupied the edge of the conversation, not a participant. Keisha sat apart, inscrutable.

At precisely five minutes, Bridget ushered them back into the conference room. Janice sat with arms and legs crossed, staring at the table. Roger Meadows spoke in a steady, firm voice. "My client's financial status has no bearing on this case. This won't be admissible at trial. Further, you obtained this information illegally, so if you do introduce it, you can expect punitive consequences. You know all that. I'm curious, *Bridge*, why you brought it in here."

Bridget glanced around the room, her eyes fixed briefly on Dennis. "For the benefit of those in the room who can't see the documents in front of Mr. Meadows, they show that shortly before Carl Barnett died, he sequestered all his assets so that Mrs. Barnett could not access any of his money. They further show that Mrs. Barnett made monthly financial contributions via cashier's checks to a foster mother named Yolonda Davis."

Meadows held up his hand. "Stop. None of that has any bearing on whether or not Dr. Winston committed malpractice."

Bridget grinned at him. "Thought you all would want to know what we know, but if you're not interested . . ."

Meadows huffed but did not respond. Bridget looked at Janice Barnett, who continued to stare at the table. Bridget shrugged. "Okay, then. Let's move on. You can keep those copies. We have others."

Ange handed Bridget another set of pages. Bridget addressed Roger. "Please refer again to the financial documents passed to you a few minutes ago. I have exact copies in front of me." Roger did so. Janice and Jerry leaned in to read along with him. "Referring to the last three pages,"

Bridget said, "please note the highlighted entries, all of which document first class plane tickets, for two people, plus hotel suites, to the following locations and venues: Bermuda, Hotel Atlantis; Key West, Eden House; Cancun, Fiesta Americana. Please also note copies of actual hotel receipts, showing in each case a luxury suite, double occupancy."

Across the table, Janice's complexion turned from pallid to fiery red. "Where did you get these?"

Bridget ignored her. "On the next page, please note a Regent cruise to the Virgin Islands, luxury suite, two occupants."

Roger fumed. "This means nothing to our case. Stop your bullying."

Bridget shot him a condescending smile but said nothing. She addressed Jerry Hartman. "Doctor Hartman, were you the plus-one with Mrs. Barnett on these trips?"

"No."

"Can you prove it?"

"I can document that during each of those time intervals I was attending to patients in my office or the hospital, or else on separate travel to different locations."

"Really?" Bridget said. "So, someone other than you has been sleeping with Mrs. Barnett in luxury beds all over the Caribbean?"

"Enough of this," Roger said.

Ange handed Bridget other photos. Bridget turned to Dennis. "Doctor King, you may want to look over Mrs. Barnett's shoulder so you can see these photos as well."

Dennis appeared shaken. For a moment he remained in place, then regained his composure. He walked around the table to stand behind Janice.

"One question for you, Doctor King. What model car do you drive?"

Dennis flushed. "Jaguar XJ."

Bridget glanced at her notes. "Maryland license plate ERDOC1?"

Dennis' eyes widened. He responded in a hoarse voice. "Yes."

Roger Meadows sat with arms folded and legs crossed. Had the ferret conceded?

Bridget pushed the first photo across the table. "Mrs. Barnett, this is your house in the photo, correct?"

Janice sat with arms and legs crossed, face livid. "You know it is."

"Right," Bridget said. "Doctor King, is that your Jaguar XJ, license number 'ERDOC1,' in the driveway?"

Dennis spoke in a near-whisper. "Yes."

Bridget continued. "Note the date and time stamp on the photo. Two days ago."

"If you say so," Janice said.

Bridget pushed a second photo across the table. "Same location, the next morning. Same Jaguar in the same spot in the driveway. Hasn't moved a centimeter." She looked from Janice to Dennis. "Did you two sleep together that night?"

Neither answered.

"Wasn't your first night together, was it?"

Roger lurched from his seat. "Stop. You might prove that Mrs. Barnett and Doctor King had an affair. Other than the personal embarrassment to them, so what? You can't bring that into court, and it has no bearing on the merits of our malpractice case." He began gathering his files. "I'm sure this has been very entertaining for you and your client, but we're done playing." He motioned to the people on his side of the table. "Let's go, folks."

As they started to move, Bridget addressed Jan and Dennis. "Your choice. You can hear the rest now, or you can hear it in open court."

Janice stopped, stared at Bridget, looked at Dennis, then resumed her seat. Dennis asked Jerry to vacate his chair, then took the seat next to Janice.

"Figured you'd see it that way," Bridget said. "Doctor Hartman, you're free to go if you choose. Roger, you may take your seat again, or stand there and gawk. I don't care."

Meadows returned to his seat. Jerry took a seat at the end of the table.

"One more reference to the documents in front of you," Bridget said, "then we'll move on to something else." Roger, Janice, and Dennis peered at the documents. "Pages thirteen and fourteen," Bridget said. "Phone records from Mrs. Barnett and Doctor King."

Dennis looked at her then Zack.

Bridget stood, towering over them, crossed her arms. "We've established a personal relationship between the two of you, so we don't need to pore over all the phone calls and texts from the last three years. I only want to point out a couple. First, a thirty-three-second conversation on the evening of Carl Barnett's death; second, a fifty-five-second call in the evening after Doctor Winston's second deposition. Rather coincidental, don't you think?"

Janice said nothing. Roger glared at Bridget. Dennis sank lower in his chair.

CHAPTER EIGHTY-TWO

Bridget looked around the table. "Does anyone need a break before we move on?" No one moved or spoke. "Very well," she said. "We really are almost done." Ange handed her another set of documents. Bridget did not pass them across the table, but set them beside her, upside down.

"Mrs. Barnett, you suffer from migraine headaches, right?"

Janice looked at Roger Meadows. He nodded. "Yes," she said.

"What medication do you take for your migraines?"

Meadows raised his hand. "Stop. You will not interrogate my client here. If you want to do that, you'll wait for trial."

Bridget shook her head. "I think she would rather answer my questions here, off the record. Right, Mrs. Barnett?"

Janice replied with an almost imperceptible nod.

"I'll take that as permission to continue." Her eyes bored into Janice. "We know you take ergotamine for your migraines."

Janice stared at her, eyes smoldering.

Bridget addressed Roger. "I planned to ask Doctors Hartman and King, as 'uninvolved' experts, to explain the actions of ergotamine, but I suppose you'll interrupt in the same way you did with Mrs. Barnett."

"Damn right," the ferret said.

"Okay, then Doctor Winston can summarize, just to be sure we're all on the same level of understanding." She turned to Zack. "Please be brief, Doc. They seem about out of patience."

Zack cleared his throat, glanced at Dennis. "Ergotamine has similar effects as epinephrine. Among other actions, in high doses it can cause coronary artery spasm, which can induce chest pain or fatal arrhythmias."

Roger started to speak, but a gesture from Bridget stopped him. "Thank you, Doctor Winston. Mr. Meadows was about to say that's not relevant, so I'll just acknowledge his concern and proceed." She turned over the pages in front of her. "Here I have a copy of Mrs. Barnett's pharmacy records."

"How would you have that?" Roger said. "Unless you invaded her private health records."

"As you did with Doctor Winston's? Pot to kettle, *Rog.*" The ferret slunk back into his hole. Beside him, Janice glowered. Dennis appeared ready to charge at Bridget.

"In brief," Bridget said, "Mrs. Barnett received regular monthly prescriptions for ergotamine from her usual physician, Dr. Hartman here, except on two occasions. The first was an extra prescription filled the day after Mr. Barnett's death; the second on the day before Dr. Winston's episode of chest pain and near-fatal ventricular fibrillation." She fixed her gaze on Janice. "Those prescriptions were ordered by Dr. Dennis King, the man with whom you've had an affair for the last three years; the man whom you've taken on expensive trips and cruises. Am I correct, Mrs. Barnett?"

"Stop it!" Janice's voice shook.

Bridget turned to Keisha. "Miss Rollins, you've been mighty quiet through all this. Are you prepared to tell us what you saw in Mr. Meadows' office?"

The ferret raged at Keisha. "If you answer, you're fired." Keisha stood, walked around the table, and sat next to Ange.

Bridget faced her. "Miss Rollins, when did you first meet Dr. King?"

"Just today, when they all came into the room."

"Have you ever seen him before today?"

"I've seen Dr. King several times in Mr. Meadows' office. I didn't know who he was then. One of those times, Mrs. Barnett was also there."

A deep pall descended over the room, and for a minute no one spoke. Roger shuffled his papers, stuffed them into his briefcase, and stood. Janice and Dennis sat like stones, staring straight ahead. Jerry studied the ceiling. Bridget picked up her briefcase and set it on the table. "No one leaves this room."

She stared at Janice, forcing the woman look back at her. "Mrs. Barnett, who is Chantal Davis?" Janice did not answer. "She was born Amanda Barnett, right?" Still no response from Janice. "She wasn't Carl Barnett's child, was she?" A tear appeared at the corner of Janice's eye, and she yielded an almost imperceptible nod. Bridget's voice turned soft. "Carl made you give her up, didn't he?" Another slight nod from Janice. "But you found her and supported her for seven years."

Janice answered in a muffled voice. "Yes."

Bridget spoke like a mother to a suffering daughter. "When Carl found out, he shut you off financially, intended to divorce you. Your nursing income couldn't keep up the payments to the foster mother, right?"

Janice's eyes moistened. "Yes."

"You and Dennis conjured a plan to get rid of Carl and make some money, right?"

Roger put a hand across Janice's mouth. "Do not answer that."

Bridget moved closer to Janice. "You overdosed Carl with ergotamine, enough the first day to cause chest pain; then a massive dose the next day to produce the fatal cardiac arrhythmia."

Roger kept his hand over Janice's mouth. "Do not speak." He snarled at Bridget. "You can't prove any of that."

Bridget shrugged. "I'm no prosecutor, but it sounds like a credible case for murder." She patted her briefcase. "As you know, I have some, uh, connection with the US Attorney."

Roger sat back, crossed his arms and legs, fuming. "How much to settle?"

Bridget shook her head. "I'm not done. After their plot to plant a damning EKG into Carl Barnett's medical record failed, these two used the same pharmacological means to strike down and frame Zack Winston while on duty." Jan and Dennis both shuffled in their chairs. Bridget spoke to them directly. "First, you tried to discredit his integrity by revealing his redacted history from the naval hospital. When that didn't work, Dr. King planted a used packet of cocaine in Dr. Winston's jeans and laced his sport drink with ergotamine. I believe you simply intended to discredit him, but you damn near killed him. At least you had enough integrity left to save his life." Dennis stared as if he could strangle her.

Roger deflated. "You win, Bridget. We'll drop the suit."

"You have no choice. It's too late for deals, Rog. Your complicit role pales in comparison to murder and attempted murder, but it appears you colluded, at least in the plot to discredit Dr. Winston. When I'm done pulling that string, you'll never practice law again."

Without a word, Meadows stormed out of the room.

Bridget glanced at Zack. His cue to watch Dennis. *"No es todo,"* she said in perfect Spanish. She patted her briefcase. *"Aqui tenemos evidencia de un cartel de drogas y su jefe, algun 'El Medico Asesino,' para compartir con las autoridades apropriadas."*

Dennis bolted from the room. His shoulder struck Bridget's as he left. On purpose. Janice hurried after him.

"Meeting over," Bridget said.

Through the glass, Zack watched Dennis stride toward the elevator. He was glad his former mentor didn't have a gun.

CHAPTER EIGHTY-THREE

After a brisk, rain-spattered walk from the office, Bridget, Ange, Keisha and Zack were trying to celebrate victory in the crowded bar at Old Ebbitt Grill. They stood together in a tight group, not talking much, each savoring the thrill of victory; or in Zack's case, the fear of what might happen next. They had not only succeeded in getting the lawsuit dropped, but they had flushed out *"El Medico Asesino."* That thought sent a shudder through his body. Bridget's mood seemed to match his own, whereas Ange and Keisha—unaware of the deeper realities—chattered like college girls on spring break.

Ange spotted a booth opening and made a beeline for it with Keisha in tow. Bridget started to follow them, but Zack touched her arm. She stopped. Due to the noise in the pub, he leaned in to make himself heard. "You were magnificent today."

Bridget returned a genuine, warm smile. "You too. We make a good team."

At a loss for words, he sipped his Oban single malt with one rock. She did the same with her Laphroaig. He looked at her, troubled. "Not over, is it?"

A serious look came over her. "The lawsuit is dead." She leaned closer to him, tone confidential. "But we woke the dragon."

Zack scowled. "Are we in danger?"

She glanced toward the ceiling. "Maybe. I'll know more after I talk to Marshall." She shrugged. "We can discuss that tomorrow. Tonight, you should celebrate."

He shrugged. "Don't feel like it."

"We should at least join the girls." She took him by the hand and led him to the booth where Ange and Keisha engaged in animated conversation. Age-wise, Bridget and Zack could be their parents. A brief wave of sadness washed over him.

Ange jumped out of the booth and hugged him, planted a wet kiss on his lips. "I am so happy for you." She released him and reclaimed her seat across from Keisha, patting the spot beside her for Zack. He glanced at Bridget, who smiled and pushed into the booth next to Keisha. As soon as Zack sat, Ange put her hand on his knee beneath the table. His other knee touched Bridget's.

Jerry Hartman appeared at the table. "Figured I might find you folks here."

Zack jumped up, shook Jerry's hand with vigor, then went all in with a bear hug. "Thank you so much, Jerry."

"Happy to help nail those two," Jerry said. "Janice has had it coming for a long time. The final straw was her attorney's shameless offer a couple weeks ago to co-opt me into helping them." A waiter brought a chair, and Jerry sat at the end of the table. "Can't stay long."

Zack grinned at him. "If you ever want to get out of medicine, you could do well as an actor, or an undercover investigator."

Ange addressed Jerry. "I heard you hated ER docs."

Jerry laughed. "It's an act. I do it for fun." He winked at Zack. "Keeps them on their toes."

"You had me fooled for a long time," Zack said. "Until the Walter Knowles case when you showed your true colors."

At the mention of Walter Knowles, they fell silent. A twinge of fear gripped Zack's chest. Ange broke the silence. She looked at Zack. "What was the deal with the cocaine lab results?"

"Dennis lied when he called about the preliminary. He planned to alter the record, like he did with the EKG, but I found the true result first."

"And the bag in your jeans?"

Bridget answered. "We had the jeans tested by a private lab. It was cocaine. I think we know who used the contents before the empty bag was planted."

The waiter brought appetizers, fresh mojitos for Ange and Keisha, and an Evolution IPA for Jerry. Zack and Bridget continued to nurse their scotches. Ange asked, "Bridget, what's going to happen to Janice and Dennis?"

Bridget's face turned sour. "Roger will get them a top-notch criminal defense lawyer. They won't spend a single night in jail."

"That ain't fair," Keisha said. "You shoulda heard the shit conversations happened in that place."

Bridget took a sip of scotch. "Our objective was to keep this malpractice case from going to trial, because we expected a jury would buy into the story of Zack's alleged substance abuse." Zack felt her knee press against his. "We never intended to make a solid case for murder. In truth, that case is weak because it's based on circumstantial evidence."

Zack frowned. "They walk?"

Bridget shrugged. "With tarnished reputations and no cash windfall. Expect them to leave town, depending on what Dennis does about his current marriage. In any event, they have to drop the lawsuit, and they think we have additional evidence to keep them at bay. We achieved our objective."

"Why did you talk in Spanish near the end? Ange asked.

"Private message," Bridget said. "Unrelated."

Ange looked skeptical. Zack raised his glass to divert attention. The others followed suit. "Thanks to you, counselor." He touched Bridget's glass and they made brief eye contact. He turned and touched Ange's glass. "And to you, dear friend." Then he touched Keisha's glass. "And to you." Finally, he touched Jerry's. "And you, sir." His gaze swept all of them. "You all saved my career. You saved my life." His eyes and Bridget's briefly met, a haze of uncertainty between them.

Keisha followed the toast with one of her own. "Here's to the best firing I've ever had."

Ange clinked her glass. "The only firing you've ever had, girlfriend."

"True," Keisha said. "I never thought I'd feel so happy about being unemployed."

Bridget turned to her. "That won't last. Wait a day or two to get some rest, then come see me. After what you did for us, we'll have a place for you in our firm."

Jerry Hartman downed the rest of his beer, swallowed a grilled oyster whole, then stood to leave. "Sorry to part such great company, but duty calls." He shook Zack's hand. "Congratulations, Zack. For the record, you can care for any of my patients, any time. You're a hell of a physician." He grinned. "For just another ER doc."

"Happy to bail your ass out of trouble any day, friend." They embraced, and Jerry left.

When Zack turned back to the table, Bridget was looking at her phone. "My husband is returning from Richmond. I need to pick him up at Union Station. She texted a reply on her phone, then motioned to the waiter. "Please ring up another round for these folks. You can bring it when they're ready, but I'll sign it now."

"We can pay," Ange said.

"You won't pay," Bridget said with such authority that Ange could not protest. She signed the tab, replaced her credit card in her wallet, and stood. "Walk me out, please, Zack."

"Of course."

CHAPTER EIGHTY-FOUR

Outside, the rain had intensified. Inside the front door, Zack helped Bridget with her raincoat. Pursing her lips, she picked up her umbrella in one hand, briefcase in the other. "I'll call you tomorrow to let you know how it goes with Marshall."

Zack hesitated, then touched her arm. "Call me anytime. About anything." He smiled. "What friends are for."

"I may take you up on that." She set down the briefcase, touched his shoulder. "What is it you navy guys say? Watch your six?"

Zack's shoulders tightened. "Did we overplay our hand?"

"We may have." She gazed into his eyes. "Be careful, Zack."

He pointed to her briefcase. "Are the contents that damning?"

She shook her head. "Not by themselves. Once I tell Marshall what happened today, he can steer the investigation in the right direction and maybe find something incontrovertible."

Zack saw fear in her eyes. "What's scaring you, Bridge? The conspiracy, or your husband?"

She looked away. "Nothing." She blinked her eyes. "I have to go. I'll call you tomorrow."

Zack shook her hand. "Thank you, Bridge, for everything." Neither let go. An awkward moment passed between them.

She cast a furtive glance around. "What the hell," she said. She hugged him, close and warm. He wanted to linger in her embrace, let her head drop onto his chest, savor the scent of her hair. She broke loose. "Take care, Zack." She pecked him on the cheek, turned, and rushed out the door into steady rain.

CHAPTER EIGHTY-FIVE

Zack lingered in the alcove. Images of Noelle in their happy days wafted through his brain; intimate moments forever lost. He should concentrate on their soul-blending times, spend less psychic energy reliving the final tragedy. Zack would always carry the pain of that night. He must allow an equal measure of joy and gratitude for the time that she was in his life. Few men had been as fortunate as he.

He weaved through the growing crowd at the bar to return to Ange and Keisha. A dark-haired woman turned and blocked his path. Noelle. "You deserve happiness, Zack. Follow your heart." Before he could react, she turned back to the bar to resume chatting with a friend. In profile, the woman was not Noelle. *An illusion?* He had heard her voice, real as it needed to be.

Back at the table, Ange and Keisha were well into the round Bridget had bought. A fresh glass of Oban with one rock waited at his place. He hesitated, then sat down next to Ange.

Keisha stood. "Glad you're back. My bladder is about to burst, but I couldn't leave the girlfriend by herself in this den of horny men. Be right back."

As soon as she left, Ange turned to him. "Is it still raining?"

He nodded. "It is."

Her eyes turned soft. "You still have that rain check."

"And we are having drinks," he said. "Except if I finish this one, you'll have to roll me out of here."

Keisha returned to the table. Zack raised his glass for another toast. "To two rising stars. I am fortunate and humbled to have you both on my team." They all clinked glasses. Zack made eye contact with both of them.

As the women worked on their drinks, Zack held his. Bridget's absence weighed on him. He thought about the strength of her personality, interspersed with moments of unadorned vulnerability. Like Noelle.

"Time for me to go," Keisha said.

"I'm ready too," Zack said.

Ange raised her eyebrows at his nearly full glass and shrugged. "Me too." She chugged the rest of her mojito.

At the front of the restaurant, they donned raincoats and retrieved umbrellas. An exiting crowd pushed them through the revolving doors. Standing on the sidewalk, they popped open umbrellas, which forced space between each of them. Ange looked at him. "Where did you park?"

"I took the Metro. Didn't want to trust myself driving home to Bethesda. Whatever the outcome of the meeting, it would not have been safe."

Keisha said, "I'll leave you two on your own. My car's down the street." She tilted her umbrella and gave Zack a big hug. "God bless you, Zack."

He hugged her back. "Thanks for what you did. Congratulations on your new job." Keisha kissed him on the cheek, hugged Ange, raised her umbrella, and headed down the sidewalk.

As Keisha walked away, Zack and Ange stood together, their umbrellas overlapping. "About that rain check," Ange said. "You're welcome to come to my place; go home in the morning when it's dry."

He returned her gaze, then shook his head a few millimeters in each direction. "I can't. Not tonight. I need to be alone."

Ange looked away. "Of course. I have no idea what you must be feeling right now."

"I don't either. Why I need to be alone. Figure it out."

She caressed his arm. "Be careful. Call me, or come over, anytime."

He nodded. "I know." They faced each other. Rain and wind whirled around them.

"My car's in our garage," she said. "We can walk together to I street."

They covered the distance within a few minutes, neither one speaking. At the corner, Ange stopped and turned to him. "Guess we say good-bye here."

Zack closed his umbrella, moved in under hers, and hugged her. "Thanks for being a true friend."

Ange tilted her face up to his. He couldn't tell if the drizzle on her cheeks was rain or tears. "Please take care."

Zack's mind swirled with the wind. "You too. I can't thank you enough for being there for me."

"Always." Ange turned, pulled her umbrella close to her head, and walked away. She didn't look back.

Cold rain pounded Zack as he watched her disappear down the sidewalk. Turning in the opposite direction, he headed toward the Metro station, his umbrella at his side. The rain drenched him, but he reveled in the feel of water soaking his hair, running down his face and neck, flowing under his jacket and shirt, down his back and legs, pooling in his Ferragamo loafers—like a cleansing shower. He ignored the passers-by who looked at him askance as he meandered at a leisurely pace, lost in thoughts of Noelle. And Bridget.

CHAPTER EIGHTY-SIX

By the time Zack reached McPherson Square Metro Station, his Ferragamos squished while icy, soaked socks chafed his feet. Entering the station, he wiped away water dripping from his hair into his eyes. He stood aside to let a clump of passengers precede him through the turnstile. Water pooled around him. As he stepped up to the turnstile, he heard a woman's voice call his name from behind. *Noelle.*

He turned. Not Noelle, but Ange. She ran toward him, her hair and clothes soaked. No umbrella. She closed the distance between them in seconds. Her frantic look and voice alarmed him. "It's Bridget. I tried to call but you didn't answer." Zack had not taken his phone off silent mode after the meeting. "Her husband called. She didn't pick him up and doesn't answer her phone."

Zack looked at his watch. Half an hour since Bridget left the restaurant. Union Station was less than fifteen minutes away. *Unless. . .* "Traffic?"

Ange shook her head, eyes desperate. "Marshall tried to call her three times and texted her twice. She never answered."

A jolt of panic seized Zack. He rushed past Ange toward the Metro exit, nearly toppling incoming commuters in his haste to get out. Clear of the bottleneck, he dropped his umbrella and broke into a full sprint—ignoring the socks rasping his feet. Ange followed. He saw her trailing a

295

block behind by the time he'd covered the two and a half blocks to the Franklin Tower parking garage.

Inside the garage, he dodged vehicles as he ran down the ramp to the private parking level. He came to an abrupt halt, searching for Bridget's Range Rover. Several vehicles were parked on that level, eerie in its subterranean stillness. No sign of hers. Had she been in an accident after she left the garage?

Zack walked in a circle around the dimly lit deck, intent on looking at every vehicle. Halfway around, his ears caught an ominous sound: rasping, desperate breathing from in front and to the left. He hurried in that direction, spotted the Range Rover almost obscured by a larger SUV.

Bridget's shoes lay strewn apart on the concrete behind the Rover's left bumper.

He rushed around the vehicle and found her, face down, blood staining her blond hair, a three-inch gash on the back of her head. Her head turned to the side in a pool of blood. Her chest and back convulsed in spasms as she gasped for air.

Zack knelt beside her and gently rolled her onto her back. She gagged, coughed, and spewed blood onto the purple blouse and white jacket already blotched with it. Her eyes widened in panic, stared at Zack. When she drew a deep breath, Zack heard a bubbling sound from her neck. He brushed away the blood-soaked hair. His heart jumped when he saw the deep, jagged slice across her throat.

Ange arrived, breathless. Her eyes went from Zack to Bridget. She gasped and grabbed her face.

"Call 911," Zack said. "Then shine your phone's light onto her face and neck so I can see." He heard Ange make the call as Bridget's breathing became more labored. She convulsed again, spewing blood into Zack's face. Her head fell back, and her breaths became irregular and shallow. She barely moved any air.

Ange knelt across from him and held the light as he'd requested. Bridget's lips had turned blue. Her eyes stared vacant into space. She stopped breathing.

Zack felt her neck. No pulse. He looked at Ange. "Do you know CPR?"

"In theory."

"Drop the phone. We need to keep her alive until EMS gets here." He grabbed her hands, pushed them together, and placed them over Bridget's sternum. "Compress."

Ange did as directed while Zack put his mouth around Bridget's lips, squeezed her nostrils shut, and blew air into her throat. Most of it bubbled out from the gash in her neck.

"Shit," he said. "Ruptured trachea." Where the hell were the paramedics? Not close enough to wait. He needed to ventilate Bridget's lungs immediately.

Half-formed images of Noelle's death and of his failure to save Melody Snyder flashed through Zack's brain. He cast a determined look at Bridget. "Not this time. Lady, you will not die."

He thrust his left pinky finger into the hole in Bridget's neck, felt for and found her trachea, then traced upwards to feel a crosswise half-inch slice between the rings of cartilage. He held his finger there as he blew air into Bridget's throat. A slight rise in her chest.

Not good enough.

Zack looked at Ange. Her purse hung in front of her from around her neck. "I hope to hell you've got a big pen in that purse. Pull it out, take it apart, and hand me the pointy end."

Ange fumbled with a pen. Blood welled up around Zack's finger. He pressed it over the hole in Bridget's trachea.

If I lose my place, I'll never find it again.

He held out his right hand. It shook as Ange placed the tubular end of the pen into it. "Give me light again."

Breathing hard, Zack tracked the tip of the pen along his finger until he felt the point next to where he was compressing the hole in Bridget's trachea.

Only get one shot.

He blinked and held his breath as he guided the pen past his fingertip through the hole and into the trachea. Stabilizing it in place with his right index finger and thumb, Zack blew into the protruding end. Bridget's chest rose. He blew again. Her chest rose again. He looked at Ange. "Resume compressions. Please don't knock this thing out of my grip."

The procedure had taken less than two minutes. They continued CPR for another minute when Zack heard a siren whoop above them, then the sound of a large vehicle descending the ramp, followed by the flashing red lights of an ambulance. Behind that, the blue lights of a police vehicle.

Two paramedics rushed to their aid. Zack addressed the first one. "Ruptured trachea, emergency airway in place. I need an endotracheal tube." The medic looked at him, skeptical. "I'm a fucking ER doc. Do it."

The medic disappeared. A police officer approached.

"I'm Dr. Zack Winston, emergency physician from Bethesda Metro Hospital and this woman will die if you interfere with what I'm doing to save her life."

The officer stepped back as the paramedic returned with an assortment of endotracheal tubes and an ambu bag. Another arrived carrying an oxygen tank and tubing.

"Give me a number six tube," Zack said. In seconds, a tube appeared in his hand. Bright auxiliary lights from the ambulance flooded the scene. His next move would be the trickiest, and potentially deadly. If he lost the trachea, he would never find it again in the welling pool of Bridget's blood.

Like Melody Snyder.

He glanced at Bridget's face. Her skin color had improved a little. Maybe they had kept her alive.

Perspiring even in the cold garage, Zack tracked the tip of the endotracheal tube alongside the pen and rested it at the edge of the hole. He took a deep breath and in one simultaneous motion withdrew the pen and slid the tube into the hole. His heart stopped when he felt resistance against the tube. Had he missed? Was the tube outside the trachea? Sweat dripped into his eyes. He took another deep breath, applied slight upward torque on the tube, then pushed it gently forward. In the bright light he saw the clear plastic tube's interior fog slightly. Air from Bridget's lungs. The tube was in the trachea. He advanced it further, a little less than two inches, so as not to enter a bronchus, and blew air into it. Bridget's chest rose, more than before. He blew again. Her chest rose again.

"I feel a slight pulse," a medic said.

"Inflate the balloon," Zack said. "Hook up the ambu with 100%. Do all those other good things you do." He held the tube in place while a medic connected it to the ambu bag and started ventilations. The other secured the tube in place so it couldn't move. Bridget's condition continued to slowly improve. Her skin color was almost normal, and her chest rose and fell with each squeeze of the bag.

Zack had saved her life.

He let go of the tube and moved aside. His face fell. Bridget remained unconscious as the medic squeezed air into her lungs. No trace of breathing on her own. Zack stepped back to let the paramedics start an IV and connect a cardiac monitor. "Sinus rhythm," one said.

He looked over the medic's shoulder. "Normal complexes. A bit of ST elevation consistent with transient hypoxia." His compartmentalized clinical assessment belied the terror in his heart. How long had she gone without oxygen? Had he rescued Bridget only to commit her to a permanent vegetative state? A fate worse than death?

A medic shone a light into Bridget's eyes. "Pupils sluggish but reactive." *Functional brainstem,* Zack thought. That said nothing about higher cortical functions like intellect, speech, cognition—the brilliant brain he admired. Tears filled his eyes, not from remorse but from rage.

CHAPTER EIGHTY-SEVEN

Zack wiped Bridget's blood from his hands to his trousers, reached into his back pocket to retrieve his wallet, then handed his photo ID and medical license to the police officer. "The victim is my attorney," he said.

Two more police cars arrived, and the officers began to set up a perimeter around the crime scene—including Bridget's Range Rover.

The officer handed Zack's documents back. "We'll need a statement, Doc."

"It will have to wait," Zack said. He pointed to where the medics were loading Bridget onto a gurney for transport to the hospital. "She's my first priority."

"At the hospital will be fine," the officer said and walked away to brief the incoming police.

What would Zack say in his statement? That Zack Winston, a disgraced emergency physician facing criminal charges, suspected his prominent leader and mentor of being a drug-dealer and murderer? Based on what evidence, Dr. Winston?

The paramedics wheeled the stretcher bearing Bridget toward the ambulance. "Will you ride along, sir? GW is the closest hospital."

Zack took a deep breath, nodded. He started to follow them when Ange appeared at his side. "I found her purse in the car, but her briefcase is missing."

His mind erupted around an array of disturbing images. Dennis storming out of the meeting room. Janice rushing out behind him. Carl Barnett. Walter Knowles. Roland Edwards. Almost Zack Winston, and now Bridget Larsen. Looking at Bridget, he decided. He whispered to Ange. "Where is your car?"

She looked puzzled. "Next level down, but why?"

The police had secured the scene and were moving on to the tedious task of investigating it. For the moment they had forgotten about Ange and him. He turned to her. "Give me your keys. Go with Bridget to the hospital. Text me what happens."

Ange stared at him in terror. "Zack—"

He held out his hand. "Keys. Now."

Ange shrank from Zack's threatening glare. A medic called to him. "Coming, Doc? We gotta go."

Zack pushed Ange toward the ambulance. "Go." She took her keys from her purse, handed them to Zack, and rushed toward the waiting vehicle.

A familiar voice whispered behind Zack. "How did Walter Knowles die?"

He turned. Noelle was not there. He rushed to the ambulance just as a paramedic was closing the back doors. "Wait. Give me an atropine autoinjector."

The medic looked askance, but the intensity in Zack's eyes and voice forced his compliance. He dug into a drawer, retrieved an autoinjector, and handed it to Zack. He closed the doors and the ambulance started to move. Zack walked along the side opposite the police gaggle. When it reached the ramp, the driver turned on the flashing red lights and the ambulance accelerated upwards. Zack was already sprinting down the ramp to the next level.

He found Ange's Honda FIT, jumped in, started it, and drove up the same ramp as the ambulance. A police officer stopped him at the exit. Zack handed over his credentials. "I'm Dr. Winston. That ambulance victim is my patient. I need to get to the hospital."

The officer nodded, handed back his ID and license, and motioned him out of the garage. As soon as he was out of sight, he pulled to the curb and opened the Waze app on his phone to find the fastest route to Potomac, Maryland. Thirty-four minutes via George Washington Parkway and I-495 to River Road. He prayed he would not be too late.

Time is life.

CHAPTER EIGHTY-EIGHT

With aggressive driving and risky lane-switching, Zack made good time on GW Parkway to I-495, where he hit snarled traffic at the American Legion Bridge crossing the Potomac River into Maryland. He knew from experience he had no escape route.

No doubt the police had begun their investigation of the attack on Bridget. Ange would tell them about the briefcase and the meeting in Bridget's office. How long would it take them to figure out why Dr. Winston had not shown up at the hospital, and where he had gone instead?

Halfway across the bridge, his phone buzzed. Text from Ange. *Bridget in surgery. Some improved. Still unconscious.*

He texted back. *Breathing?*

Not in ER.

Police?

All over me.

Stall.

A pause before she texted back. *Why?*

Best you don't know.

[Angry emoji]

Keep me posted on B.

K

He reached the end of the bridge, where traffic accelerated. In minutes, he exited on River Road and tried to remember his way to Janice Barnett's mansion.

CHAPTER EIGHTY-NINE

Zack reached Potomac in full dark of night. The rain had stopped, but remaining clouds blocked the moon and stars. After several wrong turns and dead ends, he found the circular street where he'd followed Dennis' car to what Zack now knew was Janice Barnett's home. He decided to take the longer route around the circle so he could approach from behind a strand of trees between the Barnett home and the one next to it.

As he passed the trees, he switched off the FIT's lights and swung left into the Barnett driveway. An immediate crumpling sound in front caused him to slam on the brakes. He had hit something. He slipped out of the vehicle, closed the door lightly to make no sound, and came around to see the familiar red Jaguar near the end of the driveway, pointed toward the street, its front end dented by the FIT's bumper. The license plate hung by a single screw. ERDOC1.

Positioned for a hasty exit?

Verifying the atropine injector was still in his jacket pocket, Zack edged around the Jag and continued alongside the driveway for about thirty yards to where it forked around a large evergreen, toward the garage on the right side of the house and the portico on the left. Zack went straight, bisecting the space between the two paths, and hid behind the tree. He had a clear view of the front of the house. The porch light was off.

Leaning out from behind the tree Zack scrutinized the house's windows, upstairs and down. No interior lights. Perhaps Dennis and Janice were in a rear-facing room; or they had already fled in Janice's car. Then why leave the Jag where it was? *Maybe they're in the garage.*

Zack hunched and crept around the evergreen tree toward the garage. The wind had picked up. He shivered. His clothes were damp and blood-smeared, shoes and socks soaked. They made a squishing sound with every step on the concrete. *So much for stealth.* Zack removed his shoes, dropped them to the ground, and inched toward the garage.

As he got closer, he spotted dim lights in the windows of the three garage doors. Zack took a deep breath and scurried across the driveway toward the corner of the garage. As soon as he broke out of the foliage, all the exterior house lights came on.

Motion sensor.

Zack dove between two small trees abutting the house next to the garage and hunkered down. What to do? A loud rolling noise startled him. The garage door lifted, illuminating the driveway. Janice Barnett's voice from inside. "Who's there?"

A chill ran up Zack's spine. He backed away, slowly, in the direction of the house. He bumped into something. A body. A strong left arm wrapped around his forehead, jerked his head back against someone's chest.

"Hello, Zack." Dennis King's voice. "I'm holding a number ten scalpel a half-centimeter from your carotid artery. Do as I say or I'll slice it open and watch you bleed to death here in the bushes." He pushed his body against Zack's back. "Walk to Janice, please. Slowly. Don't let me slip with this knife on your neck." Zack hesitated. He felt the sharp edge of the blade against his skin; enough to scratch but not cut it. "Now," Dennis said.

CHAPTER NINETY

Dennis pushed Zack into the garage. At the back wall, Janice activated the switch to roll the door closed. She wore a white coverall garment that protected her torso, arms, and legs.

A work bench extended along the rear of the garage; on top, an industrial spray canister that resembled a hand-held fire extinguisher, about twenty-four inches long by four inches in diameter. A wand and trigger-squeeze extended from its mouth. A device someone might use to kill weeds. Or insects. Or people.

Dennis moved around to face Zack. He also wore a protective cover-all garment. Atop his head, a military-style rubber gas mask that could be pulled over his face in a single motion. He brandished a blood-stained scalpel in Zack's face.

Bridget's blood.

"You never known when to quit, do you?"

Zack barely recognized his friend and mentor.

Eyes crazed; face twisted into diabolical grin, Dennis said, "Keep in mind I know just where to cut you."

Zack stared at him; his own eyes defiant. "You going to murder me too, Dennis? Surprised you'd resort to a knife. Why not make it look natural, like the others?"

Dennis smacked him across the face with the back of his free hand. "Shut up." He glanced at Janice and back to Zack, pointing the knife point at Zack's throat. "Don't speak or I'll do a cric and miss your trachea; like you did on Melody Snyder."

Zack held his tongue but continued to glare at Dennis. Janice approached them. Zack glanced at her, puzzled by the look in her eyes. Confusion? Panic? He looked back at Dennis and tilted his head toward the work bench, a question in his eye.

Dennis' expression turned more sinister. "Think you've figured it all out? I doubt it." Keeping the knife aimed at Zack, he moved to the workbench. Janice, nearer now to Zack, glanced between him and Dennis. In a quick, fluid motion, Dennis dropped the scalpel on the counter and picked up the canister. He faced Zack, canister in his left hand, spray wand in the other. "You don't know what you've done."

Janice moved closer, now beside Zack. She scowled at Dennis. "What are you talking about?"

Dennis recalibrated and smiled at her. "You know, love. What we did to your husband, how we tried to save your relationship with your daughter—until this idiot and his hotshot lawyer messed it up."

Zack looked at Janice. "You don't know the whole story, do you?"

Dennis pointed the spray nozzle at Zack's face. "Shut up." Zack raised his hands, signaling submission.

Janice stepped toward Dennis. "What don't I know?"

Dennis shot her a patronizing look. "Nothing."

"I don't believe you," she said. Defiant, she stepped forward, which put her between Zack and Dennis.

Dennis motioned Janice to move away from Zack. She stood her ground.

"Janice Barnett," Zack said to the back of her head, "Meet *El Medico Asesino,* the physician assassin who not only killed your husband and almost me, but also Walter Knowles, Roland Edwards, and . . ." He paused for full effect. "Almost Bridget Larsen." He stepped from behind Janice and glared at Dennis. "She's alive. Whatever you do to me, you are going down."

Dennis chortled. "How so? Not on the insipid contents of that briefcase." He gestured toward the workbench. Bridget's briefcase lay opened, the files and papers scattered around it. "She's got nothing on us."

"Us?" Zack didn't believe Dennis meant only Janice and him.

"You and your blond girlfriend have no clue how deep this goes. Neither does her philandering husband."

Zack wished he had texted Ange to send the police. He was on his own, however this played out. He needed a different approach.

"Why me, Dennis? Why did you set me up? We were friends. You rescued my career."

Dennis scoffed. "Zack, you are so naive. I marked your pitiful ass the first time you wandered into my office begging for redemption."

The harsh tone and words took Zack by surprise. "Nine years ago? You knew then you would use me?"

Dennis shrugged. "You think an elaborate plan comes together on the fly? What I'd expect from a JAFERD. You happened along at the right time. A few more pieces had to come together before we could execute."

"Execute," Zack said. "Interesting word. You executed Walter Knowles, didn't you?"

Dennis seethed. "Walter paid the price for betrayal. Just like—" He glanced at Janice and stopped talking.

Zack took note but pursued a different line. "We know about Knowles' role in your drug business, but why parathion? Why such a miserable death? Are you that sadistic?"

Dennis leered at him. "Proof of concept. For something you won't live to see." He flexed his hand over the canister's pistol grip.

Zack tilted his head toward Janice, who stood next to him. "How much does your blond girlfriend know?"

Janice spoke. "Enough to keep my daughter. All I need to know."

Zack turned toward her but kept one eye on Dennis. "You know he's used you too, right?"

"Never," she said.

"You're done, Zack." Keeping hold of the spray wand, Dennis pulled the gas mask over his face then raised the wand in Zack's direction.

Zack moved behind Janice. "He's going to kill us both. Chantal will never see you again." As Dennis advanced, Janice lunged at Dennis. Zack dove to his right, landing hard on the concrete floor.

The other two tumbled backward to the floor, Janice on top. Dennis held onto the canister, but no longer held the attached wand. She tried to pin him down and reach for the wand, but he bucked her off, pivoted, grasped the wand by its pistol grip, and shot a full blast into her face. She rolled away, gagging and coughing.

Zack covered his mouth and nose with his arm and charged at Dennis. Rising to a half-crouch, Dennis aimed the nozzle at him, but Zack deflected it away with his arm as he tackled Dennis like a rushing lineman on a quarterback about to throw a pass. As Dennis went down, the canister and attached wand clattered away.

Zack pulled the gas mask off Dennis' head, rolled off, and lunged toward the canister. Dennis seized his ankles, pulled him to a stop, then tried to crawl over him. Zack made a quarter turn and smashed his elbow into Dennis' face. Then he jumped to his feet and seized the canister. The heft of it felt like a baseball bat.

Dennis got to his feet. He retrieved the scalpel from the counter. The blade glinted in his hand as he faced Zack. "Go ahead, Zack. Hit me with the parathion." He beckoned Zack with both hands. "Come on, JAFERD. Give me what I deserve. You want to do it. You know you do."

Zack shook his head. "No. Give it up, Dennis. You've lost. Police are on their way."

Dennis chortled. "You are pathetic to think I'd fall for that line." He brandished the scalpel. "I gave you a chance. Game over." He lunged at Zack.

Zack blocked the thrust with the canister, knocking the scalpel from Dennis' hand. Dennis rushed to tackle him, but Zack swung the canister in a vicious arc like a baseball player hitting for the fences. It struck Dennis in the left temple. He went down like a felled tree. Zack stood over him.

Dennis rolled away, retrieved the scalpel, rose into a wrestling crouch, and reattacked. Zack swung the canister again, this time like a two-handed tennis backstroke. It struck Dennis in the right temple. He crashed to the ground in a motionless heap. Zack pushed him with his foot. No movement. Unconscious.

Zack rushed to Janice. She was in severe respiratory distress, gagging on her own secretions. He pulled the atropine injector from his jacket, tore open the package, uncovered the needle, plunged it into her thigh, and injected the full contents into the muscle.

A wave of panic seized him as his own breathing became labored, his eyes watered, and his heart fluttered. He slumped to the garage floor. In the distance, the gradual crescendo of approaching sirens.

Ange figured it out.

CHAPTER NINETY-ONE

Forcing himself to move, Zack crawled to the rear of the garage, grasped the edge of the workbench, and struggled to lift himself up. He swiped at the switch to open the garage doors and shouted at Janice in a raspy voice. "Get out. Breathe."

Hacking and coughing, dizzy from the effort, he stumbled to where Dennis lay lifeless on the floor. Struggling to breathe, Zack rolled him onto his back, checked to be sure his airway was open, then looked for breathing. A few shallow breaths. He felt Dennis' neck. A weak pulse. He opened the eyelids to check his pupils. The right one was dilated and non-reactive. Zack squeezed his own eyes shut to fight back the parathion-induced tears, mixed with his own of rage and terror, then rolled onto the floor next to Dennis.

Moments later, a gaggle of police and paramedics charged into the garage. "Hands! Show your hands!"

Zack sat up, raised both hands in a move-away gesture, forced his voice to work. "I'm Dr. Zack Winston. Organophosphate poison. Take precautions." The effort to speak exhausted him, and he fell back to the ground.

The response team moved away to don protective gear. When EMTs returned, Zack leaned on his elbow and pointed at Janice, who writhed on the ground gasping and drooling near the garage door. "Poisoned. Parathion. Need atropine." A paramedic hurried to his side and injected him with atropine. Another checked on Janice.

Zack's breathing eased, and his mind cleared. He pointed to Dennis. "Closed head injury, probable epidural hematoma. In extremis." He looked at the closest medic. "Intubate him."

As the atropine took full effect and the air in the garage cleared, Zack recovered from the effects of the poison to which he'd had only indirect exposure. As he got to his feet, a medic in full protective gear was having difficulty intubating Dennis. Zack started to walk away. Hesitated. Walked to the garage entrance. Stopped and turned back.

He put a hand on the paramedic's shoulder. "I can do it." The medic handed him the tube and laryngoscope. Zack willed his hands to steady as he forced turbulent emotions from his mind. In front of him, a dying emergency patient; not the deranged psychopath he'd once considered his friend; who tried to kill him; who almost killed Bridget.

ER doc is what I am.

He intubated Dennis without difficulty. The paramedic hooked the tube to an ambu bag.

Zack stepped back to let the paramedics do their work. A police officer approached him, one whom Zack recognized from past ER encounters with victims of violent crimes. He didn't wait for the question, pointed at Dennis. "He attacked us both, with a knife and parathion. I hit him in the head with that canister. Twice."

The officer nodded, scribbled into a notepad. "We'll need a full statement, Doc."

"Later," Zack said. "I need to stay with my patient." The medics had loaded Dennis onto a gurney. "I'm going with you."

Ten minutes later, Zack braced himself against the sides of the ambulance as it careened with full lights and siren to Bethesda Metro Hospital. On the monitor, Dennis' heart rate decelerated to a rate of forty. His blood pressure shot up above 200.

Cushing's sign. Brainstem dying.

The ambulance wheeled into the ER bay. Dennis lost all vital signs. Zack looked at the pupils. Mid-position, fixed, no response to light.

Brainstem gone.

He helped the paramedics move Dennis into the resus room. A physician Zack didn't know rushed in to take over. *Hired as my replacement, no doubt.* The ER team would do all they could to save Dennis, call neurosurgery to perform burr holes. No matter. Dennis King was already dead.

Zack left the resus room, pushed away the nurses trying to get him onto a gurney, walked out of the ER, out of the hospital, past the arriving police cruiser, and into the dark night.

The storm front had receded. A half-moon and a few stars poked through the thin layer of waning clouds. He pulled out his phone to summon an Uber and call Ange.

CHAPTER NINETY-TWO

Thirty minutes later, Zack startled awake when his ride stopped at the entrance to the George Washington University Hospital ER. Exhausted and drained, he had dozed off as soon as the car moved away from Bethesda Metro and the driver turned up the heater at the sight of Zack's wet clothing. He opened the car door, shook his head clear, thanked the driver, and got out of the vehicle.

Shoeless, his feet raw meat inside thin black socks still damp, he limped into the ER waiting room. His frantic eyes scrutinized each of several dozen faces in the room. *Where is Ange?* Gawking stares told him he looked a fright. The shirt and trousers he'd put on that morning for the settlement meeting clung to his skin like plastic molds, while his suit jacket hung from his shoulders like a dingy limp dish rag. His yellow silk tie bore a tapestry of multihued blood stains; burgundy spots from Dennis mixed with older umber splotches from Bridget. He rubbed a hand through his hair, a tangled mess from which he pulled dirt and small pebbles from Janice's garage floor.

A triage nurse pushed a wheelchair toward him, her expert eyes trained on the blood stains on his clothes and hands. "Sit down, sir. I'll get you right back to the treatment area."

Zack waved her off. "I'm not a patient. I'm a— a doctor, emergency physician." The nurse narrowed her eyes. "Dr. Zack Winston. I work at

Bethesda Metro. I'm looking for a patient I rescued earlier, Bridget Larsen. There was a young lady with her, name of Ange Moretti."

As if on cue, Ange appeared at his side. Her mouth fell open when she saw him. They hugged, both genuine but desperate. The triage nurse rolled her eyes, snorted, and walked away with the wheelchair. Zack broke the embrace, stepped back. "Bridget?"

"Out of surgery," Ange said. "ICU." She looked away.

"What else?"

"She'll live. That's all they would tell me." She took his hand and led him from the ER to an elevator bank. They rode up to the ICU floor in silence. When they got out of the elevator, Ange gestured toward the waiting room. "You'll have to wait for a minute."

"The hell—"

She pushed him into the chair. "Trust me." She sat in the chair next to him.

"What the . . .?"

Terrified, Zack sat on the edge of the chair, rocking back and forth. After five minutes he'd had enough. He was a physician, for God's sake. No one could stop him from seeing Bridget. *Now.* He stood.

Movement in the chair across from him caught his attention. Stern-faced Noelle pointed a finger at him. "Chill, Zack. Sit."

Zack sat. Another five minutes passed before a tall, handsome man with wavy salt-and-pepper hair and tanned complexion walked through the ICU doors. Next to him a slim teenage boy who looked to be about fourteen or fifteen, with long straight hair the color of flax. *Bridget's son.*

When they saw Ange and Zack, the pair approached. Ange stood. Zack followed suit. "Zack, this is—"

"Marshall Hilliard," Zack said. "I recognize you, sir. I'm Zack Winston." He turned to the youth. "You must be Justin." He reached out to shake their hands.

Tears came to Marshall's eyes as he ignored the proffered hand and embraced Zack. "You saved her life. Thank God you were there." Justin stood beside his father and stared at the floor.

Zack scrutinized Marshall's face. "How is she?"

Marshall sighed. "Alive. Not yet awake. Other than that, we don't know."

"Can I see her?"

"Of course." The tall man put his arm around Zack's shoulder and led him toward the ICU doors.

A nurse blocked their path. "One visitor only now."

"Go on, Doc," Marshall said. "We'll wait here with your girlfriend."

Zack started to correct him, but instead he turned and hurried into the ICU.

CHAPTER NINETY-THREE

When Zack saw Bridget, he froze. He barely recognized her. Tears welled into his eyes. She looked already dead.

Bridget lay motionless on her back, covered by a single white sheet over a gray hospital gown. The ICU staff had cleaned her up. No blood stains like Zack wore on his shirt and tie. They had washed her hair and combed it back, away from her pallid face and off her shoulders. Not how she wore it. Her eyes were closed, her face devoid of expression; despite the array of beeping machines around her, the IVs in each arm, the bulky dressing around her neck, and the new endotracheal tube protruding from her mouth, hooked to a mechanical ventilator that made a whooshing sound with every breath.

Zack inched up to the bedside and observed her in silence. He reasoned that the surgeons had repaired her trachea over the endotracheal tube and kept it in place as a splint until her wounds healed. He scanned the various monitors, relieved to see numbers within or close enough to the normal range. He stepped to the ventilator with a surge of relief. She was breathing on her own, each breath assisted by the machine to assure maximum inhalation and transfer of oxygen to her lungs, her blood, her brain.

Her brain.

A wave of fear swept over Zack. Had he restored her breathing soon enough? Did she suffer brain damage? Temporary or permanent? Even with mild to moderate hypoxic brain injury, the final outcome would not be known for days or weeks—or months. After all the brain swelling had resolved. After the rest of her body resumed normal function. Only then would they know for sure. She could land anywhere on the neurocognitive spectrum; from vegetative to full function, or with subtle but significant holes in her memory, thought processes, emotions. Would she ever practice law again?

He thought about their brief connection when she left the victory party at the Old Ebbitt Grill. Would they ever talk to each other again? Would they. . .? He squeezed his eyes shut to stifle the tears.

Zack remembered being in the OR with Noelle. She never moved. Her eyes never opened. Bridget had not moved, and her eyes stayed shut. He bit his lip, reached over the bed railing, and squeezed her hand. No response. He leaned over, spoke into her ear. "Bridge, it's Zack." No response. Overcome with a surge of grief, he looked away.

"God help us," he said aloud. "No more pain."

A slight movement under his hand caught his attention. He looked back at Bridget. Her open eyes looked straight at him. A glimmer of recognition. He squeezed her hand. She responded, a slight but definite squeeze. He moved his face close to hers. "Do you know me?" She blinked and squeezed his hand again. On the monitor, her heart rate accelerated and her breathing quickened. He gripped her hand. A return squeeze made his spirits soar.

A nurse appeared at the bedside, alarmed by the change in her patient's vital signs. "You should go," the nurse said. "Don't want to overstress her."

"Right," Zack said. "In a second."

The nurse stepped away but remained close to assure he did as promised. Zack leaned closer, looked into Bridget's eyes, and spoke. "You're going to be okay." He leaned in close to whisper in her ear. "We made it, Bridge. We survived. Together."

She blinked her eyes and gripped his hand. He would swear she smiled around the taped endotracheal tube.

CHAPTER NINETY-FOUR

Two months later, Zack got off the Washington Metro Yellow Line train at Eisenhower Station in Alexandria. The National Capitol Region had recovered from a mid-February snowstorm, but the streets and sidewalks remained treacherous. Mounds of slow-melting gray and black ice, like licorice snow cones, lined the sidewalk. Slick patches lay in wait on the sidewalk for the smooth soles of Zack's new Ferragamos. He should have worn more weather-sensible shoes, but he wanted to make the right impression. He pulled his cashmere overcoat close to his body and shuffled with care to cover the short distance to the US Attorney's office on Jamieson Avenue. When Marshall Hilliard's executive assistant had called to arrange the meeting, she had assured Zack that it would be informal, "for information sharing only." While he hoped to get answers to his own lingering questions, he agreed to the meeting mostly to learn about Bridget's condition. He'd had no communication with her, or Marshall, since her discharge from GW Hospital a month ago.

Zack had visited her in the hospital every day, pleased at her progress but alarmed that she had not yet recovered to the same dynamic advocate he'd begun to cherish as they worked his case. Her voice had not yet returned, and she showed no emotions. Now he wondered if Marshall's report would be glowing or . . .?

Half-way to his destination, he got a text from Ange. *Still on for dinner?*

He stopped to text her back. *Sure. 7 p.m.?*

Yes. Any preference?

Your choice. Anything but Indian.

She responded with a smiley emoji.

Zack looked forward to a relaxed evening, now that they had finally cemented their platonic friendship.

When the secretary ushered Zack into the US Attorney's wood-paneled office, Marshall Hilliard stood, came around his desk, and shook Zack's hand with warmth. "Dr. Winston, thank you for coming. Good to see you again." The quintessential Virginia aristocrat; tall, handsome, confident, with a booming voice that spoke in a sophisticated Southern drawl. Zack could picture him wearing a powdered wig and pontificating as a member of President Thomas Jefferson's inner circle.

"Thank you, sir," Zack said. "My pleasure." He hoped he did not appear as uneasy as he felt.

An attractive brunet thirtyish woman entered the room. Marshall introduced her as Carol, his executive assistant. "I've asked her to join our meeting."

As a witness? Zack thought. He wondered if the room was bugged. He smiled and shook Carol's hand, doing his best to be professional.

Marshall told the secretary to bring coffee and ice water, then ushered Zack to an ornate Queen Anne chair beside an antique oak coffee table. Marshall sat in an identical chair across from Zack. Carol sat at a smaller chair between them. Uncomfortable silence descended on Zack as they waited for the secretary to return. He'd never been good at small talk with relative strangers, and he didn't know how to voice the most burning question in his mind.

What the hell? Just do it. He cleared his throat. "How is Bridget?"

Marshall sucked in a thin wisp of air before answering. "Doing well, all things considered. Still foggy in the noggin' but improving. Doesn't remember the assault or what happened after it. Maybe never will. Neurologist says six months to a year before we know how much mental acuity she's retained." He grimaced. "Or lost."

The secretary returned with the coffee and water. Marshall took a long quaff. "Her voice . . ." He trailed off, gulped another sip of coffee. "The ENT surgeon says she has permanent vocal damage." He looked away. "She'll never speak above a whisper." He swallowed hard. "Even if her brain recovers 100%, she'll never address a jury again." He shook his head. "Courtroom drama is her grand passion. I don't know how she'll handle life without it."

Zack bit his lip, did not vocalize his immediate thought. *At least she's not a vegetable.* He wondered how Marshall could be comfortable showing his feelings about Bridget in front of his assistant. Had he cheated on his wife? More than once? Did he love her? Was this Carol his latest dalliance?

He had a sudden need to take his own long quaff and chose ice water over coffee. He forced his errant thoughts and emotions back to the room. "Please give her my regards."

"Of course." Marshall took a deep breath. "Bridget knows you saved her life."

"Really?"

"I told her. It was the first time she smiled after she woke up."

Not the first time since the attack. He remembered his exchange with Bridget that night in the ICU, when she smiled around the tube. He looked at Marshall with a straight face. "I need a rest room."

The US Attorney pointed to a door behind his desk. "Use mine."

CHAPTER NINETY-FIVE

When Zack returned from the rest room, Marshall had several documents and folders laid out on the coffee table. Carol sat cross-legged, with a steno pad on her lap. "Let's get down to business," Marshall said. His tone changed to no-nonsense prosecutor. "I imagine you have some questions about the investigation. I can't tell you all we know, but I'll be as candid as I can. We owe you that much."

Zack nodded. "Thank you. I understand."

"I'll have some questions for you as well." Marshall's voice was neither intimidating nor warm. He scrutinized Zack's face. "None of this discussion will be on any record." He glanced at Carol, who closed her steno pad. He swept his arm around the paneled room. "I assure you, no listening devices in here." He chuckled. "They would be illegal and inadmissible in any event."

Zack shrugged, not believing a word of it.

For the next ten minutes, the two men refreshed their common knowledge: That Dennis King had been the lynch pin of a regional prescription-drug distribution network, for which he also performed as the medical hit-man, *El Medico Asesino,* expert at making murder look like death by natural or accidental causes. The one exception had been his attack on Bridget, fueled by rage and the immediate need to steal the documents she'd obtained from Marshall.

Walter Knowles had run the procurement operation by forging prescriptions with the names of legitimate physicians, mostly those in the ER group. He'd also run the finances and laundered the money from his apartment in Adams Morgan, DC. He had performed additional duties, such as altering medical records to erase the trails of Dennis King's actions—including the bogus EKG on Carl Barnett.

"Here's what you don't know," Marshall said. "Several months before his death, Carl Barnett approached me at a political fundraiser to request a clandestine meeting. He had financed the original drug operation, from which he reaped significant return on his investment. For reasons we never understood, he turned on his co-conspirators and became our confidential informant." He took a sip of coffee. "When Dennis King stumbled onto Carl's treachery, he sparked an affair with Janice. Dennis was a serial philanderer and Janice was trapped in a loveless, sexless marriage she couldn't leave because she needed Carl's money. She was an easy mark."

Zack remembered how Dennis had glanced at Janice after he had described how Walter paid the price for treachery. "Just like—," Dennis had added then stopped. He had meant Carl Barnett.

"Dennis learned about Janice's secret support of her daughter and convinced Carl to turn on his wife. He sequestered his assets and planned to divorce her. Dennis then persuaded Janice to poison Carl, frame you for malpractice, and win a handsome settlement that would allow her continued support of her daughter."

Zack stared into the distance. "I've learned first-hand how well Dennis played the long con."

Marshall cleared his throat. "When Bridget stumbled onto the file in my home office, we didn't know details. We had no clue who was involved in the conspiracy. Carl had not supplied names. We figured he was holding out to protect himself, but I was beginning to doubt if he really wanted to help us. Perhaps he was a double agent, planted to find out how much we knew."

"Wouldn't put that past Dennis, knowing what I do now," Zack said.

Marshall changed topic, his voice and manner suddenly stern. "You and Bridget flushed Dennis out with your reckless drama in that so-called settlement meeting. Not only did you break the law, you almost got Bridget killed." He glared at Zack. "Why?"

A cold shiver ran up Zack's spine. He stiffened and looked at the floor like an errant student before an irate principal. "Why do you ask?"

Marshall said nothing.

"To be blunt, am I— are Bridget and I in trouble over that?"

Marshall huffed. "That depends on how the rest of this conversation goes." He stood. "Shall we take a break, Doctor? Ten minutes?"

CHAPTER NINETY-SIX

Zack walked through the lobby and stood outside the building to let the chilly air clear his brain. Could he trust Marshall Hilliard? Cheater or not, would the US Attorney charge his wife with breaking the law? He seemed to care for Bridget. Would he take Zack down to protect her?

No choice but to hear him out.

When he returned to the ornate office, Zack found fresh water and coffee and a more affable US Attorney. Carol was no longer present, and the secretary closed the door behind Zack. His senses on guard, Zack took his seat but didn't speak. First move had to be Marshall's.

"Before we get down to why I asked for this meeting, let me fill you in on the rest of the story as we now know it. Feel free to ask questions."

Zack nodded.

Marshall continued as if he and Zack were close confidants. "Janice Barnett knew nothing of the larger conspiracy. Dennis duped her into thinking it was all about their love affair and getting money to support her daughter. She's confessed to the attempted murder, but we'll consider the mitigating circumstances. She'll go to prison for a long time, but she won't lose contact with her daughter."

"I wouldn't be here now if she hadn't stood in front of me when Dennis was about to attack."

Marshall nodded.

"What about Walter Knowles?" Zack asked.

"He was skimming from the profits. When Dennis figured it out, he executed him in the most painful way he could imagine."

"The parathion."

"We haven't figured out that whole story. Dennis had simpler means to kill Walter Knowles. Why obtain a dangerous insecticide just to stage a sham suicide? Why entice law enforcement and Homeland Security into the picture? Why did he have that same compound in Janice's garage? One theory suggests that the cabal was working a darker conspiracy, perhaps a political target, and Walter was experimenting with the compound. Does that make sense to you, Doc?"

Zack shook his head. "I challenged Dennis in the garage about the parathion. He said it was 'proof of concept' for something I wouldn't live to see." He shook his head. "Dennis was a sociopath. Those types have no limits."

"Like many criminals and terrorists," Marshall said. "Nor is he available for interrogation." He cast a penetrating look at Zack. "That's one reason why I asked for this meeting. I'm hoping you can help us figure it out as we go forward."

Zack blinked. "I thought your investigation was done."

Marshall shook his head. "We've just scratched the surface."

Zack sat in silence, thinking about the situation. Marshall seemed to wait for Zack to ask the next question. "Does Roland Edwards' death play in this?"

Marshall smiled like a college professor with a bright student. "Right question. Roland went out of bounds when he contacted you. Dennis feared he was on the verge of discovering the conspiracy, so he eliminated him. Set up his death to look like another drug dealer gone over the edge."

Zack stared into space for some time before he spoke. "You want me to help? How?"

"Among other things, we don't see Dennis King as the ring-leader. There may be another physician, or several, driving the conspiracy. You could help us find them."

Zack smelled something odd. He sat back, folded his arms, stared at Marshall. "Your not-so-veiled threat that Bridget and I might have legal trouble was what, a stick to assure my cooperation?"

Marshall spread his hands. "I wouldn't put it that way."

Repulsed, Zack stood. "I would. I won't be threatened, and I doubt Bridget would be either. The answer is no." He turned and left the office.

Halfway to the Metro station, Zack came to an abrupt stop. His shoes slid out on the slick concrete, and he went down hard on his ass. The pain and embarrassment stifled his anger at Marshall Hilliard. He had felt no closure from walking out of the office. The grief from Dennis King's betrayal stormed his mind. He thought of Bridget, the bond that had grown between them. Would Marshall prosecute her? Doubtful. Regardless, if Zack continued toward the Metro, he would never see Bridget again. Her career taken from her, what would she do next? *Not quit.*

What would Noelle do?

Zack got up, brushed himself off, and hurried, careful not to slip again, back to the US Attorney's building. He sprinted up the stairs, ignored the secretary, and stormed into Marshall Hilliard's office. Behind the desk, the man looked up, alarmed, as if he feared imminent attack. Zack stopped in front of the desk. "I won't be threatened. Nor do I need to be. Take that crap about Bridget and me breaking the law off the table, swear never to bring it up again, and I'm in."

Marshall stared for a few seconds, then stood, reached out his hand. "Got yourself a deal, Doc."

CHAPTER NINETY-SEVEN

One mid-April morning, six weeks after Zack's agreement with Marshall Hilliard, cherry blossoms heralded the return of spring across the National Capital Region. Zack left his apartment and jogged toward the Capitol Crescent Trail. He planned a five-mile run, which would give him ample time to shower, change clothes, and commute to the US Attorney's office for his regular meeting with the task force. As an emergency physician accustomed to split-second decisions that yielded immediate life-or-death results, he'd found the plodding pace of the investigation frustrating. A year or more would pass before they completed their work—if there was anything to complete. Thus far, they had uncovered nothing new.

At the trail, he put the task force out of his mind, seeking the Zen-like tranquility that marked his current life. He picked up the pace. His brain savored an endorphin-infused pleasure state by the time he reached that special bend in the trail.

Noelle was there. They ran together in silence, their pace and strides perfectly matched, out and back to the same spot. Noelle stopped, smiled at him. "Ever get bored running the same trail all the time?"

Zack looked at her, puzzled.

"You should try Mount Vernon Trail." She winked. "Runs through Alexandria, right?"

The next morning, a Saturday, Zack rode the Metro Red Line from Bethesda, changed to the Yellow Line at Gallery Place, and got off at Crystal City Station in Arlington. After a few wrong turns in the underground commercial labyrinth, he found the right exit and jogged the few blocks to the Mt. Vernon Trail.

He headed south, running at a brisk pace to where the trail followed the Potomac River alongside Old Town Alexandria. He slowed his pace by the busy waterfront, scrutinizing every woman—runner or walker—in either direction. Many of them sported long blond hair, but none looked familiar. When he passed under the Woodrow Wilson Bridge and crossed over Cameron Run, his heart sank. Alexandria lay behind him. The trail ahead continued into remote wooded terrain.

Zack stopped, unsure. Had he come here for naught? He continued south for another mile, in which he encountered more bicyclists than runners, most of them men. Disappointed, he turned back north and quickening his pace, still scrutinizing everyone near his path. He slowed to a near-walk through Old Town, canvassing not only the runners, but anyone else strolling along the waterfront. No joy. When he reached the forested park where the trail traversed Dangerfield Island on its way back to Arlington, he stopped. He should continue to Crystal City and catch the Metro back home. Return to this trail another day.

The hell.

He turned and ran south again. After a half-mile, he saw her. Bridget jogged toward him in a smooth, lilting gait. Her blond ponytail swayed behind her like a metronome in rhythm with her stride. She looked thinner than Zack remembered.

Bridget saw him right after he spotted her. They closed the distance in seconds and caught each other in a long, tight hug. When they broke apart, his eyes strayed to the jagged, maroon-edged scar across the front of her neck. She touched it, self-conscious.

"What are you doing here?" Her voice a hoarse whisper.

"Looking for you."

She smiled and stretched out her arms. Her voice croaked like a small frog's. "Well, you found me."

They hugged again. She raised her head, looked into his eyes. "I never got to thank you for saving my life."

He whispered in her ear. "You saved mine first. You believed in me when no one else would."

She squeezed him, then broke loose from his embrace and shook her head. "You're still a BAFERD," she croaked.

Several silent seconds passed as they gazed at each other. Bridget wet her lips, beckoned southward with her head, and jogged toward Alexandria.

Zack joined her. They continued down the trail side-by-side. Without thought or effort, their strides and pace melded into one.

FINIS

MIKE KRENTZ AUTHOR

Mike Krentz writes medical suspense and military fiction featuring complex characters. His medical stories transport the reader into the stressful environment of emergency medicine, where life battles death amid terrified screams, plaintive whimpers, and shouted orders; where fallible humans strive to postpone death, restore life, or eliminate misery. These ardent heroes sometimes fail. No time to grieve. They suck it up and move on—to quiet a frightened child, relieve pain, straighten a broken limb, repair a laceration, or reassure the worried well. What evil might lurk amid such chaos?

His Flagship Series portrays the lives of servicemen and women, their challenges, and interactions; and their wounds—physical and emotional—that evolve into professional and personal conflicts more daunting than combat. Can crucial human relationships survive such brutal demands on hearts and souls?

Born and raised in Arizona, Mike Krentz earned a classical degree in English from the University of San Francisco, a Doctor of Medicine degree from the Medical College of Wisconsin, and a Master of Public Health Degree from Johns Hopkins University.

Following a civilian career as an emergency physician, Mike rededicated his professional life to serve America's Navy and Marine Corps heroes and their families, and to honor their sacrifices in defending our freedom and way of life. Serving in hospitals, ships, and air wings, he earned ten personal decorations, including five awards of the Legion of Merit. His last active duty assignment, as 7th Fleet Surgeon on board the flagship, USS *Blue Ridge*, became the inspiration for the Flagship Series.

After retiring from the US Navy, Dr. Krentz continued his service as a consultant supporting the Navy and Marine Corps Public Health Center. Upon completion of that mission, he returned to his earliest life passion as full-time writer of character-based stories.

ACKNOWLEDGEMENTS

A few years ago, faced with the inevitability of retirement from the US Navy, I made the glib decision to become a fiction writer. With humble yet ardent gratitude I acknowledge those who helped me along the way—in my life, in my navy career and in my pathway to publication:

My wife, Kathryn, who not only signed onto the great navy adventure with me, but also endured my Piscean forays into rotating hobbies and avocations. You are the perfect life companion.

My son, Matthew, who moved thirteen times in twenty years and attended seven different schools before graduating from high school in Yokosuka, Japan. You have risen to the challenge of a military child. Whatever course your life takes, I am always proud of you.

My older children, Jewls, Lisa, Debi, and Michael. You've endured more than a fair share of your imperfect dad's life wanderings yet remained loving and loyal through it all. You will always have my constant and unconditional love and gratitude.

My stepchildren, Kate and James, who suffered family disruption and turmoil in addition to the vicissitudes of living in a blended military family. Your adaptability and indomitable spirits are models for all of us.

Frank and Jayne Ann Krentz, for your encouragement, support, gentle nudges, and solid counsel—and for the blurbs on JAK's Facebook page. Your confidence helped me to believe in myself as a writer.

Sheri Williams and the staff at TouchPoint Press for opening the door for me to traditional publishing.

Jennifer Haskin, whose editing skills caught my errors, suggested clearer language, yet preserved my original voice. It's a pleasure to work with you. Best wishes on your own trilogy.

Dr. Pat Connell, fellow BAFERD and friend/college roommate/colleague since grade school, who reviewed my original manuscript and pointed out clinical anachronisms by virtue of his current emergency medicine practice.

Bill Baker, one of the world's most voracious readers. I am honored that you read my books, and grateful for your keen and thoughtful suggestions and edits.

My colleagues at The Muse Writers studios whose critiques elevated the quality of my manuscript: Kelly Sokol, Lydia Netzer, Jon Cameron, Kelley McGee, Dave Cascio, Elaine Panneton, Kimberly Engebrigtsen, Susan Paxton, Michelle Ross, Alisha Brown, Sarah Darrow, Tucker Hotte, Robin Pearson, Chris Guthrie, Kathy Hessmer, and Rachel Parris. There is something from each of you in this final version. You all are fabulous writers and your works deserve publication. A huge thanks to Michael Khandelwal, founder and guiding light of The Muse for establishing a world-class writers' community in our hometown.

Thanks also to Paula Munier and Michael Neff for providing me the "epiphany moment" for future direction of DEAD ALREADY at the Algonkian NYC Pitchfest a few years ago.

Most of all, thanks to the readers who took a chance on this book. I appreciate your investment in my story, in time as well in money. I hope you have enjoyed reading it as much as I did writing it. If you would be so inclined, I would appreciate a review on Amazon, Barnes and Noble, Goodreads, BookBub, and/or other retail platform.

CPSIA information can be obtained
at www.ICGtesting.com
Printed in the USA
FSHW011255170221
78721FS